The Book of
Intimate Grammar

David Grossman
was born in Jerusalem
in 1954 and lives there
with his family. He is the
author of two novels,
The Smile of the Lamb
and the internationally
acclaimed *See Under:*
Love, as well as two
books of journalism,
The Yellow Wind and
Sleeping on a Wire.
The latter was shortlisted
for the Waterstones/
Esquire Non-Fiction
Award in 1993.

By David Grossman

Novels

THE SMILE OF THE LAMB

SEE UNDER: LOVE

THE BOOK OF INTIMATE GRAMMAR

Non-fiction

THE YELLOW WIND

SLEEPING ON A WIRE

THE

BOOK

OF

INTIMATE

David **GRAMMAR**

Grossman

TRANSLATED FROM THE

HEBREW BY BETSY ROSENBERG

PICADOR

First published in Great Britain 1994 by Jonathan Cape Ltd.
Published by arrangement with Farrar, Straus & Giroux, Inc., New York

This edition published 1995 by Picador
an imprint of Macmillan General Books
25 Eccleston Place, London SW1W 9NF
and Basingstoke

Associated companies throughout the world

ISBN 0 330 33594 4

9 8 7 6 5 4 3 2 1

A CIP catalogue record for this book is available from
the British Library.

Printed and bound in Great Britain by
Mackays of Chatham plc, Chatham, Kent

THE

BOOK

OF

INTIMATE

GRAMMAR

1

Aron is standing on tiptoe for a better view of the street below, where Mama and Papa have just stepped out to breathe some fresh air at the end of a long hot day. They look so small from here. He can taste the dusty metal of the blinds on his lips. His eyes glow. It isn't nice to watch like this. From above. They almost seem like dolls down there, a slow tubby one and a little snippety one. It isn't nice to watch, but it is kind of funny, and kind of scary maybe. The trouble is, Zacky and Gideon see them too. Still, he can't tear himself away. Y'alla, let's go, grumbles Zacky, his nose squashed flat against the blinds. If What's-her-name turns up now we're history. Hey, whispers Aron, here come the Kaminers. Old man Kaminer is going to die, says Gideon. See how yellow he is? You can tell.

Mama and Papa stopped to talk to the Kaminers from Entrance A. They flickered in and out of sight behind the spreading fig tree. Don't ask, sighed Esther Kaminer. Snatches of conversation drifted up to the fourth-floor window. Poor Avigdor—she shook her head—it's a miracle he's still alive, and Mama clucked her tongue: God help anyone who falls into a doctor's clutches. They chop you to pieces for diploma practice. Avigdor Kaminer, slouching as usual, stared blankly at his chattering wife. And you wouldn't believe what it's costing, she moaned, what with the medication and the dietetic food, and a taxi home every time after the dialysis. If you ask me, said Mama as she and Papa continued their stroll, she can hardly wait to be rid of him, he's getting

3

too expensive for her—Aron saw her lips move and guessed what she was saying—and who does La Kaminer hope to hook after he's gone, with her hair falling out by the handful already, as if she didn't have enough of a dowry; she isn't fooling anyone with that savings-and-loan bouffant, the bald spots show a mile. Papa merely nodded as usual, distracted by a bit of litter on the sidewalk, a scrap of newspaper, a lemon rind. Don't look now, it's Strashnov, said Mama, her lips twisting into a sour smile. You think the snob will say hello? Hello, Mr. Strashnov, how's the family?

It's your father, said Aron flatly. Y'alla, let's go, said Gideon, transfixed at the window: his father, dressed to the nines in Terylene trousers, with a tie on, even in this khamsin. Mr. Strashnov nodded disdainfully and pursed his lips as he minced along. Well, that's a fine hello; thinks he's too good for us, does he? Papa blocked his way. Back from the whatsit . . . the university? Mr. Strashnov pursed his lips again. Ha, he has to make faces before he'll talk, before he'll open his mouth and say hello, afraid to let in a little air, is he? And his wife has to take in typing and work her fingers to the bone, because Professor Inallectual can't earn a decent living, hissed Mama, waving goodbye and shuddering in his chilly wake.

Come on, Ari, let's go, said Gideon, backing away from the window. But we haven't seen anything yet, whispered Aron. Why're the two of you so scared all of a sudden? Zacky and Gideon exchanged glances. Look, Ari, said Gideon, staring down at his sandals, actually . . . there's something I wanted to tell you before, before we broke in— Not now! fumed Aron, we'll go ahead as planned! And he strutted back to the center of the room, with Zacky and Gideon reluctantly following him till they too fell under the spell of this raided sanctuary, this unsuspected ice cube in a block of steamy flats, and they tiptoed after him over the rug-checkered floors, past the black leviathan of a piano in the salon; Aron pointed to a trio of ivory figures on the bookshelf, then paused to contemplate the statuettes on another shelf, a group of naked men and women holding hands as they danced, a boy with his chin resting on his hand, a curvaceous torso—and suddenly he remembered his old guitar with the crack down the middle and the strings all torn; he had taught himself to pick out tunes, his sister Yochi loved to hear him play, but Mama and Papa said he couldn't have a new one, his bar mitzvah

4　　　　　　　THE BOOK OF

was only a year and a half away and they had other plans for him. Aron paced resentfully and stopped in front of the painting with a castle carved out of a cliff that looked as if it might crash into the sea any moment. Her and her pictures, he muttered, hands on his hips, you've got to be meshuggeneh to paint like that. And Gideon said, Right, that's what my father calls "modern art." Aron could just imagine him saying those words. It's phony, it's ridiculous, I feel like taking a hammer and smashing it to bits, he ranted, kicking the wall for emphasis. And then he stopped: the piano seemed to rumble a warning.

Come on, squealed Zacky, haven't we seen enough already? No, and we don't have proof yet either, replied Aron, turning away. That was really dumb, what you said about her not having a shadow, said Zacky. Well, she doesn't, snapped Aron, surveying the book-lined shelves. Why else does she carry a parasol all summer, and what about the time we followed her, why did she slink behind the buildings and the trees? To fool us, that's why; Zacky snarled and shifted his weight, pressing his legs together in distress. His lumpish potato face glowered at Aron. Then he peeked through the blinds and recoiled.

Aron noticed and peeked out with him. Below, under the fig tree, was a heavyset man glancing anxiously over his shoulder. Gideon too peeked out. The man approached a small green Fiat and started fumbling in his pockets for the keys. Aron had never seen this man before, but with a pounding heart he knew who it was. Once he'd overheard a grownup say that Zacky's mother, Malka Smitanka, had someone on the side. He had started following her around, watching her whenever she went out, but he'd never caught a glimpse of the someone on the side before. Now the big man straightened his belt, smoothed his thinning hair, and got into the car. Zacky's lips moved in a silent curse, a scream of alarm that resounded all the way to Africa, where his father drove a bulldozer for Israel Waterworks. The boys stood frozen at the window. Aron was sad that Gideon had seen the someone on the side, his Gideon, who was so pure and noble; whenever Zacky told one of his jokes, he and Aron would laugh politely and look away. A moment passed, and they stood together in silence, afraid to budge, and then Zacky's mother stepped out on the balcony, wearing her bathrobe, and called him home for lunch. Lunch she feeds him at five in the afternoon, said Mama as the green Fiat drove by; we're not inviting *her* to the bar mitzvah, and that's that. I will not shake hands with *her* after *him*. She's calling you, said Aron quietly. Mind your own business, growled Zacky, I'm not hungry, let's look around some more.

They lingered in the semidarkness for a while, and then slowly, like sprats in a stream, began to drift through the corridor into Edna Bloom's bedroom, where they circled quietly, past the neatly made bed, the ornamental mirror above her dressing table, the tiny basin . . . and the nylon stocking draped over the chair. Zacky and Gideon peeked at each other, and bright red stains spread over their faces, but Aron noticed nothing, he had just been overwhelmed by a painting that went on for half the wall. "Get a load of him." Zacky signaled Gideon, who saw what was happening and quickly grabbed Aron's hand. Let's go, Ari, he murmured uneasily, you'll get in trouble if you hang around. But Aron only shook his hand off and continued staring at the fettered horse in the foreground, mimicking the lips that curled with strain; "Modern art" they call this crap? But his eyes bulged out with the gasping horse. Move, wake up! called Gideon, as Aron spotted the dead man under the horse, and then recognized the shape of the bull, only its eyes were in the wrong place, though strangely enough they looked right that way; and then he saw the tortured faces, the fractured bodies, and the woman hovering in the background, lamp in hand. He tried to fight it, this "modern art," and staggered out of the salon—Where'd they go, I'm stranded—but he found himself staring at the picture again, this is ridiculous, even I can draw a better horse, I can definitely draw a better bull, with all the practice I've had copying the label on Green Cow cheese. But suddenly there were tears in his eyes, big, slow drops from a secret well. What's the matter, dum-dum, you're crying like a girl? I am not. Are too. If Papa could only see you now! Who cares. Let him laugh at me. Let him run home and tell Mama. Little Aron's going "artistic" on us, going inallectual!

Ari! Gideon called impatiently from the doorway. He was sick of waiting. But Aron didn't answer. Gideon peered around the room till his eyes rested on an enormous pink-lipped conch adorning the shelf. Where does she find this sickening stuff, he sneered, thinking, Hurry up, she'll catch us, as he nearly ran out, but stopped himself and turned to stare again at the baffling conch that seemed almost to come alive and squeeze itself around an invisible object. Goodbye! He was out of there, jumping three stairs at a time with Zacky close behind him,

THE BOOK OF

shaking off the prissiness of Miss Edna Bloom, her and her paintings and her matchstick furniture, but Aron, they knew, would yell at them later for running out on him.

Aron shook a fascinating paperweight, watched the snow falling on a lonesome mountaineer, and kept him company through the blizzard. By the entrance door there was a display of soldier dolls in uniform, the kind Shimmik and Itka collected from their trips abroad, only hers were arranged in a grand parade of trim guardsmen and mustachioed gendarmes, from Greece and Turkey, and England and France, like a great international army; and then, casually, Aron went back to the painting. First he faced it, then he turned away, then he turned back to gape at it some more, shutting his eyes, surrendering with open arms, backing off with a little dance, meandering like a lost panther, like a spy colliding with his mirror image, scratching where his skin tingled, glancing over his shoulder, what if it came off the wall and started following him, and a flower blooms out of the sword in the dead man's hand, and suddenly you see the eyes everywhere, run for your life.

Edna Bloom's had purity. Oho, just look at those surfaces, hissed Mama in his brain, look at this dust, but to him it was stardust, and someday a knight would come riding into this enchanted castle and break the spell, and then— Aron shivered and hugged himself.

He paused in front of the refrigerator. You think this is a cupboard you can open any time you like? If you want something, ask me. He pulled the handle. Amazing. Starvation corner, rasped Mama's voice: a vegetarian refrigerator. A spinster's kitchen. I tell you it's unnatural! It is, he agreed, so white, so empty, no meat, no chicken, no salami, no medicine vials or stools to take to the clinic; there was hardly anything in there, except for a couple of shriveled cucumbers, a jar of sour cream, a bottle of milk, half an apple wrapped in a napkin, a bowl of cottage cheese. Yet in a way it was beautiful, unspoiled. He stood and stared, eager to learn more, the secret of her ascetic code. Are you crazy? She'll be here any minute, she'll catch you red-handed. No, she would never do anything to hurt me: My gallant knight, you've come at last. And then he hurried to the toilet and peed luxuriously, who knows, someday he might even bring himself to poop in here; to rehearse the possibility he pulled his pants down and sat on the toilet, all sweetness and light, dangling his trouser-bound legs; behind the door was another picture, of a kneeling bull and a beautiful lady stroking its back. Sure, why not, he could do it here. Masterfully he pulled the chain, smiled at the water swirling in the bowl. No fear of disgusting surprises in this toilet.

Aron took one last peek through the blinds. Mama and Papa were about to disappear into the house, but just as they reached the fig tree, Edna Bloom approached from the opposite direction, slender, boyish Edna Bloom, with her fuzzy yellow hair shining between the leaves. Okay, let's see if you have any guts now. Good evening, Miss Bloom. Good evening to you, Mrs. Kleinfeld, Mr. Kleinfeld. You seem a little tired today, Miss Bloom. Well, I have to work for a living, Mrs. Klein-feld. Yes, but you're awfully pale. Ha, did you see that, Moshe, the way she blushed when she looked at you? Oi, Hindaleh, you're imag-ining things, a girl like her and a man like me. You should relax more, take things easy, Miss Bloom, you have your whole life ahead of you. Ha, any minute she'll miss the boat. What are you talking about, Hin-daleh, she's just a girl. Allow me to be the judge of such matters, Moshe, to you she may seem young enough, but I looked at her teeth and teeth don't lie, she's thirty-eight if she's a day. So, maybe she isn't interested in men. Not interested? Ha! Don't you see the way she devours you with her eyes, the little lemaleh, butter wouldn't melt, pshhhhi, pshhhhi— Bye-bye, Miss Bloom, take care now. Yes, thank you, good-bye. And Aron watches her trail away; twenty-five seconds left to lock the door with his passkey, but he can't resist one last look, and now she's in the building, now she's walking up the stairs, now she's on the second floor, run for your life.

Wait.

Because as soon as Mama and Papa turned their backs she played a trick on them: instead of walking up the stairs to her apartment, she waited in the hallway till they disappeared into Entrance B, and then, breathless and birdlike, she reappeared, and Aron's heart soared, so she too had tricks, she too had secrets, and she rested under the leafy branches of the fig tree, surrendering to it like a girlish bride, breathing in its fragrance, her delicate hand on the massive trunk. And suddenly she trembled. Papa was there. He had returned. How did he know? He approached the tree and stood beside her. A hunk of a man, twice her size. A bull and a crane. But where was Mama? The broad leaves rustled, concealing, revealing. "Moshe!" She called Papa from afar. Papa hunched his shoulders. Then he reached up and tapped one of the

THE BOOK OF

branches. A cloud of tiny insects swarmed through the air. Edna recoiled. Papa looked away. "Moshe!" shouted Mama from the hallway, key in hand. "Where did he go?" "See, I had this feeling, Miss Bloom," said Papa, his words fluttering up to the fourth-floor window. "What feeling, Mr. Kleinfeld?" She tilted her chin up but avoided his eyes. A blush spread over her smooth white neck, visible only to Aron. "The fig tree is sick," said Papa simply. Their eyes did not meet. They spoke through the tree. "My fig tree, sick?" whispered Edna Bloom, saddened, shocked, though the tree belonged to everyone.

By the time Mama came down again, all three boys were standing under the fig tree with Edna Bloom. A single glance was enough for Mama. There was something murky in her eyes. High and low she hunted for Papa, squinting suspiciously up at the tree. At last she caught sight of his fleshy red heels flopping around. Controlling her temper she called his name. The leaves fluttered, and Papa's sunny face popped out between the branches. "Oioioi," he greeted her. "This tree is covered with sores, Mamaleh, it needs a good wiping." Mama pursed her lips and squeezed her collar tight. Then she turned abruptly and hurried home.

2

The next day, after stopping by the Romanian apothecary's on his way home from work, Papa showered, changed into a clean undershirt, and sat down at the "little cripple" table in the pantry to prepare an ointment for the fig tree. First he mixed the powders, then he added water and squeezed in a tube of smelly goo, his big red face puckering with concentration as he stirred. Mama was watching over his shoulder. When a tree is sick, she sneered, you have to be ruthless and whack off the rotten branches, as anyone with half a brain and a little instinct would tell you. That's the only way to get the healthy ones to grow. Papa merely nodded, carefully measuring out a few drops from a tiny vial, with his tongue pressed tightly between his teeth.

Then he climbed on the rickety Franzousky in the kitchen and rummaged through the storage loft. Cascades of dust spilled down as Mama watched him, till suddenly she felt the zetz in her heart, and sure enough, when she ran out to the balcony there was Grandma Lilly leaning over the rail, halfway to the next world. Mama grabbed her by the arm and dragged her back to the alcove. Lie down, Mamchu, supper isn't ready yet, why are you staring like that, it's me, Hinda, no one's going to slit your throat; there, legs up, lie down straight, stop crying, it's time for your nap; see the pretty pictures on the wall, see the parrots and the monkeys on the trees, you made them, Mamchu, that's your embroidery. Now you just rest awhile. And she covered Grandma Lilly up to her chin with the Scottish plaid, and tucked the corners under the mattress,

THE BOOK OF

and went huffing back to the kitchen. "You and your meshuggeneh schemes, Moshe," she said, slapping the nylon bags over the sink to dry with the wax paper from the margarine. "Your own mother nearly throws herself off the balcony, and here you are still futzing around; honestly, you are so stubborn." "I found it," he hollered, deep in the storage loft, and emerged with a headful of dusty curls, holding a kidney-shaped palette in his hand. "I knew I put it away up there."

Carefully he climbed off the rickety Franzousky and wiped the dust and paint from Yochi's palette. "You'd better make sure she doesn't need that anymore," whispered Mama. "You know Yochi, she'll have a fit." "Take it, go on, take everything," screamed Yochi from the bedroom, "I'll never be an artist anyway." Or a dancer either, she muttered angrily to herself, I should have kept on with my painting, though, then no one would care that my legs are fat.

Papa went out and closed the door, carefully balancing the palette with the ointment. Outside, Aron and Zacky Smitanka were playing Traffic on their bikes. Aron dipped like a matador, swerving so fast he didn't see the fierce red face coming at him till he found himself lying on the pavement with Zacky's bicycle jammed between his wheels.

Papa set the palette down and rushed over to the boys. "You rat, you dirty creep!" shrieked Aron, choking back the tears as Papa locked him in his burly arms. "Just wait, I'll make mincemeat out of you!" He waved his little fists at Zacky, kicking furiously. "Let me at him, let me at him!" Zacky, alarmed by what he'd done, thrashed back halfheartedly, cursing Aron, calling him a lousy cheater. "Trying to mess with me, Kleinfeld? Huh? Huh? Trying to mess with me?" he screamed, aiming higher because he couldn't think of anything better to say. Papa hoisted Zacky up with his free hand and roared with laughter as he held the two boys face to face, and let them swing at each other: wiry little Aron wriggled in the air, heaping abuse on Zacky and his bike, and Zacky screamed back: "You trying to mess with me? Huh? Huh?," his snub-nosed face burning with indignation. A sudden squeeze reduced them both to silence. Roaring with laughter Papa let them down, and they reeled on the ground with all the fight knocked out of them. Zacky got his wind back and started to whine that Aron was playing dirty, trying to be a wise guy. But those are the rules, burbled Aron, you ride up, you lunge, and then you ride away as fast as you can; was it his fault Zacky was such a klutz, such a golem and a turtle and a snail?

Papa frowned at the torrent of words. "All right!" he shouted. "Sha! We heard you the first time, big mouth!" Instantly he regretted his sharpness of tone, and tousled Aron's soft yellow hair; then, noticing the miserable expression in Zacky's eyes, gave him a big hug and scratched his bristly head. The two boys took comfort in the warmth of Papa's hands, and Zacky sidled up to feel the prickly hair on his leg.

"Off, you two, go play, and if I hear you brawling again, you gonna be sorry." Aron was the first to break away, and Papa patted Zacky on the shoulder. "A-shockel, Zachary, get on your bike and ride. I'll keep an eye on you from the tree."

Papa climbed up the fig tree and seated himself comfortably on a branch. Aron gripped the bike wheel between his knees and tried to straighten it. Papa parted the leaves and asked Zacky to fetch him the palette he'd left on the fence. Aron pressed down on the fender so hard it nearly cut his skin.

Papa leaned back. The leaves reached out to caress his face, to nuzzle him like friendly colts. He breathed in the muskiness of the fig tree and ran his hands around its ample trunk. Then he kicked off his plastic scuffs, startling Zacky, who was on his way back to the tree, and making him jump like a frightened kitten.

Solemnly, deliberately, like a craftsman spreading his tools out, Papa cracked his knuckles one by one. Then he shook himself and inspected the tree. There were sores on the branches: lesions infested with little white worms. The sores ran all the way up the tree, and Papa followed them with his eyes to the fourth-floor window. He thought he noticed Edna's curtain flutter and crossed his arms over his barrel chest. This would not be an easy job.

He took a roll of flannel out of his pocket, deftly tore a piece off, and poked the sore. A sticky gold fluid soaked through the cloth. He sniffed, nodded wonderingly, shrugged his shoulders, and tossed the rag down. Zacky glanced anxiously up at Papa's feet. He studied the flannel, took a whiff, made a face, and buried his nose in it, inhaling with rapture.

Papa wound a fresh piece of flannel around his finger and softly whistled a half-forgotten tune, which in his rendition sounded somber and vague: suddenly Mama poked her head out the window and searched for him between the leaves. She knew where Papa's mind was whenever he whistled that way. He began to swab the little hole. A

THE BOOK OF

bloated worm wriggled blindly in his palm, and Papa examined it, whistling out of the corner of his mouth. Long ago in Poland, a wily Communist named Zioma had talked Papa into fleeing with him over the border to join the Red Army. Oi, Zioma, Zioma, you momzer you. Mama slammed the window shut. This fig tree business was all she needed now. She tried to concentrate on polishing the fleishik knives. Papa had told her once about his childhood in Poland, about the escape to Russia and his three years in the army, about the detention camp at Komi, and his lurid flight from the taiga and the peasant's wife, but she had covered his mouth with her strong little hand and said, Enough already, Moshe, I don't want to hear any more, after I'm gone you can tell the world, you can shout it from the rooftops for all I care, but not here, not in my home, in my home I refuse to hear such things; and when the children were born, she made him swear never to speak of those terrible times. There's no reason they should know their father was an animal, so he promised her, with his patient nod and ever-ready smile; the only trouble was, she understood his whistling too. She opened the window and snapped her dust cloth on the sill. A small gray cloud flew up. The whistling ceased. Mama vanished into the house. Papa blew on the palm of his hand. The worm dropped off. He squashed it against the tree trunk with his heel, and quietly started to warble again.

Papa worked painstakingly, pausing only to explain to passing neighbors what he was doing up in the tree or to answer Hinda's calls. Two hours later, at six-thirty on the dot, when the signature tune of the evening newscast blared forth over every radio on the block, Papa rested from his labors and listened eagerly, but there was still no news of a devaluation. Aron rode up and down the street, ignoring Papa, Zacky, and the tree, veering around every so often to call his make-believe dog, Gummy, who chased his bike invisibly. Zacky stood dutifully at his post, collecting the filthy rags as they landed. How could a father leave a son like that and go off to make money in Africa, thought Papa. Then he brooded over Malka Smitanka, sending her child out so she could screw around. What does a woman like her see in that deadbeat, that slouch of an accountant, or lawyer, or whatever he was? True, he owns a car, sighed Papa, deploring the waste. Go ask Hinda for the enema bag, he shouted down to Zacky, and began to muse about the beauty mark on Malka's bosom and the sassy hair curling under her arms.

"Got it!" cried Zacky, holding up the bag and startling Papa, who only sent him off again, gloomy-eyed, to tell Hinda he would soon be home.

Papa sat back, lit a cigarette, and puffed with pleasure. From his perch in the treetop he couldn't see the building project or the street. He might have been anywhere; and if he leaned to the right he could just make out the curtains fluttering in a certain window. But he didn't move. It was June, and gallnuts hardened on the branches. A sweet fragrance enveloped him. He breathed it in.

Zacky shinned up the tree with the enema bag, and Papa winked to console him for the scolding, playfully scratching his bristly head again. "You sit here and watch," he ordered.

First he used the enema pump to dry out a sore, then he dipped a special brush into the ointment and carefully painted around the hole. Zacky stared open-mouthed at his gently moving hand. In the street below them, Aron was riding around calling "Gummy! Gummy!," his arms outstretched to make Gummy chase the bike. Papa finished painting the sore. "There," he said, looking at Zacky and passing him the enema bag. "Now you go 'phoo!' while I shmear on the ointment." Zacky pumped air into another sore, biting his tongue with the effort. They worked in silence side by side until Aron's fair head popped up between them. "How come he gets to do everything?" Aron whined. "It's my turn now."

Papa and Zacky recoiled from each other and Papa embarked on a loud explanation of how the healing process works. Zacky started cracking his knuckles, and Aron shuddered. Suddenly he had an idea. He slid down the tree and got his bicycle pump. It was a terrific idea, a brilliant idea, in fact. How quickly and efficiently the pump dried the sores. It's much faster this way, isn't it, he panted, all aglow. Yeah, growled Zacky. Noisier too.

The three of them worked together, swabbing sores, while Aron chattered to fill in the silence and make them laugh with his hilarious imitations of famous people; he did a fabulous one of the Prime Minister, even though his voice hadn't changed yet; well, what do you expect, he was only eleven and a half. Once he got started there was no stopping him, though little by little he too fell under the quiet spell of healing.

And suddenly Mama was on the balcony, calling Aron. Papa signaled the boys to keep still and they hid their heads behind the branches.

THE BOOK OF

Again she called him, certain he was there. I'm warning you, Aron, you're in for it. Papa cupped his hands over his mouth and gave a cuckoo cry, and the boys nearly burst with stifled laughter. In vain Mama searched for them, bobbing up and down, and then she turned on her heel and disappeared into the house. Now now, boys, laughed Papa, is that any way to behave? He gazed serenely at the sky and wound his thighs around the big warm tree.

3

For seven days Papa ministered to the fig tree: poking the sores, wiping them clean, daubing them with ointment. Again and again Mama stepped out on the balcony and shouted at him, what did she care who heard her, he was an idiot not to charge good money for all this work, let the Residents Association pay, they were responsible for the gardening, weren't they? But Papa knew how to sweet-talk Mama, and he stayed at his station in the tree. One day Zacky, arriving late, found Aron's little bicycle propped against the trunk and went pedaling off in circles like a jilted lover. Slowly, painstakingly, Papa and Aron worked their way up the branches. They put their heads together and examined the sores. Whenever Papa's undershirt hiked up Aron glimpsed the pale scar under his hairy red potbelly, like a silky gap in Papa's brawn that never ceased to fascinate him. You didn't get that at the camp in Komi, did you? he asked, knowing better, in an attempt to pump Papa for a trickle of forbidden memories, and Papa laughed: Not likely, not at Komi, there they left you to die like a dog. No, this is from the appendix operation in Poland, when I was about your age or a little older maybe; and then, forgetting his promise to Mama, he spoke about the terrible winter in the taiga when the earth froze so hard they couldn't bury the dead, and anyone fool enough to try to escape was found next day half-gnawed by the wolves, and some of the prisoners went crazy from hunger and fear, they went out of their minds like you go out of a room, and the worst were the inallectuals Stalin

16   THE BOOK OF

sent there, they went crazy not because they suffered more, a body is a body, same for everyone, but because . . . because . . . He shrugged his shoulders. I don't know . . . maybe they couldn't believe it was happening, they thought the world was inallectual like them, not like Stalin . . . Papa laughed and Aron laughed with him, intently watching his face.

Sometimes Edna Bloom came out for a walk and approached the tree with her dainty parasol. Papa would watch her and part the leaves, startling her every time, though she knew by now that he was a kindly giant. Oh, Mr. Kleinfeld, you gave me a fright, she gasped wide-eyed, hand on her heart, and in the silence that followed, the empty lull, she seemed suddenly transported, awaiting her own return, but then, smiling meekly, gulping solicitously, she inquired about the welfare of her fig tree. Aron thought her very beautiful, in spite of her peculiar pink coloring, which made her look almost transparent, like a newborn chick with a throbbing heart. If not for this fig tree, she confided one evening, I would have moved out of the neighborhood long ago. Uh-oh, thought Aron, she made a mistake, though what it was, he didn't know. And the next day she said she felt close to the tree, those were her words, she said that sometimes she almost felt like pouring her heart out to it, which made Aron wince again, how could she say things like that to strangers. But Edna wasn't accustomed to talking to her neighbors, even after thirteen years among them, she kept her distance. I'll show her, said Mama, I'll grab her by the roots and teach her to be civil, or at least to say hello to me. Now Aron hung his head and Papa muttered something, and he blushed even more. Edna seemed to sense she'd made a mistake, but she was in great high spirits so she quickly forgave herself, waving a jolly goodbye, and promising to return next day, same time, same place. Aron smiled at Papa. He tried to catch his eye as she walked away, but Papa avoided looking at him and said, Quick, start blowing on the sores.

Edna hurried upstairs and ran breathlessly to the curtain. A breeze was blowing, rustling the leaves, making shadows flicker on Papa's back. She could see the thick of his neck, the fleshly nape. She could put him together like a jigsaw puzzle, here a biceps, there a shin; and when he twisted his arm around she glimpsed the scar on it winding through the leaves like a tropical snake. His hefty legs swung down beside the scrawny boy's, and she wondered how the son would ever grow up to be a man. Suddenly her eyes twinkled with a rare gleam of mischief, and she dashed to the kitchen to make a pitcher of lemonade. With a giggle and a blush and an Edna-what's-come-over-you, she poured the lemon concentrate and sugar in the water and gave it a vigorous stir. But as she approached the window her hands went limp. What, would she lean out the window, call him by name, and hand him the drinks . . . maybe it wasn't such a good idea after all. Still carrying the pitcher, she paced through the rooms, vexed and disappointed with herself.

A curious silence descended over the block. In steamy kitchens, red-faced housewives looked up from their tasks. Husbands dozing under the newspaper on their balcony lounge chairs sat up and listened. The distant strains of a Chopin mazurka trickled through the dreary building project, over the rusty banisters, the spatterdash entrance walls and crooked mailboxes, and out to the sickly yellow lawn. For years she hadn't touched the piano, now she was playing again.

Up in the fig tree, Papa and Aron peered shyly into each other's eyes and quickly looked away. Papa was busy wiping a sore, patiently prob-ing it with his fingers. Aron considered asking for a new guitar as a bar mitzvah present. He remembered the time he caught Mama watching him play the old one; that was a mistake, she had walked in and seen the look in his eyes. You're giving me a hole in the head, she shouted. Go outside and play with your friends, we didn't spend half Papa's salary to buy you a bicycle so you'd stay in here hunched over your guitar all day, and really, the bike was great, he loved it, only he wanted something more. What it was, though, he couldn't say. More, that's all. But they had already decided what to give him for his bar mitzvah, a savings account, that's what, so that twenty years from now he would be able to buy an apartment for his wife. His wife? Who cared about his wife. Maybe he could still talk them into buying him a guitar. Tenderly he strummed the tree, accompanying Edna, and then he rubbed the chicken-pox scar on his chin; and Papa had another bar mitzvah present to give him, a very special one: the army shaving kit with the razor and the shaving soap and the little tray he used in the Sinai campaign. But all Aron wanted was a guitar; and again he strummed the tree and rubbed his chin and strummed again, with the dreamy look of a medieval scribe dipping his quill into the inkpot.

Even though the big event was still a year and a half away, Mama and Papa were up to their ears in arrangements. They were planning a

THE BOOK OF

grandiose affair, said Mama, they would rent the Empyrean Hall and hire an expensive photographer from Photo Gwirtz this time instead of using old Uncle Shimmik, whose hands trembled so badly at the last family affair that Mama came out looking hideous. Yochi's bat mitzvah party had been celebrated modestly at home, and now she flew into a jealous rage. On me you scrimp, she exploded, and Mama replied, with a hint of malice, that a bar mitzvah is different, like it or not. Don't worry, we'll make it up to you with your wedding, only first let's see the suitors, ha ha ha.

At night when Aron got up for a drink, he would find his parents huddled together over the big bar mitzvah ledger on the kitchen table. Cast aside were the Sick Fund stampbooks—who had time for them nowadays—the reddish-yellow stamps were glued on any which way, while the ledger was carefully bound in green shelf paper with a label on the cover: ARON'S BAR MITZVAH. Here his parents entered the menu of every bar mitzvah they attended, reckoned the costs, counted courses, criticized and compared the cuisine. In a year and a half the mortgage would be paid up, and they would take out a little loan, which, together with what they'd managed to put by already, would be enough to throw him such a bar mitzvah party, Mama clasped him to her bosom, "Their eyes will pop!"

Now she appeared on the balcony, searching high and low, her nostrils flaring. Papa yanked Aron back into the tree as stealthily as a guerrilla fighter, till both of them were safely hidden from her scrutiny. All Aron could see now through the leaves were her fingers turning white on the balcony railing.

"Moshe!" she shrieked, "how long do you intend to stay up there wiping snot?" A hush fell over the building. The tinkling of the piano died away.

Papa tucked his neck between his shoulders, then pushed it out again, thick and red, with a throbbing blue vein. Aron cringed. He had never seen Papa like this before, but Papa controlled himself, clenched his powerful jaws, and gravely, deliberately, began to smear the ointment on the sores. Mama waited, and then suddenly pounded on the railing: "A-ron!"—the sound waves encircled him like iron rings around a pole—"come home this instant to try on your boots!"

"What? But it's summer!" he whispered to Papa.

Papa nodded. His eyes still intimated danger, but his chin dredged up an old excuse: "That's Mama for you, she likes to have things ready in advance," he whispered. "Suppose we have to buy you a new pair of boots this year?"

But of course they would have to, the old pair was two years old, all worn out, with cracks in the soles. He definitely needed a new pair of boots: he and Gideon and Zacky were planning to open a tadpole farm, they were going to sell frogs to Bonaparte's, the first French restaurant in Jerusalem.

"What is it," whispered Papa. "Why the long face?"

Aron turned away so Papa wouldn't see him. "Why does she have to talk to me like that," he grumbled.

"Don't take it to heart, Aronchik, your mama loves you. She worries, that's why she talks like that."

"I'm as tall as Gideon, I'm as tall as most of the kids in my class."

"She wants you to be the best in everything, that's all. A mother is a mother."

"She hurt my feelings."

Papa stroked his head. Aron melted at the touch. Again the piano tinkled upstairs, tentative, wary, like the first green sprouts after a forest fire. Papa sat still. Only his hand moved, stroking Aron. There was still enough light to see the veins on the leaves. The music fluttered through them, plucking delicate strings. Aron peeked up at the sky, the deep blue sky of twilight. And then Papa stared into his eyes until he made him smile.

"Anyway," said Papa, "what's-his-name, Napoleon, he was a shorty, and so was Zioma Schwatznicker, now that's a fact!"

4

Aron found Mama in the kitchen, wobbling on the Franzousky with her head in the storage loft. Hearing him enter, she popped out again wearing a pink rubber bathing cap to protect her from the dust. Don't think I didn't see you in the tree, that we'll settle later, now go get a pair of woolen socks from the sock drawer in the big closet. Woolen socks? grumbled Aron. Now? In the middle of summer? How do you expect to try on boots, then? Barefoot? But in this heat, Mama, wool? I know what I'm doing, now go get the socks.

Angrily he opened the closet in his parents' bedroom. Behind the sock drawer he found a little brown envelope, like the kind that came in the mail with Papa's reserve orders, only this one had no name or address on it. Printed across the envelope were the words *Alfonso's Pussy Circus*. He peeked inside and saw something strange, a black-and-white photograph on the back of a playing card. He knew at a glance this was something he shouldn't be looking at. But when he peeked again, his hands began to tremble. Close the door and get out, he commanded himself. Close the door and get out, he whispered to save his soul, then slipped the card into the envelope and put it back, trembling so much he almost dropped the socks. He stood frozen in the middle of the bedroom. What was I looking for? And again he commanded, with a quivering voice, Get out of here now! I said now! Then he stumbled to his room and flopped down on the bed, to calm himself before Mama found the boots in the storage loft. He curled up in a ball and suddenly realized that things had not been going at all well lately. There were certain signs, like the broken guitar strings or the fights with Zacky, though what did they prove, what did they mean, he only knew that up until now, it might have been possible to turn back the wheel of signs and proofs. He didn't think, he only tried to listen to the sober voice inside him whisper: "Not good," and "Tsk tsk tsk," like a doctor's prognosis, and Aron was startled, not by the voice, but by the gravity of the "Tsk tsk tsk" and the shake of the head that accompanied it, like Mama's that time they passed a fatal road accident on the bus to Tel Aviv, and suddenly he recoiled at the thought. Nothing's changed, he told himself, it's just a mood, get up, but he didn't.

The day was over; a lazy summer evening stretched ahead. From every doorway came smells of salad finely chopped, dewy cucumbers in yogurt, herring wreathed with onion, eggs dancing sunny side up, fresh rye bread thickly sliced and ready on the table. The sultry sky began to darken at the seams. Blithe new strains floated through the fourth-floor window—hesitant at first, measured and slow, then breaking loose in a rampage of pounding. Papa sighed and collected his tools from the fig tree. He looked down at his fingers, stained yellow with the ointment, as he listened to the music, wrinkling his brow in an effort to remember where he'd heard it before. He shrugged his shoulders. Hinda's voice boomed out, she'd found the boots and was calling Aron to try them on. Just as he jumped down from the fig tree, Zacky rode over. "You mean to say you've been up there alone the whole time?" He scowled in innocent dismay. "Go on home now, it's getting dark," said Papa, and Zacky stared down at his bicycle fender and said he didn't feel like going home yet. But it's dangerous to ride around without a light, Zachary; Don't have one—dynamo's out. Remind me tomorrow and I'll fix it for you: never fear—Moishe's here. And Papa scratched his prickly hair, but his mind was elsewhere, his hand perfunctory, and Zacky drew back with indignation and quickly rode away, pouting as he leaned over the handlebars. Oh, please let a car speed by with blinding headlights, like a fist out of the blue. Around the corner he slowed to a stop, looked both ways, and kicked the taillight of the Fiat with all his might.

Mama reached into Aron's boots and pulled out the wads of newspaper. Aron trudged wearily through the hall, careful to conceal himself from her penetrating eyes, fervently praying for a last-minute reprieve.

THE BOOK OF

If only someone would explain it to him, slowly and patiently. Walking like this, in slow motion, he was reminded of David Lipschitz, the albino kid in his class. That's how David walked, dragging his feet and wagging his head from side to side. Papa was at the front door; he pressed the handle with his elbow and came in, carrying his tools and medicines. "Hey there, Aronchik, why so glum?" Papa smiled at Aron's startled face, the brush sticking out of the corner of his mouth. Aron panicked, what if he headed for the bedroom now and looked behind the winter-sock drawer. But instead he went to put the palette with the jars and the rags down on a newspaper in the bathroom. I'm going to shave now, Mamaleh, and then we can sit down to eat. At least he didn't suspect anything. Aron hurried to the bedroom, but changed his mind. Not now. His lips were dry, crusty, how would he get the pictures out of there without his parents noticing? Someone might suddenly walk in and go straight to the closet, and then what?

Mama emerged from the kitchen and found him leaning against the wall. She rushed to his side: "What's wrong, Aronchik, why are you acting like this?" Everything's all right; he waved limply. Maybe I got out of bed too fast and it made me dizzy in the head. I'll be okay in a minute probably. She gave him one of her special hugs and held him so tightly he could feel a worrisome throbbing under her skin, an intense vibration almost like an engine inside her. "Mama, you're strangling me!" Gently she let him go, and again he pressed himself into her body, into her soft, saggy waistline, her heaving bosom, and the perspiring nest under her arms, and suddenly he tore himself away, afraid to touch her even with his fingertips, and she opened her eyes wide with a strange little laugh: "Too big to hug your mama? All right, go try on the boots, they're on top of the cans in the pantry." And she went off giggling to tell Papa.

Aron reached into the old boots and pulled out a few more wads of last year's newspaper. He spread one over his face to hide from the world, but an item with a squiggly line around it caught his attention, something about a young blacksmith from a village in Armenia who died and was buried in a wooden coffin, but at night the gravekeeper heard the sound of kicking and ran away, and the next morning the police came and pried off the coffin lid and they found the blacksmith, only his face was contorted and his nails were broken, and the lid was covered with scratches. "God in heaven," said Mama in his ear, "how long does His Majesty intend to keep us waiting? Would you please try on your boots already?"

Aron slumped down on the benkaleh and leaned over to unbuckle his sandal. Where were we? David Lipschitz's father works for the Ministry of the Interior, he's a big shot, that's why the school authorities let David pass each year. Aron felt benevolent as he contemplated David Lipschitz, as though suddenly he had all the time in the world to pay an old debt. Did David wag his head like that even in his sleep, Aron wondered. Tick-tock! The big albino face with the eyes blinking out like frightened creatures in a cave . . . and the only thing he cares about is Anat Fish. The cruel and beautiful Anat Fish, who has a "freshie" boyfriend. David stares at her and smiles, he'll pay a whole sandwich for one of her pencils or a sheet of paper from her loose-leaf notebook, and if you bring him her sweater, he nuzzles it and his eyes get misty. Sometimes in winter he runs out of the classroom, and when the bell rings, you find him in the hallway, rubbing against her coat. But she's so mean, she never looks back. She has eyes like an Egyptian queen. Aron pulled the sandal strap.

The front door opened and slammed shut: Yochi was home from Madame Nikova's. She threw herself down on the bed and burst out crying. She often cried these days, especially after ballet class; he could hear Papa humming in the bathroom as he lathered his face. A year and a half from now, it all goes to me, he mused: the shaving soap and the razor and the shiny tray, but the thought of it was not particularly exciting; in fact, the certainty of it only oppressed him, and alienated him from Papa even more, and suddenly he imagined Mama there, all dressed up, with a fat banana hairdo, smiling radiantly at the company as her fingers searched under his chin for the chicken-pox scar. "Didn't I tell you whiskers would cover it one day?" Aron pulled away indignantly: he remembered the first time she said that, when he was seven years old. He had resented her deeply, she sounded as though she wanted to lock him inside the future and jangle the keys in his face.

"No bread for me, thank you," said Yochi as she sat down red-eyed.

"What, no bread? You can't live without bread."

"I said no bread!" Her lips were quivering. "You should have heard the names Madame Nikova called me."

"Yocheved," cooed Mama, wiping her hands on the apron with the

THE BOOK OF

kangaroo, "Madame Nikova may be an expert on dancing, but I know something about girls and growing up."

"Look, just look at this!" screamed Yochi, kicking her leg out and slapping her thigh where it joined the hip. The pink flesh rippled. "It's because you never sit down properly when you eat," Mama explained, "I've told you a thousand times—" "And today she put me back in the second row!"

"Yochileh," said Papa quietly, "at your age you've got to build your bones. Later on you can reduce if you want to, but now the bones need nourishment."

Yochi shook her head and squeezed her mouth shut to keep from crying.

"One slice?" asked Mama. "With butter and a little matjes herring?"

Yochi shook her head furiously, then tucked it between her shoulders as though waiting for a blow. Ever so casually Mama opened the jar of matjes herring, swirled it around in the air, and forked out three fat pieces. Then she spread a slice of bread with a thick layer of creamy butter. Yochi turned her face to the wall. From his seat in the pantry Aron could see the yellow-red eruption on her cheeks and forehead; soon she'd get the curse again and everyone would start worrying, that's what happened every month since the fateful day she flushed her curse down the toilet and there was a big eisseh-beisseh because in the middle of supper Mama raised her knife and pointed, and her face turned pale and she lost her voice, and when they looked around they saw a tiny lagoon spilling out of the bathroom, flowing through the hallway into the kitchen, and Papa ran to get the pliers from his tool chest in the pantry, and the water kept gushing out and Papa stuck his hand with the pliers all the way in to see what was clogging the toilet, which spewed up more and more muck and filth, and finally he fished out a glob of something that looked like a piece of meat, and he stood there gaping at it until Mama grabbed the pliers from him and waved the glob in front of Yochi's nose. Well well, the princess has the curse, like a million other women, including her mother, and right on time, too, so just keep it to yourself, you don't have to shout it from the rooftops, and then she waved the pliers in front of her, like a triumphant surgeon, screaming at the top of her lungs; maybe that's when Yochi developed the whistling in her ears, and Yochi, nobody's lemaleh, sat perfectly still this time, red as blood, and after that she was always careful with the curse, and Aron too learned to be careful in the toilet, and Mama said, "Nu, Aron, are you going to stand there gaping all night, can't you see the table's set?"

From the pantry he watched them sit down to supper, reflecting how cozy the kitchen was at times like this, with everyone eating and talking at once, but the wistful scene dissolved before his eyes, and an arctic fog descended, full of ghoulish apparitions, naked bodies, tangled limbs, a dog on top of a woman; he suddenly felt the blood drain from his hand as he picked a boot up and reached into the lining with its smell of old fur, glancing bleakly at Yochi slouched over the table, angling for breadcrumbs with her little finger; and from Yochi's jaundiced face to Grandma Lilly, not yet sixty and already senile, muttering to herself as she wandered around the house, and only a year ago she was so lucid, so cheerful, and then a tiny blood vessel got clogged up and that was that; how he pitied his parents, especially Mama, working so hard to keep Grandma's illness a secret, to hide it from everybody, including their rummy friends on Friday night, and then he remembered it was Tuesday, and on Tuesdays Mama served bananas in sour cream with sugar on top in those orange dessert dishes, and while he wasn't so crazy about squashed bananas, he liked to see the expression on Mama's face when she served it to him, and he felt a pang; where were we, what were we thinking about, oh yes, his film collection, the negatives he picked up outside Photo Lichtman, and the pieces of celluloid he'd found, including one really long strip from an actual movie showing a tall woman with white eyeballs, white lips, and black, flowing hair, which meant that in real life she was blond, and she was standing in the doorway, talking to someone, and the subtitles said: "Don't kid yourself, Rupert, no one is indispensable"; but what if Grandma died, she was a little girl once too, you know, there may be billions of people in the world, but there's only one Grandma, and he checked again, carefully, but knew it was hopeless, he had seen what he had seen, and he heaved a sigh, how fragile life is, he never realized that before, yes, they would have to pull together as a team, in perfect loyalty, he melted with compassion for them, for their smugness and ignorance of what lurked behind the sock drawer. Slowly and carefully he unbuckled his sandal, and nearly fell asleep again over his outstretched foot, but who could have brought such a thing into this house and hidden it in the

THE BOOK OF

bedroom, and then he had another staggering thought, what if his finding the cards behind the drawer had made him, God forbid, an accessory in the crime, his fingerprints were smeared all over the pictures, so the agent who smuggled them in could use them as evidence to blackmail him, there were stories like that in the newspaper sometimes, and it was anyone's guess what a person like that was capable of, and how would Aron be able to prove he was pure and innocent?

He felt exhausted, as if he'd just been through a terrible ordeal, like one of those poor children he read about in books who had to leave home and fend for themselves. Papa came out of the bathroom with shaving cream on his face. Aron lay low, and felt his soul evaporate into a single quivering strand; carefully he put the boot on his childish foot, and was startled to find everyone staring at him, even Yochi turned in her chair, and Grandma came closer and gawked at him, making him shrink even more, his bare foot drained white, his skin numb and cold.

Nu nu, said Papa. Nu nu what? said Mama. Nu nu, it fits, said Papa, and wrinkled his brow, as his lower lip covered the upper lip. That I can see for myself, said Mama, that much is obvious. Maybe the sock isn't thick enough, suggested Papa, his mouth a red hole in a mountain of foam. It's a heavy winter sock, said Mama, I specifically told him to get a heavy winter sock. But he's worn those boots for two years in a row; Papa suddenly raised his voice. Tell that to him, not me, said Mama, turning away. Please, Mama, please buy me a new pair! whispered Aron. In your dreams, answered Mama, pulling off the boot. You'll get new ones the day I have hair growing here, she said, indicating the palm of her hand with an arching of a furious eyebrow. Go on, y'alla. She pushed him away, stuffing last year's newspapers back in the boots. Wash your hands and come to the table, and if you know what's good for you, you'll finish every bite on your plate.

5

 There was Rosaline, and Natalie, and Lizzy and the chimp, and Angela, the blind girl, and Roxana, his favorite, and Alfonso, the whip-cracking dwarf, ringmaster of the Pussy Circus. Each picture had a caption under it scribbled in Hebrew: "Giddyap! To the Race-track of Desire," said the one showing the black stallion named Ringo with zaftig Lizzy. "Now she sees . . ." said the one showing Fritz the chimp paired off with Angela, who knows by touch. The slovenly, unfamiliar writing was full of misspellings that irked him even more than the pictures did: corruption spread like mildew from the pictures to the words. He also noticed that the newspaper Alfonso was reading in the picture where Rosaline crouched between his hairy knees was in a foreign language. Looking through a magnifying glass, he saw it wasn't English: the letters were crooked and clumsy, and he couldn't make out the date either, though the magnifying glass did reveal a number of large, greasy fingerprints on some of the photos, especially the ones of Roxana. With the eyes of a detective, he examined the pictures one by one and deduced from the evidence that this circus was in serious financial trouble: the high-heeled shoes worn by smiling Natalie turned up on Angela, the blind girl, in the card with the silver horn, and Fritz's eating trough reappeared in the picture where Alfonso uses Natalie as a saddle on Ringo. The pictures really disgusted him, yet every time his parents stepped out the door, he went running back to the sock drawer, he couldn't help it, he had to take one last peek,

THE BOOK OF

and a moment later he was at it again, frantically thumbing through the cards, God forbid he should skip one; then he would slip them back in the envelope and continue sitting there, distraught, as though he'd just seen them for the first time, these joyless men and women, naked slaves of an invisible emperor, writhing together like hammy actors in a play, with twisted grins and bulging eyes.

Who then, he wondered, had smuggled these cards into the house, who were the girls, who was the photographer, and supposing the circus was still in town, on an ordinary street nearby where crowds of lecherous adults gathered even now to pay their homage to the emperor . . . One night he woke with a start: a distant blast, like an engine backfiring, had frightened him out of a deep sleep, and he lay rigidly in his bed, certain that not too far from the building project, amid whispered confessions and ghostly groans, the emperor's slaves were pitching the circus tent, erecting the king pole for a hasty performance, and in the dim glow of the spotlight the ring looked like a huge red eyeball or a cavernous mouth, and Alfonso, in a top hat, cracked his whip while four grimacing, grease-smeared girls jumped obediently through a burning hoop . . .

He had to tell somebody. Zacky and Gideon were his two best friends, of course, but he couldn't possibly tell Gideon. That would breach their noble silence, that would be a sacrilege. And Zacky, well, Zacky was worse than ever, sadly enough, though it wasn't really his fault, it was just the change. Anyway, Zacky knew more than was good for him; what if he used dirty language and turned the mystery into something more disgusting than it already was.

At school, in class, Aron stares down at his desk. His teacher, Rivka Bar-Ilan, is talking about a rabbi who fled from Jerusalem during the Roman siege; her voice drones on, she barely moves her lips. "Now, did Rabbi Yohanan Ben-Zakai advise his followers to surrender because he was a traitor?" She hunts for names in her attendance notebook: "Michael Carny, answer the question." Aron retreats into his thoughts again. Michael Carny sits across the room. He's tall but limp, like a jellyfish. Giggly Rina Fichman at his side tries to whisper the answer out of the corner of her mouth. "No teamwork, please," says the teacher wearily, scouring the rows with heavy-lidded eyes. "Well, Michael Carny?"

Michael giggles in distress. "Rabbi Yohanan Ben-Zakai," he repeats slowly, as though the name itself should be enough to acquit him, but Rivka Bar-Ilan screws up her mouth and makes a mark in her notebook. "Hanan Schweiky." "Yes, Teach?" Poor Hanan, half reclining on the desk, is diligently drawing a picture, his head resting in the crook of his left arm with his hand perched over it, parrotlike. Aron tries to collect himself and remember the question. They were talking about some traitor. But who? The noose tightens. You never see her lose her temper, though, not Rivka Bar-Ilan. She just keeps talking in that cool, indifferent voice, making those little marks in her notebook, and if you get three X's beside your name, she sends you to the principal's office.

This is their fifth and next-to-last class today, after this there's math and then home. Meirky Blutreich in the row by the window is trying to focus sun rays on his lenses. There's a long black line of fuzz from his sideburns to his cheeks, and a couple of times when he raised his arm, Aron thought he saw a shadow there. He tried to sneak a closer glimpse in the locker room before gym class, but no luck, and according to the new rule, you have to see it three times in broad daylight for it to count as incontrovertible evidence. Aron slips his hand in and cautiously touches himself. He's as warm and smooth as a baby there. Now the teacher's asking Zacky Smitanka, who naturally doesn't know the answer either, and when she writes the X in her notebook, he spins around with a goofy smile on his face, as if to say, Fooled her, didn't I? Twenty-four minutes to go, Gil Kaplan signals the class, two fingers and four fingers over his head. He has wavy hair like a movie star, and the girls say he sleeps with a net at night. Aron looks down at the grooves on his desk: fifteen days till summer vacation. Fifteen days times five hours a day equals seventy-five hours. Oh well.

Hanan Schweiky, the class comedian, bends down, sticks a piece of balloon in his mouth, and sucks it in. Then he sits up again looking innocent and starts rolling the balloon around under his desk. Something's happening. Aliza Lieber, the redhead, takes her glasses off and sticks the sidepieces into the corners of her mouth. Aron watches her, she always does that, and suddenly it dawns on him that she's trying to stretch her lips. He sits up straight; it's a good thing the teacher is busy with Gil Kaplan now, otherwise she would have noticed the spark of interest, the gleam of light in the tedium spreading toward her. He glances furtively at Aliza Lieber. It's true! She thinks she can stretch

THE BOOK OF

her lips that way! She thinks her mouth is too small! He sure has been making a lot of discoveries lately.

A sudden pop: the balloon. Raucous laughter, groans of protest. Meirky Blutreich, the troublemaker, ducks down the row to deliver a painful swat on the neck to Michael Carny, now cross-eyed with tears, whose fellow gigglepuss, Rina Fichman, jumps up and shouts at Meirky. Rivka Bar-Ilan raps the desk with her notebook. Not angrily, but leadenly: one, two, three. Her eyes show only weary contempt for this display. To no avail: the children crackle with indignation, zigzag curses across the aisle, explode with hilarity, and flash their eyes in a great electric storm that discharges the boredom of the classroom.

Aron sits quietly at his desk. At times like this he has learned to stay calm. Regarding the class with open eyes. Maybe it's a sign that he's changing. Maturing. Gideon sits there, serious and quiet like him. But he has a disapproving, even haughty look in his eyes. Aron doesn't like that look. Next year Gideon will be a youth group leader. He quit Scouts because there wasn't enough Zionist content for him, but he has no intention of joining a kibbutz. Gideon has principles, he plans his life to the last detail: in six and a half years he will join the air force like his brother Manny. Then he'll work as a commercial pilot for El Al. Gideon gets a little puffed up at times, but the kids respect him, and even though he never goofs off in class, they know he isn't a coward or anything, he just has principles. Still, Aron can't help wondering when Gideon managed to develop such a responsible attitude—the two of them have been together practically all their lives; since they were born, in fact.

The class simmers down. Gil Kaplan flashes eighteen minutes to go. At least something worthwhile came out of that hullabaloo. "So we see that Rabbi Yohanan Ben-Zakai was neither a coward nor a traitor," says the teacher. "He was a seeker of peace, and when he realized that the inhabitants of the besieged city were not going to survive without food, he left secretly to speak to the Roman governor, Titus Vespasian. And now, who can tell me how Rabbi Yohanan Ben-Zakai managed to escape—yes, I see you, Zachary—from the besieged city? Yes, Zachary, what is it?"

Zacky is suddenly speechless. His vigorously waving hand begins to wilt. Furious with himself for being such a numskull, he slouches dumbly in his seat. Rivka Bar-Ilan throws him a sidelong glance and sighs. Then she asks another boy, and Zacky spins around with his goofy grin as if to say, Fooled you again, didn't I? Aron studies the grooves in the desk: with seventeen minutes to go, he has now entered the horse phase. Then, in descending order, come the donkey, fox, dog (these minutes run very close together), cat, rabbit, mouse, fly (the final minutes, and then the final half minutes): mosquito, amoeba, germ, atom. And next to the atom, which has to be imagined, comes the great picture of a bell and the words "Born Free."

But it isn't time yet. Don't get excited. Imagine the horse phase lasting forever, and then suddenly Gil Kaplan locks hands over his head and flashes: Surprise! Thirteen minutes! Over a minute in the fox and we didn't even notice.

In the back of the room, alone by the wall, sits David Lipschitz. His head keeps jerking to the left: click! click! Like a water sprinkler. It's huge, his head. His hair is almost white. Aron has found a sly way of watching him. He takes a good long look in his direction, and absorbs his features: the scowling pink cheeks; the eyes blinking bitterly, darting madly around in the caves under his albino eyebrows. But why is he angry? Lately Aron has been trying to guess certain things: for instance, does he have his own room at home? And when did the change take place, or maybe he was born that way because his mother happened to look at an albino while she was pregnant with him. And did his parents really love him? Did his mother scream when she saw her baby was a freak? And did he have a younger brother or sister who was a comfort to his parents? And how would it feel to have a younger brother who was smarter and more normal than you were? Aron swerves around. David Lipschitz noticed. How could he have noticed? Aron sits up and concentrates on the teacher's lips. In his film collection at home he has one negative that's exactly like David: a boy with a big white head, slumping over a desk. Sometimes Aron holds the film up to the light and searches for the aura most of them have; and he tries to imagine Mr. Lipschitz walking into David's room at night and laying his hand on David's head, the way Papa does sometimes, but for different reasons. At home in front of the mirror once, Aron put his hand on his own head and started to jerk it. Strangely enough, the touch of his hand relaxed him, and right away the jerking stopped. Okay, so David's father, the big shot from the Ministry of the Interior, comes home from work, finds David sitting in his room, staring morosely out the window at the children in the street, longing for Anat Fish. Gently he lays his hand on David's bony head, and it jerks, once, twice, but then as he spreads his palm over it like a warm cap, it slowly yields to him and stops jerking, and for a moment when Aron stood before the mirror he imagined David's scowling face becoming human, longing for comfort. He gazed in wonder at the sharp, expectant face, thinking: This is you. This is the boy you are. This is the face you have. He shut his eyes tightly and, when he opened them again, he saw only himself, okay, but that's cheating, you deliberately put on the American expression, still, you can't deny that your face shows life and hope for the future. And then he grimaced and watched himself in the mirror. Isn't it strange how one little scowl can reveal the pattern of distortion? And he arranged his features and smoothed out the kinks.

Varda Koppler turns around in her seat, searching for eyes to avoid. She's short and skinny and has tiny breasts, and she keeps stretching her blouse all the time. Varda Koppler has a grown-up face, with a big, strong nose and smoldering eyes, but she has the body of a little chick. It's strange. Like a campfire on a matchstick. Wouldn't it be interesting to know how girls feel about their breasts, or maybe it's no big deal for them, like a shoulder or a knee would be for him. Varda wears a ring on every finger. She can't wait to grow up. She has a pen pal, a soldier from the Golani unit, and she knows army secrets. Koby Kimchi in the next seat looks up at her and sighs, and Aron reflects: Here we've been together since kindergarten, yet it feels as if we're separating.

But why is he so heavy-hearted. Last year on the school trip to Tiberias they sat around the lake at night, after the teachers went back to the hostel, and built a campfire and laughed and talked till dawn, and dozed off in a heap, like some huge, weird animal that breathed with one enormous lung. Aron was the first to open his eyes in the morning. The Sea of Galilee was smooth and pure, and the morning twilight quivered upon it like a harp string.

Twelve minutes left.

Will this class never be over. And there's still math. Fifty minutes. Another countdown, then it starts all over again. And during recess he'll have to copy the answers to two math problems he didn't finish yesterday. So he won't even have ten minutes for soccer. If it takes a workman three days to tear down a wall, how many days will it take him to tear down a house . . . He turns around in his seat, wriggling in a way that lets him see Adina Ringle's watch. Still twelve minutes! I'm telling you, this lesson will go on forever. They'll be stuck in this room for the rest of their lives: while other kids go out to recess, run home, grow up, join the army, get married, their class will be forgotten, until at last, one fine day the saving bell will ring and they'll hobble out to the sun-filled schoolyard, trembling and bewildered, blinking in amazement, thronged by the children of the next generation. He smiles inside, so no one will notice he's awake. Dorit Alush, the cow in the next seat, looks up at him with her muddy eyes. Moo.

I don't believe it, still twelve minutes! Is there something wrong with all the clocks? Has some mad magician frozen time? How will I get through twelve whole minutes? Okay, here's how we do it: yes. Far, far away in Tel Mond prison lives a convicted murderer, sentenced to life. Or better yet, Papa, a Russian soldier guarding the armory for three years in the freezing cold, hopping from foot to foot in the snow, another month and he will be released, then another week, another day, another twelve minutes, oh joy, and suddenly, wait, what's this, two men approach and ask him to accompany them for five minutes, but instead they board a train, and for eight long days he wriggles in his seat, they never say a word to him, and in Moscow, the prison, Taganka, Lubyanka, Aron faints and an interrogator who looks like the Angel of Death beats his face to a steak, and what did Aron think of, what kept him going, I'll tell you what, his memories of schooldays, of the children in his class, this is what he clings to with what's left of his mind when they send him to Komi, to the frozen taiga, to chop trees for the railroad, oi Zioma, you momzer, damn you, Zioma, and all around him people are dropping like flies, from hunger, from disease, they go out of their mind like you go out of a room, and he heaves his ax, wistfully remembering the happy faces of his classmates long ago; there was that girl, yes, what was her name, Varda Koppler, a little thing with smoldering eyes, and there was Gil Kaplan, and Eli Ben-Zikri, the hood; together we passed our childhood days in a sunny classroom with pictures on the walls, and a map of Israel, and plenty of fresh air, and there was recess. Aron feels himself reviving: Hey, this is great, where were we, and all around him people are dropping like flies, but you can't bury the dead here in winter, the earth is frozen solid, hard as marble, and if you make trouble they throw you in the cellar with the

THE BOOK OF

corpses, you spend one night down there and you come out raving, eight long hours; and he doesn't give in, he fights, he seals himself off hermetically—hurry now, use your brains—in the cellar, in all this horror; think about the war you waged as a child, don't ask, someone smuggled pictures into the house, and there was nobody to turn to, he had to face the enemy alone, oh if only he could have talked to Yochi about it. Yochi, who are you kidding, he giggles. In our house you learn to hold your tongue. In our house you never hear a dirty word. Mama and Papa leave their bedroom door ajar. Aron and Yochi never talk about such things, not even when they're alone together. Even the time they fished her curse out of the toilet, and Aron was scared and wanted to ask her things, he felt too much like a traitor because he'd scowled at her with the rest of them, and now it was every man for himself, he would have to fight this war alone: but who was the enemy? Okay, let's go, we're freezing, it's pitch dark, there's a crackling sound, the dead are stirring, their bones contract in the icy cold, you could go crazy with that noise, but you know what scared him the most, what worried him more than anything, a pack of dirty pictures, that's right, and once in desperation he set a trap, he wound a yellow thread around the envelope before replacing it in the drawer. And then he stayed in the house all day, on the lookout for the enemy agent, listening for the sound of drawers opening. And the next morning when he ran to the drawer, lo and behold, the thread was gone. He could have sworn there hadn't been any strangers in the house. Nervously Aron stretches in his seat. Remember, Aron. Remember this. The way it used to be. A time will come when you'll miss all this, when you'll melt at the very thought of it! And one day, long ago, when he was seven or eight, he ran home and found Papa holding Mama against the salon wall, hugging her and squeezing her into the corner, funny he should remember that just now, and when Mama caught sight of Aron over Papa's shoulder, she tried to push Papa away—"The boy!"—but he didn't want to let her go, or maybe he couldn't, Aron had learned since then that it can happen to dogs too, Papa must have gotten stuck; he pulled his face away, but the rest of him clung to her with a will of its own, it wasn't Papa's fault, some higher force was making him do it. "Stop already! The boy!" she rasped, and finally he unstuck himself and stood in the corner, panting shamefacedly, but a little smile slithered over his lips, oozing with the slime inside him, and his arms, which a moment ago had looked too long, dangling ape-like at his sides, began to shrink to their natural proportions, and that was the last time, thank God: only Aron couldn't afford to take chances, he always coughed outside the door, he was so used to doing it, he barely remembered why anymore, though there wasn't really much point, since it had never happened again.

Eleven minutes. What is this? He's been halfway around the world and only one minute has gone by? He leans back against the uncomfortable chair. Dorit Alush is the girl Zacky likes, but Aron feels indifferent toward her. They have nothing in common. They've been deskmates for two months now. Nitza Knoller, their homeroom teacher, moved him up to Dorit's desk because she couldn't see him behind Hanan Schweiky anymore. Dorit and Aron rarely speak. All day she chews the same stick of gum, and every class she draws a picture of a boy with long, straight bangs. That's the only face she knows how to draw. She's probably drawn a thousand of them by now. At least she could add a mustache for variety. What does he know about her, though, not much. That her father has a stall at the Machaneh Yehuda market where he displays his homemade mechanical diver toys in a tank of water. Maybe their house is full of diver toys. Aron feels like scribbling on her picture. He has an urge to rip it up. What would happen if he lit a match and burned it? She'd only draw another one. And someday she'll forget Aron Kleinfeld and the millions of hours they sat together. Oops, his foot slips, he kicks the desk. At least her hand moves and she frowns at him. Maybe she will remember him after all.

Ten minutes.

Last year in English class they learned the present continuous. Aron was thrilled: I em go–eeng, I em sleep–eeng. You don't have that *eeng* tense in Hebrew. Gideon didn't understand why he was so excited. Well, Gideon was like that, dead set against anything non-Israeli, non-Zionist, especially anything English, because the British loused up our country under the Mandate, and if we had one drop of pride we wouldn't be learning their stupid language. Aron wanted to point out that the Hebrew language has just as many exceptions to the rule, but he held his tongue and reveled in "I em jum–peeng . . ." Jumping far, far out in space, halfway to infinity, and soon he was utterly absorbed and utterly alone; jum–peeng; it was like being in a glass bubble, and someone watching from the outside might think Aron ees only jum–peeng, but inside the bubble, there was so much happening, every second

THE BOOK OF

lasted an hour, and the secrets of time were revealed to him and the others who experienced time the way he did, under a magnifying glass, and inside you feel private, intimate, and the people watching you, pressing their faces against the bubble, wonder what's going on; they stand on the outside looking in, puzzled and sweaty and filthy, and again he asks himself what it will be like when his bar mitzvah comes around in a year and a half, will he start growing those stiff black hairs all over, his might be blond, though; what happens, does some mysterious force squeeze the hairs out through the epidermis, and does it hurt, and he vows that even when he's big and hairy someday, with coarse skin like Papa and other men have, he will always remember the boy he used to be, and engrave him deep in his memory, because otherwise certain things might vanish in the course of growing up, it's hard to say what, there's a quality that makes all adults seem similar, not in looks so much, or even in personality, it's this thing they have in common that makes them belong, that makes them law-abiding citizens, and when Aron grows up to be like them, he will still whisper, at least once a day, I em go–eeng; I em play–eeng; I em Aron–eeng; and that way he will always remember the individual Aron beneath the generalities. Eight minutes to go. Whew! He got so wrapped up he skipped two minutes.

There are kids in this class he's been with since kindergarten, yet he hardly knows them. Some of them are clods, some are probably smarter than he is. Take Shalom Sharabani, for instance. Now, there's one kid who knows how to avoid calling attention to himself. He's a real pro at that. He never ever gets called on in class. But when you talk to him in the yard you find out he's not a bit stupid: he has everything planned out. He will not go to high school. His father runs a stonecutter's shop near the cemetery, and in a few years Shalom will start working there too and make good money. Compared to his type, Aron feels silly, like he's wasting his time. And whenever Aron does his hilarious impersonations or his fabulous Houdini act at school parties, and the kids go wild, there in the audience sits Shalom Sharabani, scorning Aron for playing up to them, for craving their cheap, fickle love, in his ignorance about real life.

Aron looks up and down the aisles. So this is what will be left someday to turn into memories. Eli Ben-Zikri, for instance. Not twelve years old and already a hardened criminal. He has squinting eyes and wrinkles on his forehead, and his mouth never stops: he's always licking his lips, biting the gold chain he wears around his neck, or puffing on his pen like a cigarette; squirming around like a caged tomcat. What do I know about him, though? Nothing. The only time he ever talked to me was when he sold me the passkey and said those dirty words. Even the teachers leave him alone. One day I might be proud of going to school with such a famous burglar.

But who will I be? What will I be? Maybe somewhere in this world a baby girl has just been born who will be my wife in twenty years. Maybe she's in school already and she has no idea that I'm opening a savings account for us, she has a boyfriend and doesn't realize it's only a phase, that someday fate will bring us together. He smiles and shivers with anticipation, with secret joy, could it be that he's already living his fate? Mama didn't know anything about Papa either, she was busy raising her brothers and sisters in Jerusalem while he was slaving away in the taiga, in the ice, and little by little their paths converged, until suddenly, boom, like colliding stars, they knew they were made for each other.

Aron peeks around. Who can she be, he wonders. Pudgy Naomi Feingold stares straight at him. He blushes and quickly looks away. Sometimes he has the feeling that Naomi has a crush on him. Not that they ever talk in class, but once a year, on the school trip, she works up the courage to push her way into his crowd, the crowd with the good kids. He doesn't like her, though: she hangs around them and yaks all day till everyone stops listening, that's how she unwinds enough to show them who she really is—a girl who's frightened of being hurt. And she never stops eating and making fun of herself for being fat, for being a party pooper and a real flat tire; she reminds him of Yochi in certain ways, they have the same kartofel nose, the same red creases in their thighs from wearing shorts. Maybe Naomi is in love with him. Who cares. It's her sense of humor that annoys him, knowing as he does from Yochi that making fun of herself the way everybody liked —ha ha, Naomi Feingold, she's a card—is her first and last line of retreat, and what does she get out of it: a broken heart, humiliation, hate. Again he peeks around and sees her gazing dreamily at Gil Kaplan; who cares, good riddance, but just the same he feels a little pang.

Or take Anat Fish. Anat-fish. If you dare call her Anat without the Fish, she glares at you as if you invaded her privacy. Anat Fish goes steady with a "freshie" named Mickey Zik, who invited her camping in Eilat during school vacation, everybody's whispering about it, but she hasn't made up her mind yet. Aron peers around at her. She's stacked. They say she needs a bra with three hooks in the back, and she wears "fuck me" stretch pants to high-school parties. She's shameless, really. There she sits, nonchalantly, ignoring the notes that nitwit Avi Sasson keeps throwing her. Even Rivka Bar-Ilan gets flustered when she looks into those Egyptian eyes. Aron has noticed the way Rivka starts fiddling with her hair whenever Anat Fish is watching her, and then you can see that she was a little girl once too, sitting in a classroom just like this, and Aron rests his chin on his palm to contemplate Rivka Bar-Ilan, a homely girl with a big nose, she must have gotten teased about it, and there was probably some beautiful, coldhearted girl like Anat Fish in her class too; see how carefully she avoids Anat Fish's eyes, it's the same in every generation, but were any of the adults he knew like him, he wonders, and thinks of his father; but no.

Now their bottoms are wriggling on the hard seats, as they cross and uncross their legs. All eyes are fixed on Gil Kaplan's pompadour, over which he signals the five, four, three. Varda Koppler and Koby Kimchi jostle elbows on the halfway line of the desk, trespass it and you die. Zacky Smitanka, Meirky Blutreich, and Hanan Schweiky wave their hands exuberantly to rectify any bad impressions. Dorit Alush chews her gum and writes around the face with the bangs: *Dorit Alush, grade 6C, Beit Hakerem Elementary School, Jerusalem, Israel, Asia, earth, universe* . . . and then she stares out the window: what else was there? Michael Carny and Rina Fichman exchange notes and giggle behind their hands. Naomi Feingold munches pretzels under her desk. Anat Fish turns slowly with a sharklike stare at Avi Sasson, who shot a rubber band at her, and David Lipschitz's face lights up, he looks so woebegone when he smiles like that, but she looks right through him, he isn't there, can't she at least give a sign that he exists; Aron vows revenge, he'll steal something valuable from her and give it to David Lipschitz, how he loathes her, yet he can't help admiring her a little too, for her beauty, for her coldness, for making a crazy boy fall so helplessly in love with her; and then Rabbi Yohanan Ben-Zakai slipped into the coffin, and his devoted pupils carried him out through the gates of the besieged city, and that is how he made his escape and founded his new center of learning. After the destruction, after the destruction—the words grate on his nerves. Two minutes left. Redheaded Aliza Lieber stretches her mouth for all to see. Miri Tamari has a hairy mole on the side of her hand that she tries to hide. A backward glance. The albino head is still jerking, almost as if it has a gizmo inside it, a spring or something that makes it bob around like that. "After the destruction of the Temple, children, Rabbi Yohanan Ben-Zakai founded the spiritual center of Yavneh." The bell rings. Hurray. A monster with eighty arms and legs scrambles out through the narrow doorway past Rivka Bar-Ilan, who turns away with a vague look of horror in her eyes.

Aron's favorite is Roxana. He's fond of Rosaline and Natalie too, and he feels a certain sympathy for Angela, but even though he always knew it was his fate to marry a blind woman and be her eyes, he can't quite ignore that shadow of a smile on Angela's lips, that hint of pleasure in some of the pictures. He tries to mimic the smile, but stops himself, afraid he'll be noticed by the noisy crowd as they walk home together. They're fifteen strong, the boys and girls of the workers' neighborhood, as they storm through the shopping center, with Aron, as usual, in the eye of the hurricane, telling jokes and talking about his inventions, though lately he prefers to observe them from the side, from behind.

Slowly they move on. Gideon and Zacky, and Dorit Alush chewing gum, a head taller than the boys; tiny Varda Koppler, with the womanly face and a ring on every finger, doesn't seem to fit in anymore; bringing up the rear is a fifth-grader, little Yaeli Kedmi, whose mom asked them to keep an eye on her when they cross the street, but no one talks to her, she follows them meekly, practically invisible except for her wavy black hair; Michael Carny slithers along as if he were made of jelly, he only smiles when Rina Fichman's around, and Aron turns away from the gloomy expression on his face; redheaded Aliza Lieber is pensively licking her lips . . . Take a good look, he tells himself: why is everyone so withdrawn, so lost in thought, so sad, even, though outwardly they're as noisy and cheerful as ever; together they pass through the new electric door at the supermarket, and Aron is careful not to cross the threshold alone, he doesn't trust these automatic things, and the kids swarm by the food shelves, so many colors and no smell, thinks Aron, and they stop to watch Mr. Babaioff at the fish counter kill a carp with one blow, the body goes on squirming, and while the rest of them chase their tails around the aisles, Aron tarries at the fish counter till the carp lies

THE BOOK OF

motionless and the manager rushes over shouting, Shhhhh! And the chorus of children answers, Shhhhhine my shhhhhoes! and go rollicking out the automatic door, and Aron vows he'll make it through alone at least once before his bar mitzvah. Outside he sees Binyumin the gimp standing in the doorway of his father's barbershop. A year ago they had a fight. Aron beat him up and walked over him to make him stop growing, and in revenge Binyumin cursed him, well, sticks and stones can break my bones; now they file past Morduch, the crazy blind beggar, who either blesses you or curses you, depending on your charity, and as usual, Zacky finds a nail or screw in the street and sneaks up on Morduch and says in a husky voice, "Here you go, Mr. Morduch!" And the beggar stirs hopefully, groping in his direction with trembling hands, and Zacky tosses a screw into the rusty cup, and it lands with a ring. The blind man beams: "May the Holy One bless your household! May He doubly reward you, and grant you health and prosperity!" And they laugh their heads off. Gideon has given up lecturing Zacky about this daily prank, and Aron, who used to stifle his laughter for Gideon's sake, imagines Morduch coming home at night, if he has a home, spilling the coins out on his little table, and counting the day's take with his crooked fingers, and the way he must feel when he touches Zacky's screw. He can picture it vividly, as though he were actually there: the dirty room, the bare walls, the hungry children, Morduch's lips trembling with disappointment . . . Come on, y'alla, Aron shouts to the others, and starts walking faster, his head held high, and then someone makes a wisecrack behind his back, and someone else, or maybe several children, splutter with laughter.

Roxana's different, he feels, striding briskly ahead, she has a serious air about her that sets her apart. On her cheek there is a mole, which doesn't make her any less pretty as far as he's concerned; in fact, it makes her even prettier. As if the little blemish brought them closer together. And there's one picture that shows Roxana in a nurse's uniform suckling Fritz and Alfonso the dwarf. No matter how many times he looks at this picture, he always sees it differently. One thing is certain, though: there's nothing cheap or disgusting about Roxana's face. Yesterday as he shyly kissed her picture and watched his lip prints melt away, it suddenly occurred to him that even if the circus didn't exist in real life, even if it was just a filthy sham, there was still a Roxana in this world, a living girl who had her picture taken to earn money because she was poor, and had innocently fallen into the clutches of that bastard Alfonso; if only he were older, if only he had power and money, he would dedicate his life to saving Roxana from Alfonso, because how long would she remain virtuous with so much corruption around her? And again he thumbed through the pictures, maybe he would understand this time, maybe he would figure them out and stop suffering.

Once every three days—he's a stickler about this—he shuts himself in the bathroom with the cards and uses Mama's 70 percent alcohol to wipe off the big, greasy fingerprints that soil Roxana in particular. Tenderly he cleanses her from head to toe. For almost two weeks now he has been watching over Roxana like this, and he wonders whether maybe he should rub himself, the way you're probably supposed to with these pictures. But reaching down to touch himself, he knows he's only bluffing. He doesn't need to. He's empty still.

He stopped, turned around, and saw he was alone. His friends had stranded him. Or maybe they'd taken a different route home. Let them, who cares. Still, his feelings were hurt. Gideon had gone along with the others. Then he shrugged his shoulders: he had more important things to think about just now.

But later that afternoon, while Papa was working high in the fig tree, and Mama and Yochi were shopping, and Grandma was tucked under the Scottish plaid, Aron hurried to the sock drawer and rummaged through it with a practiced hand. And then his heart stood still: Roxana was gone. They were all gone. Overnight the circus had disappeared. The traitor had changed the hiding place.

6

Summer went by and winter went by, and then came spring. Nearly a year had passed. One afternoon in the middle of a soccer match against the other seventh-graders, Mama called. From the balcony to the playing field in the valley her voice assailed him. Aron was mortified, but he noticed something different, an unfamiliar tone in her voice that made him hurry home, hot and sweaty from the game. "Shvitz shvitz," said Mama, sticking her fingers down his collar. "Bren bren, look at you, hoo-haa, chasing a ball like a meshuggeneh, you wouldn't catch Zacky and Gideon running around like that, no, they have some sense, they let the donkey do the work for them while they sit back and laugh at you," she grumbled as she picked at the knot around a brown paper package. And then with a Tfu! choleria! she tried to pry it open with her teeth. Why are you staring at me like that? she rasped. I wasn't staring. If you have to stare at someone, go stare at yourself. But I wasn't staring at you, who's the package from, anyway? His bar mitzvah's less than six months away and he can still walk under a table. Who's the package from, Mama? Sit up straight, you're short enough as it is. She bit the knot off and unwrapped a familiar-looking shirt and a pair of shorts. For a moment Aron feared that the clothes had come from someone who died. Mama handed him a striped brown shirt and said, Go try it on.

What do you mean, try it on? I'm not trying on any secondhand clothes. He stood there shrugging a defiant shoulder, his face burning with impatience to get back to the soccer field, because with him gone for even a minute, the other team would charge up the pitch, and suddenly he felt a gnawing in his heart, and Mama said, These aren't secondhand clothes, Aunt Gucha sent them from Tel Aviv, from Giora, all right? From Giora? But why? Because he only wore them one season; nu, try the shirt on already so we can see.

Aron stared at her in bewilderment. Giora was the cousin he went to stay with in Tel Aviv every summer, and after only a few weeks there, Aron fit in like a native; the year he was nine he taught the kids how to see angels: you press your eyeballs and wait till these sparks appear, some of which fade, some of which don't, depending on how hard you press. And he told them about his secret ambition, to become the first Israeli bullfighter. And the following year he taught them Jerusalem stickball, Alambulik, and they taught him Red Rover at the swimming pool, and he taught them Chodorov's save from the game against Wales, where the goalkeeper dives parallel to the ground and blocks a "howitzer" shot from right field, and for the entire month that Aron was there, whoever played goalie had to dive that way, even when the ball went into the corner, no one cared as long as it looked authentic. And last year he told them about the great Houdini, master of escape, who lived in America, and demonstrated how he could free his wrists and ankles from thickly knotted ropes; and when they didn't believe him, he asked them to shut him inside the stinky cooling chest they found on the beach, and tie a rope around it and cover it with empty sugar sacks and stand back fifty paces, and when they were sure he'd suffocated in there, and started blaming each other for letting him do it, out jumped Aron, laughing and panting. The ideas your little Aronchik thinks up, Aunt Gucha wrote Mama, kineahora, you could grow fat just listening to him laugh.

And the Tel Aviv crowd introduced him to the sea. Of course he'd been to the beach at Ashkelon with his parents and their card friends lots of times, but it was always crowded there and full of tar, and they'd sit around telling dirty jokes and burping, and Aron didn't like seeing people he knew half-naked in their bathing suits, and they had a policy called "Never turn your back on a wounded kebab"; in other words, never go home with leftovers in the cooler, and they forced Aron to eat himself sick. Papa was a terrific swimmer, you could always tell he was in the water by his powerful kicking and splashing and the pranks he

THE BOOK OF

played, like diving down and attacking their card friends, trying to pull their trunks down, or to drown their wives, who would float up shouting and squealing; and Aron was very careful never to go in the water while Papa was there, he had secretly decided that only one of them should be in the water at a time; besides, he suspected Papa liked to piss in the sea, and even when Aron came out and sat on the sand, he felt as if Papa's piss had followed him; and once, in the middle of a tranquil swim, far away from the crowd, just him and the open sky, he had a sudden apprehension that something was chasing him, he knew it couldn't be, that he was imagining things, but still he felt it slithering beneath the waves; at first he thought Papa was down there, trying to scare him, which made him panic and kick and splash and swallow water, but then something tough and rubbery circled his waist like a sinewy arm, or the trunk of a giant elephant, trying to pull him down, and when he crawled up on the shore, he knew he hadn't imagined it, that something very strange had happened in the sea, and Mama and Papa's card friends ran over to ask what happened, did you forget how to swim, and they wrapped a towel around him and rubbed his shoulders, and he searched for Papa but couldn't see him, he was reading the paper under a beach umbrella, and he didn't even look up when Aron shuffled over wrapped in a towel and sat shivering beside him and said, It was just a cramp, and when Papa didn't answer, Aron sobbed and said, It could have happened to anyone, but still Papa wouldn't look at him, he merely rolled over with his face in the paper.

The Tel Aviv kids took him out to a secluded beach with nothing but moon rocks everywhere, and they taught him how to swim for real, not doggy-paddle Jerusalem-style, and how to dive underwater with his eyes open, and in the sea he felt his soul grow boundless. At night in his sleep on the narrow porch at Gucha and Efraim's, he could hear the swishing water beyond the mosquito nets, and he floundered and kicked in deep oblivion, drifting in and out of sleep with the rockabye flow of the tides. And he also dreamed awake: about building an underwater train, or organizing a marine corrida, with sharks in the ring instead of bulls; and he conducted experiments with burning sand, trying to turn it into glass like the ancient Phoenicians, and he sent letters over the waves to survivors on desert islands in sealed bottles of Tempo soda, and he tried to lure the mermaids out of the sea. Every summer the kids fell in love with the sea again, thanks to him. And his skin grew tan, his hair golden. Giora was a few months younger than he was, shy in public and moody at home, and Aunt Gucha hinted in her weekly letters to Jerusalem that maybe Giora was eppes a little bit jealous of Aronchik, who had won over all his friends. Well, never mind, she wrote her sister Hinda, he'll simply have to learn to live with it, this only child of ours who's used to being treated like a king.

Last year, as the summer vacation was drawing to a close, Aron and the kids built a raft. For three whole weeks they worked on it from morning to night, making models according to Aron's specifications, trying out different pieces of wood for the masts, stealing sheets from laundry lines for sails. The day before the official launching they finished early and went for a swim. All of a sudden a boat raced past them, slicing the waves like a sharp gray knife and barely missing them. The children huddled together in amazement: no boat had ever come this way before. There were two people aboard: a pretty woman and a much older man with a bony face and sallow skin. The man pointed at them and said something to the woman in a gravelly voice with a foreign accent. The woman held the hem of her green dress out to keep it from getting wet and smiled at the sunburned children gathered in the water like a school of fish, though maybe she was smiling at something else, maybe she didn't really see them, maybe she was the old man's prisoner, Aron worried, and he was holding her there against her will. Suddenly the man took a coin out of his wallet and tossed it over the side of the boat. The children stared in bewilderment. One of them quietly cursed the man. The man laughed hoarsely and bared his rotten teeth, and the woman laughed with him, disappointing Aron, who realized now that she was a willing accomplice. Then the man took out another coin and said, "Dis aprecious! Worth amuch!" and slyly flicked it into the water. It twirled in the air as it fell and they all dived after it under the shadow of the boat. Aron found it spinning slowly to the bottom. He caught it between his lips and pressed it under his tongue. By the time he rose to the surface the boat was gone. "Whenever you find something, hide it in your pocket and keep your mouth shut," Mama always said, and once he'd found a tennis ball in the valley with Gideon and he disobeyed and told Gideon the ball belonged to both of them, and felt triumphant. But now for some reason he kept quiet and slipped the coin down his swimsuit at the first opportunity, where it sent an eerie shiver to his private parts.

THE BOOK OF

Then the wind blew up and swelled the waves. The sea looked murky. Aron jumped to his feet and suggested that they launch the raft right away. The children hesitated, afraid the current would carry them out too far. Aron knew they were right but coaxed them anyway, to snap them out of their present gloom. He cajoled them with descriptions of the maiden voyage, how the raft would carry them across the waves, till even the skeptics were reduced to silence, and when dark clouds gathered on the horizon and he saw it was dangerous to venture out, the important thing was still to lift their spirits, to banish the dread they felt in their hearts. But they were not swayed by his eloquence. They kicked the sand and shifted their weight and rubbed their necks and looked away. He had suddenly become a stranger again, the long speech had misfired, he was too articulate for them, and their coldness cut around him like a pair of scissors and tore him out of the sunny picture. And then he gulped and asked them to wait and ran up the hill to the kiosk. With his own money, not the coin, he bought a bottle of real cognac and returned to them proudly, carrying the trophy. Let's go, let's launch her, he exulted, with an anxious undertone in his voice, but his radiant smile convinced them just the same.

The *Captain Hook* was launched with a small bottle of cognac at exactly four-thirty that afternoon. And went down in a whirlpool five minutes later. The children bailed out and scrambled ashore, looking stunned and devastated. There was one scary moment, when Aron and Giora were sucked into an eddy together, and Aron was almost sure Giora had pushed him down to save himself. The wind blew cold, and the children shivered. No one actually blamed him outright, but Aron felt as though a big hand had just snuffed out the candle in his darkened cell.

No, Mama, it'll be too small on me, he whined, staring helplessly at the shirt she thrust at his chest, at his face. Why's she so grumpy, he wondered, hoping to be back in time for the last few minutes of the game, you could always rely on him to score, and just then Papa walked in, and then Yochi, she wanted to ask Mama where the depilatory wax was, and suddenly Aron remembered that time last summer when he was trying on the boot. Perspiration trickled down his collar. Quickly, he thought, before my fingers start shaking, and he pulled off his sweaty shirt and changed into the other one, and suddenly, with his arms caught in the striped sleeves as he desperately searched for the neckhole, he started gasping and wheezing as though someone were pressing down on his chest, trying to strangle him, and a strangely familiar-looking boy appeared out of a haze, looking pale and pure, and a fine cool ripple filled his soul, and the little white boy, so white he was almost blue, sailed out into a craggy moonscape.

Frantically Aron tried to push through the neck hole, stop flapping around or Mama and Papa will see how smooth and skinny your arms are, and the fetus from science lab floated in formaldehyde, slowly decomposing and blinking its tadpole eyes, and suddenly it opened its mouth and grinned at him. And Aron groaned and finally poked his head through the hole. Papa and Yochi disappeared. Giora's shirttails hung all the way down his shorts, where his legs stuck out like matchsticks.

Aunt Gucha had enclosed a note saying that her Giora, kineahora, was outgrowing his clothes faster than dough rises; why, next to him, even Efraim is beginning to look like a raisin. These, I'm sure you'll find, Hindaleh, are just like new, he hardly wore them, and it's a shame to throw them out, he is the youngest cousin, may all five live to be strong and healthy, so why not take the clothes to Rabbi Carasso's wife, to give to the poor, even today my heart bleeds for them, wrote Gucha, who grew up in dire poverty with Mama, the family nearly starved to death in the days of the siege and the food rations in Jerusalem, and she closed with regards to everyone, hoping to have Aronchik back with them next summer.

Mama stood before him, looking grim. All of a sudden he needed a hug. Right this minute. Desperately. He needed her to hug him the way she used to. But she recoiled from him and knocked something over. Maybe the shirt had a curse on it. He racked his brains. What broke, was it the vase with the yellow apples Rivche and Dov brought to the housewarming, but no, he had seen the vase later on, right where it belonged. Was it the blue bowl with the stag and the doe chasing each other's tails that Shimmik and Itka brought from the trip to Holland? No, that too was in place, with no signs of gluing. For an instant he saw the image of his yearning face in her pupils, while her puffy cheeks stretched back to reveal the cusps of her molars. So now can I go out to play? he asked, retreating gingerly, careful not to look at the broken pieces, like a mountain climber afraid of looking down. So now can I

THE BOOK OF

go out again to play? he repeated weakly. Mama stood rigid, her lips turning pale. He could hear them singing in the valley, his team; they'd finished the game without him and struck up a song with the rival team. Whoever heard of singing after a game, with the rival team yet, I don't get it, they sound like a choir, what, did they rehearse or something, and he gazed imploringly at Mama, who split down the middle before his eyes till he could see the kernel of white hatred inside her. You know, she said, I'm beginning to think you're doing this to us deliberately.

7

And some weeks later, just before dusk, Aron, Gideon, and Zacky were together in the valley, sprawling on the big brown rock. It was blistered and rusty, tufted with shrubs, and Aron pressed his cheek against it to welcome the warmth of spring.

Languidly the three boys floated through the twilight hour, prattling about Mordechai Luk, the spy found in a suitcase last year at Rome airport wearing a gold ring with a lion seal and a secret slot for poison or microfilm, and Aron leaned forward on his elbows and said, Hey, wouldn't it be a blast to do the Houdini number out of a suitcase for this year's class party? He could picture it now: Zacky and Gideon would lock him in Uncle Shimmik's old black suitcase, tie a rope around it, hold up a Bukharan bedspread to conceal it from the audience, making drumrolls with their tongues, and then, as the audience waited breathlessly, Aron would dig two fingers into the heel of his shoe and pull out Papa's razor blade and reach into the lining of his sleeve for Mama's missing nail file and, as the seconds ticked away, because his fingers were slippery and what if he dropped the saw, how would he find it in the dark, the girls would shriek, Quick, somebody, get him out! and the boys would jump up, and presto, Aron would stand before them shouting, Hey, I'm free! Zacky snickered quietly. He had this new way of laughing, and Aron felt the ember in his bowels glow red. So what do you say, Aron asked Gideon, lying facedown so as not to blur the imprint on the rock, do we start rehearsing for the party? We'll call

THE BOOK OF

this number "The Man in the Suitcase." How about it? Gideon said he wasn't sure he had time this year. What do you mean? Aron was dismayed. I have to plan my campers' activities for the Carmel mountains trip this summer, said Gideon. But that's still a month and a half away, gasped Aron; we always do something special together for the class party. Gideon didn't reply and Zacky said, Who cares about a dumb show, I want to win the soccer championship next year. What does that have to do with anything, screamed Aron; you know we'll cinch it, our team's the best, now let's get back to the Houdini number, and Gideon said, Okay, we'll see, calm down, what's with you anyway?

Aron seethed in silence. It really irked him the way Zacky was gloating over the sudden flare-up between him and Gideon. All right, let's think. Don't provoke them. Don't tell them anything, but he did; he swallowed his spit and announced with a nervous squeak that this summer they were definitely going to catch a spy, he was sure of it. Zacky snickered again. Aron did his best to ignore him and said, This country is crawling with foreign agents, every week somebody else is caught photographing military bases, while we sit here twiddling our thumbs, and I'll tell you who the next spy will turn out to be, that student guy at Gideon's, he has a whole network of enemy contacts, remember the time we found an Arabic newspaper in his wastebasket, with certain words underlined in red, and what did we do about it? Nothing. Come off it, said Gideon impatiently, he's no spy, he's just studying Arabic. Gideon hated their stupid lodger, who acted like he owned the place, with his booming laughter, and his singing in the shower, and the way he was always sucking up to Gideon's mother, doing chores for her and bringing her flowers every Friday. Well, what about the empty apartment on the third floor, then? ventured Aron, forcing himself to continue. The owner might come back this summer and we'll find out he's a Soviet agent. Aron waited. Surprisingly enough, Zacky said nothing, but his silence was worse than his sneer. Aron ignored him and announced, as though everything had been settled, Okay, we'll take turns watching the apartment. I know he's coming this year. I can feel it in my bones. Zacky sat up. There's no spy in that apartment, he drawled. Nobody's set foot in there for years. The blinds are always down, and we've never once seen a letter in the mailbox. Why waste half the vacation on a pointless stakeout? Aron pouted and said he had a hunch, this was going to be their lucky year. Yeah, sure, said Zacky, you and your hunches.

And then because Gideon said, Quit it, you two, Aron cherished a fleeting hope that Gideon would come around to his idea, as a token of their friendship, as a sign of his loyalty. Don't kid yourself. Still, a chance in a thousand? He leaned on his elbows and glanced at Gideon, who only went on sucking a fennel stalk.

And only last year Gideon had lain there earnestly pressing his face to the rock. With his chin thrust forward he was the image of Israeli youth: courageous, determined, like his brother Manny. The idea had been Aron's, naturally, and he kept at it long after he realized how ridiculous it was; all right, maybe he was pretending, but he couldn't afford to lose now, not even with this. Something was happening; he couldn't quite put it into words but he knew, it was challenging him to hold his ground, which is why, as he sprawled on the rock in the usual position, one cheek round, the other flat, he remembered to stick his chin out, until the sound of chatter, or his anger at Zacky, or the pang he felt at Gideon's betrayal, made him forget his obligations, and Mama's chin disappeared.

Gideon raised a lazy wrist and checked his watch: time to run to his bar mitzvah lesson with the rabbi. Zacky, who was already past his bar mitzvah, said with a smirk that every morning now he prayed with his phylacteries—in the closet, haw haw haw; lately, no matter what came out of Zacky's mouth, it sounded like a personal dig at Aron. Zacky sat up and grunted. Now he'll start cracking his knuckles, thought Aron, humming a little tune in his head to drown out the obnoxious noise, he had a special voice for such occasions, and suddenly Gideon yawned and stretched luxuriously. Aron watched him. Who's he trying to impress when he stretches that way? For a few weeks now, he'd noticed a kind of dark severity clouding the candor of Gideon's face. Why that should hurt him, Aron didn't know. He peeked again: no fuzz yet, though there was definitely a toughening under the surface, a hardening of the bones that hid the light within; and yes, his jawline was thicker now, it jutted out defiantly, almost like Manny's, and you could see his cheekbones moving beneath the skin, but when did it happen; we're always together.

Aron sat up with a little cry, it just came out of him, and he stifled it and pulled his socks up to hide the baldness of his skinny shins. Once again, he saw unblinkingly, the stubborn rock had declined to immortalize Mama's features. Go on, you can't make a fossil that way, said

THE BOOK OF

Zacky, just as Aron was reflecting that maybe all he had to do was try harder; or maybe it was too difficult to fossilize Mama as she looked today; he preferred to remember her two or three years ago, when she was warmer, friendlier to him. Frantically he groped in his pockets through the crumpled notes and the rotten onion strips for writing invisible messages and the candle stubs to decipher them by, and the cigarette butts he had started collecting for that other business, till finally he found a book of airline matches and plucked one out and struck it sharply against the rock, as only he could, but why did he have to light it now, to cap the argument? He gazed at the flame for reassurance.

Zacky had launched the fossil project with the face of his absent father. Right, because that will help you remember him, Aron chimed in, overjoyed to share his excitement, which only made Zacky scowl and say, Then I won't do my father, I'll do Hezkel instead, and he put on the face of his brother Hezkel, who drove a delivery truck; and when he got tired of sticking his jaw out like Hezkel, he switched to his broad-cheeked mother, a Bulgarian who married up, but his impression of her faded fast, and he went on to some uncle of his, and in the weeks that followed he ran through a whole slew of relatives, most of the players on the Betar-Jerusalem soccer team, various comedians, Chief of Staff Yitzhak Rabin, Sean Connery, and Cassius Clay. And then he decided he would quit knocking himself out for others, and from now on the only face he'd try to immortalize would be his own, for better or for worse. For worse, quipped Aron, in the good old days when Gideon used to laugh at his jokes. At that point Zacky started scoffing at the idea and inciting Gideon; and the next day Aron found himself alone.

Gideon glanced at his watch again. A quarter to, he pouted. Why did I have to get stuck with the longest Haftorah portion in the book. And Aron murmured: *Then flew unto me one of the seraphim, with a glowing stone in his hand, which he had taken with tongs from off the altar; and He touched my mouth with it and said* . . . He hadn't started his bar mitzvah lessons with the rabbi yet, but he'd read the Haftorah portion a few times and was pleased with it. Summer's coming, he thought, soon they'll send me to Giora's in Tel Aviv. Forget it, I'm not going this year. I don't care if they kill me, I'm not going. He stood beside his friends now, twiddling sage leaves, rocking on his heels, bidding goodbye to something; okay, this was the moment to ask casual-like if there was any news of David Lipschitz, who'd been absent since

Passover, his seat was still empty. Nitza Knoller, their homeroom teacher, said David has been transferred to a more suitable environment, and that was the last mention of him, almost as if everyone had made a secret pact, but how did they know to keep their mouths shut; once there was a little boy, then he was gone, and Aron, like a character out of "The Emperor's New Clothes," was afraid to be the first to ask because then they'd know he wasn't one of them. Zacky picked a fistful of hawthorn apples from a nearby tree and began to munch and spit. Aron turned away and stared into the distance. The valley looked strange and hazy all of a sudden. He hiked his trousers, Giora's trousers, still a little large for him. I'll need to find a big enough suitcase, he blurted. I can use my Uncle Shimmik's black one, and we'll tie a rope around it, and you guys'll cover me, and three minutes later I'll be out of there. Right, that's how we'll do it. Forty-two verses, groaned Gideon, I get hoarse just reading it silently. And then Aron remembered, he reached into his pocket and held out the piece of honey candy he'd brought especially for him; Gideon and Zacky exchanged glances. Gideon looked away and said, Don't want any, Kleinfeld. Aron put his hand back in his pocket, careful not to feel rebuffed. All he did was offer Gideon a piece of candy. Just wait, this'll be the biggest Houdini number yet; he spurred himself on like a mountain climber. Bigger than the one I did in the UNWRA crate, bigger than the one in the furnace, no kidding! I'm going to see *Goldfinger* tomorrow, said Zacky nonchalantly, rippling his arm muscles and examining them with interest. Hey, that's restricted, you have to be over sixteen, said Aron, a little shocked. You coming, Gideon? asked Zacky. But they won't let you in, protested Aron, they'll check your ID's at the door. How about it, want to go see *Goldfinger* tomorrow? Zacky reiterated. We'll think about it, said Gideon, prudently evasive. Now he's being tactful, sensed Aron. Phoo, I must've eaten a hundred of these, said Zacky, spitting out a mouthful of peels. Want some? He offered the remaining hawthorn apples in his hand. Gideon grabbed a few and chewed thoughtfully. Aron declined and shook his head. Oh, I thought you liked hawthorn apples, sneered Zacky. I did but I don't, answered Aron. Go on, have some, they're good for you, said Zacky, a new levity in his voice, pushing his hand into Aron's mouth as Aron backed away. Hey, you two, cautioned Gideon, and Zacky flung the apples gleefully to the winds. Aron stood up in dismay.

Let's race up the hill, suggested Gideon. Notice how quick he is to manipulate the situation, thought Aron, certainly a lot quicker than he used to be. They went down on one knee, arching their backs. Wait, cried Aron, switching feet, and a second later switched back again, but when that still didn't feel right, he said he'd like to start from a standing position, if that was all right with them, which it was. You know you're going to win, said Gideon, and Aron flexed his muscles, and Gideon said ready-set-go and they scrambled up the slope, Aron in the lead as usual, though they had longer legs now, and he wondered whether it was true what they said, that swimming champions shave themselves before a race to minimize the friction, maybe that's why Aron ran faster than they did, so that even this little triumph turned into a humiliating proof of something, or maybe he had been propelled up the hill by the fear that seized him when Gideon said go, and for the first time ever, beyond a shadow of a doubt, Gideon's voice had cracked.

8

On Thursday nights, when the housecleaning is done, Papa takes a nice long bath. With a shiny red face and a towel around his waist he strides into the salon. "Ahh, a mechayeh," he says, and lies facedown on the sofa. Aron watches from the kitchen, where he is sitting on Farouk in front of a heap of potatoes he has to peel for the Sabbath cholent. He's a real pro at this.

As soon as they finish the thorough cleaning, Mama and Yochi wash their hands and change into comfortable housecoats. Then they fetch the towels and cotton and 70 percent alcohol and converge on Papa in the salon. Grandma Lilly joins in. She likes to be included in their cleaning sprees, but most of all she likes to work on Papa's back. It's a miracle from heaven, says Mama, misty-eyed, the way our little Mamchu comes to life for the Thursday "thorough" and Papa's back. And it's true: whenever they bring out the pails and mops, her eyes light up. She scurries out of the alcove, mumbling and waving, begging for a piece of steel wool to scrub the panels. "Good for you, Mamchu," says Mama, leading her to her corner in the kitchen under the stove, where the greasy grime collects. She sits her on the taboret and moves her hand around in circles. There, there, good, harder, till the movement gets into her system and suddenly she's cleaning all by herself. Mama watches over her a little while longer to make sure Grandma's making progress on the panel. Sometimes her mind wanders and you have to lead it back.

THE BOOK OF

When the work is done, the cleaning things go back on the kitchen porch: brooms, towels, luffa gourds, sponges, steel wool still raring to go; feather dusters; and floor rags drooping over buckets, oozing sweat, exhausted from their frenzied dance around the room. And Papa lies facedown on the sofa, with the women huddling over him. Mama has eyes like a hawk, she can spot a blackhead a kilometer away. When she does, she sounds a little battle cry and the three of them confer on how best to get rid of it—should they squeeze with their fingertips or dig in with their nails, and from which angle? Mama squeezes. Papa groans. Grandma applies the cotton and Yochi disinfects with 70 percent alcohol. Meanwhile, Mama starts hunting for a new one. When she spies an ugly whitehead they shriek with rapture and report it to Papa, cursing, threatening, exaggerating the size of it, gasping with horror, basking in anticipation of his relief. Deep inside him Aron can feel the tickling tongue of their excitement.

It's hard to concentrate on the potatoes. Slowly, discreetly, he drifts into thought, Aroning again. But he can still hear Papa groaning out there. And when they're through with his back, Papa wants to talk to him; that is, Mama asked him three times in her mustard voice, as Yochi calls it, Will you please talk to Aron, and Aron knows why, but he won't go, nothing doing, they'll have to kill him first.

Fast and furious he wields his knife, losing half a potato in the process. Nothing doing, he will not go. He'll run away to the Gaza Strip. "The Voice of Cairo" promises a paradise for anyone who gets sick of living in Israel. He laughs. Thanks but no thanks, he will not go to Tel Aviv this summer. They can't pack him off like a little kid anymore. He'll be having his bar mitzvah soon. The peels squirt out between his fingers. Nothing had been mentioned since Passover, so he was kind of hoping they'd given up, and then suddenly last week Mama told him that he was going to spend the entire vacation at Giora's, Papa said so and that's final. But I want to stay here. There's nothing more to discuss, you're going to Tel Aviv this summer, you want to grow up healthy, don't you. But I'm not sick. The fresh air and sunshine will make you big and strong, she said deviously, anyone in your shoes would jump at the chance. He tried to protest: what about his bar mitzvah, how was he supposed to learn his Haftorah portion by next winter? Brains you've got, she answered snidely, you'll manage. Aron stomped off to his bedroom and sat on the windowsill, one foot resting on the kerosene heater, which had a blanket over it. He gazed out at the street, where some little kids were playing freeze tag. He was running out of ideas. He didn't know what to do. Just before Shavuot, Aunt Gucha had sent them another package of clothes for charity. Giora's shirts reached down to Aron's knees, and the trousers were enormous. The kids outside had scampered off and now the street was deserted. He heard footsteps in the hall. Was Mama coming to tell him she'd changed her mind, that she was only testing him? No, it was Grandma Lilly, wrapped in her Scottish plaid, her lips murmuring silently and her face tremulous. What does she want from me? Go back to bed, Grandma, you shouldn't tire yourself. With an anxious glance over her shoulder Grandma Lilly grasped his hand and put something into it. But what? She dropped it into his palm and quickly pulled away, beaming proudly at him, urging him with her eyes to look. He did. But his hand was empty. He showed her it was. Go lie down now. Grandma's face appeared sallow. And suddenly she grabbed his hand and turned it over, digging between his fingers with yelps of disbelief. She wanted to give him something. What is it, Grandma? Again she glanced anxiously over her shoulder. She was terrified of Mama. Maybe she'd heard they were sending him to Tel Aviv and she wanted to give him a going-away present. Again she clasped his hand. She leaned down and examined it closely. Her breath blew softly on his palm, cooling it like you do in the finger-play: "Granny stir the porridge, Granny stir the pot." Only his granny never stirred the porridge, she was a useless old woman; for shame, how could he think such things about her when she would soon be— All right, Grandma, go lie down on your bed and look at the pretty pictures, come on, I'll help you. But suddenly her eyes lit up. She smiled at him like a baby as she searched through her bathrobe pocket, turned it inside out—what is she hunting for—and then she beamed at him again, holding out a tiny thread between her fingers, or was it a speck of lint or basting from her robe, but the robe was blue and the thread was yellow, golden really, what does she want from me, all he needed now was for Mama to have a zetz and find her out of bed and the two of them whispering together, at least he was whispering. Here, Grandma, I don't need it. She pushed his hand away impatiently. What is it, Grandma? Is this a special thread? Am I supposed to keep it or something? But instead of answering, Grandma hid behind the blanket and tripped off to bed. Go know what she was trying to tell him, maybe in her mind it was a precious treasure. Or maybe once he'd asked her to embroider him something with golden thread, but she was so muddled now that the memory of his request had popped up like a missing letter. But when did I ever ask her for anything? he brooded, twiddling the thread between his fingers, and anyway, Grandma was wacky long before the trouble in her head; it was Mama who made a mensch of her, who taught her how to behave around strangers, not to laugh too loud or tell the truth, it was Mama who civilized her, and yet, a year ago she was a regular member of the family and now she wasn't anymore, whole days went by when he ignored her and she was left entirely to poor Mama. The twirling thread was barely visible, a mere golden blur, and he felt a vague anxiety that maybe Grandma knew she was about to die, maybe people in her condition have an animal instinct about that and she wanted to give him a present, something precious to remember her by. Like an heirloom. He laughed dejectedly. Poor Grandma, she spends a lifetime embroidering, and in the end all she has to leave me is a piece of thread. When he looked again there was nothing there, but out of deference to her, he pretended to put it in his pocket for safekeeping.

"How many times do I have to call you, Aron?" Mama was standing over him, and he quickly hid his fingers. "What's the matter, why are you so jumpy these days?" She gave him one of her vivisecting looks, unaware that deep inside he was sealing himself off from her, slamming doors. "Why are you staring at me like that?" "Like what?" "Oh fine, now maybe you need glasses too." "What are you talking about? I see perfectly well!" "With eyes like this? Like a Chinaman's?" She mimicked, squinting up, and shook her head in bewilderment. "What I wouldn't give to be in your dream when you make that face." Again she mimicked him. I'm all alone in here, he thought, just me, myself, Aroning.

"And watch the potatoes. You're cutting them into snippets. I wouldn't serve cholent like that to my worst enemy. Now clean up in here, and sweep the floor, because Papa has something to say to you, right, Moshe?" Papa strode into the kitchen without a glance. Mama hurried off to help Yochi put Mamchu to bed. Slowly Aron started picking up the peels from the newspaper on the floor, and Papa sat down at the Formica table. He flipped through the Sick Fund account books and licked in the reddish-yellow stamps, making sure each one was glued in place, God forbid he should skip a month. Aron finished sweeping and stood before Papa. Papa was still poring over the account books, still ignoring him.

And suddenly Aron realized there was nothing to fear. The moment he had been waiting for had come at last: Papa was about to look into his eyes and whisper something, the secret code that went from father to son, from king to prince, or maybe he would touch him somewhere only fathers know about; it might hurt, of course it would, pain and change go hand in hand, like when you're circumcised; he blinked in anticipation, so what happens, is it like a slap on the face or a stomach punch or a knife wound that leaves a scar like Papa's, without an anesthetic, and it hurts like crazy, but if you can stand the pain, you've made it, you're in. Papa stood up. Aron stretched and straightened his shoulders. Papa approached the stove. Or did they brand you like a new calf joining the herd? Papa lit a cigarette from the burner. Watch closely, and learn what to do with your own child when the day comes. Finally Papa opened his mouth, and Aron melted with gratitude for his clumsiness, his awkwardness, not like certain strange, unreliable fathers with high-flown words and a tongue like a snake's; Papa muttered something about Tel Aviv, about summer and having fun, and how lucky he was to be going away. Aron hung his head, feeling both sheepish and relieved. Papa stammered and waved his heavy hands: Aron was old enough to do this for him, to help the family out. Silence. A pair of eyes gazed up in bewilderment, and the other pair avoided them. Nu, stop looking at me like that. Like what? Like a, like a, like a lousy commissar. Papa, it seemed, wanted Aron to save his Tel Aviv bus tickets so he could turn them in at the workers' council. You get a refund, he explained, good money too, no questions asked.

THE BOOK OF

9

Just as he feared, he did not have a good time in Tel Aviv that summer. Giora made an effort to be friendly, he was friendlier than ever, in fact, and wouldn't leave him alone for a single minute. He was always sidling up to him, jabbering at him in that new voice he had, giving out his new smell, and swinging his arms, till you had to be blind not to notice. Aron tried to avoid him; he refused to go to the beach with the gang, but much to his astonishment, Giora decided not to go either. He wanted to tell Aron about the signals a guy their age should know: like, when you meet a girl, if you rub your thumb from right to left over the palm of her hand, it's a signal. And if you swish your tongue from your right cheek to your left cheek while you're looking at her, that's a signal too. Anything can be a signal. And a girl with a build like Sophia Loren might really just be wearing falsies underneath. When Mama came to visit she tried to explain how important it was for his health and well-being that he should stay in Tel Aviv. She was wearing a flower print dress he'd never seen before that smelled of stale perspiration. Settling herself in Gucha's armchair, she told him all the latest: the Pouritz was at the upholsterer's, there were plans for a little redecorating before winter, but she hadn't made up her mind about the buffet yet; they couldn't just throw it out after eighteen years, it was almost like new, though she supposed it could do with a bit of a face-lift. And it's high time we thought about painting too, there's a moisture stain in the salon over half the ceiling, she went on in her cellophane voice, as Yochi called it, the voice she used with the neighbors in the hallway, and then, holding her coffee cup close to her mouth, she told him the good tidings: Nitza Knoller would be his homeroom teacher again next year, and Yochi was cramming for finals, Mama had seen to her army deferral and the rest of the bougeras, and also, she and Papa had decided that the way things were going now, Grandma needed to be looked after properly, somewhere nice, with a haimish atmosphere. Please, begged Aron, take me back to Jerusalem. I'll help with Grandma. I swear I will. I'll wash her for you. I'll even wipe her. You leave Grandma to me, said Mama in the old voice. It's yourself you have to worry about, you hear? Aunt Gucha, who had been listening with a blank expression on her face, remarked that this year, eppes, Aronchik didn't seem to be having much fun. He'd rather stay home and read a book than go out and play with the other children. Mama looked worried. Him, read a book? This boy cannot sit still for more than five minutes. And Aunt Gucha, to ease the tension, smiled at him and said she was sure that by the end of the summer they'd see a world of difference.

There were forty-one days left. On alternate Thursdays, when Mama came to visit, Gucha's Efraim gave up his place in the double bed for her and slept on a mattress in Giora's room. Aron would lie awake half the night listening to Mama and Gucha. Over the whirring of the water cooler he could hear them whispering together in Yiddish, about Papa and even about Uncle Efraim, and it made Aron sick the way Mama laughed. He guessed—with a flickering of the ember inside him—whenever she crossed the border between girlhood and womanhood, and he almost gagged at the memory of what he found on his search for Roxana and the others. Oi, Gucha, Gucha, said Mama at the door next day when it was time for the makisht-zich, you're the only one I ever laugh with like this, like we used to when we were girls.

Giora walked at Aron's side. His words poured out in a tedious drone. A scorching khamsin hung over the streets of Tel Aviv, and the bleach-white sun rays burst into scarlet drops on the poinciana trees. They always blossom at the same time, reflected Aron, the way cats go into heat. And a tap turns counterclockwise. And a screw turns right to left, or is it the other way around? He rubbed the coin in his pocket, the one he had caught in the sea the year before: a foreign coin, worn smooth by time, he couldn't make out the inscription on it. Obsolete, he had decided, but kept it safely in his pocket, although he was tempted to toss it away at least a thousand times and the only thing that stopped him was the vow he'd made to throw it back exactly where he found it. Giora was ambling along, full of good cheer. He took an instructive magazine clipping out of his pocket and read aloud: "Foam-rubber padding is a thing of the past. Today's brassieres have Dacron squares sewn into the lining, or ultra-thin layers of fiberglass that shape the cup." They were walking up Ben Yehuda Street and Aron found a public telephone and rang up his father at work. If you're gonna whine like a girl in Tel Aviv, I hate to think how you'll do in the army, said Papa, who kept bringing up the army lately in strangely resentful tones. The army will make a man of you yet, he said. No sooner did Aron emerge from the phone booth than Giora picked up again: "The latest designs from Rudy Gernreich, creator of the monokini, will be available this summer in a variety of colors: black, white, and flesh tone." Aron stood still, watching him wearily. Hey, you know that last part, the flesh-tone part—Giora giggled—whew, I come just thinking about it. If you want, I'll let you copy it. Aron declined politely. Suit yourself, said Giora, not minding, carefully folding the page back into his pocket. On and on he went, about sixty-nine, about the two holes in a woman's cunt, one for pissing and the other for the main thing; Aron was scarcely listening anymore. What was going on behind those winks? Giora elbowed him: Get it? They signal you when they're ready, like, if they bat their eyes and lick their lips, it means they're hot. Or, if they stick a feather in their hat, that's a sure signal. And then he told about a Moroccan girl half the neighborhood had used as a mattress till her parents got wise and married her off to a tourist. So then, like on her wedding night, while the man isn't looking, she takes a dead pigeon out of her suitcase and slits its throat to stain the sheet. Aron studied Giora's face: his complexion looked muddy somehow, lacking in transparency, there were fuzzy smudges on the cheeks and around the mouth where the skin set waxlike into the lifeless features of a stranger. When he noticed Aron staring at him, Giora offered some more of his mysterious tips: If a girl wears an anklet it means she's a homo. And if she breaks out it means she's getting the curse. He gazed darkly into Aron's eyes. I give up, said Aron, withering, let's go to the beach and see your friends. He hoped Giora would behave less crudely around them, but no such luck. The Tel Aviv kids were definitely changed. Some of them smoked openly. Their husky voices made the dirty talking easier. Aron stood limply in their midst like some elderly uncle or a tourist who didn't speak the lingo. At least Gideon is still loyal, he reassured himself, if only he remembers to take the pills I gave him for his eyes, but he winced at the memory of Gideon that last day in Jerusalem, after report cards, as usual he and Gideon got straight A's, and Zacky Smitanka ran down to the rock proudly waving a handkerchief at Gideon; mine doesn't have that yellow stuff yet, muttered Gideon, turning guiltily toward Aron. Show me, show me, cried Aron, jumping up and down behind them, trying to peek. Zacky offered a single tantalizing glimpse, then quickly hid the crumpled handkerchief; why was he getting so full of himself, why did he treat Aron with such contempt, yes, and loathing, as if all along he had been biding his time, just waiting for this moment; but why, he wondered, what did he do to them? Come on, you guys, let me see too, cried Aron, reaching out. Uh-uh-uh, cautioned Zacky, mustn't touch the merchandise! And Aron was about to say that he also had a secret, something precious to share in return—his last milk tooth, the one that wouldn't fall out, but he stopped himself. Gideon, glancing at the handkerchief again, asked with shy revulsion if it hurts when the stuff squirts out, and Zacky sprayed the air with a prolonged snicker and answered like a movie actor, looking straight at Aron for some reason, No, it feels all soft and nifty. Let me touch it, please, begged Aron, who by now had lost all pride. Zacky stared at him, wide-eyed. Whoa, Africa awakens! he said, flashing the handkerchief under Aron's nose. Here you are, ma'am, fresh as yesterday morning, and he led him backward over rock and bush, Aron's eyes transfixed by the glob in the handkerchief. Must be some kind of new substance, Aron ventured wretchedly, and Zacky howled with laughter, patting him on the head like a backward child, as Gideon turned away, shaking with stifled paroxysms. Hey, what do you say we nominate him for the Nobel Prize in chemistry, suggested Zacky, leading Aron around in hilarious circles. Where did you get it? asked Aron, well aware that he was humiliating himself. There's plenty more where that came from, shouted Zacky. Care for a peek at my secret factory? I just want to touch it, please, begged Aron, with the sound of Gideon's wheezing in his ears; all of a sudden Zacky stopped laughing and licked his lips enticingly, and then with a dramatic flourish passed Aron the handkerchief. Aron touched the tiny glob. It was hard as resin. His finger trembled. He

THE BOOK OF

forgot his erstwhile humiliation. Now he knew, whether they did or not: this glob didn't belong to stupid Zacky. It belonged to something far, far greater. And he savored the moment like a dignified beggar.

And here he sat, fully clad among the half-naked Tel Avivians, listening to their chatter with a hollow grin. Last year there were only boys in the gang, but this year there were girls too. As they talked and joked, the boys began to jab each other, right in the shoulder muscle, where it hurts the most, though luckily nobody did that to him. Nearby he could hear two kids snorting with laughter, trying to persuade Giora to steal a chicken from Gucha's freezer: Hey, it's your turn, what're you scared of, just put it back when you're finished and no one will ever know. Aron stood up. He shuffled down to the water, hands in his pockets, fiddling with the coin. Someone started humming "Pocket Ping-Pong." Raucous laughter rang out behind him as he waded into the sea. How is it that kids learn the same things everywhere, like what to say and what to do; it's as if they're plugged into the same current; "with the fowl of the air in attendance," for some reason this was the phrase that came to mind, followed, much to his annoyance, by an image of a frozen chicken, with its legs spread wide over the big round hole and Mama's hand dripping blood after wringing out the innards, but he shook off the image and sailed it away on a receding wave. Then he took the coin out of his pocket and was about to throw it, may it sink a thousand fathoms and never return, amen, when Giora walked up beside him so suddenly he barely had time to close his fist around the coin.

Don't mind them, they're only fooling, said Giora. Hey, did you hear about the chicken? I thought it up myself, brilliant, huh? Giora grinned at him as if the word "brilliant" were another sly dig, only Aron's mind was elsewhere: what if the spy had caught on when he wiped off the greasy fingerprints with 70 percent alcohol; with all his might he pitched this troubling thought into a receding wave, but Giora, staring at the sea beside him, was positively unrelenting, and jabbered on about how the players on the Italian soccer team aren't allowed to fuck before a game, it's true—look at Gianni Rivera. Aron took a tiny step backward to protect the tips of his shoes from an oncoming wave. He's really been sliding since his engagement to that sexy showgirl, have you noticed? Pay no attention, concentrate on the sea, thought Aron, trying to throw off his mounting despair; high and low he'd searched for the pictures, till finally weeks later he found them—the nerve of that spy —hidden in Papa's tool chest. Yes, Aron gasped, the tool chest Papa used at least once a day, because there's always something to fix around the house, lucky Papa's so handy or the house'd fall to pieces, the electricity and the plumbing and the blinds, screw in to the right, unscrew a light bulb counterclockwise, same direction as a tap; he used to know that stuff by heart; go, wave, go, take it away, but there was Giora, looking out to sea, his voice booming over the breakers, telling Aron about this kid named Cockeyed Sammy, who's feeling up his girlfriend for the first time and she says, Sorry, I can't, I have the curse, so he says, Don't worry, sticks and stones will break your bones, and Giora howled with laughter, staring hypnotically at the waves, and Aron thought, Away, away, but how did the pictures vanish from the tool chest, only to turn up again, after a week of frenzied searching, at the bottom of the drawer where Papa keeps the receipts, and how did they find their way from there into the first-aid box in Papa's army kit bag, that's where Aron found them, and he prayed there wouldn't be a war. So Sammy's girl keeps trying to explain, No, really, I have the curse, and Sammy says, Hey, didn't I tell you not to worry, I'll fix that son-of-a-bee. Aron groaned, the waves Giora reeled in were dark and sullen, hurling themselves at Aron's shoes with their scum and seaweed and nylon bags, and Giora said, Tide's in, and Aron searched his face for an allusion to the storm last year, which was, he suspected, when his problem began, maybe his brain had been deprived of oxygen or something, he was afraid to ask, because what if Giora gave a different answer, or blurted out more of the filthy secrets lurking behind his grin and the charcoal blotches on his coarsened features, and he slipped the coin back into his pocket, because he knew that Giora would only retrieve it if he threw it in, so he said, a little lamely, that he had to go home and rest now. Fine, said Giora, I'll walk you back.

Through virtually deserted streets they passed, Aron drooping in the heat, Giora striding briskly, going places, moving fast. And if a girl carries her handbag to the restroom, it doesn't mean she needs to rest, it means she has to change her sanitary napkin because she's bleeding; he grinned at Aron again, penetrating his obtuseness with a possibly ominous message: you never know, anything can turn out to be other than it seems, anything or anyone, and Aron started Aroning, pondering all the discoveries he'd made while searching for the lost pictures, like

THE BOOK OF

the plastic pen from the drawer in the "little cripple," with a girl floating inside, and when you pick it up, her top slides off and you see her boobs. And elsewhere he found a pile of faded photographs from Poland, one showing Grandma Lilly in a bathing suit, hugging a half-naked stranger whose arms were wound tightly around her waist. It was sickening the way her eyes and lips were opened toward him. And in the photo that showed her performing in a low-cut dress, you could see a stranger in the audience with spittle glistening on his lips; and far back in the medicine cabinet, on Mama's side, he found a lacy black brassiere he'd never seen before, though she always used to let him stay in the room while she was changing; her breasts were small and white and wonderful, he liked to peek at them through a milky haze, yearning to feel their softness against his cheek, but why did Mama handle them so roughly, and now Aron saw the blue ribbon of water between the buildings on Ben Yehuda Street, and then suddenly he stopped in his tracks, as though someone had called his name, and he turned around and started walking back in the direction of the sea. Hey, dum-dum—Giora laughed—you're going the wrong way. Who cares, muttered Aron, about to vomit lunch, hurrying to the beach while Giora talked about sumo wrestlers, who are trained from early youth to squeeze their balls up into their stomach for safety's sake, and of all the nonsense Giora had been spouting, this had the most convincing ring, and he wondered how old you have to be to start training, and then Giora said he could tell just by sniffing when a woman walked past him whether she was hot or not, and Aron lagged behind, stepping lightly, pressing his legs together in distress, fanning his face with his hand, about to rush out to the waves, yes, and what about the packet of greasy rubbers he found rolled up in Papa's army socks, or the dirty magazines he discovered in the storage loft over the bathroom, the latest issue was on top, and half the crossword puzzle was completed, in Mama's handwriting yet; and then there was that letter from Zehava, Yochi's best friend, who went to live in America and sent her a ring of kinky black hair taped to the paper with a little note saying: "My first curl!" Why had this trivia been hidden away, it was frightening; don't think about it, wait, there's still time! He headed for the water, almost running, Giora just ahead of him with his pointy nose, walking like Uncle Efraim. See, that one over there, you can tell she's hot. Giora pointed as they passed a woman in a feathered hat. Sure, wise guy, thought Aron, you can tell by the feather. Yeah, that one's hot too, said Giora, though this time there were no feathers. So's that one and so's that one and so's that one. They all were, apparently. Giora and Aron continued at a trot, down a narrow lane of rotting houses, and emerged at the seafront, on a filthy beach littered with nylon bags and cigarette butts and empty beer bottles sticking out of the sand, and Giora turned away from Aron and stared into the waves, compelling them shoreward, and explained that men have a biological need to fuck at least three or four times a week, because if the pressure builds up too much, it can be dangerous, and Aron tried to fend him off but Giora was unstoppable; there was a jingle in English he had to hear: *Eef you vant to be a bradher put yoor fadher on yoor madher!*; his voice was different suddenly, kind of quiet and alert, he seemed to be alluding to something, guiding Aron with clues and arrows and hot and cold to an understanding, an admission, but of what, and Giora scowled impatiently and added in the same tentative, cautious tone, You can always tell a woman's been laid at night if she sings in the morning, it's a fact, he said, his face crusting over with cocky ignorance, and Aron beseeched him with his eyes: Go on, say it already, but Giora stared out at the waves again and cracked his knuckles, crack, crack. Aron shuddered. What if he cracked them off, and then his hands, and his wrists, and his arms, and his shoulders, all piled neatly on the sand, and then his vertebrae and then . . . everything seemed to be removable, interchangeable, anonymous, and in his anguish Aron blurted out that at home he did hear, well, Mama singing in the morning.

With eyes like a vulture Giora veered. He forgot the waves. They lapped away. Instantly Aron regretted his betrayal. Of Mama, yet! Giora drew closer: "You mean every morning? You're kidding. What does she sing?" And Aron sensed he'd desecrated something, but the feeling blurred into limp confusion and his mounting resentment of her for abandoning him. Every morning she comes into our room to raise the blinds, singing, "We're off to work in the morning." Giora shook his head like a schoolteacher prompting a dull-witted pupil to try a little harder. "I'm telling you," said Aron. "That's what she sings." "Okay, but if she sings that every morning," Giora concluded, "it's not because she's getting laid." Aron shuddered to hear his parents spoken of like that. "But!" exclaimed Giora, guiding him toward the treasure, "does she ever sing anything else?" Aron thought awhile, and suddenly the

THE BOOK OF

wave inside him was rising again, maybe he'd feel better if he vomited. "Yes . . . sometimes she sings, nu, what's that song from the opera . . . *Carmen*, it's called . . ." "Get out of here!" Giora fumed. "What does she know about opera!?" "She went to see *Carmen* at the opera house in Tel Aviv," protested Aron, "before she married Papa." And the face of his father loomed out of the sea, grinning not at him but at Mama, the way he did when she put on airs, and hard as Aron tried to erase the vision—he needed that like a hole in the head right now—there it was against a background of ruffled seawater, bobbing and sinking below the waves, watching Mama tell how she saved her pennies for the bus fare to Tel Aviv and the ticket to the opera, in the days before she met Papa, who was starving in Jerusalem, and Aron watched him narrow his eyes at her, while she wistfully described the luxurious seats and the plush red curtain, and the gowns and hats of the shlochtas and yekketes; and Papa's eyes flashed maliciously: "She isn't just anybody, your mama, she's a regular inallectual, in case you didn't realize; who knows, if not for marrying me, she could be a great artiste, a Mozart at least, or a Whozit, the actress . . . Rovina." "You wouldn't understand!" raged Mama. "To you it means nothing, but not everyone's like you!" "Oh sure, it must have been dandy to sit there for five hours listening to all the heehaa-heehaw! Heehaa-heehaw!" Eyeball to eyeball he brayed into her face, grimacing to remind her of her treachery, of what she really was, and the smile vanished from his eyes, heehaa-heehaw! Heehaaheehaw! And he pushed till she yielded, the muscles aquiver in her face, like a savage succumbing to jungle drums. Hawheehaaheehaw! brayed Papa; heehawheehaaheehaw! Like a donkey with his tail in the air. And Aron watched her, praying, Don't give in, oh please, not this time, but behind those tears of rage and humiliation she was getting ready to laugh, preparing to surrender her pretensions and abandon her pathetic resolve to defect, and then, forsaking Aron, braying "Heehaw-heehaa," amid tearful snorts and hiccups of contrition over the treachery of Carmen, "heehaaheehaw," she sank down beside Papa, their faces moving closer, till for one horrible moment Aron could actually see the frayed heartstring only Papa knew how to pluck. "Are you telling me your mama sings opera"—he heard Giora's voice from afar—"at seven o'clock in the morning?"

In a flash he understood: Papa's hands reached out of the waves, dripping with tangled seaweed. They were unmistakably his father's hands, dangling ape-like at his side, and now he imagined them stroking his hair, tending the fig tree, leaving greasy fingerprints on the pictures, yes, oh yes, and Giora, who had been carefully observing Aron's face, exclaimed with awe: "Your papa sure must know how to bang!"

With a great, bitter howl Aron was upon him. Giora ducked, but soon recovered and began to laugh, pretending to be afraid of little Aron as he hopped around him, blocking his punches, pounding him not very playfully on the head with a heavy fist, teaching Aron a lesson to the rhythm of "Oh, tico-tico-ti, oh, tico-tico-tu." And Aron reeled like a drunkard, blinded by his tears, the tiny undefeated wrestling champion of his class, who didn't know the meaning of fear, no one had dared to mess with him before; why, when he was eight years old he'd flattened Zacky in the yard, that was the start of their friendship. Zacky stuck to him like glue after that, but now Giora was showing him what the future held in store, offering him a crash course in the strategies of avoiding danger, groveling to musclemen and reviling yourself with a crooked smile for being a little runt—suddenly Giora hammerlocked him from behind, threw him down on the sand, and sat on his back. Aron stopped breathing, not because Giora was heavy, but because he was crushed by the discovery that a boy his own age could weigh so much. "Say you're sorry."

Aron buried his face in the warm sand and choked back his tears.

"Say you're sorry."

The pain in his arm was becoming unbearable. He'll break my arm and they'll send me home.

"Repeat after me"—Giora's face loomed over him—"Eef you vant to be a bradher put yoor fadher on yoor madher." His face was red, filled with loathing. Why does he hate me so much? What did I ever do to him?

"I mean it, I'm going to kill you, now repeat after me."

Aron lay still as a new emotion welled poisonously up inside him: he was gloating, enjoying his own humiliation, the abuse of his own body. Go on, hurt it. Torture it.

"Eef you vant to be a bradher . . ."

He deserved this, he deserved this. For telling Giora about his parents, for listening to his silly prattle, for all the mistakes he'd ever made, great or small, like refusing to watch the wrestling with Papa on Lebanon TV at Peretz Atias's—he might have learned some tricks to use

THE BOOK OF

in a situation such as this—because those bloated freaks disgusted him and now they were getting revenge, through Giora.

"Repeat after me or I swear I'll finish you—"

Aron screamed. His arm felt as though it had been torn out of its socket. Giora jumped back. He approached to make sure Aron was still alive, then ran. Aron lay unmoving, his head in the filthy sand. Empty nylon bags and seaweed tangled with bird feathers splashed up on the shore. Through his open eye he could see the clouds turn pink. Maybe someday he would long for this, someday when he was all alone, fleeing across the icy taiga, going out of his mind in the frozen wastes. He closed his eyes and rested.

Finally, with great effort, he picked himself up and carefully moved his throbbing arm to bring it back to life. At least he didn't say he was sorry. At least he didn't repeat the stupid rhyme. He didn't foul his mouth. He brushed the sand off. He would learn judo, or maybe sumo. Three or four holds would do the trick. Slowly he dragged himself back to Gucha and Efraim's.

Five weeks later, at the end of a fifty-seven-day-long vacation, Aron left for home. At the central bus station in Tel Aviv he found twenty ticket stubs, and bowed down in resignation to collect them off the filthy floor.

Later, as he watched the fallow countryside roll by, he thought about his bar mitzvah. It would take place a few months from now at the beginning of winter, and there would be a lot of guests around to observe him at close quarters. The bus began to joggle up the narrow slope of Bab-el-wad, and the heavy Orthodox woman in the next seat glanced at him disapprovingly. Open the window, she ordered, it's stifling in here. He tried to open it, but it was stuck; his strength failed, so the woman stretched her hairy arms out and thrust it open herself. And still he couldn't breathe. He unbuttoned his shirt collar, but that didn't help much either. The hills rose up on the roadside and hemmed him in, and rusty auto wrecks with wreaths around them from the War of Independence blurred before his eyes. The woman leaned over and asked loudly if he was feeling sick. The driver watched him in the rearview mirror, scowling under his visor cap, and the passengers began to whisper, accusing him of being disrespectful to our valiant dead. With all his might he tried to prove his patriotism and hold it down, but the bumpy pass got the better of him, and he found the paper bag Aunt

Gucha gave him just in time. The woman beside him stood up, holding her skirt out, and started looking for another seat, and Aron burned with shame. When they arrived at the central bus station in Jerusalem, he hid his face in the paper bag until the last of the passengers got off, and then realized with a sudden start that it had been ages since Mama and Papa mentioned the loan they were going to take out to pay for his grandiose bar mitzvah.

THE BOOK OF

10

And three days after Aron's return, Mama and Papa sent Grandma Lilly to the hospital. They were afraid to tell anyone what they were planning, especially Yochi, and they waited till she'd left for ballet and Aron had gone to the supermarket with a long shopping list before calling an ambulance; only, Aron arrived home just in time to see them helping the driver pull Grandma into the van.

As soon as Aron noticed the commotion he understood. It was almost as if he had been preparing himself for this moment. He did not approach. What was the point. It was hopeless. Rigidly he walked past the ambulance, and Mama and Papa averted their eyes. He slouched up the stairs, pursued by Grandma's screams, and set the shopping bags on the Formica table in the kitchen, but then suddenly he couldn't stand it anymore, and he rushed to his window and peeked out from behind the curtain.

Grandma was going berserk down there, cursing and kicking and scratching everything in sight. For a moment old words poured out of her and it was hard to tell whether she was in her right mind or not, preferably not, though, maybe: the whole world heard her scream that they were throwing her out, her, after all the years she'd sweated and slaved for them making the kishelech Hinda peddled at fancy prices, not that she ever paid her for her work so she could go out and buy herself a dress or a pair of earrings. Mama tried to hush her, grinning apologetically on every hand, but Grandma continued to blast her in

Hebrew and Polish: For twenty years I held my tongue, because if anyone finds out what even Mauritzy doesn't know yet (Mauritzy was her name for Papa), you'll be arrested as a murderess.

Mama turned white and her hair stood on end. Then she lashed back at Grandma Lilly: "You shameless thing, you're sixty years old, sixty, not sixteen, you hear!" And Grandma made a face and said, perfectly lucid, "And you're the dried-up prune you always were, Hinda, even at sixteen!" Aron, who was listening behind the curtain, stuck his fingers in his ears and sobbed out loud, because they both had a point, especially Grandma: life for Mama was a sea of tsuris. What's happiness, he heard her say to Yochi the night of Papa's accident; a moment here, a moment there, and before you know, it's over. "Is this my thanks for taking you in and feeding you all these years!" she yelled at Grandma now, her hair flying Gorgon-like around her face. "For bathing you and dressing you and licking your ass, is this what I get?!" Papa tried to separate them, but they flared up at each other like ancient torches, in front of the neighbors yet, and the children, even Zacky Smitanka was there, leaning over his handlebars, and trust Sophie Atias to step out just then on her way to the grocery store, naturally, she wouldn't miss an opportunity like this to watch the Ashkenazim going at it, her and her gaudy Sephardic slippers; and finally, when the ambulance drove off with Papa and Grandma Lilly in the back, a kind of hush descended over the street, and Aron threw himself on his bed, utterly exhausted.

He lay there motionless. He could hear Mama pacing around her bedroom, pleading her case before an invisible jury, accusing, explaining, blowing her nose. He tucked his head under the pillow with Grandma Lilly's fancywork: there were hundreds, no, thousands of those pillowslips and coverlets: long-tailed parrots, luxuriant palm trees, brilliant butterflies, tropical fish . . . Deprived of her embroidery, Grandma withered, but hunching over her bright-hued threads again, she lit up like a lamp, and Mama would sigh and say, What are we going to do with these pillowslips, Mamchu, who's going to buy them all? But Grandma ignored her, sewing with fervor, filling the house with her plump little pillows; there wasn't much else to do, she rarely went out, and practically lived on the Pouritz, nibbling chocolates, licking her fingers like a child even in front of company, or skimming the Yiddish paper for gossip about the rich and famous. Mama wouldn't let her lift a finger around the house, except for the Thursday "thor-

THE BOOK OF

ough," and didn't allow her in the kitchen, there was room for only one woman there. And yet how could somebody like Grandma Lilly, like Grandma Lilly used to be, bury herself in the house day after day, Aron asked Yochi, and Yochi squinted at him, the gloom in her dispelled by a knowing twinkle, and said, Watch, li'l brother, watch her face and her hands, and then look closely at the embroidery. And Aron gazed into Yochi's eyes, wondering at her wisdom, and shyly asked her why she acted like that. Like what? The way she did around Mama, pretending . . . playing a role. What role, what do you mean? You know, as if you were, well, dumb or something, and he shuddered at his chutzpah, but Yochi threw her arms around him and hugged him tight, and murmured into his neck while he smelled her haimish fragrance, You're a smart kid, Aron, smarter than I am in certain ways, but there's one thing I know that maybe you don't. She giggled, or did she gasp, his neck was damp, I know how to stay alive around here.

Silence. Papa wasn't home from the hospital yet. Yochi was still at ballet. And Mama was pacing in her room, up and down, to and fro. Again he tucked his head beneath the pillow and sniffed the mesh of embroidery, remembering something that happened once, on this very bed he was lying on, it was mean of him to think about it now that she was practically dead and about to become a saint, but long ago, when he was six or seven and Mama and Papa went away for their annual vacation at the Sea Breeze pension, and Grandma Lilly stayed home in charge, well actually Yochi was in charge, she was only ten, but even then she was more mature than Grandma, and Grandma put on such a show for them, here in this room, he shuddered to remember, she climbed up on the bed and acted out a scene from the detention camp in Cyprus, how she was released and sailed to Palestine after the war, and how—oh, why didn't Yochi stop her—she was introduced to Mama.

Aron couldn't remember the details, all he managed to bring to light was an image of Grandma Lilly with her dress between her knees, jumping up on his bed and announcing in her artful baby voice, Now I show how I met your Hindaleh.

Aron turned to Yochi, too young to understand, but troubled by Grandma's roguish eyes. Yochi hesitated: early on she had chosen Grandma as her ally, partly to spite Mama, and she had her reasons for wanting Aron there to watch. Grandma covered her face as if in prayer, slowly seeping herself in memory, and suddenly she broke into a smile and started prancing on the bed. She carried herself with grace, old as she was, and you could tell she was remembering how she used to dance on the stage. "Ho, the zop I had me, you should have seen it, kinderlach, the braid was thick like so, down to my tuchis!" Her hand slid longingly to her nape, where Mama had shorn her hair in a charmless bowl shape long ago, Mama was her hairdresser too. "I used to dance the polka-waltz at the Kaffe Theater! And my cavalier, Mauritzy Wolfin, loved to watch his stomping 'shiksa mit a ponytail'!" She threw her silvery head back and laughed. Aron drew closer to Yochi. "And when we lay in bed," she whispered, "he spread my zop around me, black as sable, and said, This is the night sky, Lilly, and you're my demilune . . ."

Aron's mouth dropped and Yochi smiled. She knew all those stories, like the one about how Grandma ran away from home when she was thirteen to join a traveling theater, and how she had Papa out of wedlock, though Mama better not find out she knew, it made her sick to see the blank in Papa's identity card. "You see, kinderlach," said Lilly, "I was only forty-one when I come to Eretz Yisrael. Forty-two at most, and still a beauty, even after three years in a dark cellar in Poland, and after the camp in Cyprus, eyes like fire, I had, a figure like fine champagne, they said, everywhere I go heads turn; and boobies, Yochileh, firm like this! And a pair of legs on me, aiaiai . . ." And she rolled up her dress again, gazing wistfully at her legs, which were still pretty good. "Even Lieutenant Stanley, the one at the camp in Cyprus, said my body was good enough for a certificate, so I board a ship for Palestine." She sailed the bed with a dreamy smile. "And when I step off on land, I see Mauritzy, only the curls he had in Poland were gone! Kaput! And beside him was standing your mama, your Hindaleh." She pronounced the name with a little smile, and Aron glanced anxiously at Yochi, but she didn't glance back. "Mauritzy wore a coat like an old man, it was the first time I saw him since he was sixteen, when he turned Communist and ran away, and he didn't write a letter from where he was in the war. I never knew, was he alive? was he dead? But now I took one look, like this"—she shook her head, arched a furious eyebrow, and melted into a smile—"and I saw Mauritzy was gestorben. Finished. Back in Poland he was strong, a little meshuggeneh maybe, like an animal, but a cavalier, with a fine smile and teeth like Jan Kipura. And

THE BOOK OF

when we walk through the streets together *engagé*, the people take him for my husband, and he had muscles, Yochi, the Polacks never guessed he was a Jidovsky, and now when I step down from the ship I take one look at him, and vish!" Again she arched her eyebrow and squinted. "I know it: he's through, kaput! And when he runs to me crying, Mamaleh, Mamchu, I cover his mouth and tell him, Sha! Shtill! Don't call me Mamchu! Call me Lilly! What, everyone should know I'm the mother of this shlimazel. So then Mauritzy says to me"—she mimicked Papa's lumpy, long-suffering face, and Aron giggled and felt a pang of guilt, and turned to Yochi, but Yochi stared past him, studying something of infinite interest out there—"And now, Lilly, meet my wife, I married her in Israel, and she's practically a Sabra, she came from Poland when she was only two, and her name is Hinda Mintz, now Kleinfeld, the name she has from me." Grandma Lilly nodded. "And your mama put her sweaty hand in mine and said, I will call you Mamchu now, only please remember, Mamchu, in Eretz Yisrael his name is Moshe, not Mauritzy. Tfu!" spat Grandma. Aron recoiled and Grandma gave a throaty chuckle. He hated the sound of it. Why was he stuck with her for a grandmother, why couldn't he get one who was kind and loving, who liked to spoil you like a regular grandmother?

Grandma's eyes grew misty: her thin brown hand reached up to caress her shingled hair. "And that's how it started," she told them quietly in a voice so changed that Aron was astounded. "Yes, that's how I met your darling mother." Again she grimaced as though about to cry. "And she made me feel as small as a pencil stub that could fit behind your ear." Yochi's arm turned rigid at his side. "But she was even smaller, she was maybe twenty-six, it's hard to guess her age, but she told Mauritzy she was twenty-one, she had him eating out of her hand, and I was forty-two at most, but she had the Hebrew and the brains, and education—all right, a kindergarten teacher's diploma, but they call it education, and what did I have, Yochileh? My figure, my pearly teeth, and my kavalieren, and she had to go and cut off my zop!" She said this as though realizing it for the first time. Yochi jumped up on the bed with Grandma and hugged her around the waist. "She took her scissors and zip-zip-zip! And then she—" Grandma choked on her sobs. "She laughed at my kavalieren, the ones I had in Tel Aviv when we were living there! Casanovas, she called them! Criminals! Hochsta-plerin! Go home to your wives and children! And they were so good to me . . . so kind . . . we laughed together, they wrote me poetry, poems for Lilly . . . and drank champagne from Lilly's slipper . . . get out, go home, she said, Casanovas! Tramps! Klezmers! Artistes!" Grandma clutched at Yochi, who was only ten. "And I'll tell you something else . . ." She wiped her tears and runny nose on the back of her hand like a child. "Maybe one in a thousand klezmers he's a . . . Mozart someday . . . maybe one in a thousand poets he's a Mickiewicz, but if Hinda ever came across a Yehudi Menuhin, you can be sure she would call him a klezmer artiste . . ." Aron didn't know why she said that, nor did he care, he just wanted this irksome performance over with so he could run out and play with Gideon and Zacky.

"And there are other things, Yochileh, things I shouldn't tell you—" "Enough, Grandma, enough crying, no more now." Who knows what secrets Grandma whispered when Yochi crept into her bed at night and the two of them giggled till Mama put a stop to it. "Hinda always gets her way . . . you have to behave yourself around her and make yourself small, good morning, Hindaleh, good night, Hindaleh, because if you don't watch out she'll dig into your kishkes like you were a chicken not a person . . ." Yochi signaled to him sharply behind Grandma's back to leave the room. He heard the gloom in Grandma's voice, like a bitter secret behind her youthful brow, calling him to stay, but Yochi's hand swept him resolutely away, and he stood at the door still holding the handle. "She led me like this, and threw me into a tub of boiling water, and said, Now, Lilly-Mamchu, we're going to wash off the slime of your wonderful Casanovas . . ." She choked on the words and shivered like a leaf. Aron ran out.

The door opened and slammed. Aron froze: Yochi was home. She took a few steps forward. And stopped. He imagined her sniffing the air. Suddenly she turned around and walked into Grandma's alcove. How did she know? Dead silence. The door to Hussein, the little cupboard in the alcove, swung open and slowly shut. Mama stopped pacing. Yochi hurried into the room.

"Aron."

"What?"

"Look at me."

"What?"

"No. Raise your head."

"All right, satisfied?"

THE BOOK OF

"Did they send her away?"

"Leave me alone, I don't know anything."

"Her pajamas and bathrobe are missing. Did they throw her out? Did you see?"

"No. I was at the super. They sent me shopping."

"You'd better be telling the truth."

She didn't go to Mama. Or say anything about anything. She didn't even ask where Grandma was. At seven o'clock Papa came home, silent and sweaty. There was a fresh scratch on his cheek, but he wouldn't let Mama put a bandage on it. His mouth was tightly shut. Mama set the table, looking flustered, but her eyes were dry. Yochi sat in silence, and Aron averted his face. How stupid of me, said Mama quietly, I set five places. And suddenly she blurted, What do you want from me, Yochi, why are you staring at me like that! Aron was aghast, Mama wasn't allowed to scream at Yochi anymore, she was forbidden to because of the squeaking in Yochi's ears. And all this time I let her stay in my home! Show me another woman in my place who would agree to take her schweiger in and treat her with so much respect and consideration! Who else would have given her the time of day if they knew the kind of woman she was! Her voice was choked, and she hid her tearful face behind the apron with the kangaroo. You can't even cry, Yochi's eyes accused her silently, you can't allow yourself to shed a tear for her. No one is going to have that pleasure, especially not you, Yocheved; last year, when she started going meshuggeh in the head, who took care of her? You will not look at me like that! Yochi had been sitting silently, cupping her ear. Tell me, who washed her dirty underwear? Who rubbed her feet five times a day? And what did you do for her? Well, what? What did you do besides reading the paper and telling her the news of the day, as if she knew the difference between Gamal Abdel Nasser and Levi Eshkol! I don't want to hear a word out of you! Understand? Not a word!

Yochi said nothing. She didn't touch her fork. The steam from the mashed potatoes fogged her eyes. Papa bowed over his plate and looked away. Aron took a bite, but the food stuck in his throat. He wouldn't swallow a single crumb for her. Mama must have known what he was thinking. She slapped a drumstick on his plate. It's a chicken's leg! If he had any guts he would stop eating meat. Starting tomorrow he would become a vegetarian. How can you chew something that used to be alive. He chewed a little mouthful and stored it in his cheeks. Where was Grandma now, who was taking care of her? And what was she thinking? Did she understand? He glanced at Mama out of the corner of his eye. She was toying with her fork, not eating, moving her lips, mumbling explanations. He tried to control himself, but again and again his eyes darted to Grandma's empty chair. In front of strangers you were not allowed to call her Grandma, she was Lilly. This she had taught him from earliest childhood. Yochi told him Lilly wasn't her real name either, it was the name she made up for the cabaret. Funny how Papa insisted she live with them. You'd think they kept her around just so Mama would have somebody to take care of and civilize. And now she was gone. But he felt her presence even more, his strange little grandmother, a granny-child like a half-baked roll, except when she was embroidering, then she became another person; it was kind of scary to watch her muttering over the pillowslips, wearing a thousand different expressions: hate, fear, revenge; it was murder, not a jungle scene she was embroidering, with the parrots and monkeys and fish, shimmering pink and gold, and Mama would beg her, Please, Mamchu, slow down, there's no one left to sell your kishelech to, no more orders from the dry-goods store, and Grandma looked away, and Mama humbly clutched her hand. Do you have to make them so gaudy, Mamchu, she pleaded. Can't you try using softer colors, does it have to be purple and turquoise and gold like the Arabers; our customers are respectable people who want something decorative for their salon, fershteist, Mamchu, we're not selling dreck to Zigeuners here, but Grandma only sucked her breath in, snorting away any trace of respectability, and Aron remembered her look of contempt whenever the relatives got together, how she would sit apart watching them out of the corner of her eye, scowling at the matronly shrieks of laughter when Rivche's Dov told one of his dirty jokes. Let's be reasonable, Mama cajoled, keeping her distance from Grandma's embroidery, try shmearing a little less red! The house was suddenly silent. Mama's hand trembled at her mouth, and she stared at Grandma remorsefully. Grandma sat perfectly still. The crimson thread hovered briefly in the air. Slowly Grandma raised her eyes. She glared at Mama like a wounded animal and let out a mighty howl, and Mama shrank back as though faced with the proof of a forgotten crime.

No one said a word after supper either. Yochi sat down at her desk and started scribbling, doing homework or writing letters to her pen pals. Aron lay in bed. It was so quiet in the house. Where was Grandma now? Did she know what they did to her? Papa's cigarette smoke wafted in from the balcony. Maybe it would float off to Grandma's window in the new place. And when she smelled it, she would rise like a sleep-walker and follow it home. Maybe they could send her some nice homemade smells, like the smell of chicken soup mit lokshen. Of moth-balls in the closet. Anuga hand lotion. Tuesday-night bananas-in-sour-cream. If only they'd hidden a piece of bread in the pocket of her bathrobe, she would have been able to scatter crumbs from the am-bulance window, like Hansel and Gretel, and find her way back. Or a ball of string to trail behind. He could hear the sound of scrubbing from the living room: it wasn't the Thursday "thorough," Mama was in there alone. Scouring the panels with steel wool. Scraping the cracks in the floor tiles with a knife. What would Thursdays be like without Grandma? Even Grandma came to life for the "thorough." It's sad that I didn't really love her, though.

"Yochi."

"Hmn?"

"What are you doing?"

"None of your business."

"Where do you find so much to write about?"

Silence. She's writing so furiously, her collar flutters.

"Do you tell them things about the family? Like about Grandma?"

"I'm warning you, leave me alone—"

"Or you'll come to grief." He finishes her pet phrase on such occa-sions. "Just tell me one thing." He pauses, gauges his chances, her anger, and gives up.

"Nu! I'm all ears."

"Never mind. I forget what I wanted to ask you." Why doesn't she meet those pen pals of hers? But he'd better keep quiet.

He lay down, took off his clothes, and crawled under the covers. It was still early, but he tried to drift into sleep. Night fell slowly. Yochi too undressed and climbed into bed. From Mama and Papa's room he heard an unfamiliar gasping sound. Aron was mortified: it was Papa crying. A rough-hewn wailing sound from deep within him. Aron lay rigid. The wailing grew blunter, as though from having bored through many layers of rock. Aron got up and went to the window. He pressed his face against the screen and tasted the acid metal with his tongue. I've never heard my father cry before, he whispered solemnly to himself. I didn't realize he felt so close to her, he murmured. Yochi sat up under the covers, her face hard. "He didn't," she said. "He turned her over to Mama, right?" "Then why is he crying?" "Not about Grandma, believe me."

Aron nodded, though he didn't really understand. He grieved for Papa sobbing in there, and experienced the mingling of two fresh sorrows, for Grandma and for Papa, an ache of separation from both of them, though for Papa it was tinged with disappointment and also a kind of relief, as if one had shrunk so the other would breathe a little easier.

Mama went out to the balcony. Aron drew back. He peeked at her from behind the curtain: grasping the rail, inhaling deeply, breathing in the night, tilting her chin to the sky, and for a moment it seemed as if the slender moon had wasted away and would remain a crescent forever.

At four o'clock in the morning there were loud sounds of kicking, scratching, and screeching at the door. Papa jumped up, his thick lips sputtering Polish, and when he opened the front door, there stood Grandma Lilly, shivering in her Hadassah Hospital gown and unfamiliar slippers: how on earth had she found her way home, where did she wander all night, what had she been thinking? Bleary-eyed and tremulous, she didn't even recognize Papa; when he tried to hug her, she pushed him away, and when Mama approached her, pale with horror, but also quivering with childish joy at the triumph of Good, Grandma gave a piercing scream, and it wasn't until Yochi came and stood beside her that her shoulders relaxed and her head drooped, and she threw her skinny arms around her and cooed like a baby.

THE BOOK OF

11

At five in the afternoon Aron was playing soccer with Pelé on the asphalt behind the building project. The game had been going on for over an hour and he was getting bored. Gideon wasn't home yet, and Aron didn't feel like hanging around with Zacky, so he sat down on the narrow steps of the Wizo Nursery School, smashed a few pine-cones against the cement, and started pecking at the dusty piñones. Time stood still. Utterly still. There were gray November clouds in the sky and birds on the wires fluffing their feathers against the cold. The pantry screens at the Atiases' were coming off, and Esther and Avigdor Kaminer were out on their kitchen porch cleaning the grill of their kerosene heater. Aron was practicing his signature, forefinger in the dirt, an impressive autograph for soccer fans to collect someday. He didn't like his name. Aron Aron Aron. He pronounced it with deep concentration till it wrapped around him like a heavy overcoat, a hand-me-down from an old relation, Aron Aron Aron, a subtle pulsing of his selfhood was alive and calling to him out of his somber name, like a twinkling eye, like a squeal of glee in the gloomy vowels, but the more he said it, the further his tiny selfhood receded, the faster it faded, like a match flaring with elation, how strange; he forced himself to go on, though, just for fun, to keep repeating his name in search of the twinkle, until there was no reaction anymore when Aron said Aron, so Aron quit.

He called Gideon's name a couple of times, maybe he was back by now. Then he whistled for Gummy, his invisible dog, at a frequency only a dog can hear, and charged up the pitch with him to score a few more points behind the building project, and ran out of breath and sat down again. It had to be ten past five already. Time was standing still. For his bar mitzvah they promised him a watch, a present from Grandma Lilly. Out of her savings. Out of what Mama put aside from selling her embroidered pillows. Maybe she didn't even know about it. Who was he waiting for? Oh right, Gideon. Or was it someone else? Some guest, some relative from far away? To judge by his excitement, there were a lot of people coming. Whole crowds of them. Go on. He scratched Gummy's belly, ran his fingers through his fur, and tickled him where it makes their leg jerk; it's a canine reflex, even if their brain resists, they can't help jerking when you tickle them there; and then he made a little earth mound, glancing around to see if anyone was watching, the Kaminers were still on the kitchen porch with their backs to him; he wondered whether Avigdor Kaminer would live long enough to warm himself beside the kerosene heater that winter, or would Esther Kaminer be left alone, he did seem to be doing his best to stay alive for her, and Aron blew into the mound of earth and said, Let there be man, but he blew too hard as usual and the dust flew to the four winds. Nothing was going right today. How did that brainteaser go? Can God make a mountain so high even He can't get over it? He turned it around in his brain till it sickened him, and then he called out quietly, Gideon, Gideon. Had he been religiously inclined, he would have prayed for Divine intervention with his problem. But he had stopped believing in early childhood, seeing that his parents only went to synagogue twice a year, on Yom Kippur and Rosh Hashanah, and didn't keep the Sabbath. How come? And once they slapped his face for telling company that Papa ate salami sandwiches with butter. Go know. What time was it? He rolled a leaf and made a whistle out of it, and first he played "Skipping Like a Ram," and then what he'd learned to chant so far from his bar mitzvah Haftorah, Isaiah, Chapter 6, in his lessons with the hairy rabbi, who yelled at him for daring to ask if God is always just. Gideon, Gideon, come on already. In his heart he reckoned the days: today's menu: beans, buttermilk, bananas; tomorrow we have corn and cabbage, and maybe a little chicken soup would be in order too. That wasn't enough though, probably. You need carrots for your eyes, cheese for your bones, meat for your muscles. And more too, something to build up your willpower, otherwise how would you ever get rid of that stubborn baby tooth. From his pocket he took a small round mirror and looked for the tooth. There it was, white and tiny, sticking up between two permanent teeth. Right in the middle of his mouth. But he knew how to grin without letting it show. That was him all right, civilized down to his smiles. He turned the mirror over. He'd like to engrave Anat Fish's name there with a knife and give it to David Lipschitz. He'd risked his neck swiping the mirror out of her school bag. That he had the guts to do, but not to go knocking on the Lipschitzes' door and say to David's big-shot dad, Here, this is for David, it belongs to Anat Fish, so he'll have something to remember her by in his new environment. He looked at himself in the mirror. Stuck his tongue out between his teeth. He had three lips this way. Hey, he could work out a special lip number and perform it someday. He twisted his mouth and suddenly felt the scornful eyes of Anat Fish on him, her cold Egyptian stare; he probably seemed like a moron to her. What did he care. It must be twenty to five by now. His lips felt numb. How come there's no such thing as a lip massage. Peter Piper picked a peck of pickled peppers, how many pecks of pickled peppers did Peter Piper pick. Not bad. He tried "Hey, Beebo, hey, baibo" and got through the "hefti befti belabelabefti" like a whiz, thousands of tiny tongue muscles, how amazingly well they worked together; in a little while he'd go upstairs and knock on Gideon's door. Maybe Gideon was avoiding him. No, that was silly. Just the same he ran out through the entrance hall and walked around for a couple of minutes, one foot in the street, the other on the curb, that seemed like the appropriate thing to do, from now on that would be his walk, though he knew the look Gideon would give him, like he was a real pain in the neck, a huge embarrassment, and he stopped and glanced casually in the direction of Gideon's balcony. Empty. Hmm. What if he really did go to see *Dr. No* with Zacky. Aron walked out behind the building and practiced the glorious fall of a soldier shot in the back, writhing on the ground, full of pathos, then suddenly leaping up and spraying the air with his submachine gun. Who was supposed to be coming today? A relative maybe, from Tel Aviv or Holon? Something was definitely in the air. Now Sophie Atias, the young wife of old Peretz Atias, came out to the trash bins wearing those pink zapatos Mama can't stand, noticeably waddling though she's only three months gone, she doesn't even have a belly yet and already she wants to show off. He decided to be a gentleman, ran up to Sophie, and offered to carry the garbage. Don't be silly, Aron. She flashed a toothy white smile. Come on, give it to me, I'm strong. Well, I am too, thank God, but he tried to grab it anyway, that was the most they'd ever spoken. Let go, Aron, she said, not smiling anymore. But you shouldn't be carrying things, he blurted as they struggled over the handle. Watch it, she shrilled at him, then yanked the pail away and toddled off, leaving Aron frozen there, feeling scared, all he needed now was for Sophie to have a miscarriage thanks to his good intentions. He sprinted after her and waited by the trash bins, pale and tense, practically standing at attention in an effort to see what would happen now and whether she would look at him or not. She emerged from the bins and walked blindly past his rigid, upturned face. What's your problem? She scowled at him, menacingly rough, not at all like a married woman speaking to the child next door, and suddenly he saw her crudeness, he saw a cheap young girl breaking out under her panic, people said landing old Peretz Atias was the only way she could get herself a furnished apartment with all the accessories; she used to sit with Peretz and Papa and Aron and her little boy sometimes to watch wrestling on Lebanon TV, and once she kidded Peretz that it was good for him to watch because it got him hot, and then she poked him in the ribs and they all laughed, and Aron suddenly realized how close to his age she was; maybe she was afraid they'd find out now, and that's why she wouldn't look at him; sure, that must be it, the guttersnipe. He watched her waddle away like a duck, and again he started pacing up and down behind the building project, kicking the gas canisters, sipping water from the highest tap just for the heck of it, not because he was thirsty, the way a dog pees on a tree, and then he saw a shiny beetle on its back, attacked by a column of ants. He, Gideon, and Zacky had been slacking their FBBF Patrols (Flip Beetles Back on their Feet) for quite a while, and they used to be so conscientious, too, checking around the electric poles, rescuing beetles from certain death, till Zacky became bored and the project fizzled out; damn that Sophie Atias anyway, who does she think she is. It would serve her right not to see anybody but Peretz for nine months, then she'd give birth to a bald-headed baby with a mustache. Oh help, who's coming, what now. Is it the lottery, could that be it? Did he forget something, is there a big drawing today for valuable prizes? He ran through his list: not the Tempo bottle caps that win you a weekend

THE BOOK OF

for two at the Galei Kinneret Hotel in Tiberias, or the Popsicle sticks with the letters that spell out "bicycle," and there were three days left before the Toto results came in, so it wasn't that. Five-twenty-five. What if they really did go to the movies. He kicked a crumpled pack of El Al cigarettes, then picked it up. Examined it carefully. Sniffed it: it didn't smell like onions, but you never know. He struck a match from the matchbook Uncle Shimmik got in the airplane. He held it up to the pack of cigarettes. Nothing. Maybe we're talking about an extremely resistant kind of invisible writing here. He found the old strip of onion in his pocket, rubbed it against the pack, his own discovery: when the invisible onion sniffs the visible onion it reveals itself, only this time it didn't, not one letter of the invisible writing showed, maybe the juice was used up and he needed a new onion strip.

Three cats loped by.

Aron felt so miserable he jumped up and ran after them; instinctively, like a child, with the persistence of a child. They slipped through a hole in the fence at the Wizo Nursery School, and Aron hid his ball under a pile of leaves in the hollow of a poplar tree and followed the cats, picking up two sharp stones as he chased them, till suddenly he recognized Mutzi-Chaim, and he held his fire. Mutzi's mother had kittened her about two years before in the furnace room of the building project with everyone standing around to watch. Mutzi was the sixth and last of the litter, and she looked so puny coming out that the neighbors clicked their tongues. She'd be better off dead, in her condition, said mealy-mouthed Esther Kaminer, whose meaning was lost on no one. But Papa picked up the blind little kitten and hurried home. He put it in Aron's hands for safekeeping, stuck a tiny dropper down its throat, and gently pumped. The dropper filled with a golden fluid and the kitten sputtered and started to squirm. It has to have a name, thought Aron, we have to name it right away. Papa repeated the procedure with consummate skill, while Aron racked his brains for a name. A name, is that all you can think about at a time like this, he chided himself, if you name the kitten you'll get attached to it, but he couldn't refrain from whispering Poppet, Kitty, Checkers (because it was black-and-white), Mitzi, when Papa told him to massage it very gently and Aron obeyed, slowly, with a palpitating heart, and finally he decided on Mutzi, a common name, too common, but there was no time, and Mutzi, Mutzi, he murmured, tenderly transfusing the warmth of his breath into the kitten, fervently blowing on it, as on a dying ember; suddenly the kitten heaved its tiny rib cage and lay motionless in his palm, and Aron's heart stopped beating. It seemed to be struggling against some powerful force till finally with a mighty spasm, it jerked itself free, squeaked and wriggled, and began to breathe. Papa and Aron smiled at each other. For a week they dropper-fed the kitten, which, as it turned out, was female, and Aron decided to add the word "life" to her name, the way Minister Moshe Chaim Shapira did when he miraculously escaped from death.

She was a beauty, Mutzi-Chaim. Plump and graceful, black-and-white. Aron gazed at her affectionately, he hadn't seen her for a very long time, they had parted on bad terms, long ago, it seemed, but he wasn't angry anymore, he smiled at her and decided to head back, at his age cats weren't that exciting anymore. But all of a sudden Mutzi yowled and rolled over, rubbing her neck voluptuously in the dust, and Aron realized that the other two cats must be rutty males, and he had to smirk as he watched them, the way their eyes never left her as she lay there licking her inner thigh. The pads on her paws were pink and puffy. The yellow tomcat howled in pain. Mutzi regarded him a moment, then licked herself all the way up her thigh, where suddenly her tongue met the other little mouth that opened there. Aron cleared his throat. He could feel their maleness bristle at the sight of her rosy penetralia. The big black tom approached with an almost martial rigidity of limb, slowly swishing his tail, till Aron could feel the panther-python movements winding around his waist. He kneeled down cautiously, parting the shafts of wild wheat to peek out at the cats.

For a moment they remained perfectly still. Evening sounds from the building project reverberated in his ears. Pots clattering, a song on the radio, water running in the shower; Edna Bloom on the telephone, talking to her parents in Hungarian, raising her voice till it cracked, as usual. Windows closed, blinds rolled down. Then the yellow tom leaped in the air and smacked the black one under the eye, and the two of them tumbled in the dust, fierce with the knowledge of things to come, ripping each other to pieces, howling and yowling, drenched in darkness, and Aron squatted and gasped with astonishment, even his recalcitrant ofzeluchi brain momentarily drank in the frothy blood his heart had been withholding so long. Presently the black cat surrendered and slinked away, sloughing off the disgrace of innumerable lost futures, and the yellow one, panting and prickly with the terrors of war, ap-

THE BOOK OF

proached the female and started yowling in her ear. Mutzi-Chaim turned her head as though she wanted to think it over, but then she let out an identical yowl, how did she make that sound, he wondered, and again he envisioned Mutzi-Chaim in the early days, his lithesome kitten, poised like an elastic muscle with a triangular head you could hold in your palm, and he decided to raise her as a vegetarian, he wouldn't let anyone feed her meat or bones, he had this idea, he wanted to prove it could be done, that you could prevent a cat from growing up carnivorous; he even thought of training her to perform with pigeons, to add a little variety to the Houdini act, but his parents laughed at him; Gideon was skeptical too, which made Aron all the more determined to prove that nothing was impossible, and for the next few weeks, or maybe months, he kept Mutzi-Chaim locked in the bomb shelter and fed her out of his own hands, and felt a surge of pride as she sidled up with eyes only for him, and rubbed against him though he hadn't brought her a single bite of meat; and one day he came down to the shelter and found her gone—there was a hole in the ventilator grid—but he never lost faith in her, he defended her to tears whenever Mama and Papa teased him about the way she ransacked the garbage cans at night behind his back and feasted on chicken legs, and when he screamed that they were lying and pounded the floor with his fists, they laughed their heads off and said, Why don't we conduct a little experiment, then: go call your vegetarian pussy and let's find out, and he refused, but Papa opened the door and went "Pssss" and in she pranced with her tail held high, kitty-catting over and rubbing against his legs, purring loudly, and then Aron really blew up and told them to leave her alone, but Papa grabbed him, roaring with laughter, and pinned his arms down, and Mama exploded with hilarious gurgling noises, and then she took a piece of dripping red liver out of the refrigerator, he couldn't believe it, she was about to waste a good piece of liver on a cat, and Aron screamed as loud as he could, Watch out, Mutzi-Chaim, it's poisoned, but she scurried to the liver Mama had put in the saucer from the table service Gamliel and Rochaleh gave them for their wedding, and Mutzi-Chaim, humming electrically from her ears to the tip of her tail, grabbed the liver with her bare teeth, which looked different all of a sudden, and Papa let go of Aron, exchanging secret glances with Mama, and together they watched him approach Mutzi-Chaim, recoiling at the sound that came, not from her mouth, but from deep inside her, a strange new sound, like a throaty snarl; she had turned into a stranger, clenching the liver between fiercely bared teeth, her ears flattened ominously; and then she arched her back, crouched down, and slinked out of the house, and Aron burst into tears and ran around wailing that the Houdini act was ruined, till he bumped into something soft, his magnanimous Mama, who forgave him everything, and hugged him tightly to her breasts with pity, with love, effacing the memory of the arching cat and that awful sound he could hear again now, though it didn't frighten him anymore. The cats' ears were so flat it seemed as if an invisible presence were trying to strip them of their earthly guise, and Aron crawled forward, and the tall grass brushed against his face as the triangular heads of the male and Mutzi-Chaim came together and they yowled their gravelly song, so loudly Aron couldn't stand it anymore. Suddenly Mutzi-Chaim veered around and Aron let out a shameful moan. At that she blinked with annoyance and streaked away, the male in pursuit, and Aron after them. An old woman playing with her grandchildren watched him from the sandbox, so he pretended to be a child, a child chasing cats, diving into the rosemary bushes, where he found them snuggling together like sweethearts.

This was a rude invasion of their privacy, and they turned to him with quiet dignity, their furry triangular heads merging first, then one behind the other, coolly studying him, till he bowed before the scepters in their eyes. And then they scampered away.

Aron chased after them, cutting across footpaths, jumping fences. Stop it, Aron, are you crazy, he panted; the cats aligned their backs in search of another refuge, and Aron practically stumbled over them into their honeysuckle hideaway. The two stared at him in sheer amazement, and Aron could imagine how he must appear to them. Then a look flashed between them, their ears twitched. An agreement had been reached. With a sudden shiver they leaped out into the street. Aron gave up the chase. What did he care about cats, a boy his age. See that, you've gone and torn your shirt. And suddenly he was bounding after them.

He followed them up Hechalutz Boulevard, and around the corner to Hagai Street, where they surprised him and scampered into the valley. He'd never seen cats in the valley before. Panting hard, he chased them, his face aflame, calling silently, Stop, stop; they were going too fast, and though he knew it was wrong to do what he was doing, he realized he couldn't stop himself now. The cats paused a minute, okay, now turn around and go home, accept defeat, and again they took off with Aron after them, and he peeled himself off, layer by layer, and inside him there was something that ebbed and flowed and flooded his consciousness, but what did he care, Mutzi-Chaim used to nestle in the palm of his hand, and now look at her, strutting around with her tail in the air, to show off that pinkiness opening up, and the yellow tomcat pointed his ear at the little mouth. Hey, wait a minute, be fair, but they wouldn't stop, they lagged behind just long enough for him to catch up and then sprang full speed ahead, past the campfire sites where the fourth-grade Scouts came for their initiations, past the soccer field, and the rock ledge, and the cave where he sometimes took a shit; he could barely see, could barely breathe, he scanned the twilight for their eyes, which flashed at him like yellow droplets, thick as resin, blinking out of the bushes, and suddenly he noticed they were no longer in front but flanking him, like a pair of jailors past the tiny sewage stream and into the junkyard, where he collapsed in a heap.

When Aron caught his breath again he saw that the cats had vanished in the dusk. He lay heaving on the ground in the wavy shadow of an ancient Tupolino. Last year he'd used this car for practice, but it was too easy, all four doors were a cinch to open, and he decided not to drag it across the valley, after all, to use in his act for the end-of-the-school-year party. He tried to prop himself up against the car door or the refrigerator next to it, but he didn't have the strength. Next year he'd show them. He'd get hold of a suitcase with steel locks. He'd escape out of a barrel nailed shut with a sheet of canvas around it, or maybe a big glass cage. He giggled to himself: How silly to go chasing cats like that. He struggled to his feet and made his way up the path to the building project. Those cats, what a riot. He really had them hypnotized.

When he reached the sidewalk in front of the building project he peered this way and that. No sign of Gideon. That was strange. He went through the hallway into the back yard. On the asphalt, outside the trash bins, he signed his autograph in piss, but ran out because there were too many letters in Kleinfeld. Phew, what a fright he gave those cats. What persistence. He shook it once, he shook it twice, the last drop fell in his pants, as usual.

And suddenly, somehow, he was knocking at the door upstairs, and

Manny, Gideon's big brother, opened it wearing a gym shirt and said Gideon wasn't home yet, but come in, he'll probably be back soon. Aron said he just dropped by to check, and Manny said Sure, sure, and went back to his calisthenics on the carpet. Aron sat down on the sofa, now he realized how exhausted he was from all that running. Never mind. It keeps you fit. He leafed abstractedly through the *Guinness Book of World Records* in English, glancing up from time to time to follow Manny's muscles bulging walnutlike as he got in shape to be a pilot in the air force. Aron mouthed the English captions: the fastest man in the world, the biggest omelette, the longest fingernail. Still, Gideon didn't come home. Eddy, the student lodger, had opened the door twice already to ask if Mira was back yet. He's waiting for her like I'm waiting for Gideon, mused Aron as he sprawled on the sofa, closed his eyes, and fell to Aroning, thinking about Mira, Gideon's mother, smiling behind dark reading glasses, a petite, retiring woman, he imagined her mouth now, red and soft; what time is it, twenty to six.

Manny's breathing was starting to grate on him. The guy's a fitness freak, he said to himself in the language of the boys at school. The words didn't suit him. Manny had the same ears as Gideon and their mother. Little pointy ones. Manny's sweat smelled like the locker room at school after the eighth-graders' gym class. Only a few of the boys in his class had that smell. Let's see, Avi Sasson had it, and Hanan Schweiky had it, and Eli Ben-Zikri the hood had it for sure, and what about Meirky Blutreich and Meirky Ganz . . . He counted on his fingers. Quite a few, actually. This smell too would have to be added to the list, ah, screw 'em. What's this, he chided himself, talking dirty like you know who. But the clock on the buffet showed a quarter to six, so maybe Gideon really did go to the early show of *Dr. No.*

"So, Aharon, you've come again, I see," said Gideon's father, entering in his bathrobe, his hairy legs showing. "Gideon isn't home yet. How about a nice cup of tea?"

Gideon's father pronounced his name the way they do on the radio, Aharon, with the accent on the last syllable, which sounded a little silly; ridiculous, in fact. Aron had once heard him telling Gideon: "I'll always love you as a son, but you have to earn my friendship." It made Aron cringe to hear Gideon's father say those words in the course of some

THE BOOK OF

trivial argument. Aron was aghast, how could he talk like that to another human being, even if he was his son.

"Please, don't be shy," he said, holding out a box of cat tongues. Aron shrugged politely, the way he'd been taught. In this house manners were important. It wasn't phoniness. It was refinement.

"Go on, have some. Gideon just loves them. Cat tongues are his favorite chocolates."

Chocolates, he drawled, in a voice both disdainful and self-deprecating, always wary, always sly. How could Gideon stand him. And on top of everything, he didn't have a job. He wasn't prepared to go out and work from eight to four like other people. That's why they had to take in a lodger, and Gideon's mother, Mira, wore her fingers to the bone typing. Once or twice Gideon had mentioned that his father was doing research for a book or something, but none of the neighbors thought much of him. In the morning you'd see him mincing across the valley to the university, maybe he sat in the library there. But usually he stayed at home, stinking up the house; he even did the cooking and the ironing, and hung the laundry out to dry. You'd have to shoot me before I let a man in my kitchen, said Aron's mother. What, let a man futz around with the pots all day.

Mr. Strashnov was tall and limp, with prematurely sagging cheeks and chiselled lips that were permanently pursed, as though keeping in a secret. He would shout down to Gideon from the balcony, "Gi-deon!" like a radio announcer, as though Gideon were some personage out of the Bible, instead of an ordinary kid from the building project. "Gi-deon!" he called again, though the whole neighborhood heard him the first time, including Papa on his balcony, cooling his feet after a hard day at work. Aron would rush upstairs in time to see the evening paper flutter over Papa's smile, as he muttered a silent curse at Gideon's father.

And something else that's strange: when you see him outside you think he's a snob. That he looks down his nose on everyone, frowns instead of saying hello. But alone with him in the kitchen like this, he's almost pleasant. He's nice to Aron, pours him a cup of tea from the flowered-ceramic kettle and asks him questions about himself and his opinions on various topics, and for a moment you actually believe that grownups care what goes on inside a kid these days. Not that Aron enjoys sitting around the kitchen so long waiting for Gideon, maybe they managed to sneak in somehow without having to show their ID's, but anyway, it's sort of cozy here with Gideon's father, with the tea and the cat tongues melting in his mouth, seeping sweetly into him; he almost feels like the winner of the Vita Queen for a Day contest, as though an important celebrity, or an actor impersonating one, had invited him into his home.

The lodger, Eddy, poked his curly head into the kitchen to see if Mira was home yet. Aron turned around for a better look. Eddy explained that he needed some typing he'd given her, explaining too much. Gideon's father regarded Eddy with mild derision: "Our young student is impatient today, it would appear . . . would he condescend to join us for a nice cup of tea?" The student muttered a confused excuse. "Of course," drawled Gideon's father in his high-pitched voice. "The gentleman wants our Mira, he requires our Mira right away, and all I have to offer him is tea. Milk he desires, water he gets . . ." The lodger waved dismissively, smiled forlornly, and walked away. Aron saw the smile fade from Mr. Strashnov's lips. There was a long silence.

Aron couldn't bear it anymore and he turned around to peek at the clock on the buffet again. Six-thirty. Now's when they'd have to leave to get to the early show on time. Someone hesitated, yes or no. He swiped another cat tongue, chewed hard, and swallowed fast, without enjoyment. And then, grim-faced, he quickly ate another one. He stared at the empty box in dismay and apologized. How could he. Gideon's father nodded, this time without malevolence, with a certain curiosity even. "It's all right, Aharon. I knew you'd like them." How did he know? How could he tell? For shame. Aron wanted to dig a hole and bury himself. He was full up to here with chocolate cat tongues, and the oozing sweetness cloyed. "The older you get," Mr. Strashnov opined in his nasal voice, "the more you realize how unhappy and complicated life can be, eh?" Aron stared incredulously, certain he hadn't heard right. Gideon's father had an annoying way of saying things it took hours to scrape off, like dog-do from a shoe. What right does he have to interfere, seethed Aron. "Ah no," said Gideon's father, peering deeply into Aron's soul, as he tried to wriggle free. "Life isn't easy. I can tell you that from experience: it may seem as though your years are passing with friends and frolic; you think everyone is dancing to the same tune, but later on you realize it'll take the rest of your life to understand what was happening to you, all the loneliness, yes, and the humiliation. And

THE BOOK OF

here's Gideon now," he said in an utterly changed voice that startled Aron. "Will you join us for a nice cup of tea, Gideon?"

Gideon returned looking grouchy and tired. We used to be so close, thought Aron, and he doesn't even notice what's going on with me. Aron knew at a glance that Gideon had held out against Zacky. Traces of the argument still showed all over Gideon's face. You could practically smell it. So this time Aron was the winner in the secret tug-of-war, but there was no satisfaction there when the very sight of him seemed to infuriate Gideon. Gideon hurled down the navy-blue knapsack he'd taken to carrying lately, declined the tea, and gulped a glass of water. There it is, noted Aron a second time, his Adam's apple in broad daylight. And so thirstily, almost greedily even. He'd have to remember that too.

"I'm going to rest awhile," said Gideon, noticing the box of cat tongues on the table. He poked it with disappointment, turned quizzically to his father, who made his face a blank, and walked out of the kitchen. Aron got up to follow, started to say something, and sat down again, shamefaced. "Gideon has been looking awfully tired lately, it seems to me," said Mr. Strashnov, and Aron averted his eyes. "Have you any idea what's going on?" Aron did his best to evade the question, swallowed his spit, and firmly shook his head. "He's always yawning, always sleepy," said Gideon's father, his eyes drifting off. "Tell me"— Gideon's father leaned forward and lowered his voice—"please tell me, does my Gideon go out with girls?" Suddenly he broke into a smile, a smile of bitter resignation, and the mask of cruelty, his outward layer of disdain, was peeled away. "He doesn't tell me things, you know how it is, I daresay you don't tell your parents either, but you see, it's important to me, I want to know, what is he like with girls? Is he keen on them? Maybe he's out gallivanting with a girl when he tells us he's with Zacky?" He pushed his face closer and closer to Aron, who flinched as he watched him. For a split second Aron saw something like the negative of Gideon's father: the leprous eye sockets and lips a deadly pale. There was something vexing and unresolved about the man, like a latent disease, that contaminated him. Aron didn't know what to say in reply. What was Gideon's father so worried about? He nearly blurted out that he and Gideon weren't interested in that. Not yet, he screamed inwardly, not yet!

Gideon strode back into the kitchen in that fast, disturbingly aggressive way of his. "We're going down to the rock," he decreed. "Gideon," called Mr. Strashnov softly. "I'll be back soon," Gideon said, bolting, and Aron thought: Soon. He has no time for me. He just wants me out of here, away from his father. But which of us is Gideon more ashamed of? "Y'alla, let's go." Gideon went back for his knapsack—why does he have to take the knapsack—strapped it on, and rushed out again, with Aron behind him, smiling sheepishly, strangely sympathetic to Gideon's father, who seemed utterly helpless now.

12

They raced downstairs, and Gideon jumped three at a time, rankling with resentment. In silence they ran past the stump of the fig tree —one day a person named Eisen had phoned the municipal inspector to report a sick tree, only there was nobody named Eisen in the building project—and as Gideon dashed across the road, forgetting to look both ways, Aron remembered how he and Gideon used to risk their lives at street crossings, accidentally on purpose, just so they could overflow with gratitude when one pulled the other back to safety in the nick of time. They headed for the valley. A cool November wind blew in their faces. Gideon trudged ahead, weighed down by his silly knapsack. "He went to see *Dr. No* again," he said accusingly to Aron, looking away. "How come? He's seen it twice already," called Aron, trying to catch up, aware that his lagging behind like this was yet another proof, and stumbling as he thought: My legs are short.

Suddenly Gideon veered around. For a moment Aron hoped he was going to smooth over those snarls between them, but instead Gideon spluttered in his face: "Look, Kleinfeld—"

"Call me Ari! Ari!" cried Aron, so bitterly that Gideon cooled down, reminded of their four blood pacts and the basalt stone they hid in a cave.

They squatted on the path together to absorb this latest shock. "Well, Kleinfeld's your name too, isn't it?" asked Gideon with a hint of caution.

Aron sifted dust between his fingers. He was afraid he might start trembling if he opened his mouth. At school the kids had taken to calling each other by their last names. The Tel Aviv crowd started last summer, and now it was catching on here too. Strashnov and Smitanka and Blutreich and Schweiky—the well-blended ingredients of a delicious cake were slowly disintegrating into dry components: Ricklin, Sharabi, Kolodny. Names that belong on official envelopes, on checkbooks and draft notices. On the rough, shroudlike covering of skin.

"So why didn't you go to the movies with him?"

"I didn't feel like it today."

In other words, tomorrow he might. But Aron would take it in his stride. He'd plan the day wisely, to avoid being stranded all afternoon. He would practice escaping out of something with a lock. He had been neglecting his Houdini act lately. The trouble was, he needed another person there to lock him in.

"So why don't you come along," Gideon suggested limply.

"I hate James Bond." Silence. Shut up, stupid. "What's so great about going to see an English movie with a lot of girls in makeup and all that spy baloney?"

"For your information, even the"—he lowered his voice, peering cautiously around—"Mossad uses James Bond movies as part of their training for spies. Manny told me. Seriously, to help develop their intelligence and instincts."

What do you know about spies, thought Aron wearily, about secrecy and being on your guard all the time, acting as if you belong, when you're only playing a part, abandoned forever in enemy territory.

"Why don't you come with us sometime and see for yourself?"

Then too: there's the risk of being misclassified with a hasty glance: by movie ushers, for instance; or the new nurse at school; nearsighted old ladies who think you're a little child; the substitute teacher who, without any warning, moves you from the third row to the front; first-graders staring at you open-mouthed as you walk by with your friends, though maybe that was his imagination; or muddleheaded gym teachers on field day; or the crow that raids the trash bins who isn't quite sure whether Aron has reached the age when they stop throwing stones; or Grandma Lilly, who wanted to buy him a fire engine for his bar mitzvah, well, she is a bit daffy.

Keep quiet. Bite your cheeks. "And anyway," he blurted, "how do you know they'll let you in? What if they check your ID's at the door?"

THE BOOK OF

"We'll see," said Gideon, gratuitously and in the wrong tone of voice. But now there were dusky shadows in the sky and around the two of them, and Aron wondered, Why is there such a lovely word for something as disgusting as peach fuzz, and he peered around to dry his tears, observing the little valley through an evening mist, his eyes resting on the blistered rock, on the stream of sewage that flowed into the valley from the building project, on the junk heap with the rusty Tupolino and the stinky old refrigerator . . . What was it about him that made Sophie Atias so nervous, what harm was she afraid he would do her, and he felt something so bitter and heavy inside him, he had to blurt out that tomorrow he was going to break into that apartment upstairs and see if anyone was hiding there. And he swallowed his spit and asked Gideon if he would stand guard outside the door.

He'd noticed that look on Gideon's face before: not far from where they were sitting, in fact, three years ago at their Scout initiation. The "freshies" had built a glorious campfire, crowned with torches and flaming pinecone letters you could see for miles. Parents gathered on the edge of the valley to watch as the initiates lined up in their neatly ironed khaki uniforms. When the speeches and cheering were over, the "freshies" quickly crossed hands around the campfire, and the troop leader announced that all initiates would now break into the circle to prove they were worthy of becoming Scouts. Aron's group tittered anxiously, because the story went that each year there was somebody who didn't make it through and had to join another youth movement.

Aron, in the first wave of invaders, scuffled with a scrawny-looking "freshie," kicked him in the shins as hard as he could, broke through the circle, and sat down by the fire. Panting with relief, he suddenly noticed that deep tickle inside that often made him show off or do crazy things, though it also gave rise to some of his best ideas, like adding a final flourish to an already fantastic drawing, or taking one last spectacularly risky spin before kicking the ball into the goal cage. Gideon had broken through the circle too and was sitting beside him, all aglow. Aron examined Gideon's red little ears. They were pointy like his brother Manny's, and their mother's. The family ears. Kids were always teasing Gideon about his ears, but looking at them in the firelight now, as though for the first time, Aron couldn't help admiring their delicate form, the proud sense of lineage they conferred upon him, like a family crest in cartilage, duly preserved, faithfully imparted. Gideon's children would probably inherit those ears, how could they help it, and suddenly Aron felt a vague irritation; maybe it was the smoke blowing in his face, making him choke and fidget, as yet unconscious of himself amid the tumult of runners and blockers and the crackling of the fire, and he rose to his feet, aware of nothing but the spasm of dread that beckoned to him, forcing him to wake and listen: because there is a narrow path through the visible realm which Aron alone could tread; and he could spell mysterious new words out of old familiar letters; he was churning, feverish. For a moment he stood bewildered, and the children who were already sitting in the circle began to stare at him. Maybe they thought he didn't feel well, but he felt great. This was a declaration, of what, he didn't know yet; and it was also an outcry, against what, he didn't understand, though he reveled in the possibilities that glittered between the wires, flitting in and out, to and fro; and in the process something would melt, and unfold to him in all its glory, yes, oh yes, that's what he wanted, free passage through the fortified wall.

And he remembered that his mother and father were up there now with the other parents, Mama and Papa dressed up and solemn, and someday he too would stand on the rim of such a valley, a serious adult, watching his own child breaking through the circle, doing his family proud, from father to son, in a long succession without shirkers or traitors. And all at once he took off. This was freedom, this joy welling up as he burst through the circle a moment later, waving his arms like a little airplane; yes, he was free, but now he was an outcast, too. Crushed by the ceremony and its cruel attendants. Maybe that's when it started, in the days before cousin Giora outgrew the striped shirt, and Mama and Papa were still planning to hire an expensive photographer from Photo Gwirtz for his bar mitzvah instead of Uncle Shimmik with his trembling hands and old box camera, and they would sit in the kitchen every night going over menus; that was when Aron broke through the wall of "freshies" and ran into the furry cassia bushes, then stopped, turned around, and astounded them all by charging in again.

He hurled himself at the wall, only to be repulsed by the antagonized "freshies," who banded against him, driving him back with a rhythmic chant. Initiates who had failed before now broke easily into the circle. Again and again he charged at them, till he was too exhausted to plan his next onslaught. The beating he took no longer hurt, it merely an-

THE BOOK OF

noyed him, like a persistent tapping on the shoulder. When at last he came up for air, doubled over in the darkness, he could see the others around the campfire. There in the circle sat Gideon and Zacky, talking together; what were they talking about at a time like this, why didn't they do something, why didn't they rush to his side? Already he regretted his folly, but mostly he felt their vengeance trickling into him like poison; how swiftly they had joined the rank and file. They were ruthless in their zeal. In their cliquishness. He charged and was confronted by a cast-iron body. Panting, dripping sweat, he charged again: Touch me, I'm burning. "Hey-hop," they clamored, and it was their most effective weapon, his hidden weakness; again he fell and rose and charged at them, bellowing blindly, while they, unwitting, with the instinct of the herd, exploited his Joseph-like transcendence and offered him up in sacrifice, the victim of their unity.

Finally Gideon turned toward him with a withering look and Aron stopped in his tracks before the circle, devastated by Gideon's haste to condemn him for his one silly weakness when he was missing the point. Oh, he knew exactly how he seemed to Gideon just then: like a fighter pilot whose plane crashes while he's showing off over the air base. And suddenly Aron's legs turned to jelly and the scene dissolved before his eyes. If Gideon could be so wrong about him— And he turned from them in resignation and slinked away into the darkness.

"Hey, tell me something," said Aron flimsily, searching for words to fill the heavy silence, "how're your eyes?" "Pretty lousy, thank you," answered Gideon, stiffly polite. His left eye was still weak and he kept seeing this crooked little thread in front of him all the time, so his mom told him to have it checked at the Sick Fund clinic, but he was sure it would go away in time. Aron suggested that perhaps he ought to start taking three pills a week instead of two, and Gideon answered that it might do more harm than good. What harm, asked Aron distantly, his lips pursed with lies: Grandma Lilly and Mama have been taking those pills for years, which is why they don't need glasses. He put his hand in his back pocket and pulled out the square of waxed paper with a yellow pill inside. Gideon reached for it, and Aron's split-second hesitation upset the little bubble on the level between them; once he wouldn't have noticed, it all started with that awful business: now he was forced to learn the language of exile; and then he added, all innocence, "I hear they can be real bastards at flight school," and he felt the chilly contraction of Gideon inside him. "I read somewhere that they have instruments they poke in your eyes." He still hadn't given the pill to Gideon, who continued to hold out his hand, pretending not to notice the delay. A coarse-haired bow had scratched against the catgut of his new malevolence. Suddenly Aron turned around, whistled for Gummy, and said, "Here, boy, good dog," and scratched him under the chin, and on the belly, where it makes their leg jerk, and he knew that Gideon was boiling mad now and fed up to here and that he was only controlling himself because he needed the pill. "Knock it off, Aron," cried Gideon. "Quit acting like such a nitwit over some dog who's probably dead by now, I mean, what are you trying to prove?!" Aron looked up at him and said in a tremulous voice that he could do what he wanted with Gummy; Gideon, relenting on account of the pill, said Aron knew darned well that his mother got rid of Gummy two years ago after she saw him mounting the Boteneros' bitch out by the trash bins, but Aron protested that he would go on raising Gummy any way he liked till it was Gummy's time to die, in about twelve years, so Gideon could mind his own business; Gideon stared back at him and said, "You know, Aron, sometimes I just can't figure you out," and Aron pouted and wanted to scream, Oh yeah? And how about you and your stupid knapsack, what are you trying to prove, strapping it on like an army tracker, and why does your pal Zacky wear a gold chain around his neck and carry that six-blade pocketknife he keeps snapping all the time; he didn't really know what Gummy had to do with the knapsack or the pocketknife; he only knew that he personally couldn't stand toting all that stuff around. "Go ahead, take it!" He suddenly raised his voice, distressed to be in this unsought position.

Gideon gulped down the pill without water.

"Listen," he said all of a sudden, "I . . . Count me out this time."

Aron stared at him blankly till he realized that Gideon was referring to the stakeout. "So you're turning chicken on me? Like Zacky? Terrific." He said it like an actor delivering the wrong line.

"I'm no chicken and you know it." Again they were silent and withdrawn, as though all their energy had ebbed away. Adults, Aron reflected, carry things around with them, like wallets and pens and cards and stuff, and coins and beads and rings and key chains; why have I been breaking so many pencils lately, and losing pens, he frowned at his hand, and yesterday at supper I knocked my glass over again, and at school I slammed the door on my finger, and what about the way I always miss a few times before I get the straw in the bottle? And he wondered if anyone had noticed yet, a few days ago when Papa asked him to change a light bulb, he screwed it the wrong way and it shattered in his hand.

"You want to know what I think?" said Gideon, "we've been going along with your ideas since age zero, every summer you come up with a spy or a buried treasure, or we spend months trying to discover an unknown substance"; he rattled off the list as though proving a point, but despite himself, he softened. "And remember the time you convinced us old Kaminer was a werewolf . . ." Gideon chuckled and Aron smiled. "And we sneaked into their apartment." "And found a woman's wig," Gideon recalled. "See? I told you. It must have come from one of his victims!" "Oh sure, and there was this huge carpenter's file there, and you told us that's what he used to file his teeth . . ." "Well, whåt about that calendar? How do you explain that?" "What calendar?" "The one with the red marks that show when the moon is full!" And Gideon shook his head and sighed. "Oi, Ari, the ideas you used to come up with," and Aron thought, And still do, if you're with me. "And remember the last time we sneaked into What's-her-name's?" Aron nodded silently. Little did Gideon suspect that Aron had been back there at least once a week ever since. "Do you still have the key, that passkey?" Aron pulled it out of his pocket and showed it to Gideon. He'd bought it three years before from Eli Ben-Zikri, who had initiated him into the mystery of locks and keys with obscene allusions which to this day excited him whenever he tried a new lock. In return Aron had given Eli the key to the bomb shelter of the building project, the long, narrow cellar where people stored what they didn't have room for in their crowded apartments. And suddenly the shelter began to expand; no matter how much stuff people brought down, miraculously there was always room for more; and Aron shivered at the thought of what would happen if anyone found out.

"And remember the time Kaminer came back from dialysis and almost caught us?" "Lucky I made Zacky stand guard outside," said Aron proudly. Aron and his foolproof plans. "Poor Zacky, you always made him wait outside, didn't you?" Gideon chuckled.

They smiled at each other, a wan smile of complicity. A brief respite. "And remember the time you decided Peretz Atias was a member of the Ku Klux Klan." Gideon groaned with mirth, stretching this thread of grace even more, till Aron began to suspect he would try to shirk his duty. "And you would suddenly decide someone walking down the street was an Egyptian spy, and we'd follow him until he started getting suspicious . . ."

Aron cleared his throat, to release the nectar of longing. "Okay, then, who's Yigal Flusser?!"

"Yigal Flu . . . oh, right: twenty-seven years old."

"Twenty-four."

"Twenty-four. He escaped to Egypt and spied against Israel. And he fell in love with the wife of What's-his-name . . . Altshuller, the guy who was in prison there! But which prison?"

"Abassia Prison! And who else was in with them?"

"Just a second, don't tell me . . . Victor Gershon from Pardes Hanna. And Nissim Abusarrur."

"Not bad. And what was the name of the Egyptian interrogator?"

"Uh . . . I forget." Gideon shrugged his shoulders.

"You forget? Colonel Shams of Egyptian counterintelligence."

"Right. Shams . . . and you wanted to train us to survive his interrogations . . . You really had a thing about spies and traitors."

"I still do, I guess." Aron giggled. "And remember, nu, what was I going to say, oh yes, sometimes I still wonder about that guy they said looked like a kibbutznik, the one in prison, with the private cell?"

"They said it was hard to believe anyone who looked like that would want to spy against Israel."

"And where was Simon Kramer from?"

"Hey." Gideon smiled. "Remember the time you made us believe you were a double agent?"

"Uh-uh. Simon Kramer was from Rishon LeZion. He crossed the border into Gaza and joined Egyptian intelligence."

"You were always pretending you knew spy secrets . . . you'd draw marks on the sidewalk, to signal planes . . ." Something flashed in Gideon's eyes, and Aron turned hastily around. "You're wrong," he said. "I drew those marks for a different reason. I thought them up in fifth grade, after our big fight."

"Ah, I remember!" cheered Gideon, misled. "Right, we had this big fight, but what was it about? We thought the world had ended." It had. And when they made up again, the friendship changed: from a habit

THE BOOK OF

of childhood it became an earnest choice. They laughed together quietly. They laughed too much. A farewell sigh wafted in the words. Aron wasn't certain what had happened in the last few minutes, he only hoped that Gideon would take pity and relent.

"Right," Gideon recalled, running his hand through his hair. "You worked out some complicated system of signs; seven signs, remember?"

"Did I?" asked Aron cautiously. "Funny, I don't remember anymore."

"Sure, you must: that red T-shirt from day camp, you said that if an emergency came up while you and I were feuding, we could hang the shirt on the laundry line and then the other would see it and know to hurry down to the rock. Our feuds never lasted for more than a week, you made sure of that."

"Hmm. Anything else?"

"We were supposed to tear the three bottom leaves on the ficus plant in the hallway. That was the first sign. And on Mondays there was a different one . . . Oh yes, leave the tap dripping in the back yard; if one of us saw that, he'd rush to the rock, no matter what. As soon as we woke up from our naps, you said, at four o'clock sharp."

"See that, I can't remember anything," said Aron, choking.

"Sure! You used to draw tails on the sidewalk arrows, don't you remember?"

"No. Remind me."

"And . . . we'd pour sand into the holes in the sewer caps. I can't believe you've forgotten that."

"It's beginning to come back to me now, wait, wait." He dragged out the suspense. "Wasn't there one last sign that would rally us from the ends of the earth?"

"I'm amazed at you, forgetting that, with a mind like yours." Aron squinted at his moving lips. "If one of us was in bad trouble all he had to do was climb on the rock and SOS with a mirror. Flashing at the other's bedroom ceiling."

"Hmm . . . do you still remember how to SOS? I'm sure I don't."

Gideon knitted his brow. "Like this: dot dot dot, dash dash dash, and dot dot dot again: fast, slow, fast. Morse code is something I will never forget."

"That's terrific," said Aron, leaning back, breathing deeply.

"The ideas you used to have."

Shut up now. Control yourself. "Better than James Bond, I can tell you that"—he went and spoiled it.

"Those were the days . . ." sighed Gideon. And Aron echoed, Those were the days. Again the silence interrupted them. Gideon yawned broadly, and Aron stared into his open mouth; why is Gideon so exhausted all the time, Mr. Stashnov wanted to know. Shut your mouth, Aron begged silently, and burrowed into his thoughts, looking for something to distract him from his guilt and shame, to fan the tiny flame that had flickered between them a moment ago. What would he say? He knew a blow was coming at the end of this conversation. Full of anguish, he reached into his pocket and pulled out the coin. Gideon studied it: "Seems like it's been rubbed with a stone." "But maybe it's a rare coin?" said Aron. "Looks obsolete to me. Ask my dad to take a look. He has a coin collection." "Right, a coin collection. I forgot. See how forgetful I am today." He was playing for time. Again he mustered the strength to say, What do you think, should we throw it to Morduch, and with a wavering smile he added that he knew it wasn't right to cheat a blind man, and Gideon, carefully looking away, said Morduch wouldn't know the difference, and Aron whispered, That's true, he wouldn't know the difference. He blesses you no matter what you throw into his cup, said Gideon. Right, no matter what, Aron repeated listlessly, drawing out the endings of Gideon's pithy utterances, as if secret caresses emanated from them.

They continued this game of peek-a-boo, then stopped and fell silent. Aron's head drooped between his shoulders, revealing his slender nape, and still he waited, but Gideon said nothing. Aron was too tired to wait anymore. He couldn't understand why Gideon seemed so strange and threatening. Absentmindedly he touched the knapsack, stroked the puppylike padding inside. Gideon glanced at his fingers in surprise. Aron pulled them away.

"Now that we finally have the chance to capture a genuine spy, or maybe even a hired assassin, you want to drop out, well thanks a heap . . ." He didn't know why he was talking such nonsense. He tried to act the injured party, but his voice sounded too whiny and high-pitched, and his face appeared suddenly devoid of itself, revealing his strange, dejected depths. If only Gideon had looked at him just then, he would have seen into the heart of his anguish. But alas, with the egotism children need in order to survive, with the amazing detachment

THE BOOK OF

that maintains their loyal friendships, and with a vestigial sense of caution, Gideon turned away and was spared. He looked out into the distance, remaining sensitive and decent. And Aron knew that all was lost.

"Zacky says he's getting sick of your make-believe." Gideon embarked on his mission, tossing off "make-believe" with dignified haste.

He might have said "babyish" instead or, worse, "childish." And Aron, both grateful and humiliated, knew that Gideon had taken it upon himself to break the news and shield him from Zacky's tactlessness.

"I was making up adventures for you," whispered Aron, his lower lip trembling.

"Adventures are fine . . ." Gideon squirmed, and in the silence that followed Aron reached into his pocket, touched the onion strip that reveals the invisible workings of the mind, and heard Gideon thinking: But we're about to set off on the greatest adventure of our lives. Aron dropped the onion strip as though burned.

"So what, are you saying you don't want to do the Houdini act anymore either?" Better to hear it now, the bare truth; he had always secretly felt protected, having Gideon there to lock him in and tie the ropes.

"Okay, but explain one thing," said Aron, perishing. "I want to understand, because maybe I'm a little slow, so tell it to me straight, why did it used to be fun to sneak into a strange house two years ago and now suddenly it isn't anymore? What's changed?"

"I don't know, it's just different now." Gideon was evasive again, and a warning flashed from the tower of his self-control.

What's different, who's different, oh God, please let there be a spy this year, that'll show them, that'll clear this whole big mess . . . Here's Gideon, pursing his lips with the heartrending expression of a gladiator forced to kill his own brother before a bloodthirsty mob, but where is the mob, who are the invisible spectators goading them on, and where is the emperor; and Aron looked up and for one last moment saw the bird of Gideon's love for him fluttering across his features, as though trying to rouse him. Get up, Aron, get up, it whispered behind the mosquito netting draped over the sleeping child. Get up, we're going on a long journey, as Aron curled around himself, bloodless, fleshless. If you were loyal to me you would wait as long as it takes, and Gideon retreated further into the brightly lit corridor, where a sturdy truck or tank appeared, and on it, in a blinding light, he distinguished his class-mates, noisy boys and girls with their knapsacks and ropes and poles and pocketknives. No, no, I can't come yet, he whispered, his eyes filling with regret. You see, I'm going away for a while, I'm entering the chrysalis phase of my disaster, Aroning into a cocoon. "Will you listen to me for a minute, Ari." It was his caution and tact that made Aron decide. "For your own sake, just listen to me, you have to, you have to get hold of yourself—"

"To hell with you!" screamed Aron savagely. "To hell with all of you. I'll go in alone! All alone!" And he stood up and ran away, with one last shriek in Gideon's dumbstruck face, racing blindly through pitch darkness, into the huge black maw of the valley, sobbing and choking and screaming inside that he would never stop, he would break into strange houses, and escape out of boxes and trunks and cars, he would stay as he was, himself, forever.

13

One pleasant winter morning, the Sabbath of his bar mitzvah, Aron was called up to read from the Torah. As soon as he saw the scroll spread open with the tufted symbols, his nerves were calmed and he chanted jubilantly: *Then flew unto me one of the seraphim, with a glowing stone in his hand, which he had taken with tongs from off the altar*; Papa was standing beside him, looking clumsy in his prayer shawl, his red face bobbing after the rabbi's finger as Aron quavered: *And He touched my mouth with it and said, Lo, this hath touched thy lips, and thine iniquity is taken away, and thy sin is expiated.* The diminutive rabbi kept a vigilant eye on him, every pore on his face squeezed shut with concentration. Maybe he remembered that impertinent question Aron asked about Divine justice; narrowly suspicious, he watched the radiant son dance before his father with outstretched arms in the shower of sweets pelting down from the women's gallery, and Aron, at the height of his rejoicing, felt the sudden sting of the rabbi's eyes upon him.

Afterward the family went home and found two Orthodox Jews waiting at the door. They'd wheeled an old baby carriage all the way from Mea Shearim with a huge pot of noodle kugel swathed in towels to keep it warm. Mama hurried to the kitchen with Yochi, to cut the kugel and make last-minute changes in the refreshments, and Aron went to his room and sat in the window, one foot on the heater, looking out at the street, stabbing himself over and over with the daggerlike memory of his rabbi's side glance. When Shimmik and Itka's Volkswagen pulled up, Aron jumped off the windowsill and lay supinely on his bed.

Two weeks before the bar mitzvah Mama took one of his shoes to the Persian cobbler in the market and gave him precise instructions, but the idiot made the shoes too big and Aron had to wear insoles. Mama bought him a pair of thick new socks, too, and when she rolled them around his fist to check the size she saw they were too big, but just this once, she asked, he could wear them, couldn't he? Aron looked at the sock around his fist and said he'd heard that a person's heart is the same size as his fist. Mama took one look at his fist and grabbed the sock, tfu, don't believe everything you hear. When Aron put on the shoes he felt suddenly taller. Bending down he discovered they were elevator shoes. Mama was preoccupied with a speck of schmutz she'd found on her blouse, which she tried to rub out with a little spit. Aron was quiet. So, already he was starting to betray himself; how he despised himself for keeping silent.

Two by two, some trailing children, the relatives assembled in the salon. From time to time, Yochi peeked in to smile at him encouragingly and bring him the presents that had been left for him at the desk, as she put it. He received *A Thousand Historical Characters* and *An Answer for Every Question*; the Kapa'i Kipnis Hebrew-English dictionary; two army mess kits with plates and cup; the six volumes of the collected works of Winston Churchill; and from Itka and Shimmik the *Guinness Book of World Records* they'd promised him long ago, when he was interested in that stuff. What would he do with it now, though? From the salon he heard a great commotion, but he made up his mind to stay in his room a little while longer. To pull himself together. He felt hot in his choking bow tie, in the heavy sweater Mama had knitted especially for him, in the outlandish jacket they'd bought him with the shoulder pads; Mama would skin him alive if he dared take anything off before the last of the guests left. He lay on his bed, joylessly leafing through the *Guinness Book of World Records*, exactly like the one at Gideon's, which he already knew by heart, and thanks to which, you might say, he was top of his class in English; now he read about a farmer who stuffed a goose till it weighed fifty-eight kilos, and about bonsai trees in Japan, and about Robert Wadlow, the tallest man in the world, who died at the age of twenty-three because people of that type have a short lifespan, and he yawned as hard as he could for emphasis. The doorbell rang and Aron heard Mama and Papa merrily welcoming Ruja and Loniu, the parents of his cousin Omri, and after them, Efraim and Gucha, who had arrived from Tel Aviv. He waited a moment, yes, no, yes, no, but it was *yes*. "Efraim!" said Mama in a tight, sweet voice, "I see that Giora's left you flatfooted!"

Aron pulled back the sleeves of his jacket and sweater and shirt, and glanced at the wristwatch from Grandma Lilly, a big heavy Duxa, with two movable metal rings. The idiot cobbler had pierced another three holes in the leather band, so the watch would fit snugly. Grandma Lilly didn't even know she'd bought him such an expensive gift out of the savings Mama put aside for her. In honor of his bar mitzvah Mama had reupholstered her Pouritz, and tied her down with a colorful Bukharan shawl, to keep her from falling, she explained to everyone. Most of the guests were seeing Grandma in this state of rapid deterioration for the first time, and Mama finally opened her heart to Ruja and Rivche and told them what a gehinneh-geheinam she and Papa were living in, it was impossible, and for the first time she admitted to an outsider that one day they might be forced to put her in a home or the geriatric ward, not at Hadassah Hospital, where they don't know the meaning of responsibility, but in Bikkur Holim Hospital, where the family had a little protectzia; there they would take good care of her, and watch her during the day and especially at night. Aron, in his room, sat up on his elbows and listened, but none of the guests seemed to object to their packing Grandma off. Even Yochi, who was standing in the kitchen so Mama knew she heard—that Yochi, she never misses a thing—even she resigned herself in silence to Grandma Lilly's banishment, and none of them standing in a circle around the Pouritz asked whether a specialist had been consulted, whether she had had all the necessary tests, not that Aron asked either, he knew doctors only want to chop the patients up for diploma practice, and yet, in the hush around Grandma, who sat among them with bowed head, he longed to hear a voice ring out, the innocent voice of a child asking why they didn't try to find proper treatment for her, maybe there were new medicines available, she wasn't that old, sixty at most, and at her age a person could still be saved, but the silence around her grew heavier, and even without touching the onion strip he could hear them sigh and say, When it comes, it comes, it's the will of God, man is a fly-by-night, here today, gone tomorrow.

And the doorbell rang and in walked Rochaleh and Gamliel. Mama hadn't spoken to Gamliel for the twenty years or so since she married Papa, and now everyone was happy again, there were kisses and cheers and compliments all around, and Grandma's doom was sealed. Aron in his bedroom let out a startled laugh: That's it! It's over. *Finita la commedia*. He rolled over on his side and pressed his knees to his stomach and made a stomach muscle with all his might. Gradually he relaxed. Straightened out. In the watch that Grandma gave him there were two more tiny watches: when you press the left button a blue space opens up and the watch tells the depth of the sea—to hell with the sea, he wasn't going to Tel Aviv again this year even if they killed him—and when you press the right button you see what time it is in Alaska and New York and Moscow and Tokyo. He'd worn the watch for a week already and was living according to New York time, which is seven hours later than here, and seven hours is an eternity.

Soon he'll go out. He can hear them all crowding around, having a good time. Yochi enters with another gift. Gamliel and Rochaleh brought him Fisher's *The History of Europe* in three volumes, which they bought at a discount from their union, a present to match their faces, said Mama later that evening, as they were making a list of what everyone gave; they already had one set from Yochi's bat mitzvah, and in any case, books go straight to the storage loft so they won't bring dust into the salon. Yochi kneels beside him and gently strokes his sweat-moistened hair, careful not to intrude on his privacy. But next year she'll be in the army, and he'll be alone. She's breaking out again with red and yellow pimples and Mama made a crack about it, why didn't Yochi mention that the bar mitzvah date fell on her curse, now she'll stay that way forever in the family photographs, she should have known, it comes like clockwork, you have to plan ahead. Yochi blows on his cowlick, trying to make him laugh. She gave him the most wonderful present of all, a Yamaha guitar; three years after the crummy one cracked and all the strings broke, and his parents refused to have it fixed, she took out her savings and bought him a brand-new professional guitar. It was incredible: he, who spent a lifetime entering contests so he could get a Yamaha, had just received one for his bar mitzvah! Yochi follows his gaze back to the black case. "Will you play something for me?" "Later. When they've gone." They giggle. He looks into her eyes. Her face has changed. Once, she was a pretty little girl. She had a great sense of humor. Nowadays you rarely hear a peep out of her.

She eats and she sleeps and gets fatter and fatter: she has Papa's appetite and Mama's constipation.

"Brace yourself and go out, Aronaleh." "I can't handle those people." "Hey, you want a massage?" "A massage? What, now?" "A fast one. To relax you." "No." He recoiled at the thought of anyone touching his body just then. "Aron." "What?" "Sooner or later you'll have to go out." "One more minute. Don't go." "Everyone loves you out there." "Yeah." They were silent again. "Yochi?" "Yes, sweetie." "What did you mean that time, about knowing how to survive around here?" "It's not important." "It is important." "Not now. They're waiting for you." "Yochi."

She gazed into his imploring eyes and tousled his hair again. "I didn't mean anything. Just that—how can I explain it"—she ran her fingers through his curls and noticed they were a darker shade of blond than before—"say you were in the desert, okay?" "Okay." "Without any shade, and the sun beating down on you." Silently she envisioned the fingerlike rays, prying into every recess of her life, opening letters, leafing through her secret diary, peeking behind the door when she was deep in conversation with her girl friend Zehava, the only friend she'd ever had, and then Zehava moved to America. And Yochi didn't try to make new friends. Because the heat was so debilitating. "In the desert, li'l brother," she hums, winding a ringlet of his hair around her finger, maybe he was too young to speak to this way, though maybe you could still save him, give him a clue, you owe him that much, you've been using him as a decoy. "Ouch, Yochi!" "Sorry." She loosened the ringlet. It's a lie, it isn't true, I've always loved him, I've never been jealous. Okay, you weren't jealous, but you did use him as your decoy. Nonsense, he's always been better than me at everything. When they said he was intelligent, you called him a genius. Exactly, I never envied him. Yochi's lips are moving: I was mature about it; when the art teacher told Mama how well he drew, I said he would be another Picasso. A decoy, to divert attention. Not true. I've always been proud of him; and when he played the guitar, I said he has a light . . . a special light in his eyes . . . right in front of Mama I said that . . . Admit it, admit it, you feel guilty about him. She looked at him lying on his bed in that ridiculous outfit, mummified in Mama's shame. "Because plants that grow in the desert," she said softly, "have to be wary of the sun, and send out tiny pleated leaves to keep from being burned right away. It's a hard life in the desert." She falls silent. She can see in his eyes that he doesn't understand. Maybe he really is too young.

"Yochi."

"Yes, Aronaleh."

"Look into my eyes."

"Why?"

"Is there a different look in them now? Have they changed? Tell me the truth."

She doesn't even ask what he's talking about. She peers deep into his eyes and says nothing.

"I think I used to have a puppylike look in my eyes. An innocent look."

"People mature."

"No, it isn't that."

She stood up so he wouldn't see her faking a smile. "I think I'll write that down for you." She rummaged in her drawer for the notebook where she used to record his adorable sayings.

"Come on, what am I, a baby?"

"It's just so we'll remember. Someday you'll get a kick out of it."

He leaned over her shoulder and read the last entry: "21st of Shevat. Aronaleh is ten and one month. He made up a story about why bambis are brown. Once upon a time, bambis were as colorful as peacocks. And one bambi went out with his parents and the herd but they came to a swamp, and the other deer lay down and cried, because they couldn't cross it, so the bambi went in first, shouting that he would teach them how to skip across the swamp without drowning, and his parents begged him not to, because God would punish him . . ."

"Stop it, that's enough!" Aron shut the notebook in her face. He was pale and earnest. "I don't want you to write about me anymore. That's for little kids. That's over." But inside he was appalled. Had three whole years gone by without a single noteworthy utterance? Had he been like this for three years already?

Yochi put the notebook back in the drawer. She stood before him limply. There was growing commotion in the salon and cries of Let's see the bar mitzvah groom.

"I'll go out and say you're coming, okay?"

A moment more and he would go out. He peeked at his watch. In New York we're still asleep. It's five o'clock in the morning, so it might still be possible, theoretically, to call expensive Photo Gwirtz and hire them for the occasion at the last minute. Why not? Outside, there was shouting and laughter. Most of the guests were from out of town, Netanya, Holon, Tel Aviv, and some of them hadn't seen Aron in two years, since the bar mitzvah of Chomek and Hassia's son Gidi, when Aron was eleven. What had he been doing for the past two years? Wasting time, that's what. He stared at the squares on the salon carpet they'd moved into his bedroom for the party. Vichtig, they called the carpet, because the man who sold it to them never stopped talking about himself. Two years. God in heaven. If you add up all the centimeters and kilograms the kids at school have put on in that time you'd have enough to make a whale. He chuckled. Or imagine that they didn't grow at all, and instead, between rows 2 and 3, there'd be an enormous slippery whale swelling up more and more every minute. Again he hid himself in bed, practicing that sumo technique. Out there, Rivche's Dov asked hoarsely, What's happened to the bar mitzvah groom, why are they hiding him? and Mama shouted from the kitchen that he should eat a little tongue meanwhile, she knows how much he loves her tongue. Just thinking about it makes his mouth water, he jested, and Aron remembered Lealeh, his daughter, no one had ever seen her, she'd been in an institution all her life, and you weren't even allowed to ask how she was.

Suddenly there was a knock on the door. Uncle Shimmik's bald head peeked in, with those dangerous brown spots. Aron quickly reached into his pocket and touched the onion, a fresh, new strip he prepared especially for today. Shimmik saw him. He stood up close. He was thinking. Aron squeezed the onion and looked down. Shimmik was silent. He was secretly thinking, according to the onion, It's been two years since I've seen you, Aronchik, and in my imagination you'd grown tall as the ceiling. Yes yes, answered Aron; he knew they were waiting for him, he just had something to finish here first and then he'd come out to celebrate with everyone. "Can I bring you a little something to eat in here? Your mama, God bless her, has made such a feast—a mechayeh!" And Shimmik touched three fingers to his big thick lips. Aron said it wasn't necessary really, but now Ruja pushed in behind him, small and fast as a rat. "I will not give up!" she said to Shimmik with her crooked palsy smile. "We came here all the way from Haifa!" Shimmik managed to shut the door before she got in and Aron could hear the two of them whispering outside. Through the onion Ruja told Shimmik that she planned to saunter in casual-like, and see if it's true what they said about him. And Shimmik answered: It's much worse than I thought. Juice from the onion strip dripped over his fingers. Now Ruja was saying that she'd only go in for a minute, to see if he's mentally retarded as well, and Shimmik answered, deliberately loud, "It won't do any good, Rujinka, I've been trying to persuade him." But Ruja was determined. "You leave it to me." And she barged into Aron's room with her crooked smile. You can count on Ruja not to miss a chance to gall me, said Mama to Papa later that night when they were writing the gift list, she'd worm her way into my kishkes if she could.

Ruja spoke gaily, nonchalantly, and Aron felt compelled to answer with the highest-sounding words he knew. Seeing her eyes fixed on his thin, smooth leg, he was forced to utter, "I regret to say," his "regret to say" wriggling between them like the tail a lizard sheds to distract a predator. Even when her eyes grew wide at his intelligence and she was convinced that at least his brains were all right, Aron knew what she was thinking. Only her lipstick smiled at him. She sniffed the air and went to open the window. It's stifling in here, Aronaleh, aren't you hot, and she also said that there was an onion smell, and smiled at him again. Come, Aronaleh, everyone's waiting, they'll think you're angry or something, and my Omri is here, it's been two years since you've seen each other, and you used to be such good friends, we still have the pictures of you from that Purim party. Aron stole a glance at his watch. Maybe a doctor in New York had just discovered the cure, maybe a plane was even now approaching our shores, carrying the medicine.

Ruja dragged him out by the hand, making a fuss. Nu sure, Mama rasped through the onion, so that everyone can share my happiness. As he stood in the hallway he could hear Shimmik organizing the cousins for a family portrait and asking about the bar mitzvah groom. Aron said excuse me to Ruja and went into the bathroom to piss. Nothing new there. Shimmik ordered the cousins to stand up straight, not to move, not to breathe. Aron tried to imagine how they looked together, tall and strong as evergreens, or like the wall of players blocking a penalty kick, their hands protecting them below. He threw a piece of paper into the water so he wouldn't have to pull the chain and cause a flood. Someone knocked on the door impatiently. He stepped out,

THE BOOK OF

turning the bathroom over to Mama, who pushed her way in quickly with Grandma Lilly. "Don't ask what she did to me," Mama seethed, her face pinched and her eyes evasive. "Such humiliation, in front of company! Nu, get in already, Mamchu!" And she closed the door behind them.

Aron took a deep breath and went out to the salon, where, of all people, he bumped into Giora, and suddenly felt himself diminishing, and the burny place in his stomach flashed red. He stood as straight as he could, conscious that everyone was looking at him and that they knew, and then he slumped again. But he had no choice because there he was. He put his hands on his hips, and let them down; he put one foot out, then pulled it back; he folded his arms over his chest; it was only four months since he'd been with Giora, yet he barely recognized him anymore. With downcast eyes he stood before him, trying to hold a conversation with his gergeleh. A perfect gergeleh it was, too, moving up and down like a pump to give Giora just the right voice. He tried his best to ignore the aunts and uncles, and the children beside their parents, staring at him, and the sudden hush that fell over the house. At last it dawned on him why Mama had been in such a hurry to lock herself in the bathroom with Grandma. Giora asked him if he would be coming again next summer, and Aron stared at him in amazement, remembering how he had tormented him, and answered that this summer, he regretted to say, he would be too busy getting ready for eighth grade, but as he spoke, he realized that if he did go to Tel Aviv next summer, Giora would no longer be cruel to him, that his cruelty the previous summer had erupted at a transitional moment which he was now well beyond.

Pretending to ignore what was happening around him, Aron continued to chat with Giora and tug at his stiff little bow tie. He asked with feigned smugness about one or another of the boys in Giora's crowd, and casually mentioned the sunken raft, to gauge whether Giora felt guilty or embarrassed about it, because he had a dim impression—no, that was a lie, pretty words—he'd thought about it thousands of times, trying to bring back the moment; sometimes he would dwell on it for an entire lesson, it was not impossible that his difficulty had started at that moment when scarcely any oxygen reached his brain; yes, how often he had pictured that scene to himself, the murderous expression on Giora's face in the gray-green water, how he ruthlessly climbed over

Aron to save himself, turning Aron into an enemy, and maybe that was the turning point for Giora too, when he began to change into what he was today, as though they had both been through a kind of secret ordeal, which only Giora had passed, though he barely remembered it, or at least pretended not to, and Aron, amazed at how well he dissembled his feelings, had to ask him, nonchalantly, whether he remembered their walks through the streets of Tel Aviv, in the khamsin. Giora shrugged and said, Yeah, those were the days. And to seal their prolonged conversation, Aron shook his hand, startling Giora with that new air of gravity, which seemed to suggest he had arrived at some final realm of maturity, notwithstanding his physical appearance.

Giora had to leave with his father in the middle of the party to get back to Tel Aviv in time for a Scouting event. Aunt Gucha stood on tiptoe to kiss his cheek. No sooner was he out the door than she hurried to tell everyone he had a girlfriend, for thirty minutes he stands in front of the mirror before he leaves the house. Aunt Ruja said, "What do you know," and then she told them in a half whisper everyone could hear about her Omri and his blond doll. All these fat, floury women, Aron saw, began to titter around her like young girls, secretly hankering to be Omri's blond doll, and through the hissing of the ember inside him, Aron knew this was somehow connected with those pictures that still turned up occasionally in different hiding places around the house (when he bothered to look for them), and also with that embrace, and the slimy smile, and the way Mama elbows Papa when they walk down the street, husti gezein? Did you see her? Aron turned sharply to the window and ordered himself to prepare to dive inward and start Aroning; it used to be like going into a colorful market, the thoughts and ideas would leap and swirl before him, but now the pleasure of it was the quiet in there, the empty stillness where you could rest, unwind. He pressed his forehead to the windowpane and looked across the valley, at the hawthorn trees and the little junkyard. If he moved, he could also see the cave where he and Gideon hid the basalt stone; he never did explain to Gideon why that was necessary, he merely insisted, because for all their covenants, the notes they swallowed and the wine they drank, the words they carved on the tree and the blood they mingled from cuts in their arms, Aron still needed something more, something undefinable that flickered enigmatically in the depths of their friendship. Was it still there, he wondered. He lingered in the memory awhile, but perceived himself floating fast to the surface, against his will, because it was obvious now what an idiot he'd been, it was Papa who hid the pictures, not merely from him, but also, how could he have missed it, from Mama, yes definitely, that explained the secrecy and the mystery, and when their friends came over to play rummy on Friday nights, Mama and Papa used different cards, as Aron knew because on Friday nights he always stayed home. He and Yochi. Like two inseparable fogies, Mama exploded, Munish mit Zalman, and she implored Yochi to stay in her room with him while their friends were there. Maybe she even tried to bribe her with money, sure, every ruse ties in with another, and a few months ago something happened while he and Yochi were lying on their beds pretending to read, and the guests in the salon were playing rummy for shillings, and talking about their children, and Mama started bragging about how popular Aron and Yochi were at school, and about all the fun they had at parties: I tell you, since we had our phone installed, Yochi's boyfriends never stop calling. He and Yochi were lying rigidly on their beds, staring blindly at their books, when Yochi sprang up suddenly. Stand straight, Aron, let me see you, she said, looking him over with an expert eye, aggressively buttoning his pajama top and combing his hair with a part on the side. Then she put on the Golda dress that gave her a big tuchis and the old glasses she hadn't worn in years, and as if this wasn't enough, she found the retainer from her braces in the cupboard, and stuck it in her mouth, and she emerged from the bedroom, with Aron in tow, and walked straight up to Mama in the salon; and then—how could he have been so stupid— he saw their playing cards were from an ordinary deck with no pictures on the back. He stared at the windowpane: yes, he kept the pictures hidden from Mama too! What else was he hiding? Who was he anyway?! Over his shoulder he could hear Ruja whisper something to the women, which was answered by snorts of laughter. Schrechlich, said Gucha, it seems like only yesterday they were young enough to take to the ladies' room and today they're men, I don't remember that happening so early in our day. Hardly! cried Ruja, at their age we were innocents, we didn't know from nothing. I certainly didn't, added Itka in a naughty whisper, not until my wedding night, when Hindaleh, bless her, came in and explained the whole megillah, and scared me half to death, I still thought children came from— She lowered her voice still more, and Aron sealed himself off inside to keep out the whispers, so all he heard was their cachinnations; Rivche, laughing convulsively, nearly knocked over the blue bowl with the doe and the stag chasing each other, and stained her dress with a drip of mayonnaise from her triangular sandwich; Aron got ready to pick up the pieces, but Mama caught it without even looking, she just reached out and snapped it up in mid-air. Go wash the stain off with water and a little soap, Rivche, and when she finally stopped laughing she said, It's all right for you, you have boys, but think about me, with a teenage daughter, oi, don't ask. You did right, dear Hindaleh, slobbered Zipporah, a distant cousin who had three sons. You had a girl and a boy, the way it says you should in the Bible. And your three boys, Mama reciprocated, will bring you ready-made daughters. Here's wishing the same for you, Hindaleh, said Zipporah. Nu nu, said Mama, lowering her voice, trust my Yochi not to waste any time. And she winked a huge ugly wink at her that pulled down half her face. Lucky thing Yochi was in the kitchen just then.

When will it end? He was utterly exhausted from the squirming and the phony smiles and the whispering onion; and also from this new effort he had to make, because for the first time he understood with his brain how intricately conversations are woven and how many invisible threads there are in the corners of a smile. Yochi came in from the kitchen with another tray of chicken, how many poor hens had given their lives for his bar mitzvah, and Mama tried to grab it from her, but Yochi held fast, and the two of them took a few steps that way, with the tray held high in the air, smiling at the guests, and because they couldn't quite decide which way to turn, they headed straight to him, the bar mitzvah groom. Have some pupiklach, said Mama, they're simply delicious. No no, said Yochi sweetly, have a wing. But my gizzards came out like butter today, Mama cajoled him with a cheery face. Hmm, but the wings are really yummy too. Yochi curtsied to him, almost shoving the chicken into his mouth, till he pulled away in alarm. The pupiklach melt in your mouth, urged Mama, fending Yochi off with her shoulder. Try the wings, whispered Yochi conspiratorially, and the aromas swirled around like fog, condensing into heavy drops of gravy. I've had enough, I don't want any more! he protested, why were they jumping on him like that, in front of everyone. With his back to the wall, confused and flushed, he forced himself into his thoughts again: It's fun to think, it's relaxing, it fills you with love, where were we, ah yes, he'd always thought it was a family sham, but today a thin mem-

THE BOOK OF

brane seemed to peel from his eyes and he could see something new here, a delicate beauty, even compassion, because everyone knew everyone else's secrets, everyone was a hostage in someone else's hands, at their mercy or their cruelty. Why are you thinking these thoughts? Think like a boy your age. It all goes back to your problem. This is just another symptom. You think you're winning, but you keep losing. And you have to be so careful and conscientious in order to make a single statement without hurting or shaming someone: for instance, Mama was just telling the women they were lucky to have daughters, but she only said it when Rivche, poor Lealeh's mother, went out to the kitchen. That was a minor mercy, but the air was full of tiny darts, phrases waiting to burst with poison, compliments with false bottoms, the caress of secrets shared, and carefully circumvented topics. These he discerned, as he opened his eyes to them in benevolent wonder. And he too, it seemed, would be spared today.

Three of his cousins came in from the balcony, glanced at him, and stopped their conversation. Go on, join them; no, they're too young, they don't know the rules yet the way he does. Go ahead, join the conversation, or was it an argument: which is better, hand brakes or pedal brakes, and how far can a tutu ball fly? But Shimmik wants to take his picture with them, to immortalize them standing together. He turned to the window, pretending to be engrossed in the view. Straighten your shoulders. Try to have a good time. Always be watchful, always be cunning, with grownups, with children, with grownups and children together, like all he needed now was for one of the boys to hear him talking to a grownup, he knew exactly how he sounded. On the other hand, when he was obliged to talk to one of them, to one of the guys, he was careful to use the old language, though it made him feel phony, like a tourist trying to be friendly with the natives, or like a spy in enemy territory, fighting for his life. He smiled a crooked smile as he stood by the window. Who knows, said his smile, what sort of life you'll have. And he turned away, nervously touching his chest, his waist. Who could say how much life there was in a body like this.

Little Uncle Loniu, Ruja's husband, found one of Leo Pold's recordings on top of the phonograph and put it on, balancing a full bottle of wine on his forehead as he danced to the rhythm. The women gathered around him and clapped their hands. Rivche's Dov stood at the center of the men's group waving a fat drumstick and telling dirty jokes. Rivche warned him to lower his voice, little pitchers have big ears, and she glanced at Aron with embarrassment. Aron watched the men out of the corner of his eye. They were heavy, tired-looking, all of them, like patient beasts of burden. Their features seemed to have been engraved as monuments to grief, yet they exuded a lukewarm air of failure and monotony. And once they had been his age. Perhaps they even looked like him. He would never look like them, though. Mama called Papa with her pinchy smile to help her put Mamchu on Yochi's bed and cover her with the Scottish plaid—She's so tired, she doesn't realize how tired she is—but Papa was raptly listening to Dov's joke about the rabbit who came back to the jungle and told the other animals that he'd shown the lion how to do it right. A smile of lewd anticipation spread over Papa's face. His lower lip, cracked in the middle, moved in unison with Dov's. Aron put down the glass of juice he had been holding since the beginning of the party and went to help Mama drag Grandma to his and Yochi's room. When the door closed behind them and they had tucked in the blanket, Mama said tomorrow, so help her, she was going to throw Grandma out of the house, like a curse she needed her here, he should see what she just did in the bathroom, she ruined everything.

Aron stayed in the room a little longer to look at Grandma. Compassionately he stroked her porcelain face, which was hardly wrinkled because fools never grow old, and for a moment she opened her foggy eyes, trying to recognize him or tell him something, maybe she didn't remember where words came from anymore. Maybe she was scurrying around inside, crying and searching for the way out. That was exactly how she looked when she came to give him that heirloom. The golden thread. Too bad he hadn't kept it. He could have shown it to her now and brought her a little happiness. On a sudden impulse, stupidly, he touched her mouth, offering a hint that this was where words come out, and her soft, surprisingly supple lips wound around his finger. For a moment she sucked with the fierceness of a baby, and he drew his hand back in alarm.

Her lips groped blindly for his finger, which was wet with the embarrassing moisture of life, but he managed to hide it just in time. In walked Mama and stood by the door, sensing something, not comprehending. "You leave Grandma alone, you hear? You hear?" she whispered furiously. "You let us take care of her. Go do what a kid your age should do, you hear?!" Again he was dispatched to the salon, where he stood alone, confused and agitated. Someone tapped him roughly on the shoulder, frightening him before he had a chance to tense the muscle and disguise his scrawniness. "What's with you, nebbich?" called Uncle Loniu, who was small and round as a button. "What's with him, Hindaleh," he cackled, and everyone heard. "Don't you feed your bar mitzvah boy?" And a few months later, these words of Uncle Loniu's spelled the beginning of the end of Aron's leaps on the rock, as rough-hewn sobs erupted from deep inside, more like the crude ore of the soul than an outburst of tears. He leaped and fell, lacerated by the thorn-bushes and bruised by the stones, his eyes clogged with tears, but he couldn't do it, so he tried to envision everything that had happened to him over the past two years, all the facets and figments of his problem, and still he crooked his arm at the last moment, till finally, when his strength failed, and all he remembered was that he had to get up and fall, get up and fall on his arm, though sometimes he only imagined he was up, then he suddenly remembered the time at his bar mitzvah when smart little Aunt Rivche caught Loniu by the arm and whispered, What do you want from the boy, give him a rest today, and Loniu shook off her hand and said, "Is this why we came to Israel with the sun and the vitamins and the oranges?" And Rivche caught his arm again and said quietly, tensely, Leave him alone, Loniu. Luz im nuch, what do you think, somebody's doing something on purpose here? And Loniu crooked his arm and said, "At his age he should be starting to packa packa!" And he looked around, with a grin, and Rivche pressed her face up close and crackled as only the women in the family could: People in glass houses, Loniu. It seems to me the coat rack at our house hangs pretty low too, but again he evaded her and came back to Aron, who was by now completely paralyzed, living, say, in New York, where he read about this sad case in *Woman's* magazine; Aron, who survived a night among the corpses in the cellar at Komi by remembering his magnificent bar mitzvah. And Loniu stood screaming at the top of his lungs, "Take a tip from Omri! Look at him! Body-building! Body-building!" And poor tormented Aron peered into his eyes and beheld the vengeance his butterball uncle had wreaked upon nature by means of his son, and for a moment he almost felt compassion for the stupid man, who had burst the bounds of family etiquette and screamed through the lump of anguish that was stuck in everyone's throat, and then came the blessed moment, two months later, when grief and loneliness overwhelmed his ofzeluchi brain and Aron leaped up and plummeted from the rock and heard, with a mixture of shock and relief, the bone in his arm go crack.

14

Another year went by. And nothing. Like egg white folded evenly into batter, so his days were stirred into time. It was a weird winter: icy cold, with storms and piercing winds, but not a drop of rain. They were already talking about a drought. An arctic winter, they said on the radio, and Aron shivered.

One evening he's sitting on Farouk in the kitchen, peeling potatoes for the Sabbath cholent. The balcony window keeps banging in the wind. It gets dark by five these days, and people stay indoors. The cozy smell of kerosene pervades the house, and if you keep perfectly still you hear the old Friedman heater breathing. Mainly, though, you hear Papa moaning on the sofa. Mama and Yochi are busy on his back, Mama working her way up and Yochi working her way down, so they'll meet in the middle. It goes faster without Grandma. She always insisted on helping, poking everywhere, giggling like a girl, tickling poor Papa under the arm, and sometimes, recalls Aron, peeling faster, concentrating with all his might because of the chirring sound he'd started hearing lately, and when Grandma was in an especially good mood, she would squeeze in between Mama and Yochi and throw herself on Papa with her cheek to his back, singing a Polish song into his rib cage with a sly peek at Mama, and Papa would start writhing with ticklishness or stifled laughter, maybe it was one of those songs Mama forbade him to sing, from Grandma Lilly's nightclub days; the chirring sound is shrill and it's a signal, he knows, he figured out when he gets it, for instance—when he's using a kitchen utensil, holding something in his hands, touching a tool or some other object, even a person, right away he hears the *tsss tsss tsss*, like an electric discharge, like a warning or a hiss of mockery, and then his fingers slowly open, and go numb, that's how he broke the glass at supper yesterday, it fell out of his hand; he heard the chirring and gripped the glass, but the sound continued, and his fingers started trembling, getting weaker and weaker, and Mama saw it happening, she stood there, watching his trembling fingers slowly unclench, who knows, maybe she heard it too, and now, with the knife and Papa's groans, Meirky Blutreich has it under his arm, today Aron saw the third proof in broad daylight, during gym class, and the third proof is final; the chirring is persistent, like a fluttering outside his ear on the left, and inside it, and Hanan Schweiky is clearly entitled to a gergeleh, it's amazing how fast he developed it, only yesterday Aron noticed it for the first time, and already it's official, it just hatched overnight, but still, for the sake of protocol, as they say, he would only confirm it after two more sightings, a day apart. Enough already! He lets the peeling knife drop. Thank God. A little quiet. It's cold in the kitchen. What is this, we have central heating and a radiator in every room, but all the neighbors have been using their kerosene heaters for the past three years to get even with Mrs. Pinkus, the divorcée who lives over the Boteneros and refuses to pay her dues to the Residents Association. Where were we? He quickly counts on his fingers. Seventeen boys in his class have at least one item. The armpit list's the longest. Though interestingly enough, some boys, like Asa Kolodny or Haim Saportas, for instance, have a lot under the arm, practically a forest, but hardly any on their legs, proving that in these matters too a variety of strategies exists, so maybe there's a certain, well, arbitrariness, and things sometimes get bungled the way they do in bustling offices, like the office of the army reserves. And think what would happen if someone started tidying up, it would be all over. Oh sure, sure. He stops. Listens. Nothing. Good riddance. Carefully he picks up the red knife, so the knife won't notice and neither will he. But no cheating. There it goes again, the chirring. There's no end to the ingenuity of this problem. Sometimes the sound seems to be addressing him. It's hard to understand what it's saying, though. Scolding him or threatening. He glances warily into the salon, where Papa lies writhing in ecstasy under one or another pair of feminine hands, signifying by the tone of his groans that the end is near, here it

THE BOOK OF

comes, hmmmm, Aron hums against the chirring, a special hum he has that's so shrill, it sets the pipes inside him quivering, and then the chirring goes away. Hmmm—he hones the hum, feeling his teeth vibrate; hurry, fill the silence, and how furious Mama used to get whenever Papa and Grandma Lilly spoke Polish together, which she didn't understand; before she married him she made him promise to speak nothing but Hebrew. But there are some things I can only say in Polish, Papa protested once, during the big fight they had after Yochi's bat mitzvah. It's our language! But you promised! She wagged a finger at him, because Grandma sang one of her songs at the bat mitzvah and Papa joined in, and suddenly you could tell they were related, their eyes shone with the same light, and when the song was over they sat in the corner chattering in Polish, loudly interrupting each other as Mama stomped by them at least a hundred times. Aron had never heard Papa talking like that to Grandma Lilly, or anyone else for that matter, so lively and cheerful, and after the guests left there was a big fight, the walls shook; *ntzz ntzz ntzz*, it hisses like a snake now, and Aron slows down. He nearly cut his finger.

Just then, when Papa got up off the Bordeaux sofa and heaved a sigh, and put on his shorts and the haimish shirt that was accidentally dyed blue in the wash, there was a knock on the door. It was such a muffled knock that at first they didn't realize it was a knock at all, they thought maybe the pantry window was banging again, that maybe Sophie Atias slammed the door the way Sephardim do, but then came another knock, and then a quick loud rap that shuddered at itself, and the whole family ran to the door and who should be standing there but their upstairs neighbor Edna Bloom, huddling in her enormous overcoat, trying to smile with trembling lips. Aron's heart froze at the sight of her: Uh-oh, she found out, I left signs, she's here to tell them. The potato knife was still in his hand. Edna Bloom hesitated in the doorway. Papa, in his spotted haimisheh, stood up straight and suddenly shrank and apologized for the way he looked, and hurried off to change his shirt. A wrinkle of amazement zigzagged over Mama's right eye. Do come in, Miss Bloom, why are you standing in the doorway, such a rare visitor, of course you're no bother, a cup of coffee?

Edna teetered in, with little bobs and curtsies at Yochi, at the oval photograph of Mama's father on the buffet, at the new lamp fixture, at anything and everything in the room. Aron walked behind her. How would he explain. Where would he begin. Maybe he should run away before they were ready. Maybe he should faint. What could they do to him if he fainted. Maybe he would stab her with the knife and then kill himself, but just then the chirring started, mocking him, Aron who didn't even know which way you screw in a screw, let alone how to hold a glass, if he tried to switch off his body, he'd only wind up with another silly defect. Edna cast a wonder-filled glance around the salon, with the reupholstered Methuselah and the Pouritz, and the big new lampshade; they redecorated after Grandma, and she'd never seen their apartment inside, because she didn't attend the Residents Association meetings, and Mama noticed and showed her the salon with a sweeping gesture, more sweeping than necessary, and apologized for the mess, though everything was shiny clean as usual, it was Thursday night, you could eat off her floor, and she prided herself on the fresh paint job and the new buffet, it had a modern bar, and a light went on behind a red plush curtain whenever you opened the door, the bottles were reflected in the mirrors. Why don't you take off your coat, Miss Bloom. No no. Edna Bloom shivered, diving deeper into her overcoat and glancing wide-eyed at the modern bar, though maybe she was surprised to see such a grand buffet but no books anywhere.

Papa returned in his checkered blue-and-white, his hair slicked down with water. Mama's face was unchanged; Edna Bloom seated herself daintily on the edge of the Bordeaux sofa, clasping her rosy fingers and shaking her head with giggly coruscations as though in the midst of some deeply discomfiting inner dialogue, which only her blushing cheeks evinced. Papa sat down facing her on Methuselah, clenching the armrests with his powerful hands. You see, Miss Bloom, he began ineptly, trying in vain to hide his bulky legs, even in winter I wear shorts around the house; and he smiled at her foolishly. I get hot from inside, I'm like an oven, summer and winter both. Edna gazed up in bewildered silence. Mama cleared her throat and waited. Again the silence enveloped them. Aron coughed. Such a cough he's developed, Mama threw him an angry glance, everything has to be a chendelach with that boy, but he did have to cough, really, he coughed with all his heart, maybe he was ill. Maybe he would die.

Edna Bloom leaned over, accidentally touching the lemon in the bowl on the coffee table, and then sharply withdrew her hand as though guilty of unspeakable rudeness. The family wriggled in their seats; Aron gave another nervous cough, the prelude to an imminent storm; who knows, with a little effort he might even spit blood, and you can't argue with blood. But he knew it was hopeless. These were his last moments among them. No explanation would convince them of what he was doing at her house, and anyway, they'd probably been preparing themselves for someone to come in and break the terrible news about him. Suddenly the words burst out of her in a high, strained voice, and she recoiled into herself with a shudder. Aron stopped coughing and gaped at her.

"But I don't . . . I'm not a workman that knows how to . . . no . . ." Papa laughed in surprise. "What you need is a real professional. Me, I'm just a handyman." He was embarrassed and fell silent. "I really believe, Mr. Kleinfeld, in fact I'm almost certain, that you would do it as it should be done." She blinked and giggled and craned her neck like a bird shaking off a drop of water. "I heard how you fixed the electricity at the Atiases' and the kitchen pipes at Mrs. Botenero's. I'm sure you will succeed, Mr. Kleinfeld." "But those were small jobs," murmured Papa, carefully gauging Mama out of the corner of his eye, did she see how hard he was trying to refuse the offer? But her face remained impassive; though she wavered, studying the anemic complexion of Edna Bloom, her swollen red eyelids and her teeth; forty, she decided, not one day less, with a wasp waist Moshe could easily fit his hands around, and her untried womb and unsuckled breasts . . . "It's true, Moshe is a good worker," she weighed the pros and cons. "Only he's not much of an expert in what you want, and he has a little trouble with his back in winter, so I don't know what to tell you, Miss Bloom, maybe you should look for someone else? Everyone is replaceable, no?"

Aron watched Edna's eyes grow wide. "Not exactly, Mrs. Kleinfeld." She shook her head. "I wonder if anyone is truly replaceable." His heart went out to her for speaking so well, even though the conversation was about something ordinary and boring. But Mama too was alert to the strange scintillation in Edna Bloom's voice: she shook her head and no longer smiled.

"I will pay generously," said the visitor.

"We're not talking about money yet," muttered Papa.

"Just how much are you prepared to pay, Miss Bloom?" asked Mama, appraising her coolly with a broker's eye.

"Why up to . . . fifty pounds," blurted Edna Bloom; you could see that she herself was staggered by the offer, but she continued to nod insistently. Red blotches spread over her throat. You could feel how damp her delicate pink fingers were, the fingers which had tinkled over the piano that day. Papa groaned, and the big blue vein on the side of his neck began to throb. Fifty pounds was enough to close off the balcony, to start redecorating the kitchen, to buy a secondhand motorscooter he could ride to work in the morning . . . Mama leaned back and gulped. Papa mumbled, That really is too much, Miss Bloom, but he too fell silent and studied his hands. Mama hadn't yet uttered a word. Her eyes were darting around in her head, her chin was quivering. A shadow like a slinky martin fluttered under her lips. So—a dog wouldn't stick his snout out in this storm, yet she leaves her nice warm flat and comes here? The ravishing Miss Bloom couldn't wait? Edna twisted under Mama's invidious eye; that look, thought Yochi despondently, poking and probing everywhere. Edna raised her heavy lids and searched Mama's eyes for a verdict; she and Papa seemed to await Mama's blessings over something infinitely more complex than tearing down a wall between the bedroom and salon.

"And when do you intend to pay?" Mama's crassness shocked him; suddenly he saw that there was something not quite honorable here that made polite behavior superfluous, and his heart melted for Edna Bloom and what she had endured here, in their home. Because some people can tolerate vulgarity, he felt, while others get used to it little by little, but Edna Bloom was far too vulnerable. He was astounded at how fast she grew inured to Mama's tone: why didn't she just leave and slam the door behind her; but her long thin neck continued to writhe in agony, as though she had swallowed the rusks of her pride. "If Mr. Kleinfeld agrees to take the job, I will pay half the sum immediately and the other half when the job is completed," she said, using the language she learned at work, in the office of a notary public named Lombroso.

"Mr. Kleinfeld will work for you three hours every afternoon until he finishes," decided Mama. "And either I or the boy or Yocheved will be there to assist him at all times."

Edna bowed her head in surrender. The tiny bracelets jingling on her rosy wrists disturbed her equanimity. She clasped them with her fingertips and tried to hide them: Aron's heart went out to her again, calling her over and over like a cuckoo clock.

Then she opened her red leather purse, fumbled with the zipper, giggled with embarrassment, blushed crimson, and took out several bills. She waved them limply in the air, and when she saw that Mama wasn't going to reach out for them, she set them on the edge of the coffee table, from where they instantly flew off.

"You'll tear down her wall and we'll buy a new Friedman heater, the old one stinks, and then we'll forget about it. Tfu on her," said Mama afterward, furiously scrambling eggs in the frying pan, livid at having been conned by the money of that Hungarian. Notice how she walks, like the living dead, and the way she talks, *ta ta ta ta*, rasped Mama, maliciously mimicking the cranelike ways of Edna Bloom, but even this outburst failed to relieve her: she always said she was no pigeon, yet this time she felt an itch in her navel that told her she'd made a big mistake.

15

One gray Monday Papa left to tear down the wall that separated Edna's bedroom from her salon. The job was expected to take two days. He arrived at four-thirty, after a shift at the Jerusalem Workers' Council, a proper meal at home, and a siesta. Wearing the blue shirt from his days at the Angel bakery, he picked up his toolbox, watched closely by Aron, who made sure no stray Roxanas slipped out; then he went down to the furnace room to fetch Og, the giant ladder he'd made with his own hands in 1948, when he and Mama first set up house-keeping, and plodded over to Entrance A and up four flights of stairs to Edna Bloom's. Yochi trailed behind him, her arms full of old news-papers for collecting the rubble of the soon-to-be-demolished wall; after Yochi came Aron, lugging Papa's sledgehammer; yes, he was back in her house again, this time in broad daylight and with permission, maybe he would even do it in there, with Mama and Papa around, who knows; and last in line, at Aron's heels, stepped Mama, wearing her dreary brown cassock, grim as a brooding hen, with her hair in a stiff topknot and her knitting bag under her arm, carrying a thermos full of tea, because, she forked her tongue, you won't be getting anything to drink from that cuckoo.

Edna Bloom greeted them with a festive smile, and Aron gasped at the sight of her in the doorway. She had dressed casually for the oc-casion, in jeans and a yellow blouse, frayed at the seams, that fell softly over her small, round breasts; her wispy hair framed her features like

THE BOOK OF

a halo, and her face was polished to such a fragile and radiant symmetry that her beauty seemed almost pathological. Mama, Papa, and Yochi stared down at her slender bare feet, the feet of a bird that rarely alights. Edna invited them to sit down on the squeaky white leather armchairs. Before them on the coffee table there were plates with slices of pie she'd bought from Kravitz the gonif, who uses three eggs when the recipe calls for eight. Did you imagine the balebusteh would slave in the kitchen all day in your honor? And there was a pitcher of golden juice, and a bowl of fruit that looked as beautiful as a picture in one of her heavy art books, so beautiful you might have doubted it was real. Suddenly Mama—his well-mannered mama, who never touches food at a stranger's house—groped through the fruit bowl as though she were choosing apples at the market, snatched a ripe guava, and sank her teeth into it. Edna cringed with a private pain and offered Mama a saucer for the peels, or ends, she whispered, and Mama quite deliberately, Aron realized, explained with a mouth full of fragrant pulp that she liked to eat guavas whole. Edna nodded meekly, then offered Aron and Yochi a box of Turkish delight with powdered sugar. "This I bought in Izmir," she murmured, adding confidentially, "Every summer I take a trip to Turkey."

"Thank you. It's not good for their teeth," decreed Mama. "And Mr. Kleinfeld would like to get started already."

Edna Bloom was fading fast. She apologized and explained that she had wanted to launch the enterprise with a little celebration, but Mama gave her such a look she immediately shut up.

Papa began by taking down the pictures and stacking them carefully against the far wall. They're only reproductions, said Edna modestly, and Mama let out an ugly whistle of amazement, meant for Yochi and Aron's ears. These are Degas dancers, and this is Magritte, and this of course is Van Gogh's chair, and that's one of Dalí's, and this one is an abstract, and that's a still life by Renoir or Gauguin; Papa carried them in his arms, and Aron was afraid to help because of the chirring; he sat in the white leather armchair staring at the faded squares left by the pictures, and thought of Grandma Lilly's thick old braid, all wrapped up in newspaper, which he'd found at the bottom of the trash bin; maybe people leave faded squares like this too after they die.

Papa dismantled the black bookcase. He respectfully removed the snow-filled globes Edna had collected in the lands she visited; when

Aron sneaked in he liked to shake them, it was a little ritual he had; the melancholy magic of fairy tales would envelop him at the sight of these lonely mountaineers, swans, clowns, orchids, dancers, children, trapped under glass, surveying each other through the silent snow-storms, and then Papa took down the heavy art books Aron never tired of leafing through, where there were pictures of naked men and women, but with nothing dirty about them, and then, carefully, biting his tongue, Papa carried off the delicate prism and the pitcher with the long lips that seemed puckered for a heavenly kiss, in which there was a bouquet of straw flowers. And the princess didn't lift a finger, she let you do all the work, like a Sudanese slave, but Mama was wrong: Edna took the pieces from Papa one at a time and set them down in a special place, and everyone witnessed that slippery moment when the tips of her slender fingers met his, and he tried with all his might not to feel this strange contact, this airy caress, hurling himself into work, work, work. Only when he held up the carving of a sad, old Negro did they see he was losing control, because he ran his finger over the wise forehead, the broad, flat nose, the full lips; Mama gave a snort of contempt, and Papa stood up a little straighter. Sealing his face, he continued passing Edna the ebony figurines she brought back from her two trips to Kenya; and the statue of a slender youth, lost in reverie; and forms suggestive of feminine curves embossed in a piece of wood; when Aron was here on his own sometimes he would mischievously imitate their poses as he ran his fingers over them. The big secret was not what he did in her bathroom but the fact that he kept company with the pictures and the books and the sculptures. Pleasure trickled into him: he wanted to remain here, like one of her statues, so that when she came back from her Spanish class or her flower-arranging course, she would find him and allow him to stay, and she would gradually mold him till he was perfect in her hands.

"There, finished," Edna panted when the wall stood bare, almost indecently.

Papa smiled, flashing his strong white teeth at her: "There are two sides to every coin, Miss Bloom, you must have pictures and things on the other side of the wall, am I right or am I wrong?"

And truth to tell, Edna had failed to take into account what was about to happen in her home. Her face turned ashen: she wanted to tear down a wall, the decision had required an immense effort of will,

THE BOOK OF

it required all her stamina just to imagine a hammer striking the wall on one side, let alone the other. And the huge space that would be created. She stood there limply, head bowed.

"Miss Bloom," said Papa with unfamiliar gentleness in his voice, "maybe you didn't think out what would happen here . . . tearing down a wall means dirt and noise and a big mess. Maybe you'd rather we put everything back in place and we'll shake hands like friends, no hard feelings, really."

He tried to protect her, this wisp of a woman, floating embryonically in her sac of skin: they were facing one another now, and suddenly Aron saw how handsome Papa must have been, before he became so lummoxy with fat and his fixed expression, and Mama saw too, she was struck dumb, because she'd seen it once before, she couldn't decide whether to sit there goggling at him, or to tear her eyes away and lose the moment forever; he had been so young then, a few years younger than herself when she first met him late in '46, not yet handsome, practically starved to death, hollow-eyed and befuddled, but with a prominent forehead that radiated something, a kind of wildness and abandon, the longing of a child, of a generous urchin. In the middle of the street I found him, I took your papa in from the street, where he slept at night on a discarded door, half-dead; somehow he'd crossed the steppes of Russia and arrived in Palestine without friends or family and without knowing a word of Hebrew. Mama was a spinster, twenty-five years old, an orphan who'd raised five brothers and sisters, when he came into her life; she valiantly ignored the gossip of the neighbors and certain members of the family too, whom she didn't forgive to this day, why, she hadn't made up with Gamliel and Rochaleh until Aron's bar mitzvah, and for five whole months, with threats and promises, she kept him from leaving her home; now it was coming back to her, here of all places, like a fountain bursting through layers of grief and oblivion, she felt her old love for him briefly stir. Hinda is Hinda, Gucha laughed to tears once, telling Yochi about those days, she let him think the British were hunting Communist infiltrators, so your papa, nebbich, did her bidding, spread honey on the ground she trod, and what touched his heart most was the way she took care of us little ones; there were five of us around her neck, motherless chicks, with Hinda this, Hinda that, and we saw the way he watched her as she fed us or dressed us or helped us with our homework, we thought he missed his own mama;

we hadn't met Lilly yet, of course, it was only when she turned up that we realized the opposite was true; it was your mama's strictness, I think, that he liked so much, and then, schrechlich, he started playing the child; so help me, Yochileh, he slipped back to babyhood, cooing at Hinda, pestering her at the dinner table, playing hide-and-seek with us like an overgrown boy, and once, Mama recalled, when I came home from a hard day as a cleaning lady for a rich couple in Rehavia—what I didn't do for a slice of bread and a couple of olives in those days—I found him rolling on the floor with Gucha and Rivche and Itka and Ruja and Isser, laughing like he didn't have a care in the world, and I felt a zetz right here in my heart, maybe I spoiled him too much and now I would have to push him forward fast, and that was when I took him in hand and began to teach him Hebrew, and at night, by the light of a kerosene lamp, Yochi, I would sit with him and show him the letters and spell out words, he had a good mind for things like that when we were young, and I wouldn't let him speak Polish anymore so he'd stop thinking about what happened and not waste any more time being homesick, and whenever he said something in Polish to me, I would say, What? and he would say it again, and again I'd say, What?, till he finally gave up, and Yochi asked wistfully, You mean you were together all that time without being married? And Mama answered, Now, Yochileh, he never laid a finger on me, not him or anyone before him, not like girls these days who serve the compote before the forspeiz, though I won't tell you he didn't try, he is a man, after all, but you can rest assured that on our wedding night I was like an apple he was the first to bite. Other food she fed him, recounted Gucha, don't think your mama was quiet like now, she has more in her little finger than all of us put together, she knew how to hold on to a man, sometimes she went without to give him the best of everything, and we little ones were happy as can be, whoever heard of fresh eggs for breakfast in Jerusalem during the siege, or a roast chicken, Yochileh, imagine, Hinda went all the way to Kibbutz Kiryat Anavim and gave fifty haircuts, snip, snip, snip, in exchange for one poor starving hen, and the feasts she prepared over the Primus stove, first she would brown it, and while other folks were eating dandelion greens, your mama made kreplach and knishes stuffed with potatoes, and all around us people were practically starving to death, but your mama, when she sets her mind to something, nothing can stand in her way. It's true, Yochileh, recalled Mama, her face veiled with pleasure, in no time your papa started to improve, the hollows of his cheeks filled out . . . And now Yochi watched her with amazement, with pity, sitting here in Edna Bloom's salon with her hands in her lap, defused for the moment, drifting away into the memories she shared so rarely. What was, was. When I retire I'll write my memoirs and tell you all, oho oho, but now is not the time, Yochi, children don't like to think what their parents did before they were born and why they turned into who they are, and it's a well-known fact, she would laugh whenever Yochi screamed that they didn't understand her, that only the children have psychology nowadays, not the parents, but Yochi perceived from the expressions she wore, from Rivche's stories and Gucha's giggles, that little by little Papa put on weight, and the man emerged from the skeleton; even he was amazed at the sight, he had been all of eighteen at the camp in the taiga, and was only now meeting himself as a full-grown man. You should have seen him in front of the mirror, Yochileh, laughed plump little Gucha, combing his hair for hours, slicking it down with brilliantine, that's right, your papa, and one time our neighbor Miss Hemda Kotlarsky came over to borrow three tablespoons of flour, what else was there to borrow in those days, and when she saw him there, half-naked, fixing a broken window, she started grinning like a fool and forgot to leave, nu, and your mama, Yochi, took the jewels left by the grandmother you never knew out of her kifat, the gold watch, the silver pins, and some Bukharan rug they kept rolled up, and she went on the warpath, as they say; she would disappear from the house for days—where did you go, our Hinda?— but she held her tongue, and it was only years later that she told me, it made me sick, how she wandered through the alleys of the Old City, in those days it was dangerous for Jews there, and a woman alone yet, and she would stalk the suq in Bethlehem and the casbah in Hebron, that's how crazy she was, you know Hinda, once she sets her mind to something; so one time she dressed up like a beauty queen—Where are you going, Hinda?—no answer, and she set off to pay a call on that shit, you should pardon the expression, Professor Meislish, and she offered to sell him our own father's prayer book for the High Holidays, if I'd known I would have killed her, the Venice machzor, he would have turned in his grave; that's the power of love, you see; and after each excursion she came home exhausted and trembling and pale, and right away she would lift her skirt and unload a veritable market, and then she would quickly cover the windows with blankets and stuff the keyhole with a garlic-soaked rag—the neighbors shouldn't be jealous, God forbid, and give us the evil eye, we were living on top of each other in the Kerem Avraham quarter—and when she started cooking, Yochi, her face would light up, with your papa hanging on her apron, devouring the chicken with his eyes and her too, poor girl, he was that hungry, and she would feed him with a teaspoon out of the pot, choosing the fattest morsels, allowing him to lick the gravy, that's right, you heard me, and there was a look in his eyes, like an animal grateful for its life. You mean our mama let him eat out of the pot? Strange but true, though only until the wedding, five months later, and she even managed to get hold of six eggs, six eggs, you hear, the grandest wedding cake in all Jerusalem, and you should have seen their eyes when they looked at the cake, or better yet, when they looked at your papa. Hinda ran a limp hand over her face, it was like magic, a miracle, how this poor refugee had been transformed, he even had a little goider on him; she smiled to herself, whirling like a queen among the astonished wedding guests, secretly following their gazes, her heart flying high: she saw their scorn and their amazement at the luxury which had fleshed him out, hiding his eyes behind mountainous cheeks, this in the days of austerity, when goldsmiths waxed rich melting down wedding rings, well, at least the women stopped ogling him. No more neighborhood spinsters gulping at the sight of him, or if they did—your mama acknowledged forbearingly—it was only a confusion of appetites, a derangement of gluttony, while she, Hinda, could look inside him and forge his manly charms out of that hulking carcass, like a miner striking gold, but suddenly she understood, she was shocked to her very soul, she felt knives twisting inside her, for Edna Bloom had seen HIM too, the forgotten handsome one, and it was to him she smiled softly now, while Yochi and Mama and Aron watched the way it permeated like precious oil through the rhinoceros hide his soul had grown. His face turned red. Mama burned, but it was too late.

Edna and Papa walked out of the salon together and into Edna's bedroom. With an arching of her eyebrow Mama sent Yochi after them. Aron stayed. He wanted to go with Papa, but he didn't dare, out of loyalty to Mama perhaps, or maybe he couldn't go in there with him just as he couldn't go into the water at the seashore when Papa was there. He sat in silence, avoiding Mama's flashing eyes: Look at you,

THE BOOK OF

sit up straight, stop sniffing, and now Papa was encountering Edna's bedroom, the picture with the bull and the dressing table and the tiny basin she had installed in the corner for some inscrutable reason, and of course the big bed; sometimes Aron made so bold as to lie down on it, incredibly comfortable, he would say to himself to excuse the languor that came over him there, it was like being carried off to a warm den of sleep, and if you ran your hand over the bed, it too would fall asleep. Once he had drowsed off there, but luckily the news beeps from the apartment next door woke him up a quarter of an hour before Edna was due home; just think, what if she'd found you fast asleep on her bed.

A screech and a groan, a giggle and a gasp were heard, they must have moved the bed into the center of the room. And what if Papa accidentally tripped and fell into it. Aron chuckled to himself. Big Papa lying spreadeagled forever in that bed. What if. Then Aron would have no choice, he would have to tear the wall down by himself. He stifled a smile, so as not to annoy Mama, but she noticed nothing. She was sitting stiffly in the white leather armchair, cursing herself for the greed which had landed her in this miserable trap. Get the green felt board, Aron prompted Papa from afar, where she tacks the snapshots of herself in strange, exotic places; once a year she took a trip, and then for two weeks he had the bathroom all to himself; in one of the snapshots she wore a glamorous straw hat; in another, a tall round turban; she posed in front of a pagoda, or a totem, or she peeked out behind a pair of enormous sunglasses in a piazza flocked with pigeons, or looked down on a grassy meadow from a cable car; and there were train tickets tacked on the felt board too, and picture postcards, museum tickets, theater programs, receipts from hotels, a matchbox with a photograph of her and some dark-skinned man with a droopy mustache. The snapshots, though taken at various locations, always showed Edna wearing the same expression, which Aron had seen for the first time when she greeted them at the door: she was bursting with joy.

They returned to the salon, the three of them, and Yochi blushed, avoiding Mama's eyes. "Time to get to work," growled Papa, staring at the floor.

"Just a moment, please!" cried Edna Bloom, and ran to get her camera. "This is history," she explained to Mama, who almost choked. Again she tingled with excitement, with minuscule emotions, her fingers quivering. She asked Papa to wave his sledgehammer in the air. He was helpless before her; she peeked through the eye of the camera and saw him, and kept him waiting a little longer. What could I do, insult her? You saw how she was. And what if she told you to yowl like a tomcat, would you do that too? And then Edna squealed "Berdi berdi!" and Papa was bathed in magnesium light, and for an instant he looked smaller, more compact than he actually was; frozen and frightened like a hunted animal. And Edna Bloom whispered, "Now please," and sank into the white leather armchair, winding around herself as though she had no bones, and then, inexplicably, she began to suck her thumb with a dreamy, faraway look on her face, and those strangers, those silent potato eaters all but vanished from her elegant salon.

THE BOOK OF

16

Three sounds reverberated through the air: hammer blows as the wall gave way, the rumbling of thunder after weeks of drought, and Edna's piercing shrieks.

At the age of forty, after a red-eyed birthday, she had made the rash decision to give herself this frightening gift. Again Papa struck the wall and again Edna shrieked. It meant she wouldn't have enough money for a trip abroad this year; it also meant perhaps that for the very reason she had dared to destroy something, she would have to stay in this apartment forever; and in such an apartment, with a big salon and a single bedroom, there would be no child.

Again and again he stormed the wall, and Edna screamed instinctively, her hands fluttering at her sides; she wanted him to stop, she tried to stall, to breathe, but there was no going back, Papa pounded mercilessly, and the three of them sat watching her with startled eyes. Mama waved to Papa, signaling him to let up, but he was hard at work now, or at least pretending to be, deaf to her wild-goose cries, and not until the wall was properly smashed did he slowly turn to Aron and the women. With the back of his hand he wiped the sweat off his brow. How agile he was: the moment he picked up the hammer he seemed to plug into a source of power and grace; he smiled at her and said, Well, that's that. And Edna bowed her head.

He had worked for an hour, stopping only twice, to take off his blue work shirt, leaving his undershirt on, and a little while later, to take that off too, with his back to the attentive audience. The smell of his sweat was overpowering, but it was Mama, not Edna, who finally went to open the window. Peeking out she saw a number of neighbors gathered on the sidewalk, Peretz and Sophie Atias with their new baby, the Kaminers, Felix and Zlateh Botenero anxiously clutching their little dog, all of them gazing up as though waiting for a mysterious communication. Pshi! she almost spat at them. They looked like fish down there, opening their O-shaped mouths in the hope of catching crumbs. When Papa noticed the expression on her face he too approached the window. Smiling down at them, he waved his hammer at the puffy gray sky. Don't you worry, he joked, defying the elephantine clouds with his three-kilo hammer, we'll show 'em what thunder is, and smiling roguishly, he vanished from the window and returned to pound the walls.

Edna Bloom sat in her armchair, one of her virginal white leather armchairs; she had neglected to try them out at the store, and was mortified to hear the squeaks, the demon of reality mocking her again. Her eyes were half-closed now, her lips were parted, as though she was burning inside. Now and then she would listlessly offer Mama or Aron the snack she had prepared, though it was clear to them that this was but a last hollow gesture of gentility.

Papa swung like a sledgehammer. Heavy chunks of stone and plaster piled up at his feet, as he vanished behind a thick white cloud of dust and slowly reappeared. He pounded the wall hundreds of times that day, trading his three-kilo hammer for the five-kilo hammer, sending shivers up the wall with his chisel and screwdriver. Every blow was solemn and precise, expressing his respect for inert matter, his high regard for the adversary and the rites of war. And the wall surrendered to Papa, yielding to him more and more, holding in the pain, the extent of which was slowly manifested in the jagged blocks and exposed wires, and the rusty rods protruding from its side. "This wall is thick," said Papa, stopping to catch his breath. "They don't make them like this anymore." He patted the wall the way you might pat a good horse. Edna trembled.

Every blow was a shock to her, goring her inside. Only when the destruction began did she realize how deeply the house possessed her after thirteen years; for there was a bedroom Edna and a salon Edna and a kitchen Edna too; in each she became a different person, and

THE BOOK OF

passing from one to the other, she still experienced a subtle shift, an alteration of her spirit, different filings rising to meet the magnet; and there were things and people she could contemplate only in one particular room, by the light of one dear lamp and no other, and it was unthinkable that there should be a room without a basin, without, that is, even the hope of running water, which is why just as soon as she moved in, and for a considerable sum of money, Edna had installed little washbasins everywhere: in the hall, on the balcony, even in a niche of her bedroom; and of course there were the paintings, her reproductions, as she liked to call them, savoring the word like melting chocolate, and she even owned an original she had purchased in Montmartre, representing a shipwreck in a stormy sea, the bearded painter had a braid and a shiny gold earring, and his eyes were disquieting, like the painting, though she wasn't really sure it was art, and then there were her books, many of which she hadn't read yet, reading was a sacred duty, she would wait for a time of perfect peace, but she liked to feel them like a protective wall around her keeping out the world, and there was her collection of paperweights, shake them and dream, and her dolls of the world on display, and her elegant desk with back issues of *National Geographic* neatly arranged on it and her PROJECT notebooks, as she modestly referred to them, and, of course, the twenty-one afghans and carpets and scatter rugs side to side throughout the apartment, one from each country she had visited, so that as she walked over them in her bare feet she was stepping lightly from Mexico to Portugal, from Kenya to Finland, camel's hair and sheep's wool and leopardskin and broadloom, like a stroll through the pages of a colorful stamp album, and there was Edna aged twenty-six and Edna aged thirty, and Edna the bitter-hearted after her love affair with a married man, he deceived her, no, you deceived yourself, and those faceless men who did what they did; she was like a frightened child on a runaway train, and when she finally got off she sank into a torpor, isolation petrifying all around her; how had she passed through all those stages that lead two strangers, two labyrinths, from the sublime to the animal, and once a year, when she traveled abroad, she would wink her inner eye, entwining with another body from a different world, an ephemeral lover picked up for the night, only she wouldn't allow anyone to kiss her mouth; but once she fell in love, in "Lisboa," she pronounced, "Bliss-boa," at a tourist club she had ventured into, what a man you had for a night, you drove him mad with passion till he swore he would leave his wife and children for you, and you had to persuade him to be reasonable, you brave and noble girl, and there was Edna of the university, with a single seminar paper left unfinished, and Edna after the removal of a growth in her womb, and Edna who spent weeks chewing dough to feed the gosling that fell into her nest and died in her hand, and Edna of the highs and lows, who sat here writing a letter all night long, but didn't swallow an overdose in the end, and now, after a few blows from a sledgehammer, everything collapsed in a heap, her wall, the rooms of her soul.

At six-thirty that evening Mama cried "Enough!" and her voice was hoarse from the dust and the silent curses, as if she had spent the whole time screaming the same word over and over. Papa heard. His red neck, gleaming with drops of sweat, contracted. He swung a few times more. For a moment he seemed about to rebel, as though he didn't want to stop yet. She moved her lips to speak, but no sound came out. Papa slowed to a halt. And dropped the hammer. He reassumed his erstwhile shape, spreading out and thickening. As he swept up the rubble and the dust and the chunks of plaster, Edna waved limply and said, Never mind now. Go. Tomorrow at the same time. Papa glanced back at her. He was bewildered. He had not turned his head in the past hour, or seen the transformation taking place. His own face was also transformed now, though Aron couldn't say how.

That's just the way Moshe looked, fixing up the house for me when we were newlyweds.

"The ladder I'll leave here," he said.

"Yes, do," whispered Edna.

"Tomorrow I'll come again," he said.

"I'll look after it for you," she murmured.

"How about that rain?" he asked too loudly, hurrying to the window, massaging his right arm.

But the heavy clouds were moping over their interrupted journey. Far away, beyond the rocky hills, winter was closing in, galloping its chariots; a grim commander hurrying to a remote province where cries of mutiny had been heard. And the startled procession emerged through the door of Edna Bloom's into the cold of the evening, with Mama in the lead, followed by Yochi, and then Aron, and Papa bringing up the rear, head bowed, like a bull led back to his pen for the night.

THE BOOK OF

17

Supper was lapped in unbearable silence. Papa chewed and swallowed and asked for more, the work must have whet his appetite, and Mama dished his food out carefully, as though feeding the flames of an insatiable fire. Woodenly she watched him lean over his plate, his forehead glowing red in a rising crescendo of sucking and gasping and gulping. After supper Aron took the garbage out, but as soon as Mama handed him the pail, he knew; he knew by her face and her sideways glance. Near the rusty barrel of heating oil behind the building, Aron crouched down and stuck his hand in. He groped around in the muck until he found it: a stiff package tied with string. He took it out and unwrapped it: inside he found an old pair of high heels, but there was no whiff of champagne. When he finished dumping the garbage, he took the shoes down to the furnace room and hid them in his lair, together with the flowered dress, the striped bathing suit, and the shorn braid, now full of mildew.

A year had passed since Mama and Papa put Grandma in the hospital, after the scenes she made at his bar mitzvah. Again she had fought like an animal, spitting and scratching and cursing at them, though without words this time, she could only cry and snort, so it was easy for Mama to help Papa load her into the ambulance. And later, at home, Mama put on her brown-check dress and packed some sandwiches and jars of sour cream and a bottle of tomato juice and a few squares of Grandma's favorite chocolate, wrapped in wax paper and nylon, with a label on every sandwich and a rubber band, and she put it all in her bag and set off for the hospital accompanied by Aron and Yochi.

They found Grandma Lilly lying in the ward, after her sedative. She quietly gazed at the visitors but didn't seem to recognize them. It's me, Aron, he whispered with a chill of dismay. See, Grandma, it's me, but she didn't remember him. Mama, who was ready to cry, with a hanky in her hand, rose swiftly to the occasion and went to work, wiping the goo from Grandma's eyes, arranging her pillows, massaging the soles of her swollen feet. She handled her without disgust, moving over her like a nimble spider. A pockmarked nurse with a scowling face brought supper in. She was about to feed Grandma when Mama grabbed the tray from her with a benevolent smile, rinsed Grandma's dentures in the sink, stuck them carefully back in her mouth, jiggled her jaws till they were firmly in place, propped her up, tilted her head back, and started patiently spooning yogurt into her.

Every day they went to visit her. Sometimes Aron ate lunch at home by himself, and then hurried to the hospital. Mama and Papa would already be there, next to Grandma's bed, and usually Yochi too. Grandma lay in her bed, lost and tiny, barely moving. Maybe she didn't notice the commotion around her, all the effort his parents had put into giving her a haimish feeling. She had a little cupboard by the bed, which Mama arranged for her as only she knew how: Grandma's bathrobe, her soap dish, a glass for her dentures, a pillowcase from home, an embroidered serviette, her favorite comb, the elastic bandages for her swollen feet, a tube of hand cream, a jar of special face lotion, and a hot-water bottle—she had everything she needed, it was beautiful to see. With tender devotion his parents watched over her, Yochi and Aron at their side, quietly discussing the concerns of the day or the news of the world: about the Kaminers' youngest daughter who landed herself a fiancé, but they're keeping it a secret that her father is sick, because kidneys are hereditary, or about the latest invention, Papa told them, designed to help people like him fill in the Toto automatically, it guesses where to put the X's all by itself, and mark my words, a hundred years from now everything will be automatic, they won't need people anymore, everyone will be replaced by robots, there'll be robots, robots everywhere, and Mama told them about the new counter at the supermarket, with delicacies like fish roe and lox and moldy green cheese at seventeen pounds for two hundred grams, horrid-looking stuff, but still, there's a feeling of culture, a modern, European atmosphere. Every now and then she would get up to rearrange Grandma's pillow, to change her position or wipe her nose. She performed her duties with lofty dedication, refusing to entrust her to anyone else, and there were already arguments at the hospital, with the nurses and with Yochi too, till Mama finally relented and gave Yochi the task of combing Grandma's hair, and Yochi fought like a lion to stop Mama from cutting it when it started growing long, and Papa's task, besides his calming influence, was to pick Grandma up so Mama could smooth the sheets or put the bedpan under her, and even though he was very strong, his face would turn a bright red. Mamchu's getting heavy, he blurted, she looks like a bird, but she weighs a ton, and Aron, whose special task was to make sure Grandma's little toe, the rebel, didn't start sneaking up on its neighbor, reflected that maybe she was heavy because there wasn't enough life left in her, it's life that gives lightness, and a moment later the sneaky little toe was curling up again.

By now he knew all the labyrinths of the hospital. On his way to the canteen at four o'clock, he would slip away, peek in at patients, accidentally on purpose walk through corridors marked FOR STAFF ONLY; he had a little game he played with the cracks in the tiles: on the fourth floor there were big tiles, and once a day he would stroll nonchalantly past the children in their blue hospital robes, not all of them looked sick, and whenever they tried to talk to him he simply wouldn't answer, he was a tourist, no speak Hebrew, he would walk to the end of the ward, pause, turn around, and walk right back again through a double file of children, amusing himself with his private game—never stepping on the cracks. All the doctors and nurses on Grandma's ward knew him already. Every day he checked the roster to see who was on duty, and he would offer to do errands for the nurses and doctors, and when they saw they could rely on him, they even let him answer the telephone; he would pick up the receiver and say: Neurology, good afternoon. When Purim came around he volunteered (What are you volunteering for, they're lousy with money, these hospitals) to premiere his new Houdini act for the staff and patients of the hospital, and he could hardly wait, he went over and over it in his head, it was a long time since his last show, he imagined himself escaping out of boxes and crates and vaults, they would stream in from all the wards to see him. And now, ladies and gentlemen, the dignified administrator would announce, the wonder boy, our own Israeli Houdini, will show us his breathtaking feats, and then a pair of twin musclemen would lock him in a medicine cabinet, the kind with a skull and crossbones painted on it, and Aron would be inside, his wrists handcuffed, running out of air, and a worried murmur passes through the audience. Sixty seconds of oxygen left, whispers the administrator in his black top hat, and Aron pries the little saw blade he swiped from shop class out of his trouser cuff and cuts through the knots with his sweaty fingers. Thirty seconds left, counts the administrator with a worried frown, and there in the darkness, he inhales the medicine smells and nearly suffocates, but reassures himself that it's only a cabinet, made of steel; yet it emanates a certain nastiness the way a seemingly courteous salesman can be nasty, or the way a teacher can be really vicious behind a façade of decency. So sorry, my boy, I have my orders, they made me into what I am, a padlocked medicine cabinet, and from under the label on his corduroy trousers he takes out the passkey, turns it coolly, coolly my eye, just thinking about it makes him break out in a sweat, yes, he turns this celebrated key in the lock of the handcuffs, with precision and finesse, the way Eli Ben-Zikri, the hood, taught him, and suddenly he touches it, that tiny thing that makes them squeal, Stick it in, stick it in, and then there's a click and his hands are free. Twenty seconds to go, whispers the administrator, anxiously running his finger over the whip in his hand, and the crowd begins to swish like foam in the sea, the crowd of strangers, that's how it always is, strangers, maybe there were people there who secretly hoped Aron would fail this time and stay locked up forever, and that was weird, because if he came out alive, they would be happier than anybody, they would burst with happiness, for they, most of all, would be redeemed, and he turns his belt buckle inside out, feels around for his black lead nail, and with the virtuoso fingers of a guitarist, he fits it into the padlock on the cabinet; five seconds left, four, three, two, and at the last second, when the oxygen's almost gone and the administrator cracks his whip, out bursts Aron, and the audience goes wild: What a feat, how did he do it, and Aron stands blinking in the light, his name on their lips, shouted to the rhythm of their applause; without his name they would be sitting in silence like frozen statues, but his name on their lips fills them with life, go explain that to someone like Shalom Sharabani, who sneers at him whenever he performs at parties, go explain what it means to burst out like the dawn, beloved as a baby, as if hearing your name for the first time on their breath, feeling like a person who has been allowed to peek at his cherished guitar in a dark pawnshop, but Aron pays no notice to the applause, he scorns the cheap fleeting love of the audience, he leaps off the stage, pursued by the spotlight, and the people stand up to look for him: Where is he going, who is that old woman in the wheelchair, what's so special about her, still pretty, with a porcelain complexion but vacant eyes, and he leans over her, his hands on the arms of her chair, and watches the excitement in the air stirring her back to life, making her lashes flutter. It's me, Grandma; a finger goes up, trembles antennalike in front of his face. It's me, look at me, see; her lips wind around the core of his name, because she has to remember, she has to dredge it out of the mire. So what if she's confused, he revolts, so what if she doesn't even recognize Papa, her own son, she's not allowed to forget my name, I'm not him, I'm me . . .

Even Sima, the pockmarked nurse with the scowling face, started to like him and sang his praises to Mama and Papa: he is the brightest most helpful child she has ever seen, not like other children, who have no use for the sick and elderly. He's an old-fashioned boy, she said, and Aron noticed Mama watching her face so she'd know how to imitate her later at home. Even the doctors spoke highly of him, and he loved to accompany them on their rounds before supper, tagging modestly along, waiting behind the hospital curtains, where he could hear the soothing hum of the long words they used to describe symptoms and medicines and treatments; how awesome death is, sending out a thousand dread diseases like long, thin arms to embrace humanity, and maybe every illness is different somehow from the same illness when another person has it, maybe doctors are wrong to call them by the same name, who knows, because how can you compare. From his hiding place behind the curtain he peeked at the doctors and nurses around the bed. All he could see of the groaning patient was his long, crooked fingers, speckled brown, gripping the mattress, hanging on to it for dear life; maybe the man had never even heard of the disease he was about to die of, maybe he'd lived his life contentedly, in ignorance of the new disease that would come into the world, especially for him, and Aron wanted to escape, it wasn't right to peek, those fingers were very disturbing, the way they clutched the mattress like they would never let go, refusing to acknowledge what even Aron knew, that a week ago someone else had been lying there, and a week from now this man too would be gone, and suddenly he heard a gasp, and the doctors' coats began to flutter as though a breeze were blowing on them, and the man sat up with a supreme effort, and for a minute his face was reflected in the window, hollow and bony like the skull of a prophet or an animal, vouchsafed a glimpse of the eternal. And now the haggard eyes saw Aron hiding, and gaped at him with the toothless mouth, and Aron was petrified: I've had it, he found me out and he'll expose me so everyone will know—he froze at the idea—but that's ridiculous, what could they do, and suddenly the head turned and vanished. Only the groans persisted. Aron drew the curtain and quickly fled through the ward, annoyed with the patients for lying on their beds and squawking at the nurses, never realizing that death was on its way, their own terrible death, and what did they complain about, that their slippers were too tight, that they didn't get a boiled egg for supper; but why is he trembling. Death, death, he whispered to himself to see if anything would happen, if anyone would peek out at him to see who was calling; nothing happened, of course, and yet he trembled inwardly as he said it again, as he whispered "Death" behind his hand, so they wouldn't see him and be suspicious, who wouldn't, it's all in your mind, maybe this was what his bar mitzvah rabbi had sensed about him, and what if you were, say, a secret agent sent by Death to prepare humanity for its sorrows. "Is that you again?" He was startled by an amiable old doctor with a croaking voice, the one who told the family that Grandma could be cured simply by draining the blood from her brain. "A minor surgical procedure," he said, but Mama and Papa weren't about to entrust Grandma to the likes of him. "Know what I think, boychik, I think that after hanging around us doctors so long, you too may wind up, God forbid, a doctor." And the nurses joked with him and asked him what he wanted to be when he grew up, but they said it in the false-impression voice, one of them even patted his head, so he answered in his corrective tone: "I'm still debating whether to become a brain surgeon or a classical guitarist," hoping that would set them straight, but as they walked away, amazed at his maturity, he felt a pang of regret, maybe he should have been a little more direct about their error, so they'd understand, why not, they were used to problems, that was their job, after all.

He wanted to share his experiences with Gideon: once on their way home from school he tried to describe the special emotion he felt when the family was together at Grandma's bedside, and how rewarding it was, truly rewarding, to care for her down to the smallest details, like her meals and medicines and laundry, even her evacuation, that's what they called it now, and the hospital generally—the wards and corridors and intercoms, and the charts and the daily roster, with everything so neat and orderly and serious, said Aron, knowing that the word "orderly" would grab Gideon's attention, and you get a sense that everything in life and in the hospital and in the body is logically planned, like math, like an equation, and when you put the details together you see the larger picture, you start to understand what it's all about. Gideon was quiet a moment, and then said with a sideways glance that personally he wouldn't want to be involved with things like that for so many hours a day, and Aron answered, vaguely superior, Sure, oh naturally. And then he said, "Okay, bye, see you tomorrow, they're waiting for me," and just like that he walked away. Who cares about Gideon. Who cares about Zacky. Who cares that spring is bursting out with a warmth and a golden light that made everyone in class seem a little tipsy, and the girls were wearing their minis, those new short dresses that let you see practically everything, and Zacky invented a special mirror tied to his sandal with a rubber band, you stick your foot out in front of a girl, that's the kind of thing he's good at, and the girls haven't caught on yet, it's the boys' secret, they walk up and burst out laughing, it's pathetic, while here he is, at the center of a battlefield, striving against suffering and death, shoulder to shoulder with Papa and Mama and Yochi, marching to a single drum, with grim determination and nerves of steel.

Their devotion to Grandma was simply incredible, how quickly they had grown accustomed to the changes and disruptions she brought into their lives: all their leisure was spent at Grandma's bedside, observing her expressions, guessing her unspoken wishes, rolling her over to prevent bedsores, spoon-feeding her water when she had the hiccups, and thinking up a thousand and one ways to make her take another bite of egg, another sip of tea . . . Never a grumble or word of complaint, as they put everything else aside and concentrated on Grandma, though they didn't deceive themselves, they knew exactly what lay in store, when it comes it comes, the will of heaven, it was a miracle she'd lasted this long, but they treated her with so much dignity, their every movement appropriate and precise, that Aron was proud to take part in this ancient rite of leading Grandma Lilly out of the family and into the outstretched arms of Death.

Only once was the rite spoiled for him: he was alone at home with Mama when suddenly she rushed to his side. What happened, what did I do? And then she grabbed him and hugged him so hard she nearly cracked his bones. She never behaved like that unless he was sick. With trembling fingers she held his chin and he saw that her eyes were full of tears. He was frightened. Mama, who didn't let anyone see her cry, was biting her lip to control herself, and suddenly she started sobbing: For God's sake, haven't we paid our debts with interest on the interest; oh please, let the troubles with Mamchu make amends so from now on, everything will turn out, and everything . . . Aron buried his face in Mama's hand, alarmed at the urgency in her voice, because it wasn't him she was talking to; she gripped his face with flinty fingers, tilting it reproachfully, as though exhibiting a piece of evidence to a judge, and her sadness made him want to be even smaller and he was scared suddenly that he, a child, had been privy to the procedure, the mysterious balancing of the family accounts with Fate.

They also gave up their social life. There were no more evenings with the few friends they had, and Papa stopped going over to Peretz Atias's on Sunday afternoons to watch wrestling on Lebanon TV, and Aron was relieved not to have to watch those cruel giants anymore, in front of Sophie Atias yet, who kept parading around with her baby and showing her off. And there were no more Friday-night rummy games either. Mama confessed she hadn't enjoyed them in years, enough already, she said, it was fine when we were younger, the cards and the joking, but we have to act our age, she said, and suddenly Aron realized that his parents were getting older, soon they would be forty-five. They'd even stopped listening to the news every hour on the hour. "So what could happen already?" Papa would say, and Aron would think, A currency devaluation, but then he realized that what was happening here overshadowed everything else in their lives, effacing it completely, it almost seemed.

And once, or maybe twice, as the four of them sat around Grandma's bed, figuring out how long the effect of the tranquillizers lasted or reviewing the food she'd eaten that day and the number of times she had evacuated since they started feeding her pablum, and talked about

THE BOOK OF

clipping her nails on Friday, and the new ointment Mama discovered at the Romanian pharmacy, and about the Araber from Abu-Gosh who was going to whitewash the apartment, because there were stains on the walls again, pretty soon there would be people coming to pay condolence calls, once or maybe twice it happened that Aron was startled out of the peace that bore him gently over the voices and the words: as he looked up at Mama and Papa and gratefully beheld their serious faces, the way they kept pondering those unknowns with silent sighs like an endless lament, and beside them, Yochi, who was equally devoted and probably loved Grandma Lilly more than anyone, though as usual she barely spoke, she merely listened blankly to what they said, as if here too there were things to be learned which would one day serve her in good stead, like an anthropologist collecting specimens of conversation about the coldhearted nurse who had changed for the better, about white blood corpuscles and the social security forms that cheated them out of welfare money only because Grandma could still be continent sometimes, Aron suddenly looked up and caught sight of something in Yochi's face—she was choking with rage, shuddering with hatred.

Aron trudged upstairs from the furnace room, wiping the expression off his face so Mama wouldn't know. Seven months had gone by since his last visit to Grandma. Just before his parents fizzled out: he'd seen it coming, he was really sensitive to things like that these days, so he stayed away. They didn't even know they were fizzling out. They simply started grumbling to each other, in front of him and Yochi, that it was hopeless, neither here nor there, said Mama sadly, like not being able to swallow or to vomit either, and Aron understood and kept silent. And then they started explaining on the phone to Gucha and to Rivche that it didn't matter anyway, since Grandma didn't know whether she was dead or alive. It's a wonder she's still breathing. She only wakes up to take another sleeping pill. It's true she's young, relatively speaking, but when it comes it comes, once it has you by the claws it never lets go. And then just before Passover they did some redecorating, the house looked like a hovel, so they painted and hung new curtains and wallpaper, and they bought a buffet; at first they considered fixing up the old one but the carpenter found a worm in it, and Mama swore it didn't get the worm in our house but from a stranger's furniture at the carpenter's shop, and she would never let it back in our salon; and then they bought a new lamp fixture. All this kept them busy for a couple of weeks, months, months and months of shopping and checking and comparing prices and debating half the night, and there wasn't always time left for other things. Occasionally Mama went to feed Grandma and roll her over and put the ointment on her bedsores, but when she came home she didn't tell what was new anymore, and no one asked. So what could be new already? Once, though, she confessed to Yochi that sometimes when she was taking care of Grandma Lilly she would pour out her heart to her, to her body, that is, the way you do when you visit a grave, and Yochi thought, Ah, I guess I have to die before you'll talk to me like that, but eventually Mama gave up, she wasn't made of steel, you know, and at first Mama's heart pounded every time the phone rang, maybe they were calling from the hospital to tell them it was over, but she got over that in time as well; Grandma wasn't living in the street, she was in a proper institution, receiving excellent care; and sometimes a whole week went by without anyone saying, Grandma.

The alcove stayed empty. They offered it to Yochi, with your exams coming up and all, said Mama unctuously, if you want top marks and an army deferral you'll need a little peace and quiet, won't you, dear? And then Yochi let her have it: In the first place, who said she wanted an army deferral, and in the second place, she wouldn't set foot in the alcove as long as Grandma was alive, and Mama shut her mouth, and Aron saw that look in her eyes again, as if she were remembering a terrible crime she had committed long ago, and the alcove door stayed shut, though sometimes Aron would peek in, which is how he discovered that Grandma's embroidery with the parrots and the monkeys and the palm trees had disappeared. For a moment he was mortified and wanted to run to Mama and tell her something horrible had happened, maybe a robber had stolen it, but suddenly he remembered what Yochi told him once, that he had to learn how to survive around here, and he controlled himself and didn't say a word to anyone, and now he kept his eyes open as only he knew how; in fact, two days later the hook for the embroidery had also disappeared, and the day after that, the hole in the wall was filled with toothpaste. And then things started turning up in the trash bin, like Grandma's dresses and shoes, and her hairpins and ribbons, and her braid. And Aron gathered them in secret and hid them away.

THE BOOK OF

Now he took the empty can out to the pantry and noticed Mama watching his face. Spiegler, Spiegel, Primo, Bellow, Drucker, Talby, Rosenthal, and Young—he named the players on the soccer team, enabling himself to walk past her without revealing anything. Papa was on the Bordeaux sofa in the salon already with a newspaper over his face. They had barely spoken to each other since the day Edna Bloom came in asking him to work at her house. Aron went to his room. Under a halo of light behind her desk sat Yochi writing, homework or letters, soon he'd know.

"Yochi."

"What?"

By the tone of her voice, he guessed it was letters. When she was doing homework she welcomed interruptions. Better keep mum, though. But the memory of those high heels in the garbage—

"Yochi."

She was silent. There was a little brown envelope under her elbow. A sign she was answering her soldier. She had six or seven pen pals collected from the newspaper over the years and she wrote them each a letter a week. Aron recognized them by their envelopes: the university student she'd corresponded with since he was in high school, the kibbutznik from Mizra, and the guy from the agricultural center, and there was one who was training to be an able-bodied seaman and sent her letters from the *Shalom* liner, and a religious guy, and someone by the name of Evyatar, an Israeli who lived in Australia and was a cripple.

"My valiant soldier, you will not believe what happened to me today . . ." says Aron artfully, and Yochi veers around with daggers in her eyes: "If you ever so much as touch my letters! . . ." "Who the heck cares about your letters. You always lock them up anyway. Tell me, don't you get bored writing the same thing over and over seven times?"

"It's none of your business what I write."

"Just tell me that much."

"Who says I write the same thing to each of them?"

"I hear that in America they invented this robot thing that can copy a thousand pages a second."

"Aron!"

"Okay, okay, just kidding. Go on and write your boring letters. Just don't forget to change the names each time."

He sank down on his bed, tossed this way and that, folded his arms under his head, pulled a coiling thread out of the hole in his mattress, tickled his nose with it; he'd been thinking of changing his sneeze for a while, because Gideon does this loud *hutchoo* thing as opposed to his own *hutchee*, but he can't even come through with a sneeze today. What now? What time is it? It's pitch-black outside. I wonder if Edna Bloom keeps going to check the broken wall.

"Yochi is a nice name. Kind of like yokel. Or yucky. Or yak yak yak."

"Watch it."

"Okay okay. What are you getting so mad about. All I did was say your name. I can say anything I want."

She turned to him: "What do you want? Why are you being such a brat?"

"Aww, why don't you write me a letter too. That way at least you'll ask how I am."

Again he sprawled out on his bed. He was pretty tired already. Watching Papa break down a wall had proven exhausting. He could fall asleep like nothing now and wake up fresh tomorrow.

"Aron."

"Yes?" He quickly turned to face her.

"Why are you so jumpy? I was just wondering something."

"About me?"

"About us. How is it that we never have real fights. I don't remember the two of us ever having a real fight. Do you?"

"You mean, being mad at each other for a long time? And hitting? No, you're right. Is that considered good or bad?"

"I don't know. Brothers and sisters usually fight. And you and I are always together, we even share a bedroom, but whenever I get even the teensiest bit angry with you, right away I feel guilty. Don't you think that's a little strange?"

"I don't know. Never mind. Hey, tell me, if What's-her-name, Edna Bloom, got married, could she still have kids?"

"Until the age of thirty-five. Or maybe it's thirty-nine. Once I read about an Egyptian woman who gave birth at the age of forty-seven."

"Forty-seven?!"

"Yes, but that's Egypt."

"And how old do you suppose What's-her-name is?"

THE BOOK OF

"I don't know and I don't care. But before, while you were talking, I was thinking something."

"I know, you'll match her up with one of your pen pals?"

"No, stupid, I was thinking about why we never fight."

"Or hey, we could find her somebody in the personal column."

"See, you made me forget. That's what happens when you start to blabber."

Silence. How stiff her shoulders were. He tried to imagine her walking into class that morning. Taking her seat. And suddenly he saw the scene, someone shot a rubber band at her and she ignored it. His heart melted with compassion for her. Couldn't the other kids see that she was special? No one ever sees a person's home self. If they did see, thought Aron, there wouldn't be cruelty in the world. He needed to give her something, a present.

"Did you see the picture she has in the bathroom with the half-man, half-bull?"

"Shush, Aron, you're being a pest."

"And there's this woman stroking his back. Yochi, tell me—"

"Okay, one question, and I don't want to hear another word out of you!"

"What's going to happen to Grandma?" How did that pop out of his mouth.

She turned to him in surprise. "It's about time. So you finally remembered to ask."

"Why don't we visit her anymore?"

Yochi thought awhile. "I go."

"You? Liar. When?"

"Twice a week, at least. I go to visit her straight from school."

"Does Mama know?"

"No one knows. And if you dare—"

"So—how is she?"

"Same as she was. Poor thing."

"Does she still sleep all the time?"

"No."

"You mean she woke up? She's awake?"

"She doesn't take the sleeping pills anymore."

"Then . . . then how . . . she has to!"

"The fact is, she doesn't. She's awake. She lies in bed looking at the sky. There's a tree outside her window. She stares at it." Yochi spoke gently: "The leaves are falling. I tell her things."

"You mean she . . ." Oh God. "You mean she recognizes you?"

"No. But I think she feels it's me. She holds my hand."

"Hey, could I come with you sometime?"

"Sure. It's a free country."

"I really want to come."

"You don't scare me. Come if you want to."

"I mean it, I will."

"Uh-huh, sure."

Silence. Yochi returned to her letter. Aron mulled over this fantastic bit of news. Yochi did, but Mama and Papa didn't? From now on, he too would go. Starting tomorrow. Or maybe the day after, when Papa finished the work at Edna's. Enough. The age of betrayal is over. How could he have behaved that way. He stood up determinedly. Rummaged through his school bag. It was pretty interesting that he and Yochi never fought. Who had the strength to fight. The little red mirror. That's what he'd bring her as a present. Maybe she did understand something after all. Maybe she still had feelings. It would make her happy. A memento from Aron. For his little grandma, swaddled in blankets, staring through the window at the night. Maybe she was like an animal now and could see things in the darkness. He lifted the mirror to his face and held his breath. And the mirror stayed clear. There. Caught you, spy! With all his might he blew on it, fogging his reflection.

THE BOOK OF

18

For three days Papa battered the wall at Edna Bloom's. He smashed it till the iron rods and the rusty grating and the slender water pipe showed through the gaping holes and the silky bedroom was revealed to the audience in the salon. Once in a while Papa rested, luxuriously kneading his arm and shoulder on his way to the window to smoke a cigarette, whereupon the onlookers realized how long they'd been holding their breath and began to unfreeze, to clear their throats and stretch. And Papa inhaled the smoke as he looked out at the sagging gray clouds, so pregnant they almost touched the ground. Then he nodded wordlessly at the naked plane tree outside, stubbed the cigarette on his work boot, and returned to pound the wall.

Mama went to Edna's every day, with her big brown knitting bag, set down a bulky ball of yarn at her feet, and crisscrossed the air with her needles. Not a word passed between her and Edna Bloom, who sat sequestered in her armchair from four to seven every day, staring through her, lost in reverie. Papa applied himself with zeal—how had he kept his talents buried so long—and little by little his body began to manifest itself in all its glory: brawny, rugged, full of beef. Yes, he was still fat and clumsy, but to Edna's eye, the eye of the artist from her sculpture class at the civic center, that "still" was pure delight.

Papa continued excavating in silence, save for the grunts accompanying his hammer blows, which grew deeper and throatier the more he let himself be carried away by the rhythm. With Edna's money he'd purchased some black rubber bushel baskets into which he would rake the scraps of plaster and chunks of wall every half hour, and then load them on his shoulders and empty them through the window onto the growing mound behind the building.

Three days. The guts spilled out of the wall, and Edna hardly budged where she sat or reclined, snuggling into the vague, elemental horror that touched her with a thrill too fierce to endure, like a child hiding under the covers at the approaching footsteps of a mother about to extricate her from the void. A cloud of white dust hovered over the house long after working hours, and there was a permanent trace in her nostrils now of Papa's pungent-smelling sweat: to remember him she only had to breathe. After the second day of work, when she was left alone to fix her supper—an orange, a slice of whole-wheat bread, and cottage cheese—she suddenly stopped and raised her head with a cunning smile. She dropped the bread, blushed pink, and, with a giggle and an Edna-are-you-mad, danced into the empty salon, daintily holding out an imaginary dress, and sank luxuriously into her armchair: soon the white cloud would disperse and she would see the burly arm again, the magnificent paunch.

And Aron too came every day and leaned back against the leather armchair, following Papa's movements through half-closed eyes. Sometimes he would lazily turn his head to look at Mama. At the way she knitted. So vigorously. Her elbows rising and falling sharply. And the holes in the wall gaped wider. A pleasurable weakness seeped through him here. Slowly the hammer blows were converted into heartbeats, then into footsteps, the footsteps of a giant, the giant inside him who was searching, step, boom, step, boom, turning this way and that, groping forlornly; Aron couldn't interfere, he wasn't there, he was unconscious, off in another world, merely tracking the muffled footsteps from the outside, he could sit still like this for three hours, he, Aron, with the ants in his pants, curling into himself; he knew perfectly well it made him look like a runt, a caricature, but suddenly he didn't care, like the sole survivor on a desert island who maintains his dignity somehow but, when he finally sees help on the horizon, allows himself to let go and weep. Only when Edna turned to look at him did Aron sit up a little and puff himself out, but she was so engrossed in herself, he was free to sink again, running idly in his mind through the four laundry-powder box tops—don't forget to write down the names of four Shemen products on one of the box tops, send in two box tops from Telma's Yemenite-style falafel and you'll be eligible for a host of prizes, including stylish jersey outfits, suede and leather overcoats, and Arctic ice cream has this special offer for you, win a gorgeous key ring, and tomorrow, Thursday, was the day of the national lottery, with a first prize of fifty thousand pounds; his ticket was in his pocket, you wouldn't catch him unprepared for the grand drawing or the fabulous prizes, he'd been ready for a month already, what are you talking about, a month, six weeks, and at the beginning of April there were gala prizes from Yitzhar, he even bought three bottles of their oil instead of one at the grocery store, accidentally on purpose, for the special red labels, was there a more knowledgeable boy in all the land, and suddenly Aron felt restless and started squirming in his chair, as though the grand drawing were about to take place right here, in this room, and he jumped to his feet and asked politely if he could use the bathroom. "Of course," answered Edna Bloom today as yesterday, with the same abstracted look on her face, and Mama arched an eyebrow, but what did he care, she'd noticed that he never missed a chance and asked him whether he was trying to grow roses in that cuckoo's house, and said she'd skin him alive if he ever did it again, and today, before they left for Edna's, Mama sent him to the bathroom and told him she'd wait. How come I didn't hear the water? she asked when he emerged. I didn't have to go, he muttered, looking down, and Mama squinted at him and said, How long has it been like this? And he said, I don't know, leave me alone, but he realized what she was thinking, that he was starting to get her constipation now, and at least Yochi had Papa's appetite to go with it, but after an hour here he couldn't hold it in anymore, and Edna whispered, Of course, watching Papa as Aron walked past the daggers in Mama's eyes.

He slipped into the little bathroom, lingering over her soft "Of course," and sat there rocking back and forth, staring blindly at the picture of the girl leaning down to caress the bull—she alone took pity on him, the others had cold Egyptian eyes—and slowly his own eyes close with fervent prayer, and the hammer blows reverberate, the bathroom quakes with everything inside him. Papa must be incredibly strong. It's thundering outside, getting closer and closer, any minute now, and his body goes limp as he listens from within, from his kishkes. You're fourteen years old, booms the hammer inside him; fourteen years, three weeks, and two days, it resounds around him; and she says, You're doing it on purpose, but I don't believe that; Aron is deeply shocked and bows to the mighty rumble passing through him. But you gotta fight it, Aronchik, never say die; you gotta try with all your might; atta boy, with all your might! The hammering ceased. Aron leaned back, caught his breath. Silence. He raised his head and waited. The sledge-hammer was replaced for the moment by a giant screwdriver that dug out chunks of gently crumbling plaster; and what's this new mishegoss of yours, Aronchik, whispers the new voice, you won't eat meat, you won't eat chicken, we've never had anything like that in the family, how do you expect to grow big and strong, Aronaleh. Listen, murmurs the voice, maybe I'm not explaining too good, and I wish I could help you; you are my son, and I hope someday we will walk together, shoulder to shoulder, like the father and son in *Capture the Hill or Die*. Aron nodded, full of emotion: how inspiring Papa was; again the house reverberated to a mighty blow. Harder! Harder! Help me help you! Aronchik!

Suddenly the pounding ceased. Too bad. Well almost. Silence. And a different sound entered the world: the sound of rain. A driving rain at last. No more arctic winter. He sat awhile longer, rain, rain, beautiful rain, everything was flowing now. A few seconds more just to make sure, but it was no use, and yet—this was an omen. The first rain! He got up quickly, filled with excitement, he felt as if the rain were falling just for him. Fearlessly he pulled the chain and flushed the toilet, what a torrent, what a surge. Too bad he couldn't make today, though. In here of all places, where he had never had any problem before.

When he entered the salon Mama gave him a scathing look, she heard the water flush, what did he care, it was his body, and Papa was at the window, leaning halfway out, whooping joyfully at the rain. When he ducked back in, his hair was wet and there were drops of laughter in his eyes. He scratched his Poseidon-like mane and set to work again with redoubled zeal, hopping over to the wall like the Transcaucasian Butcher from the wrestling matches on Lebanon TV. Aron quickly returned to his seat and sank inside himself, listening to his blood throb with the mighty hammer blows, with the ponderous footsteps anxiously pursuing him.

Papa banged uninterruptedly for a time, during which Aron never

THE BOOK OF

once opened his eyes. At seven o'clock Mama proclaimed "Enough!" but Papa shook his head defiantly and continued to strike the wall, and Mama shouted "Enough!" again. Aron lazily opened his eyes, amazed to find that a whole hour had gone by, where was I all that time, and again Papa assailed the wall, drunk with the rain, or maybe he hadn't heard her, but he didn't stop when she shouted a third time either, everyone was sitting up by then, looking from Mama to him; he was like a giant coil unsprung, and the holes in the wall gaped wider, sometimes a single blow was enough to join two holes together, but Papa would purposely delay the final blow, as if sensing Edna's anticipation behind him; ten minutes went by, and still he didn't stop, and Aron sat attentively, with his feet pressed together and an impassioned smile on his face; this is Papa, my papa, without shame, without guile, like Samson the hero, a runaway lion, a giant geyser suddenly erupting; and there before Mama's monumental silence and Edna's languishing eyes, Papa ran through the gamut of his styles; circus ponies and elephants, torches and tigers, acrobats and clowns, sheer talent he displayed, his body as the paintbrush of his soul, though he unabashedly wore the motley too: because it was him, and he was in command, he could even play the fool with dignity: he could strike the wall like a whirling dervish, or deliver a side blow with an elegant flourish, transform it into a mountain cliff or a coquettish woman with a gleam in her eye. And there were rousing, one-handed blows; and hammer slides across the wall like a caress on the head of a darling child; or the sudden assaults of a hero rescuing his damsel from an enchanted rock. Watch, thought Aron, watch carefully.

Papa's magnificent encore lasted forty-five minutes. Edna Bloom leaned forward, staring so hard she seemed to see strange new vistas inside her, cleaved by the blade of a giant plow, or the huge propellor of a ship. Even the noise didn't disturb her, she who had always slept with cotton flying out of her ears; she who had been taught the secret of Tantra yoga by a gentle Indian student in London some years before but had never dared to take that plunge in her building, because what if, at the supreme moment of silent meditation, when the kundalini serpent rose up from the lowest chakra and wound its way through the five brains to the third eye, the locus of union, she should happen to hear a disturbing shout from a nearby balcony or a toilet flushing somewhere. She knew now that she was longingly anticipating not merely the reverberation of the sledgehammer in her bowels but everything that went with it: the smell of his exertion, the beads of sweat, and the words exchanged over the past three days among her visitors, and the ensuing silences, all abuzz with secret communications, unintelligible to her; the father, and the son watching him with adoration; and the pudgy teenage daughter glowering at her mother; how wrong she had been about them! She rebuked herself: they had seemed so pathetic to her with their lumpish sheep faces. You were wrong, you were wrong, Edna, see how the air around them shimmers, and learn a lesson from this; maybe you were wrong not only about them but about life itself, about everything, go on, have a good cry, maybe you came close to dying, and maybe you were almost, she gulped and uttered the ghastly word, barren.

In silent gratitude she bowed to Mama, who only turned away. Then she glanced imploringly at Aron, whose eyes widened at her, and her heart soared for a moment, till Mama glared at him, and like a chick warned by the mother bird of approaching danger, he sealed his face to hide the living glow in his eyes, but he blushed for shame. What we have here is a tiny tribe with strict, even pitiless laws—she melted—a violent and repressed civilization. She had not felt such a trembling inside since the day she arranged her *National Geographic*s according to subject and country.

At a quarter to eight that evening Papa flourished his hammer one last time. A snag of plaster, hanging from the ceiling, crumbled down. The wall disappeared and there on the opposite wall was *Guernica*. Papa stood still, his hammer on his shoulder, studying the picture as though he had just noticed it the first time. Mama took a deep breath. Carefully she folded her knitting. Edna Bloom, worn out and blearyeyed, could barely sit up in her dusty chair.

"Schoin," said Mama. "Pay what you owe and we'll be leaving."

Papa laid his hammer down and slumped as he hesitated before turning to look at the women.

"I have an idea," said Edna nervously.

Mama froze.

"I will pay Mr. Kleinfeld another fifty pounds to tear down the other wall as well." She pointed limply to the second bedroom wall. Without so much as a glance at Mama she revealed the wad of moist bills she had been clutching for the past four hours and set them on the table.

Mama looked down at the five-pound notes, with the picture of a muscular farmer holding a hoe, young and virile, staring out at her. "Miss Bloom," she said, her bosom rising, "I spit on your money." Never had Aron seen her so red. "There's something wrong with you, you're not normal. You let everyone see what's going on in your head. My husband is a respectable man, Miss Bloom, and what I think is that you should go live in an insane asylum, where you'll be taken care of." Aron's knees began to shake. It wasn't like Mama to tell strangers to their faces what she usually said behind their backs.

"Sixty pounds, then," said Edna Bloom, turning to Papa.

"Over my dead body," said Mama, not budging.

"Seventy."

Mama gasped. Before her eyes danced fur-lined boots, a new set of dinner dishes to replace the old ones from their wedding that looked as if they came from the flea market, a new steam iron, a modern foam-rubber mattress to replace the straw one, a new marble counter for the kitchen to replace the cracked . . .

"Your money is dirty," croaked Mama, never taking her eyes off the moistened wad, which seemed to come to life and reach out to her. "I spit on it," she muttered weakly, but didn't spit.

"A hundred," ordained Edna with astonishing composure.

"If Moshe's willing. I'm not." She tottered out the door as scalding tears of humiliation ran down her cheeks, and this was Mama, Mama who would rather die than give anyone the satisfaction of seeing her cry.

Papa gathered up his tools, glanced at Edna with gratitude and stifled excitement, and went out the door, followed by Yochi. Aron remained behind a moment more, obscured between the piano and the wall. Here, this was his big chance to speak to her alone. To confess: I feel so happy in your house, so at home, and you're nice, pay no attention to what they said to you. It's only words. But she didn't even know he was there, she stood with her back to him and began to gasp with laughter. Aron crouched down. She raised her voice again, wreathing herself round with sobs of pleasure, ticklish spasms, as though this laughter could release her very soul. Her wispy yellow hair floated around her face. Aron dared not move. For a moment he didn't even recognize her. It was as if a stranger in her skin were shaking her. Slowly she calmed herself, raised a slender forefinger, and pointed thoughtfully at the bedroom wall. Then another wall. And another, and another, while endless tears of mirth rained down over her dust-powdered cheeks.

THE BOOK OF

19

Mama declared she would not set foot in Edna Bloom's or speak to Papa until he finished the work there. At night Papa took out the scrimpy Gandhi mattress he brought back from reserve duty once and slept in the salon. Mama ordered Yochi to fill in for her at Edna's, but Yochi had exams coming up, so was excused. I'll go, ventured Aron cautiously, and Mama gave him a dirty look; she didn't trust him, maybe she thought he was too young, or then again, maybe she thought he was getting to be too much like Papa. If only he could bring himself to ask her why now, he wouldn't have to agonize endlessly over that look on her face, but at least she didn't say he wasn't allowed to go, and if he went, he would be representing the family.

How long does it take to tear down a simple wall? About four hours. But how long did it take Papa to tear down the second wall at Edna Bloom's? Five days. God Almighty, Mama screamed in silence from the Bordeaux sofa, where she lay with an ice pack on her head, that's enough time to create the earth and the moon with the stars thrown in, and to the neighbors listening outside, Papa seemed to be prolonging every blow, searching for the vulnerable point in the wall, the tender nerve center of wires and pipes and rods, so it would collapse at his feet in perfect resignation. As soon as he arrived each day Edna would serve him a glass of freshly squeezed orange juice, a large glass for him and a small one for Aron. But she isn't smart like Mama yet, thought Aron, she doesn't know you're supposed to cover the glass with a little saucer so the vitamins stay in till Papa gets there, though the juice was no less delicious for that. Papa slurped and gulped while Aron sipped politely to correct the bad impression. "L'chaim," whispered Edna, beaming a smile, and took the glass from Papa's hand; a blush spread over their faces, and Papa stammered, Nu, where's the hammer, and Edna giggled, Here it is, it's waiting just for you; and before he'd even taken off his shirt, Papa struck a few blows at the wall to hide his embarrassment, or maybe he wanted to show the wall who's boss, but eventually he relaxed and got into his stride, and Edna swooned in her armchair.

Five whole days. Rapture. Too bad his wife stopped coming, though, reflected Edna, really and truly this is what she thought; despite the woman's coarseness and her perplexing insults, Edna regretted that she and the girl had disappeared: because they too were needed here, to complete the picture and the pleasure too; she was fond of the quiet, sad-looking boy, but didn't they once have a bigger child, no, she was probably mistaken; sometimes he would look up at her in a way that made her want to hug him, to comfort him. There was something wrong with the boy. Worms perhaps: he headed for the bathroom almost as soon as they stepped through the door, and sometimes he stayed in there for hours, whatever did he . . . a naughty smile played on her lips. Ooo, such dirty thoughts! she scolded herself, but who knows, maybe it's true about little boys that age. She stretched her limbs with mild sensual surprise, no, it couldn't be, here, in my house? And again she giggled, coyly, magnanimously: Oh, let him have a little pleasure, there's plenty to go around, and she bit her lip, surprised and blushing with the sudden realization of what the woman meant by those insults which only last night had seemed so preposterous, the charge that Edna and her husband were— She tittered at the notion, what an insane idea, to suspect her of THAT?! With HIM?! Or maybe it was the child the woman wanted to protect with her animal instincts? Edna threw her head back the way she had been doing these past few days, with a thrill of release and lightheartedness that ran all the way down her spine, and then to perpetuate this new private joke of hers, she left Aron a treat in the bathroom, a kind of friendly wink, nothing cheap or vulgar, heaven forbid, just a book of erotic Indian art, conspicuously placed on top of the magazine basket after she had leafed through it, it had been years since she looked at it, she remembered that picture of the prince and

THE BOOK OF

his inamorata, the prince inside his inamorata, drinking tea to prolong their ecstasy.

Aron would emerge from her bathroom looking weary and a little dejected; Edna watched him out of the corner of her eye, absorbed in the pounding of the heavy sledgehammer, as he staggered giddily back to his place like a sailor crossing the deck in a howling gale, and sat down with a sigh on one of her carpets; she noticed his favorite was the Armenian one, so she left a cushion there for him with a Bukharan coverlet, and he would stumble over—it was alarming to see a boy so tired—and curl up on it with drooping lids. From time to time she would glance over. Ah, the capacity of the young to sleep: in this horrible noise, with all the hammering and the storms outside, the boy would doze like a kitten. Inside her linen closet she found him a blanket imbued with memories, the one they had wrapped around three-year-old Nona on the long journey from Hungary to Palestine, with which, *ai-lee-lu-lee*, she covered him now. When the work was done, Papa would wake him. Son-of-a-gun, you fell asleep again. I did not. Go on, look how red your eyes are. I was awake, Papa, really. Were not, were not, you were sound asleep; and sometimes he could hardly wake him up, he had to shake him gently, or roughly, the boy was out like a light. Then Papa would raise him slowly to his feet, surprised at the way his drowsy limbs kept slumping back to the floor, and he would kneel before him, his big Gepetto face waxing serious, and lift him effortlessly in his arms, and Edna would pull his cap on over Papa's shoulder: Wait, it's covering his eyes, and he would whisper goodbye to her, and she would whisper goodbye to him, so as not to wake Aron, and on the way out Aron would cock an eye and nestle close to Papa, shivering with the cold, with the screaming black wind, and together now, they were together, they fled through the forest at midnight, in a wagon, in the storm, but yesterday something happened, shame on you, Edna, she and Papa forgot he was there, they simply forgot him, he was huddled in the corner, Edna didn't find him till later that evening when she heard Hinda calling his name from the balcony; she was alarmed and quickly went to search for him, and sure enough, there he was, sleeping fitfully on her carpet, gripping the fringe as though he were afraid to fall back to earth, his head tucked underneath the blanket, and for a moment, oh, let him stay, hide him here like one of the souvenir dolls, like the Greek legionnaire with the red hat and the long black tassel who so resembled the mustachioed gendarme she had tried to outface as he stood on guard at the palace in Athens, staring into his eyes for three sultry days, five hours at a time, until his duty was almost over, and then she would run off, only to reappear the following day; yes, she would keep the boy as a souvenir of the renovations, to remind her what happened here and how the wall trembled, and softly she woke him, and dressed him in his uniform, the thick green sweater and the oversized coat and woolen cap, and she led him, sleepwalking, leaning unsteadily against her shoulder, smiling out of a dream, down the stairs and along the path into his building, where she left him in a heap on the mat outside the apartment, knocked on the door for him, and fled.

In the morning as usual Papa went to the office. He would peek at his watch every other minute and push away the piles of tedious paperwork, musing, for the first time, that perhaps he had been wrong to listen to Hinda after the accident at the bakery seven years ago: for while he lay groaning with pain in the hospital, Hinda had been pulling strings, pleading, threatening, and when he finally regained consciousness, he learned that he had lost his cherished job at the bakery, and that Mama, with her own ten fingers, had converted him into an office clerk with pension rights. So his good friends at the bakery gave him a gold wristwatch, which he never wore, and the life of the night shift was suddenly over, the rugged labor he liked so well, the companionship on the dogwatch, the smell of baking dough, the soft plump rolls, a friendly grin under a floury mustache, a glowing cigarette outside the main door, the right to sleep through most of the day, hiding under his blanket from the burning rays of at least one fiery orb . . . Boy, those were the days, and look at him now, a paper pusher bickering with former friends about overtime and seniority.

Impatiently he reckoned the minutes, aching to get his hands on the sledgehammer, snatching pencils and snapping them in two like toothpicks. He couldn't wait to begin again: the constant hammering never weighed on his spirits; on the contrary, with every blow he felt that slowly, stealthily, something was being chiseled inside him: the delicate contours of his soul.

At six-thirty every day he would lay down his hammer and ask Edna with a wink to turn her radio on so he could listen to Reuma Eldar discuss recent flash floods in the northern Negev; Aron, sequestered on

THE BOOK OF

the carpet, opened a bleary eye to watch him, wondering why he had stopped hammering, and Edna too watched him nodding his heavy head. He seemed to be trying to decipher a secret message behind the simple words, intended for his ears alone. Never fear, Moshe's here, thought Aron, but why doesn't he keep working; the radio announcer spoke about vehicles trapped in riverbeds, and about crop damage at Kibbutz Or Haner. Papa pursed his lips and struck the wall, and Aron's head drooped down on his shoulder . . .

And one day Edna worked up the courage to fix Papa a whopping sandwich of spicy Hungarian salami, which she set down silently beside his glass of juice. For Aron too she prepared a roll with salami. Papa said nothing. Only his eyebrows twitched and his forehead turned red. Aron stared down at this sandwich. Oh no, he thought, oh no. "Aren't you hungry, then?" she asked distractedly, glancing at Papa. Oh no. Aron's head swerved right and left, this whopping sandwich with the fat salami slices. But she's a vegetarian, he screamed inside, unnerved, as Papa devoured the sandwich with gusto, emitting deep guttural noises; where are his manners, where's his breeding, lucky for him Mama isn't around to see, and he felt himself turn pale in the presence of those teeth, because she seemed to be mouthing the chewing sounds with Papa, and Aron stumbled off to the bathroom, perturbed and whimpering to himself, I should never have come here, with his left hand unconsciously clutching the right, choking the blood off at the wrist, but no, enough, you promised, you swore not to do that anymore, he loosened his fingers and stared at the white mark on his flesh. I should never have come, what's so great about watching him tear down a wall, but Papa's blows resounded in his heart, swiftly entering his bloodstream, forcing him to surrender; harder, harder he blinked, till tears came; maybe this way he could get rid of the bulge that was like a fist clenched inside, maybe a great gear would grind down, splitting it open, breaking through, and Papa seemed to overhear him: how strong he is today, the salami must have given him energy. It's for your own good, listen to the hammering, soon he'll burst through the blockage; this has been going on for almost two weeks, more problems, he's never had it so long before. Harder, harder, groans Aron, his lips compressed with pain, and out there, beyond the wall, Edna was feeding Papa more of that succulent salami to nourish the mighty machine of his body; he nibbles from her hand and goes on working, blasting and chewing. Be careful, Edna, be careful, but when she wasn't careful, the greedy jaws snapped shut on her slender pink finger, on her delicate palm, her dainty wrist, and still she didn't run; then her shoulder, her neck, he was gobbling and slurping and gnawing the fragile body . . .

The next day Edna asked Mr. Lombroso's permission to leave work for an hour. She walked into a grocery store in the old Nachlaot quarter, searched through the crowded shelves, and bought a jar of peppery Yemenite *skhug*. Later that evening Papa devoured the salami with *skhug* on both sides, and smiled at Edna with an appreciation that gave her butterflies. A few days later, instead of munching a sandwich during her ten o'clock break, she went out to the Machaneh Yehuda market, tremulously treading a sunbeam that illumined her path from behind the gloomy clouds, and arrived at the shish kebab grill. How beautifully unspoiled the market is, she mused, till a voice within her observed derisively, Really, Edna, have you forgotten that course on naïve art at the civic center? And she joined the voice in ridiculing herself. She stammered her order to the waiter, one Jerusalem mixed grill, and watched with trepidation as the swarthy young cook spread chunks of raw meat on the sizzling griddle, chopped an onion very small, and sprinkled out a handful of seasonings. Then she laced her fingers, shut her eyes, and waited.

A heaping plate of savory meat appeared under her nose. She took a breath, raised her shoulders, and set to. Zealously she ate up the spicy meat, drawing the attention of passersby with her big straw hat and the conspicuous gesturing of a benevolent tourist—oh yes, she noticed; suddenly she could see herself from the outside, devoid of self-hatred. Take your hat off, Edna, there, that's better, now ruffle your hair and smile at the boy who's watching you. Her shoulders dropped. Her buttocks relaxed into a pear shape on the seat of her chair. The waiter came over and asked if Madame wished for anything more. There was a suspicion of irony in his voice, but she managed to overcome a haughty twinge and see that he was young and smiling and awake, reminding her, to her surprise, of someone she might have met on her trips to Spain and Italy and Greece, or even the man in Portugal; why had it never occurred to her before that there were exciting men so close to home. She began to joke with the waiter, and flushed with pride at his approval of her homely wit and fluency in market slang, why, he might have thought she'd roamed the Machaneh Yehuda alleys all her life.

THE BOOK OF

She asked for a side order of fries and hummus, and the waiter, grasping her by the wrist, gave a demonstration of the proper way to roll the pita while you wipe your plate, like a fisherman, she noted, casting a net around her flanks. A squeal of triumph filled her throat: It's me, Edna! Perkily she dressed him up in her mind's eye, her waiter, shall we say, in baggy pantaloons with a golden sash, and perhaps a fez with a long black tassel and bandoliers crisscrossing his chest; sometimes a demon would possess her on her travels; she always made sure to visit a city that had a palace with a sentinel standing at the entrance, tall and proud, his eyes smoldering or furious, in a frenzy to prove to her he was a man of flesh, forced to stand immobile five or six hours a day—in Stockholm it was four—and the thought of this dark curly-haired young waiter guarding the gates of the palace, her palace, yes, she would be queen, was so thrilling that she threw back her head and let the pleasure slide down her spine. The waiter smiled at her, but quizzically. She called him over, joined heads with him, and sweetly entreated: Would he be willing to sell her, *ya habibi*, the meat for that dish, and would he tell her the secret, *ya habibi*, of the right way to season it? She winked at him mischievously and felt her cheek muscles contract; the waiter returned a tentative wink and hurried back to the grill, with a comment to his helper. Edna felt happy. Outside, the rain was pouring down, and she thought of the half-demolished wall awaiting her at home. Waves of cold befogged the restaurant window, and Edna unbuttoned her sweater, exposing her slender pink throat as she brushed back her yellow hair and saw herself briefly reflected in a mirror strapped to the roof of a passing car; oh, the wonderful surprises life can bring, perhaps she needed a new hairdo, something youthful, she would dye her hair red; she dipped her pita in the saucer of *skhug*, and her tongue caught fire. She fanned it with her hand like a Parisian saying *Oo-la-la*.

At home she roasted the hearts and livers and gizzards, and served them to Papa on a steaming platter. "You need your strength, Mr. Kleinfeld," she murmured, red-faced, her shyness seeming natural now, because finally, she reflected, after a twenty-five-year delay, she was becoming an adolescent.

What? Oh no! Not again! How could she, a woman with two years of university education, a world traveler who attended the theater and surrounded herself with paintings and sculpture and books—how could she have missed it. Oh, Edna, she giggled, let it happen this once, what harm would it do to lose your head like a heroine in a novel and fall in love, for a while, at least, with a donkey? But it couldn't be, she knew that. So what was this? What was happening to her all of a sudden? Edna laughed; she emitted another of those new squeals, releasing a knot in the top of her head. What a ridiculous idea, Edna! A person like you with a person like him . . . Why, I could toss him out of my life with a flick of my little finger, like this: but she stopped herself: Oh no you don't, you wicked little finger!

To her office mates she described at length the upheaval caused by renovating an apartment and the nuisance of having workmen about; they had never heard her talk so much before, some even complained to the boss, who called her in and asked solicitously if he could be of any help, and Edna with a little giggle said, Oi, Mr. Lombroso, dear, dear Mr. Lombroso, if only you could help me get rid of those workmen . . . But when she tried, for the fun of it, to replace him in her imagination with someone else, any other man waving a sledgehammer and grunting with exertion, she suddenly realized that the thrill was Moshe. And she was amazed. She tried to deny it. What's happening, Edna, where's our little finger, and the following day she made him a cheese and cucumber sandwich which he ate with indignation, even the boy stayed awake to watch, staring at her wide-eyed, in utter bafflement, as the man redoubled his blows that day, giving her to understand that at this rate he would finish the wall in no time.

Therefore, the following day she prepared him a whole roast chicken on a bed of olives she had purchased from the one-armed vendor at the market. They were getting to know and like her there; everywhere she turned they winked at her. Welcome, Madame, they greeted her in English. If you like eat very spicy, come to me, they called after her, slapping their thighs ecstatically when they saw her winking back; Papa devoured the chicken and sucked the bones in awe and gratitude, and Edna sank down in her armchair, abandoning herself to the delightful dance of man and wall. Now and then, after a particularly stunning blow, he would turn to Edna heroically, as though dedicating a modest feat to her, which she acknowledged with a nod. His stately Roman muscles would swell and throb for her. And sometimes, in the middle of a whirl, he would throw her a special look, shy but lusty, that seemed to pinch her spine out through the nape of her neck like a fishbone, till

THE BOOK OF

all she had left inside was mushy organs, sliding around in a ravenous cosmic mouth.

Outside, a storm was brewing, and the street, though it was early still, grew dark. For a while the only sound in the apartment was the pounding of the sledgehammer against the wall. On the six-thirty newscast there was a report about flash floods in the Negev again, two soldiers swept away in the overflowing Shikma River. Papa glowered out the window. When he struck a blow, erupting with fury, the heavens trembled and the lights blinked off.

Edna hurried to get a candle and lit it, shading the tiny flame with her hands. Papa struck another blow, his face hard as rock. Under cover of darkness Aron slinked off to the toilet, where he sat down, and shut his eyes in pain. He had to get away. Papa was out there smashing the wall, and the whole house trembled, boom, crash, boom, crash, like a relentless engine with hammers and pistons and boilers and compressors and crankshafts going up and down, banging and bashing, although maybe something was missing, he sensed vaguely through the surging waves of pain, hallucinating rods and pulleys, and iron arms to stoke the fire because there's not enough steam from the boiler room, and he writhes in agony, wringing himself, bearing down with his hands, pressing in from the waist, help, the pain would surely split him in two, squeezing his eyeballs with his fists till the sparks flew; his little angels of light, he turned them into shining stars, chose three that exploded with a flash, he could always find the flashing stars on the pages of the newspaper announcing: One thousand prizes! Send in six wrappers, win a cruise! There was soup mix and the Ampisal knitting machine deluxe, and for a smoother shave, use Diplomat; he managed to enter that one too somehow, but didn't win the gold watch or a ride in the glass-bottom boat in Eilat with Be Lovely as a Rose in Sabrina Hose, or even the consolation prize; three pounds he stole out of her purse each week, and again he was overcome with the pain, God knows what he had in there, what was that story in *Ripley's Believe It or Not*, "Three Hundred Amazing Cases," about the boy with the terrible stomachache, maybe he was about to give birth to something, maybe that's what happens with this disease, at the age of fourteen you give birth to a creature just like you, but maybe he ought to talk to someone about it, like Yochi for instance, because it's turning into a serious problem, two weeks to the day, and again he clasped his wrist to strangle it, to stop the circulation, then shook it disgustedly, no more of that, we quit for good, and he leaned back, perspiring, utterly spent.

Lightning slashed the somber sky. Thunder roared, and Papa retaliated with more pounding and smashing; Aron was out, asleep, unconscious, while deep inside him stalked the heavy giant, the lonely giant who ran after the children crying, Children, come back, come back to my garden, stumbling in his heavy boots, pounding his head in despair, and suddenly: What's this under the leafless tree, a little bundle. Why, it's a boy, the boy who didn't get away, lying in a faint, at the giant's mercy, and the giant bends down and gently lifts him in his arms; but suddenly Aron came to, sat up. Did you hear that, that hammering, it sounds different now. What do you mean different? It's hard to say, but Aron had learned to distinguish, and this was something new, maybe because of the storm outside, it was the first stormy day all winter, or maybe because of the roast chicken she served for his dinner, did you see the way he stuffed it into his mouth with both hands and gobbled it like a tiger; listen carefully, the rhythm is different, the tempo, the dynamics, and he leaned out the better to listen, and suddenly—what was that?—like someone tapping him on the shoulder as he slept, shaking him and whispering, Get up, it's starting, and now he was wide-awake; he pulled his pants on and ran quickly out to Edna, who sank deeper in her armchair, sucking her thumb, her eyes round with wonder, like a child listening to a bedtime story, he thought on the way to his seat by the window, fighting the heaviness that weighed on his lids—I am not falling asleep—he curled up under the blanket trying to get warm. Oh, why did I come, I decided to keep out of Papa's way, and how long can you sit here watching him tear down a wall, but will you listen to that; he listens: the hammering, the grunting, the hammering, the groaning, uh-huh, uh-huh, the hammering, the grunting, the hammering, the groaning, and Aron's head drooped down as though an invisible hypnotist had snapped his fingers, not sleeping, just dozing, mustering the strength to return, to return. Edna noticed him: What's happened to the child, he falls into a stupor, it's strange, a little worrisome, the way he has to struggle to stay awake, as soon as he gets here and curls up on the carpet, with all the noise, he falls asleep. The hammering grows louder, compelling, demanding. Me, me, it calls her, listen to me, but the sight of Aron troubles her, sleeping feverishly, whatever could have exhausted him so, and why here of all places, in her apartment, as though he only came for this, a kind of hypnotherapy, an operation performed under a general anesthetic . . . But the hammering. Listen, Edna, the grunting, the hammering, the groaning, the hammering, pay attention, there's something different there; it's driven, exasperated, running for shelter. She sat up in her armchair, nodding her head like an anxious bird, and Papa's hammer cried to her, cleaved to her: sometimes it struck despairingly, as though caught in a storm, calling SOS like a telegraph key; sometimes it was more like a prisoner tapping to find out if there was anyone in the neighboring cell. Oh yes, she nodded vigorously, oh yes, oh yes, there is, and then a mild shudder trickled through her, like a drop of aphrodisiac, even Aron heaved a sigh in his sleep, and she cocked an ear: Oh no, it can't be, but it was, it was addressed to her, intended for her, the hidden signs, the invisible writing, the secret letter smuggled in, and she stretched and listened, closing her eyes, throbbing and shivering like a delicate salamander from her head to her toes.

20

Once, at Komi, at the end of the day's work in the quarry, a stranger turned to Papa and asked to speak to him later that night, outside the barracks. Papa had qualms about him, but the man looked so puny, he figured he could beat him if it came to that.

The man's name was Molochinko, and he was one of the Urkas, the criminal element, who were brutal as animals, the only prisoners ever to attempt an escape across the frozen steppes. When a group of them broke out, they would take along a couple of lucky "politicals," this being—Papa traced a bitter smile across the wall—a political's only hope of leaving the camp alive. Molochinko informed Papa that a couple of Urkas were planning to break out the following night, and he had been chosen to go with them, since he looked strong enough to carry the provisions they would need on such an arduous trek. Papa was terror-stricken, but he agreed to join them. He had managed to survive two winters in Komi; a third, he knew, would kill him, and he would die again each day till then regretting the lost opportunity. That's how I was. Papa hacked at the wall, arching the muscles of his back like steel!

Crowds of big black clouds peeked into Edna's window, their cheeks swelling furiously over childish mouths. And one moonlit night the Urkas made their getaway. They had lavishly bribed the guards, who in any case did not believe they would survive in the taiga. After a few hours' march by the light of the icy moon, Molochinko sprained his

THE BOOK OF

ankle and had to stop. The Urkas huddled together and quietly conferred while the three politicals stood apart, in vague trepidation. At last the Urka chief, a murderer from Lithuania, announced that they would abandon Molochinko there. No one protested, and they set off again, but a little farther on Papa dropped out and sneaked back to the casualty: What could I do, I felt sorry for the mutt.

Molochinko was staggered to see him and wept in gratitude, clutching Papa's hands with his iron claws. The taiga wolves had caught his scent and were prowling nearby in the darkness. Papa lifted Molochinko onto his shoulders and carried him for days. After almost a week without any food, Papa cut himself with a knife and let Molochinko lick his blood. Molochinko sucked his arm, gazing up like an overgrown calf. When he finished he blurted out that the Urkas took politicals along to use for meat on the journey, and fell to his knees, begging Papa's forgiveness for having tricked him into joining the escape, with the excuse that he hadn't really known him at the time.

Now the hammer boomed to a heavy cadence, louder than the storm outside. And so, for weeks—or was it months, who knows—Papa and Molochinko roamed the taiga. They lost their way, and the howling wolves that trailed them expectantly drove them half insane. Once they came across a skeleton with the cap of a political lying beside it. Molochinko crossed himself and peered at Papa anxiously. The sledgehammer reverberated, hard and dull, pausing each time like a cannon saluting the dead. There was nothing but pine forest and tundra as far as the eye could see. They slogged around in circles, up to their knees in the snow, stranded on the vast palm of Nature, terrified of disappearing without a trace in these infinite expanses. If not for Molochinko, said Papa, I would have sunk in the snow and waited for the Angel of Death.

Ai, Molochinko. Papa struck again, while Edna cringed in anticipation of what she read on his rippling back. Molochinko was a petty thief, a sardine from Odessa. He was arrested for stealing a consignment of streetlamps, so they sent him to the Hotel Komi for the rest of his life. Papa chuckled to himself, and Edna saw Molochinko on the wall, sketched with a few crude strokes as a shapeless but sprightly man full of merriment and chatter. Uh-huh, nodded Papa, that's him all right.

Molochinko spouted witty anecdotes, hollow abstractions; he joked obscenely, flattered Papa, and exasperated him, working hard to maintain a kind of standard of human emotion in the heart of the ice. Together they learned to hunt birds with a slingshot and eat them raw, those brightly feathered birds, Miss Bloom, that sang so prettily, it was a shame to eat them, and once they had to fight a pack of dogs off a deer carcass. And there were herds of wild horses, small and lithe, galloping fleetly over the horizon. At night he and Molochinko would sleep in a tree, tying themselves to the trunk by a rope like criminals hanging from the gallows. One night Papa awoke with a feverish start, and saw that the taiga, glowing pale in the moonlight, was aswarm with crouching wolves that gazed patiently up at him like masked humans with cold, indifferent eyes, the faceless members of a thousand committees, who sent the likes of him to die in the taiga, and he began to beg them for mercy, he was a man like them, he wanted to live, to love a woman, but then he woke out of the trance, realizing he was delirious. Actually I was more afraid of Molochinko than I was of the wolves, because if he'd seen how weak I was, he would have butchered me on the spot, that's right.

At last, after endless days of wandering, they reached the outskirts of a tiny village. Edna Bloom took her thumb out of her mouth and listened intently. Papa's chest heaved like a bellows, and Aron cocked his eye: the low clouds overhanging the window seemed to have rallied to a secret cry; they puffed their cheeks and spat, as if trying to put out a forbidden flame. Papa and Molochinko lay low: the villagers were ignorant serfs who subsisted by growing beets and stealing the logs that floated down the river. Papa smashed the wall, tucking his head between his shoulders to hide from the resounding boom: the entire building groaned like a ship ramming into an iceberg, the naked plane tree screeched like a topmast; three days later, Papa and the robber of streetlamps discovered a woman locked up in the farthermost hut of the village. The captive's husband worked outside the village and forbade his wife to leave their home. Twice a day some old crone would pass her a bowl of pottage through a hatch at the back. The two men ogled the slender arm reaching out to take the dish. Go to him now, murmured Edna all of a sudden. Go to him, wipe the sweat from his brow, bring him a glass of water. Without ulterior motives. Just to let him know there's another human being in the room.

The following night Papa kneeled down on the frozen ground, and Molochinko climbed on his back and slipped in through the hatch. Papa

THE BOOK OF

could hear a muffled cry of surprise inside. Then a thud and a curse. Then silence, panting, and a startled groan. And silence again. And gentle weeping. Papa crouched in the darkness, in the shadow of the hut. Then, after a pause, he heard a harmonica tweedling inside, slowly and shyly at first, then mounting and bursting with life—Aron's eyes were opened now: Come on, it's time to go, I have homework to do, what's taking so long? In the early dawn Molochinko shook his shoulder to wake him and they hurried back to the forest. In his hands he held a quarter of a sausage, a whole potato, and a chicken egg. A smile of pride spread over his lips. He held his fingers under Papa's nose. Papa sniffed the fingers and shivered, then grabbed them and licked them and sucked them, unconscious that his feet were taking him back to the hut: Molochinko had to hit him over the head to bring him to his senses. And that's the truth, Miss Bloom, I'm sorry to say.

Molochinko babbled frenziedly, explaining that the door was latched shut and the serf had the key. That the hatch was too small for Papa to climb through. But inside, he told him, there was fresh food and enough provisions to keep them going for days, and the woman, *aiaiai*, he drew two undulating curves in the air. Papa hung on to the robber's every word and asked a thousand times if there might not be some way of getting him into the hut. Again the taiga seemed to him like a massive prison where his youth would wither in the bud.

Papa gulped hard, as though swallowing the bitter memory. Then he started hammering again. Edna listened, but the blows sounded hollow, reluctant somehow. Why did he have to break his story off? Pale and pouting, Edna stood up. She paced the room, nearly tripping over Aron, advancing toward Papa, then stumbling backward, till suddenly she was sitting at the piano; not bothering to wipe the dust away, her fingers flitted over the keyboard, searching for something, scanning her repertoire. Aron listened with his mouth open: what a strange, wispy melody. A slow, disorderly tinkling that burst wildly into song. He had heard it before. Papa too stood motionless, then nodded his heavy head as he followed the slippery tune with his lips, lighting after it, amazed at how it spurted out of the piano, and suddenly he could feel it hovering over his face, twisting and frolicking; he stuck out his tongue and snatched it up and licked it, beaming as it clung to his puffy lips, and he flourished his hammer and struck again with a silent whistle, the one that irritates Mama, and even kept time with his foot till Edna smiled to herself and slowly shut the piano: We don't need you anymore, we found what we were looking for . . .

The following night they returned to the hut. And they did it again: inside, Molochinko copulated with the woman, while outside, Papa kneeled, his ear to the wall, listening for their groans of pleasure, for the dregs of a passionate moan. Molochinko came out with a great supply of words for him. The way she smiled; the tender flesh of her inner thigh; her soft flowing hair . . . Papa listened, swallowing his spit. Molochinko allowed him to sniff his fingertips: Remember now, no biting.

And then one night . . . Papa hammered gently, with a trembling heart, and Aron jumped up and threw the blanket off: Why does she always have to cover me up, why do I come here day after day, it's a miracle my head doesn't explode from all the hammering, how long can you sit and watch someone tearing down a wall, and he tiptoed out, afraid they might stop him in his tracks with a resounding shout, or the boom of the sledge, and force him back to listen, and so, sidling up to the door, he stood there dizzily, with his hand on the knob: Maybe I got up too suddenly, it'll pass, another second and I'll be out of here and I'll never come back, what a bore.

. . . One night Papa caught a glimpse of the crone in the next hut peering out the window. He decided not to wait for Molochinko and went back to their hideout in the forest. The robber of streetlamps returned around dawn, bragging and swaggering without cease. An unfamiliar urge for vengeance seeped into Papa's heart. An ancient outrage. He said nothing to Molochinko about the old crone next door. The enraptured lover described the bright-colored cap the woman had started knitting him, and the holy icon over the bed which she piously turned to the wall each time, and the fullness of her lips as she blew on the harmonica—there was a look on Papa's face that made Molochinko uneasy, and he slowed down but couldn't stop entirely: her breasts, he said, raising a hand to caress them, so warm and soft beneath his cheeks, sending out their milky vapor; and Papa's eyes never left Molochinko, stunned by the murderous hatred in his heart, the hatred of the meek for the braggart, the hatred of Cain for Abel.

The night after, I crouched outside the hut again as usual; there were eyes in the back of my head, though, and Molochinko jumped up on me, hippety-hop, and in through the hatch, and I turned and ran in the opposite direction; I was an animal in those days, for better or worse I was an animal, that's how I got out of the ice, Miss Edna; he was pounding with his whole body now, pressing his chest and loins against the wall, and Aron thrust the door open and fled, down four steps at a time, home through the rain, through the darkness, straight into bed with all his clothes on, with the blanket over his head, training himself in secret like a sumo. And so, Miss Bloom, Miss Edna, I ran for maybe half the night, till I couldn't hear the dogs barking or the people shouting anymore, but all night long I saw the smoke rising out of the hut, and I never even knew the woman, only her smell.

With all his might he smashed the wall. A last chunk of stone was stuck between the bricks and he waved his hammer at it. Another bolt of lightning zigzagged across the sky, but lassitude leaked in between the raindrops, as though all the spunk had gone out of winter. Papa bellowed hoarsely and struck again. And again. Edna sprawled in her armchair, all-seeing though her eyes were shut tight, with an unfamiliar violence whirling up from the abyss inside her, causing her little frame to tremble and shake; a spark flew out of the somber sky, and a bolt of lightning spat fire, but the rain had relented. Papa groaned again and paused: the rest of the wall caved in. Lightning hissed with rancor and recoiled, and there was a moment's silence. Then the clouds began to fade into the distance, withering as they mounted higher, like an assembly of grumbly old men.

Somewhere a window opened. The lamps in the street went on. The apartment was filled with a gentle light. Papa sank down, utterly exhausted. He raised his heavy head in search of Edna and was surprised to find her crouching under the piano, her arms crossed over her knees. Her eyes caressed him with tender compassion. And he smiled at her apologetically, as though waking from a dream, reflecting how young she looked, how fragile, not much older than his Aron.

"This wall is finished," he said at last in a husky voice.

Edna stood up and stumbled and sank down again. She laced her fingers as tightly as she could to stop the trembling. Papa approached and stood limply before her, waiting for her to say something. When he looked he saw her bashful smile, the gleam of mischief in her eyes, and her finger pointing at the kitchen wall.

"Hinda will want more money," he said. This was his first mention of Mama, and the way he said her name filled Edna with glee, as though the two of them had become conspirators against her.

She thought a moment. Her bank clerk, a little man who behaved like a tall one and always tried to flirt with her, had warned: profits on the fund that paid for her annual summer trip were poor this year; she shuddered at the thought, but suddenly imagined the way he moved his hips, and something inside her, a bucking bronco, whinnied and stamped before the gaping bespectacled eyes of the clerk. "A hundred and twenty," she said in a scintillating voice.

"No, no," said Aron's father. "That's too much. It isn't a very big wall."

"But it may be tricky. It's probably crawling with electric wires." She smiled.

"Excuse me for asking, Miss Bloom, but where do you get all the money?"

She smiled a little smile, cryptically feminine, the kind of smile she'd always despised. It succeeded nicely. She smiled again.

"It's late now," said Papa, peering out the window. The gloomy clouds were drifting away, gnawing each other spitefully. Papa weighed the hammer in his hand and brandished it at the window. "We can't start today," he said, "we have to wait until tomorrow, if that's okay with you, Miss Bloom."

"Tomorrow is Friday," she answered, still smiling. "And my name is Edna."

He blinked at her, distraught, recalling something faraway, impossible, staring wildly at the swift yellow animal flapping her tail, and Edna was amazed to see that even his eyes were throbbing. Like a giant he towered over her, her narrow waist, her slender thighs, and on the wall outside that led to her entrance some brat, maybe Zacky Smitanka, had scribbled a nasty jingle about a bull and a mouse who want to play house, the coarseness of which estranged them. Suddenly, Papa swerved around, waved his hammer high, and struck a blow at the kitchen wall. Aron shivered in his sleep. The hammer remained at Edna's over the Sabbath, implanted like an ax inside her wall, where it vibrated uninterruptedly, emitting shock waves in concentric circles.

THE BOOK OF

21

Mama stood in the kitchen, cooking lunch. Her hands went through the motions like a pair of trusty horses as she sank in contemplation of the sudden turn her life had taken, thanks to a certain Hungarian Miss Eegan-meegan; thanks to her idiot of a husband too, who, like all men, had a tendency to lose his head at the first scent of fresh meat; three weeks, she reckoned, this farce had been going on, sapping her strength, preventing her from attending to any number of tasks; when was the last time she repapered the kitchen cupboards, for instance, or changed the mothballs in the linen closet, or sat down for a talk with Aron; the child was going out like a candle before her eyes, what was happening to him, it wrenched her heart, he would doze for days like somebody's grandfather, it was having an effect on him, all this, all this . . . She searched for the appropriate word, but caught a whiff of a strange odor that made her lose her train of thought, and she turned her attention back to the pot in front of her, stirring gradually.

Who would have believed it, such a thing happening to us, she sighed, a model family. Mechanically she tasted the soup, added a pinch of salt, stirred joylessly. She had even stopped worrying her head about Edna Bloom in the past few days. If nothing had happened so far, chances were it wouldn't. Passions are like fruit, she whispered to her image in the shiny pot, pick them when they're ripe or they rot on the tree. Again she caught a whiff of the unfamiliar odor, impelling her hands to stir more vigorously, and when this is over, and Moshe comes home with his tail between his legs . . . she crushed a clove of garlic, added a tablespoon of oil, and began to peel the vegetables for another soup: a vegetarian I've got me now, on top of everything, the food I make him isn't good enough anymore, the boy's a regular fein-schmecker. He has more pity for a chicken than he does for me here, killing myself to cook his dinner. But then the odor pierced her nose and startled her out of these ruminations.

For a full fifteen years Mama had lived in this dingy-gray building project, and she knew the luncheon menus and baking repertory of the housewives inside out, shrewdly identifying each curlicue of smell in the tangled skein of aromas that wafted out of their kitchens.

So it must have been appalling, a veritable stab in the belly, when these undreamed-of smells infiltrated the familiar ranks, assailing her nostrils with a gypsy effrontery, a fandango of exotic spice. Still ablaze with the memory of her debacle, Mama lost her head, picked up her umbrella, put on her heavy Khrushchev, and walked out the door. Down the stairs to the muddy, neglected garden she hurried, turning left and right. She sniffed the air. Where was it coming from? Dreary gray rain had been drizzling down for the past few days. She flared her nostrils, shut her umbrella so it wouldn't get in the way, and marched ahead, nose in the air, her goiter bulging toadishly till, all at once, in back of the house, she inhaled an aromatic cluster that burst in her nose like a bustling bazaar and filled her heart with foreboding.

It was almost noon. The children were not yet home from school. The rain fell dully, undeviatingly down. The days of heavy downpours were over, it seemed; winter had reached its peak too soon, and now there were only wishy-washy showers. She scrambled up the growing mound of debris under Edna's window and sniffed the air. Here, on top of this monument to her own defeat, with her nose in the clouds, she was struck by a distinctive odor—no mere kitchen scent with sea-sonings this, but a rarefied female perspiration mingling with the cook-ing, that special smell Mama remembered all too well from bygone days, which came of a woman's stirring herself into the pot and spraying it with the musk of her intimate longings. Mama climbed down the mound, like a hen deposed from a refuse heap, and shambled home, brokenhearted.

She stood in the kitchen, wearing her apron, leaning against the marble counter, which had been stained and cracked over the years in a faithful, unflattering reflection of her life. Furtively, tormentedly, she took another whiff, and shuddered: it wasn't just an unfamiliar smell anymore but a whole new language. Like an animal she sniffed, holding back her tears so as not to lose the scent. The humiliating part was that Papa had never so much as hinted he was dissatisfied with her cooking, or susceptible to a craving for other food; suddenly she remembered and cringed with pain, his farts had a different smell to them lately; as a matter of fact, she realized to her indignity, for the first time since she'd met him, he let them out on the sly instead of tooting unabashed. Again she sniffed and flared her nostrils, drawing in all the errant odors. And thus, with fists clenched on the kitchen counter, did Mama learn the culinary language of her rival. Despondently she returned to the chicken soup mit lokshen, the noodles floating in the watery broth Moshe liked so well. Tfu! She almost spat out her biliousness, then settled herself on the "little cripple," crossed her arms over her breasts, and stared in the air. Only when Aron's nervous cough reached her ears did she shake herself out of it, disappointed to discover that for the first time since early youth she was sitting in her kitchen as she worked.

Aron slinked off to his room and lay on his bed with open eyes, kneading his sore, distended belly. Rain fell outside the window, blurry, watery, insipid. Sure has been raining, reflected Aron, listening to the pitter-patter; first there were floods, and the tree out front, that plane tree, almost collapsed, I mean the entire building creaked and groaned. He yawned. Shut his eyes. Maybe he would catch a few winks before lunch. Before the main siesta from two to four. Or the nap from four to seven. Brilliant of those grownups to come up with the siesta. It used to drive him crazy to have to lie down after lunch when there was a whole world out there. But he was calmer nowadays. And in any case, there wasn't much to do, he'd been having a kind of dead spell lately, like a hibernating bear, and what was the use of going out in this rain, in this spray like a thick gray veil, in this mizzle and drizzle. And Papa was missing beyond it.

Aron hadn't been to Edna Bloom's for days. The booms were heard less frequently now. Papa was working with a drill, with a chipping hammer and a chisel; his tools were getting smaller and smaller. Sometimes he seemed to be doing nothing at all, maybe he was just sitting on the floor there, lost in thought, listening, wondering. From time to time a passerby would see him loom statuelike in the window, staring out at the tepid rain. Then he would suddenly shake himself awake, rub his eyes ill-humoredly, and start pounding the wall again, only to languish a moment later. And once or twice a day, his powder-white mane would lean out the window as he threw a bucketful of debris onto the rising mound below. Yesterday on Aron's way home from the trash bins, he saw Papa in the window like that. Papa stared blearily, meshed with sleep, not quite seeing or recognizing him. Aron stood motionless, with arms outstretched, hidden in the coat with the sleeves that came down over his hands, his tummy sticking out for all to see: his little pregnancy, a medical specimen, a dry fact. For a moment Papa's eyes grew wide. A trace of disillusion shot through them. I've been like this for three whole weeks, Aron thought at him with all his might, you have no idea how much it hurts. Papa shook his head in disbelief. Or maybe he was only shaking the dust off, because he promptly went in and shut the window, and curtains of trickling rain closed over it, and once more his hammer blows resounded, urgent, angry, like banging on the doors of a moving train, and Aron hurried to his secret hiding place at the Wizo Nursery School, maybe now, at long last; he looked down with revulsion at his little potbelly, calling to Papa in his heart, encouraging him: Harder, harder, come on, we'll make it, but he knew Papa was too far gone by now, he recognized this wordlessly, trudging through the snow-covered steppes, hunching his shoulders as he thrust deep into winter, and Aron stood up and shuffled wearily home. He dived under the blanket, under the roots of lights, forgetting Papa, who had disappeared, who had wandered beyond the storms, beyond thunder and lightning, those childish displays of an amateur-winter, and who would tell him he was going astray, that he was running in circles like a huge, blinkered mule around a grindstone, inscribing frozen rings on the ice, but Papa doesn't hear as he goes on pounding, soullessly, with lackluster eyes, striving to destroy the site where winter was begotten, the place where there is no day or night, a barren clifftop, gleaming blue like a marble egg, the winter's heart where the winds draw their chill, which Papa will smash to release a warm little chick . . .

From the kitchen he could hear the clatter of dishes. Mama was setting the table. Soon she would call him in to eat. But how would he put anything in his mouth. As if there were any room left for food in there.

THE BOOK OF

He curled up on his side, not daring to lie on his stomach. If he were a mensch, if he had the strength, he would get up and do something: he had a math quiz tomorrow, there was Bible homework to do, at the very least he could straighten out the mess in his bottom drawer. It was impossible to find anything in there with all the bottle caps and labels and newspaper clippings and trademarks and Popsicle sticks and lottery tickets, who would have believed there were so many contests, and this morning he made a vow that from now on he would send in at least one a day, a brain twister or a completed jingle or a crossword puzzle, or "Find the Seven Differences," at least that much he ought to do, because what else did he have to occupy him lately, sleeping, waiting, wasting his life. And he heaved a sigh. Once he loved summer. Then he started preferring winter. The pale colors, the warm steam of his breath that left a smell in the woolly mouth of his stocking cap; and winter clothes are thick, so at least they make you look a little bigger. But this winter has been tough for him. And the rain is deceptive: like nothing much, but the cold pierces through. Every day on the radio they tell about chickens freezing to death. Crops destroyed by frost. Aron feels cold too. Like not enough blood is circulating maybe. He nestles inward. Worn out.

"What's with you?" Yochi walked in, home from school, and threw down her satchel. Up went his knee. So they'd know there was a body under the blanket. "Open the window, how can you breathe in here?" Why did everybody open the window whenever he was in the room. "But it's cold out." She relented and lay down on her bed, massaging her temples, panting with stifled rage, with misery. Who knows what was going on with her friends at school. How they treated her there. She never discussed them with him. Never mentioned names or admitted she was jealous of the ones who had boyfriends now. Never went to parties at school. Maybe Yochi was the Shalom Sharabani of her class. Quiet. Unobtrusive. Knowing. Once she used to share her thoughts with him. They would have these little talks at night before they fell asleep. They'd hide in their parents' linen closet, leaving the door open just a crack for air, and Yochi would make up stories for him, what a wild imagination she had; he didn't remember the details, only her soft, flowing voice, and the smell she gave off as she sat facing him on the chest of drawers, a special girl scent that got stronger and stronger as the story reached its climax, and then there was their secret code, the last one home from school would ask: Is A B? Meaning: Is Mama angry? And what about that friend of hers, Zehava, thought Aron, straining, indifferently, to fulfill an old duty. Who was Yochi to him now? When did they start to drift apart? Until a couple of weeks ago they had been close, they loved each other. Where were the beautiful years of their togetherness? And maybe she'd wind up marrying a big fat rich guy, dumb but sensitive, who would build a special room in the house for Aron. That would be Yochi's condition for marrying a man she didn't really love. And her children would play with him. One of them would look a lot like Aron, and they would be very dear to each other, but he would die young. And the other two, a son and a daughter, would be wilder and brattier. They would throw Aron around like a ball and take away his Houdini equipment and seal him in an enormous pickling jar, and sit there staring at him from outside, pressing their noses against the glass, it's a good thing Yochi walked in just in time to rescue him. And when Mama and Papa came to visit them once a year, Yochi would bring Aron out. And they'd sit around the table on her dainty chairs, while Aron and Yochi conversed in refined phrases, fragile words. And the salesman, Yochi's husband, would watch them with a contented smile on his face, though he wouldn't really understand. And Mama and Papa would sit there, meek and gray, awkwardly twiddling their forks, wondering whether it's okay to eat chicken with your fingers.

"Want a massage?"

"A massage?" he squealed. "How come?"

"No special reason. To thaw you out. You look frozen."

"Uh-uh . . . A massage, are you joking?" He shrank even more. With a little giggle. Staring fervently at the ceiling.

"You wait here. Take off all those layers of clothes, meanwhile." She jumped up a little overzealously and hurried to the bathroom, pursing her lips. He feared these militant moods of hers. It was exactly how she looked the time she took him into the living room to embarrass Mama in front of her card friends. He lay still. A little frightened. Unconsciously clasping the binding of his sweater. Drawers flew open in the kitchen. Plates clattered. Mama's angry. Don't move. Squinch yourself up and wait. It will all be over soon. How long can it take to wreck a house?

Yochi came back with a towel. And some cotton. And a bottle of 70

THE BOOK OF

percent alcohol. "Hey, come on. Start stripping." What did she want from him? Where'd she get all that vigor and vitality? "Come on, Aron. I know, you feel a little neglected, don't you? Everyone's busy with their own problems, huh? Say, how many layers of clothes are you wearing? How do you expect your body to breathe under all that armor?" She yanked off his sweater, his Leibeleh pullover, his undershirt. He shivered. Covered himself. Afraid she'd notice his swollen belly. "I can't believe you're shy in front of your own sister." She giggled irritably, tickling him under the arm. "Gitchy-gitchy-goo!" Her eyes were shining, but not with happiness. She was relentlessly playful. Rigorously jocular. Maybe she was going through something, the thought occurred to him, maybe someone had hurt her, insulted her. "Lie down straight. Nu, will you please lie down already!" He did. He rolled over, facedown. His stomach was distended. It looked weird. How long before he simply exploded. Yochi leaned over his half-naked body. A fresh, lemony fragrance bloomed in his nostrils. He knew with his eyes closed that she was rubbing in the cream Uncle Shimmik brought her from Paris. Lemon can be used for invisible writing. Now he cringed in anticipation of her touch. His impetuous body. "What are you— Hey, quit it, Yochi, I don't need—" "Shhhh! The whole world can hear you." Her palm was on his back. Near his spine. A cool, smooth hand, rubbing in the cream. Slowly warming. Drawing little whirls of softness on his skin to take away the chill. He squashed his face against the pillow. "Your back is in knots," she muttered. His finger drilled into the side of the mattress, found the hole there, poked at the crisp, curly fronds of Algerian seaweed, that's what it said on the label; what strength she has in her hands, her fingers press down on him, they crack him and knead him, she probably misses giving Papa massages, it's almost a month since he got one after the "thorough" but Papa has the kind of back you can really go wild on. "You're purring like a happy kitten," she whispered in his ear, giggling. "I hadn't noticed." Why was he whispering? Why were they both whispering? Under his helplessly goofy face, there was a sudden rustling of invisible seaweed as his finger bored deeper into the widening gap, into the tangled mass of kinky roots. All he could hear now was the sound of her grunts, who would have believed she was so strong. She was bursting with all that strength inside her. Why didn't she go out and tear down a couple of walls? He managed to open an eye in his pancake face, saw her pudgy little foot beside the bed, pink and swollen, and breathed in the wondrous strangeness of it, that foot, God, you could sink your teeth into it and eat it up. Now Yochi settled on his tailbone, but it didn't weigh down or hurt too much, though the residue of his brains squirted out with a final groan, and the mattress creaked rhythmically beneath him, and Yochi's breathing in his ear, muffled, powerful, like his own, and her fingers and palms moving over his back and shoulders and down to his waist, unloosing, dissolving, flattening his flesh like a rolling pin, dividing him lengthwise, widthwise, propelling him onward, till a knife dropped suddenly, somewhere faraway; but she didn't stop, she galloped ahead, instilling in him a rhythm of open spaces, onward, onward, to the new frontier, rubbing him with her lemon cream, squeezing out an admission he denied before he even heard it: Stop, Yochi, enough. What is this—a few minutes ago he was lying here Aroning, and now, this; all right, he would make in his bed, like a baby, if only he could, at last, even in bed, but suddenly he felt a mysterious honey trickling down his spine, his neck and shoulders were imbued with strength and straightened out, awash in pungent perspiration; smooth and bold he rose from the mattress like the darkly glistening belly of a monster of the netherworld, spangled with a thousand papillary eyes. It's coming, it's coming, but where is it coming from, it's great, it's marvelous, only don't make a mess, and suddenly, before his dazed and blurry eyes, a figure approaches—watch out, it's all over—the figure of his mother, Mama, a sidelong gleam in her eye, an electric flash that fizzles out in the well of her pupil, and her mouth bolts shut, and with the kitchen towel in her hand she reaches out and swats at Yochi, at his burning back. What's the matter with you, have you both gone crazy, I've got my own tribulations, I don't need you two fighting like a couple of five-year-olds, and Yochi held her hands up to protect her face, yowling and spitting at her like a cat: Just you wait, I'll enlist in the army right away. Too late, dearie, you've already signed up for a deferment and they'll never let you out of it. Oh yeah? Watch me, I'll declare myself a soldier without family and I'll never set foot in this house again. Who needs you home, you dirty cow, let your precious army pay your way; and Yochi covered her right ear with her hand, as Mama screeched to a desperate halt: We'll see how long they keep you in the army when they see the way you eat. Isn't the whistling supposed to be in her left ear, Aron suddenly wonders. Watch me, I'll marry a Kurd, you wait and see who I bring home to you. Who'd have you? Seen any amorous Kurds around here lately? And Aron buried his face in the pillow, which also retained the heat of his childhood, and the whisper, the trembling that seized him a moment ago and was severed halfway down his spine, where it retreated with a cool hiss, so what was that big thing that gripped the creatures of his back in one tyrannical fist and almost succeeded in squeezing something out of him, in bursting the bounds, before it melted, faded away.

Mama thrust the window open. You stunk up the whole room with your roughhousing, she grumbled, feigning anger, wide-eyed with a concern, with an astonishment that Aron could only sense. Are you a couple of little tots, raising such a rumpus and hitting each other, and she steered Yochi out of the room to set the table and, leaning over Aron, whispered, Who started it, tell me the truth now, who started it? And Aron, bewildered, gave the answer she demanded like one possessed: She started it. And even sobbed: Yochi did. She started it. Mama stood over him. Look what she's done to your back, the murderess, feh, why didn't you call me right away, it's a good thing I heard you. Lie down a minute. I see a big one with a yellow head. Lie still.

He buried his face in the pillow. No longer there. He didn't have the strength for this. Quietly he sobbed out the grief Yochi had caused him, he couldn't quite remember how, and nevertheless, his phony sadness choked his throat, a lozenge of misery melting down to relieve the bitterness of heartbreak.

Mama pinched the skin around the pimple. The hem of her bathrobe brushed against his puffy flesh. He waited for the prickle of pain, for the quick spurt. He arched his back: let it come already, let it out, let it hurt and be done with, but she suddenly winced. Pulled angrily away from his protruding rib cage, from his puny, disappointing body. Nu, get dressed already. I don't have time for you right now. Why are you looking at me like that? Take a look at yourself instead, why don't you ever wash? I can smell you clear over to here. And what have you done to your mattress! Look! With upraised fingers she charged at the mattress and tried to stuff the seaweed back in, You throw dancing parties on your mattress at night? You think we have the money to buy you a new mattress every other day? She gripped the frayed edges of the fabric and stuffed in more of the crimpy tangles, which managed to slip out between her fingers. Choleria take it, with you and your sister, will you look at this room, feh, how you stink, I pity the woman who marries you, and what are you doing lounging around here in the middle of the afternoon, you think this is a hotel or something?

"I'm tired."

"So I noticed. A boy your age, you should be"—she searched for the words—"sucking out life till it dribbles down your chin." Ha, what a life she thought, his father's turning into a regular he-goat and this one's like a piece of stale bread.

She was pacing up and down the little room, swatting his desk with the kitchen towel. Dusting. Grimly her arm went up and down. Aron felt sorry for her. Almost unconsciously he rolled over on his side, bowed his head, got ready for her to notice his ear.

"This morning I ran into Whozit—Zacky Smitanka," she said with an edge to her voice. Angrily she folded Yochi's blouse. In the army they'll make a mensch of her, she won't have any servants there; and still she hadn't noticed his expectant ear. "That Zacky, look at him and look at you." Aron was silent. He and Zacky hadn't spoken in months. Neither at school nor around the building. And in the interim Zacky built himself a Lambretta out of spare parts he'd found or acquired or maybe even stolen. His big brother Hezkel said he'd kill him if he ever caught him riding it before his sixteenth birthday, but when Hezkel isn't around, Zacky rides, and how he rides. Once he rode by Aron in the street, at night, on his Lambretta, with a girl hugging him from behind, maybe even Dorit Alush, because the legs around the Lambretta reminded him of those toy divers her father sold in his stall at the market. "He's miles ahead of you." Aron didn't utter a sound. He forgave her, in advance, for everything she was about to say. He could tell how miserable she was. Let her know at least that Aron was faithful to her. Maybe he had been a little confused at first. The hammering drove him crazy. Now it only bored him. The minute Papa started hammering, Aron fell asleep. He didn't even bother going to What's-her-name's to watch anymore. Faithful to the end, to Mama, in ways she couldn't even imagine. A dozen torturers wouldn't break him down on that score. "I saw him with his mother, Malka; she barely comes up to his shoulder. They almost look like a couple together." There was a different shade of envy in her voice, not the envy of a mother. Again he proffered his ear. A peace offering, a modest declaration of his loyalty. And she stood there, mocking him, holding out her

THE BOOK OF

hands despairingly, till finally, she was trapped: "What's that in your ear. It's like a warehouse in there." He concentrated on her eyes. The blank expression. The steely look when she forgets him and focuses on the yellow in his ear. But at least she wasn't thinking about her problems now. He took his time and studied her: first she wiped her finger on the other fingers. Little rubbing motions, like a fly about to dine. "Sit up straight. Let me get it out."

She sat him down. Bent his head. Carefully inserted her finger and began to pick. Digging deep. Saying, as if to herself, Zacky's miles ahead of you, what a physique, oho, what a walk, he's a man already, wait, stop squirming; he surrendered to the burrowing finger. But through it he made his way into her, into her ever-swelling heart, like a huge purple grape bursting with juice, the heart she used to clasp him to once upon a time, when he was a little boy, before the problems started, and thinking about it he could feel what was sticking in her throat, a pillar of salt she had sticking in there, sternly separating her kindly heart from the words she uttered. She was more bitter than ever today. Something must have happened. She still wasn't over it. Pouring out her wretchedness, not to him, he felt, but to the dirt, her ancient adversary, her ally in reverse. "How long have you been storing that filth in there? Fourteen years old and your mother has to clean your ears for you. It's unbelievable. Give me the other one."

He turned his head obediently. Following her. She didn't even notice. She just kept digging, muttering to herself. And what a voice. Baaaa! Like a bull! When he talked I could feel the rumbling in my stomach! Would you mind explaining, just so I'll know, why your voice still goes peep-peep-peep, while his has changed already. And now you're turning into a vegetarian. As if one dowry wasn't enough. Look at those spindle legs. How do you expect to grow on lettuce and carrots? She wiped her finger on the kangaroo apron. Spreading the harvest around in little swirls. Suddenly she noticed his watchful, scientific gaze. Jumped up. Hid the apron behind her back, suspicious of an affront here. "Go look at yourself, Helen Keller Kleinfeld."

22

It took five days, by fits and starts, to tear down the walls in the kitchen and the hallway. Edna, meanwhile, went off to visit her parents in Bat Yam, where, much to the astonishment of her aged mother, she asked for instruction in the spellcraft of Hungarian cooking. Sitting beside her in their dingy grocery store, she recorded her mother's every wise, long-suffering word, with notes in the margins, and joked with her father as never before. In the evening the three of them went out to a restaurant. They asked no questions, were loath to interfere. Though they must have sensed something was amiss, they were too kind to spoil their daughter's pleasure. Edna gazed at them through eyes of love, cherishing their meekness, the old cobwebs of intimacy, the crumbs of merriment they allowed themselves. For thirty-seven years, since arriving in Israel, they had lived behind the store counter, and the only way Edna could envisage them was huddled together in the back like frightened sheep. And then, suddenly, for no apparent reason, she began to tell them things: about a romantic episode in Portugal eight years before with the banjo player from a little club, and their night together, which was more like a year; he was ready to give up everything and marry her, he was so foolishly smitten he asked for her ring as a keepsake, yes, the little red one they'd given her when she turned eighteen, and now she had a little diamond in Portugal . . . She shrugged with regret, with disillusionment, and they nodded silently, staring down at the plastic tablecloth. She'd written him several post-

THE BOOK OF

cards, first in English and, when he didn't reply, in Hebrew; she laughed, not because she missed him, but because she missed the person she had been with him, and maybe too, she realized only now, as she spoke, because she longed to transport a part of herself to a more lovely site. And then she told them of her years at the university, about her disappointments there, strange that she had never shared this with them before, and they could hear what she left untold, the story of acquaintances never made, friendships never formed; she had felt like a little mouse among the sophisticated students with their silver tongues, but when she needed blood after her operation, nobody came forward except you, Father, you took the bus all the way to Jerusalem and gave your blood . . . She clasped his hand on the checkered tablecloth and held it there, small and twisted, dry and furrowed, but soft and warm inside. And when her tears stopped flowing, they began to reminisce about her childhood, evoking a past she had been afraid to remember: the arduous journey by boat and train, and the many lands they had fared through, so happy together they were almost reluctant to arrive at their destination, and how delighted Edna had been at sea, our little princess, Nona del Mar, the captain called her, and in Italy a street singer fell in love with her and serenaded her for an hour as she stood before him in a wide-brimmed hat, a three-year-old beauty with yellow curls, and in Athens a gendarme took her for a ride on his shiny black horse, but the horse bolted, it was a wonder the gendarme managed to draw rein . . . The light glowed softly over the table as they exchanged their airy offerings. Once a week we go to a movie. But why didn't you tell me? she asked, amazed. You would have laughed at us, two oldtimers out on a date . . . What sort of films do you like? she asked them eagerly. Well, probably not the sort you like, just simple entertainment for folks like us. Tell me, tell me, tell me, she entreated, anticipating further revelations; sheepishly they named a few. What do you know! she exclaimed with tears in her eyes, I saw those too. And later that night, back at their tiny apartment, they embraced in their overcoats, tremulous with emotion, with the joy of meeting and the joy of parting.

But Mama was not about to sit idly by. It was more difficult in her case, though, having to begin from the beginning in an area where she had earned much glory and self-esteem. Not that she would stoop to buying a cookbook; there wasn't a woman on earth whose tutelage in the culinary arts she was prepared to accept, *pshee!* Instead, she rallied her senses in a sly campaign of espionage: memories overwhelmed her as she set off once more on shopping expeditions to out-of-the-way markets, to remote and tiny stores in neighborhoods she would not have set foot in as a rule. Cleverly, wisely, for she was nobody's fool, she scarcely altered her cooking style, at least, not all at once: with the subtlety of an artist she seasoned her chicken soup, a dash of coriander, a hint of Indian curry, in minuscule amounts at first, like drops of precious perfume, and then more boldly, with a reckless flourish, almost grateful to What's-her-name for kindling this rivalry and her blood . . . Slowly but surely she varied the menus; she was cooking with more than her hands again, as she had for her starving refugee long ago in their home in the old neighborhood: she cooked with her heart and soul, serving up vegetable side dishes with the chicken, grape leaves stuffed with spicy rice, stuffed cabbage and peppers, and even tomatoes. And she garnished every course with a ribbon of cucumber or pimiento, just for the beauty of it; we're not animals, you know. And she invested much of the pay from Edna in a variety of fancy foods. Suddenly the dinner dishes came alive, evoking colorful market stalls. And a dying winter pressed its pallid face against the window, watching them with famished eyes.

It's a heavy gray dinner hour. Aron tries to swallow, but he can't. He just can't. The food sticks in his throat. He mustn't, mustn't, put any more in. There's no room left. Through lowered lids he peeks at Papa. At his slowly grinding jaws. Nothing will ever stand in their way. Throw in a hunk of meat and watch them devour it. Throw in a plastic box or a tin can or even an old car, they'll tear up anything. Furtively he counts on his fingers: twenty-five days now since Mama and Papa stopped talking. And she doesn't sing anymore, not even "We're off to work in the morning." You're staring at me again. No, I'm not. I want you to eat, you hear, not sit there dreaming with your mouth open. I'm not dreaming. Everyone else is . . . The last few words are swallowed in an angry murmur. She sticks the serving spoon in the mashed potatoes and fills up Papa's plate again. He watches, sighing, swallowing spit, and once again he lifts his fork. Slowly he consumes everything. Down to the last crumb. But the question is, will Papa eat the third helping Mama inevitably offers when he's done? Because a few hours from now What's-her-name will be serving him another huge meal. As Mama very well knows. As everyone in the building knows. All the same she heaps

THE BOOK OF

his plate full. At precisely one-fifty-five Papa ate chicken. Aron is scientific about these things. Yochi eats in silence, her soft greasy face glued to the plate. Aron is watching her out of the corner of his eye in her desperate struggle with the appetite she inherited from Papa. Her hand goes out to the bread basket, with a will of its own. She summons it back. A few more mouthfuls of chicken and the hand slides out to the bread basket again. Next time, the third time, he knows she will succumb. Aron chews and chews and chews, swirling the mush around in his cheeks: if he swallows this, he will explode. It will mix with the pasty mush churning in his stomach. Yochi's hand goes out and snatches the bread—I was right—which she devours pleasurelessly. No one speaks. Aron picks at the food on his plate. To make sure Mama didn't sneak in any chicken. The way she does in the vegetable soup. No one would catch him eating food that used to be alive. He chews with downcast eyes to avoid the chicken-wing remains on their plates. He moves the soda squirter in front of him to block out Mama's plate, and furtively overturns the saltcellar from the Galei Kinneret Hotel on the bread board to eclipse what he can of Papa's plate. Slowly he masticates the bread and mashed potatoes till he can't tell the bread from the mashed potatoes, using his cheeks as warehouses. Twenty-five days. And Giora said a man has to do it three or four times a week, at least, otherwise he might burst. Papa's jaws go up and down. Up and down. And in Aron's tummy there's a month's worth of food spinning round and round. He can feel it spin: like the revolving drum of a washing machine. There go the tomatoes and the mashed potatoes, there goes the eggplant. There goes the rice and the bread and the bananas and sour cream they made him eat the day before yesterday. Yochi asks him to pass the borscht. "With pleasure," he responds. And Yochi stares at him quizzically, then smiles and says with a perfectly straight face, "Oh, thank you ever so." Silence. Everyone eats. Those jaws again. Mama scoops another mound of mashed potatoes onto Papa's plate. The plate he just cleared, gasps Aron. Papa contemplates this latest mound. The steam from the mashed potatoes condenses into beads of sweat around his chin and down his cheeks. He breathes in deeply and lets out a groan. Breadcrumbs fly across the table. Aron grips the edge of the table. Papa unbuckles his belt and lets his body spill out into the room. Aron says: "Would you be so kind as to pass the bread." Yochi smiles wanly. "The pumpernickel, sir?" Aron laughs. "If you please." He looks around with a smile. But Mama buries her face in the plate, and Papa turns red. Aron is mortified: what if Papa thinks they're making fun of him with their formal Hebrew? But they aren't making fun of him, honestly. Aron uses words like that in his imagination all the time, when he pretends he lives with gentlefolk who found him as a baby. Maybe he and Yochi should talk like that whenever they're at home alone together. She's so good at it. Not that it's surprising, when all she does is read books or write letters. Aron wants to add something, but first he has to check on how things are going out there; Papa's forgotten about him; he eyes the heaping plateful before him with dismay, picks up a thick piece of bread, weighs it in his hand, tears out a chunk of snow-white dough, and impales it on the tip of his finger: in his day at the bakery, bread was bread. He squooshes the unfortunate crumb and flicks it at the sink. Then he concentrates on his plate again, picking at the potatoes, noisily sucking on a drumstick. Aron waits till Papa's eyes turn glassy with the drumstick in his mouth and mutters to Yochi: "How very delectable," and ducks his head and stuffs more mashed potatoes into his mouth, and more bread, and pickles, anything and everything to avoid looking up again. Because the drumstick has frozen in Papa's hand. Yochi too buries her face in her plate. Some secret thing inside him, a hazy memory, a quiver of joy, swims minnow-like, shimmering in his blood, while Aron plunges faithfully on, toward the one chance in a million, the flare of union and the spark of life, with Papa behind him, gloomy, dark, thrusting his body forward, and his flabby flesh gets stuck in the entrance—pow!

Mama hurries to the refrigerator, and a strange blush spreads over her cheeks, but Aron peeks and sees she's trying not to smile. She's on my side. She understands that I'm loyal to her. Now he feels a little like a matador, advancing and retreating, cheered on by beautiful women. They continue to eat. In silence. And suddenly Papa says with his mouth full, "Pass me the salt whatzit."

Unthinkingly Aron blurts out, "The saltcellar."

A terrible silence follows. You can hear the drumming of the rain. Papa bulges invincibly. "What did you say?"

Aron is silent. He turns pale. Caught out. The quivering inside him has stopped, the pleasure has vanished.

"Repeat what you just said."

"Here, take it, Papa." He holds the saltcellar upside down. He dare not turn it right side up. It trickles into his hand.

"What's that you call it?"

"It's . . . a saltcellar."

"Now listen here, Mr. Inallectual: you open your ears and hear me good: I say we call it 'the salt whatzit.' "

"Okay. Here, take it."

"No. First repeat after me: 'the salt whatzit.' "

"Please, Papa, take it." His whiny voice, his boy-soprano shame. He is pouting and the tears well in his eyes. The salt trickles out on the table. Mama is silent. Yochi is silent.

"You say 'the salt whatzit' or so help me, I'll take my belt with the brass buckle to you."

"Say it already!" shrieks Mama, who only a moment ago was gloating at the sink. "God in heaven! Say it already so we can have some quiet!"

Aron tries. He really does, but he can't. The words just won't come out of him. His lips twist and tremble. Let me go, Mr. Lion, and one day I shall help you in return; how can a mouse like you help the king of beasts; I have a plan: I'll win the lottery, I'll win the Toto, you won't have to work so hard at the workers' council anymore, I'll save our home, the light will shine again. Yochi watches pityingly. Her mouth is full. Papa cages him in, his face swelling ever larger.

"Let him be, Moshe!" screams Mama, throwing down the drumstick. "Never mind all the food I cooked. What do you want with him? Eat and be quiet!"

"I won't have him laughing at me! What does he think, he can laugh at me in my own house? He won't eat his dinner, our food's not good enough for him! And the way he talks, just like a girl, tatee-tatee-tata! Thinks he can look down on me, like a, like some damned commissar. And I'm supposed to keep my mouth shut. You say 'the salt whatzit' right now or else!"

"Nu, Aron, say 'the salt whatzit' already, so we can eat in peace!" shouts Mama, and Aron gives her a long look; he really does feel sorry for her, slaving in the kitchen all day to feed him so he can grow up and be normal. He shuts his ears from inside, Aroning slowly down, till suddenly they're speaking a language he doesn't understand, these strangers from far, far away, and he vows to stay with them, to help them cope, to bring a little sunshine into their trying lives; see them scowl as they tell him the news of some terrible disaster, some evil, hateful person has hurt them. Saltcellar, thinks Aron, somersaultcellar, his heart leaps: what a funny word, but something has happened meanwhile, a wicked emperor captured Mama and Papa, and he's threatening to execute them unless Aron swallows a bite of the "birdy" in his defiant mouth; he swivels his head from side to side. Locks his lips. A heavy hand, red and hairy, squeezes his cheeks together, forces his mouth open, and thrusts the wing inside. Okay, maybe it'll accidentally knock out his milk tooth. And his poor, poor parents, tied to the stake, they know he took a vow, they'd never ask him to do such an ignoble thing. His eyes blur with tears. I'll do it for your sake, he whispers, with the tender flesh between his teeth, and he takes a bite of this once living chicken and chews it and swallows it, and the drum in his tummy spins the yellow meat around. But don't worry, he bravely reassures his weeping parents as the emperor's men untie their fetters, they may defile my lips, they may defile my body, but the essence of me will be pure forever. Long live the saltcellar, long live the somersaultcellar, and Aron, with a chicken wing sticking out of his mouth, flies blissful as a light beam, in the radiant splendor of his word.

They ate in perfect silence again. Aron swallowed. But he never betrayed himself, he never said "the salt whatzit." Papa sat down, growling with malevolence. Staring at the heaping plate. Yochi's foot touched Aron's reassuringly. Forks scraped. In a gnarly, tearful voice Mama asked Papa if he wanted more, the chicken came out so good today. With great effort Papa raised his head. He stared at her in horror. Slowly he turned to the clock on the wall. His bull neck reappeared between his shoulders. Shutting his eyes, he nodded in reply.

THE BOOK OF

23

Two kitchen walls; the wall in the hallway; the little storage loft over the bathroom; the wall between the kitchen and the pantry; half the wall between the hallway and the salon . . . The neighbors, expert by now at deciphering Papa's moods, recognized the difference instantly: after a long spell of fatigue, Papa was back to his old self again, smashing the walls with renewed vigor, till they crumbled into dust. He shattered the bathroom and, one by one, knocked out the delicate tiles, cracking the basin in the process as well as the laundry rack and the ornamental mirror where Edna had beheld herself rising from the bath. It was difficult for him to be careful, to curb his ambitions. His flexing smithy muscles twisted over his back and shoulders and ripped through his dark blue work shirt. Once when he needed some wooden beams and Edna pointed to a stack of doors, he sawed up two of them without a moment's hesitation. During most of the next few days he worked on Og, the giant ladder, demolishing the storage loft in the hallway, indifferent to the peculiar rain of picture postcards and maps of distant lands, high-school papers and university notebooks, gaudy albums and collections of trading cards and silver foil and "gold stars," and frilly dresses, and broken dolls, and little red shoes, and a cuddly teddy bear with a faint smell of urine, and scores of black-and-white photos pelting down on his back like arrows. For three hours a day the building project trembled, the Boteneros, the Smitankas, the Kaminers, the Strashnovs; the plaster crumbled in their apartments, the furniture jiggled like herons aflutter in an aviary as the beating wings of their migrant friends pass overhead, and the dust from the ruins of Edna's apartment fell upon the dying grass and the laundry lines on their balconies, but no one dared complain to Papa, right, that's all they needed, he looked like a wild beast; poor Hinda, she must be made of steel to put up with a man like that.

And a terrible thing happened in the building one morning: Esther Kaminer, wife of Avigdor Kaminer, did not wake up: she went to sleep a healthy woman and never opened her eyes again. All the neighbors, except for Papa and Edna Bloom, came outside and bowed their heads as the diminutive body was lifted into the ambulance. In the fifteen years since the project was constructed this was the first time anyone had died there. Avigdor Kaminer stood by, arms dangling, and the onlookers watched his hunched figure full of pity and concern: who would take care of him now that she was gone, who would keep him going? She fought like a tiger over him. Mama, who had a soft spot for Esther Kaminer, came home feeling suddenly old. It was a dreadful blow. But she gritted her teeth and baked a torte and a sesame cake so poor Kaminer would have something to serve his guests during the seven days of mourning; he's as helpless as a baby, doesn't even know how to fix himself a cup of tea, how will he manage with the laundry, how will he manage with the ironing? She heaved a sigh, remembering Mamchu, of all people, with a vague irritation; maybe there was a link here, between poor Esther Kaminer and Mamchu holding on to life like an animal, to the point of indecency. Some people just don't know when their time has come, she grumbled, watching the margarine melt in the frying pan, and again with a pang she remembered Grandma Lilly, whose very survival seemed to clog the bowels of death and upset the laws of the universe.

But the others blamed Papa and Edna Bloom in their hearts, him on account of the sledgehammer which must have jolted Esther's internal plumbing—why, even a healthy person could break down from all that hammering day after day—and Edna they blamed on account of the air of repression she broadcast to the entire neighborhood. Mrs. Pinkus, the divorcée with the spotty face who never paid her house dues, lost control one time when Edna passed her on the stairway, looking pale and fragile with her new hair swirling around her brow like flames, and screamed at her, Stop the torture already, give in and be done with it

THE BOOK OF

—you think you have a diamond growing there, if you can't satisfy him, pass him on to them that can. Edna stared silently at the hysterical woman and dizzily grabbed hold of the banister. If only he'd dare, she mused, tearing herself away from Mrs. Pinkus's distorted face and trudging numbly up to her apartment. Why doesn't he, though, what is he afraid of? Her thoughts were thick and murky, filling up her head. What is he afraid of? A fine thread of blood trickled out behind her as she carried her heavy basket with tomorrow's dinner up the stairs. At the Atiases' door she stopped to catch her breath. Maybe he was shy. But why should he be shy with her? A sealed letter with Mr. Lombroso's signature had been lying under her bed for days, her bank clerk notified her sternly but with secret satisfaction that her account had been closed, red paper birds from the electric company and the gas people glided through the apartment, or glued themselves to the door, but she could always cook on the old Primus, and when she ran out of money for kerosene she could saw up the doors and the furniture and make a bonfire in the middle of the living room, and throw in her *National Geographics*, arranged and catalogued according to subject, the glory of her modest enterprise, and the oversized pages of her art books, born for burning, and her wooden sculptures and dolls from around the world. She started to climb the stairs again, shuffling her feet, how did everything get so complicated, wake up, save your soul, but where does he go when the hammering begins, as if she no longer existed for him, disappearing into the wall, forgetting all about her, all about her; she laughed out loud, shattered like a bottle on the prow of his ship as he sailed into the distance. And she leaned against the door of her apartment and saw the rash that had broken out over her slender legs. From hunger maybe. But food didn't satisfy her anymore.

And one night the telephone rang at the Kleinfelds'. Mama picked up the receiver, and, vey-is-mir, turned very white. Then she sent Aron to fetch Papa from What's-her-name's and sank down on the Pouritz. Mama, Mama, who was it, what happened? But only her finger moved, waving at him. Go already, bring him home right now even if he's in the middle of Kol Nidre.

He climbed the stairs of Entrance A, which reverberated to Papa's blows, four flights up, slowly, cautiously, his legs wide apart, every footfall hurting more, stirring the mush in his tummy. He stopped and coughed in front of the door, to announce his presence, as usual, and knocked softly. And knocked again, a little harder; it was impossible to hear anything with all the noise. And again he coughed, and rang the bell, but didn't hear it ring. Maybe the electricity had been cut off. What to do now, he couldn't go home, he couldn't just open the door. Till finally he dared, he closed his eyes and opened the door a narrow crack, and then he knew, he was certain that when he opened his eyes he would see Papa's arms dangling to the floor, and the dirty smile smeared over his face, while some ingenious machine produced the sounds of hammering. But all he found was a cloud of dust, behind which he dimly discerned his papa's bare back, as he smashed the wall of the bathroom down the hall.

The house was in ruins. Bricks jutted out like bones from the walls still standing. Extended cracks crawled over the ceiling, and the floor was littered with plaster and dust and newspapers and electric wires and leftover food. Four or five doors were stacked against a wall, leaning on each other's backs, hugging in silence.

But when he glanced around the ruins he discovered Edna: doubled over in a swoon on one of her lacerated armchairs, a shabby blanket wrapped around her. Her face was dusty white like a death mask, and the crown of her head glowed red.

Aron took a few steps forward, went limp at the sight, and sank to the floor in the corner by the piano. The outer walls and a few supporting pillars were left, but the apartment seemed bleak, exposed to raging winter winds. He shivered. Soon it will be spring, he thought, but who knows, maybe spring won't come this year, winter might go on forever, orbiting around itself . . . The persistent pounding penetrated his stomach and head now, and he let it in, a little top-heavy, but he had a job to do, he had been sent for a purpose; wake up, shake an arm or a leg, show you're alive, but first, rest here, unwind from your rigorous journey, let yourself go a little, who knows, maybe now at last, but he was tight as a fist from head to toe; and he leaned against the wall, yielding to the hammer blows, to their dull reverberation inside him, and he realized that this wasn't it either; the hammering was loud, true, but it didn't sound right somehow, it lacked spirit, maybe Papa wasn't up to more than that, too bad, too bad, and he shut his eyes, sliding down the wall, taking a breather; let's see now, where were we, this Saturday the Jerusalem Hapoel team is playing Hapoel Haifa and he bet 2–0, but now he regrets his betrayal of the home team, he should have bet

THE BOOK OF

at least a tie score, and in tomorrow's paper the winners of the Blueband contest will be announced, and he sent in ten wrappers; he dozes, organizing next week's missions in his head: to snatch three pounds out of Mama's wallet again and buy a lottery ticket, how come he never even won the small purse, or at least let him find the white Valiant, license number 327–933, that was stolen in Jerusalem, or the German shepherd with the brown collar who answers to the name of Flash, generous reward for the honest finder, that would be okay too, and in the afternoon paper it said Coca-Cola will be opening a plant in Israel this year, maybe they'll have a contest for a Hebrew slogan, how about "From Dan to Elat, Coca-Cola hits the spot," though maybe he wouldn't have to wait that long if he won the lottery first, or the Toto, or even the "Find the Seven Differences"; he was getting closer all the time, he could feel it in his bones, why, one of his letters or postcards or bottle caps or Popsicle sticks had probably just arrived at the editor's desk or at the factory where the boss opens the envelope and reads the entry, and a wide grin spreads over his face, his gold tooth positively gleams with joy, and he stands up and beckons the workers; they leave their cumbersome machines that go up and down, pounding, groaning. "Folks, we have a winner!" shouts the boss, jumping on his big black top hat, crushing it in jubilation. At long last, somebody's found the answer! It's incredible! Like a ray of light straight to the core of the problem! We have been redeemed!" And the workers return to the production line, their voices lifting in a mighty song, and the machines steam up, shooting sparks through their pistons, flamboyant fireworks in the air. Aron trembled, he thought he heard a scream in his ear, he opened his eyes, looked around; Papa was still pounding down the hall, boom, groan, boom, groan, but Aron could no longer believe, and he knew he had missed a unique opportunity.

But it really was a scream. Mama was calling him from down the stairs. He had completely forgotten his errand. How could he stop Papa in the middle? Mama yelled his name again. God knows what the urgent thing whoever it was had called about. Mama did turn white as a wall. She did clutch her heart. Aron shuddered: maybe Grandma was dead.

He let out a whimper of grief: His own dear grandma—how . . . but . . . it can't be . . . and then quickly restrained himself; yes, when it comes it comes, the will of heaven, here today, gone tomorrow, he mumbled as if in prayer, but deep inside he felt a disagreeable chill.

And you, what did you ever do for Grandma? Me? I spent loads of time with her. Oh sure, in the beginning, when it was all new and exciting. And I took her clothes and her shoes and her braid out of the trash bin and hid them in the furnace room. Traitor, deserter, did you once ask Yochi to take you there? Well no, but I thought of going, I even had a little present for her: a little red mirror. Right, presents you're good at, and writing sentimental cards to go with them, but when it comes to action, you're as bad as the others, you traitor, you lousy traitor. Some such muttering went on inside him, though both the plaintiff and the defendant were hollow, false, and what he was really thinking about was the beard Papa would have to grow during the seven days of mourning.

Sudden blasts resounded. Papa stopped what he was doing and listened to the clouds, ready to answer them, to send them back to the four winds. But the blasts came not from the sky but from the door. He veered around in amazement and wiped the sweat from his brow. His eyes were filled with bloody froth. Then he noticed Aron and wasn't even startled.

"Aron!" boomed Mama outside the door. "Tell him to come out here right away!" Aron gazed questioningly up at Papa.

"I know you're in there, Aron! Tell him to come home immediately! Because I wouldn't go in there if my life depended on it!"

Papa looked at Edna Bloom, but she seemed to have lost all touch with her surroundings, and was rocking back and forth with her eyes shut tight, to the rhythm of an imaginary hammer. He crossed to Aron. What did she want now? Aron shrugged. Papa grumbled again. At Edna Bloom's, his voice sounded gravelly, as though he hadn't used it for a long time. Impatiently he glanced at the pyramid of bricks awaiting him at the far end of the shattered wall. Then he instructed Aron to put his hammer in the bathtub and turned to go. Aron grasped the heavy tool. Something stirred inside him, inside his head. A barely audible hissing sound. How could Papa lift a thing this heavy? Edna Bloom woke out of her stupor and watched him, waiting to see what he would do. Aron cast a bewildered glance around the room and noticed the dismantled doors, stacked against each other like a giant deck of cards; he tore himself away and headed for the bathroom. He trudged down the hallway looking out for mounds of rubble, carefully stepping over the torn remains of a picture showing a kindly outstretched arm. Edna stood up to watch him. Slowly she shook her crimson head from left to right. One blow, just one, thought Aron, struggling with the heavy hammer, with the piercing hiss of mockery. Papa will be glad I finished the job for him, he said, trying to swing the hammer over his head. *Tsss tsss tsss*. But Mama, he thought. He dropped it heavily in the broken tub. Edna went on shaking her head like a metronome as he passed her with downcast eyes on his way out the door. At home he heard the news from Mama.

24

When Mama heard that Papa was going back to tear out the tiles at Edna Bloom's, she announced her intention of supervising the job. Once more the gloomy procession wound its way from Entrance B to Entrance A, with Mama in the lead, lofty and imposing in a turquoise sheath; she had wisely ruled out the brown cassock of the first visit on the grounds that it was too austere; she tried on and eventually decided against the checkered jersey, which, though respectable enough, created an ill-advised impression of severity; the bottle green was out because under the circumstances it might appear too frivolous, too gay; in the end she opted for the turquoise sheath, because it was sufficiently respectable but had softer lines that emphasized her bosom and rippled over her ample thighs, calling to mind the children tugging at it long ago; thus dressed, she marched up the stairs, clutching her knitting bag under her arm, jutting her chin out like Ben-Gurion.

Edna opened the door for her and slinked off like an ailing cat. When Mama set eyes on the islands of debris, all the color drained from her face. Only now did she grasp the extent of the damage. Such wreckage, such excess, called for retribution, demanded a victim. In a flash she understood that this was no longer the concern of three individuals but that a mighty struggle was in progress here between the forces of chaos and order civilization and insanity. Dauntless, copper-faced, she stamped over the ruins, enthroned herself on one of the torn leather armchairs, and crossed her arms over her bosom.

THE BOOK OF

"Begin," she said to Papa.

Edna Bloom, wearing a hollow expression, did not interrupt the ceremony. She walked in from the kitchen bearing a goodly tray with Papa's second lunch. Papa looked from her to Mama. An hour and forty minutes ago at home he had polished off a plate of pupiklach drowning in gravy, vegetable soup Moroccan-style, a thick slice of turkey in curry sauce garnished with tawny onion rings, and a generous helping of rice; only Mama knew the rice should have been served with piñones, but that stinking one-armed vendor from the spice shop in the market charged such a price, to hell with him; and for dessert, home-made applesauce with the peels removed. Now she inspected the regal feast that Edna Bloom was serving him. Papa pulled up his usual chair and, fixing his eyes on Mama with a little gasp, proceeded to tuck in.

He devoured the first course of eggplant in tomato sauce glistening with pearly garlic cloves; he lapped up the creamy onion soup with the crispy croutons on top; he feasted on succulent tongue of veal, seasoned Hungarian-style and flanked by heaping mounds of rice studded with piñones.

He dined in silence, his great jaws occupied with course after course. Mama watched him with a new look of empathy and wonder. She had never believed there was love between him and What's-her-name; in fact, she didn't really believe in love at all. What's love anyway, she once said to Yochi, a moment or two in a lifetime of putting up with another person's craziness. Now she was beginning to appreciate the earthier dimensions of Papa's victim. Edna brought in the dessert: stewed fruit, a glass of orange juice, and a square of Splendid chocolate, and Papa ate, and wiped his lips on a lily-white napkin with a wooden ring around it, and cleaned his teeth with a fine little toothpick, con-cealing his mouth behind his hand—he forgets where I found him, you'd think at his mother's they ate off Rosenthal—and, finally, belched, quickly excused himself, and returned to the job.

Wielding a small-sized hammer and chisel, he set about removing the floor in what used to be the hallway at Edna Bloom's; he cracked the tiles like so many eggshells, working slowly with an air of doom: while he was tearing down the walls it was a comfort to imagine something growing here, gestating in the stone; but as he pulled out the tiles, formerly overlaid with brightly colored carpets—which Edna sold to the rag man for money to pay Mama and to buy the food she sacrificed to Papa—the nubbly concrete exposed underneath, the rusty rods, and especially the stratum of sand below them, gave off a gloomy chill. Papa tapped and uprooted and slowly excavated the floor as Edna sat gaping at him, nodding her head and humming in a monotone.

Solemnly Mama picked up her needles and plied them uninterruptedly throughout the ensuing days of Papa's labors, knitting her surroundings into the fabric that soon became a woolly gray sweater; even when clouds of dust blew up she restrained herself from coughing. At last she realized how badly her rival was beating her, how cunningly she had laid bare that which Mama tried so hard to cover up over nineteen years of marriage.

Next morning, as she hung the winter quilts out the windows to air before putting them in storage, Mama caught sight of two rugged-looking movers hauling Edna's dusty black Bechstein piano. A number of neighbors had gathered on the sidewalk to watch: Sophie and Peretz Atias, Felix and Zlateh Botenero, Avigdor Kaminer, who seemed to have perked up a bit since the death of his wife and even started dyeing his hair. When they noticed Mama looking down, they angrily turned away: they knew it was Mama's greed that had made Edna sell her piano. But another thought had occurred to them too, that she was selling the expensive instrument because there was no room left for it in her little apartment.

It had been the only piano in the building, the only one on the block perhaps. And though Edna had played it no more than once or twice in the past few years, there were some among them who could still remember the occasion of its arrival here, and how Edna would practice a little Chopin in the afternoon sometimes. Mama had backed away when she saw them glaring at her, and now she reappeared in the window in all her majesty, shaking out the quilts with lofty indifference. But suddenly she too was seized with sadness. She stopped what she was doing and wadded up the rag in her hands as though to salute a passing coffin. She too, in those bygone days, had sometimes paused to listen, wiping her hands on a kitchen towel. Sighing. When the movers drove off, the neighbors bowed their heads a moment, and a shiver of woe passed through the building.

And in the midst of all this, Grandma appeared. For months she had lain immobile, till the elderly doctor who suggested a new treatment the year before broached the subject again to Yochi one evening as she

THE BOOK OF

sat beside Grandma at the hospital; the doctor had been watching Yochi take care of Grandma for quite some time. Now he showed her Grandma's records. What a shame, he said in his broken voice, and waited for an answer as her childish blue eyes stared down at the floor. How he must suffer, thought Yochi, with his voice cracking every minute. "Your grandmother could go on living," he whispered again, and Yochi thought, He certainly doesn't look like someone who chops people up for diploma practice. She said she needed time to decide, and pondered the dilemma without consulting anyone. A few days later she told him she simply didn't have the strength to make a life-or-death decision. Let him decide and she would hope for the best. And the following day the doctor wheeled Grandma to surgery and did the deed: he cut a tiny drainage canal in her brain; the fog lifted, and one week later Grandma Lilly blinked an eye, sat up, and smiled, and when they showed her how, she started to walk again.

It was truly wonderful, but terrible too. Grandma was home, but no one dared to look at her—they were ashamed of leaving her like that, like a dog, alone in the hospital, but they were also ashamed of having seen her in such a pitiful state, of having handled her body as if it were their own. Mama gasped, remembering the things she had divulged while Grandma was ill. She blamed it on Papa, on the banging at Edna's, it had shocked the foundations of order and reason, he'd raised the dead with his boom boom boom, and she bit her fingers with an anxious glance at Aron, as the three of them grasped what Mama would never acknowledge: that the family accounts with Fate were a mess; the letters had been switched.

Grandma came home by taxi. Papa went to fetch her at the hospital, stuffed respectfully into his only suit, the fusty one from his wedding day, and he had to breathe carefully not to pop the buttons on his barrel chest. Mama served coffee and a fallen torte, and they all sat frozenly around her, afraid to open their mouths. Grandma regarded them with her seeing eye, and the crooked new expression on her face looked sharp, disdainful. Her eye roved to the new buffet, the recently painted walls. "Remember, Mamchu, remember the mildew and the stains on the ceiling," Mama gushed, "you were still here the time we had the leak from the sink upstairs at the Boteneros', weren't you?" A bitter smile floated over Grandma's lips. Mama tormented herself for having trusted Grandma even on her deathbed. Still Grandma said nothing and they couldn't tell whether she knew how to talk or not. The whole left side of her body was paralyzed, but her face was barely wrinkled at all, as though she'd been living in a state of suspended animation beyond the ravages of time. One lid drooped over her eye, and from the side she looked like a fortune-telling gypsy. When Papa started cracking his knuckles she turned to him with amazing speed and he froze under her gaze. Mutely she examined the armature of his body, the new might of its bulwarks, and right away she knew everything, as though someone had whispered the story in her ear. There was no doubt that she knew. Slowly she turned to Mama and transfixed her with a long, apocalyptic stare, which only Mama understood.

Then she turned to Yochi. She stripped her naked with her eye and embossed a design of wasted youth. Yochi squirmed. Mama smiled encouragingly and whispered, "This is Yochi, Mamchu, you remember Yochi. She'll be graduating from high school soon, she'll get a deferment from the army and go to the university! Maybe she'll be a doctor someday, a doctor!" Yochi didn't even bother to protest. Grandma's eye twinkled. Maybe she remembered something, a special moment out of her many hours in Yochi's care. She smiled at her. Yochi wept softly, not bothering to wipe her eyes. Mama held out a handkerchief, but Yochi ignored her outstretched hand. The tears welled in her eyes and flowed down her cheeks, onto the chair and the carpet, and Mama watched in deep amazement, thrusting the handkerchief in Yochi's face. "Enough already, nu, you'll cause a flood, wipe your tears now, aren't we happy to have Grandma home," and Aron peeped at the tiny drops: what if Yochi went on crying forever, till her tears became a trickle, then a stream, then a mighty waterway coursing over the floor in search of Mama . . .

Then Grandma turned to Aron. Astonishment spread over her face, and her mouth skewed up inquiringly. Mama, Papa, and Yochi hung their heads. She seemed to be trying to say his name. They all looked up, surprised, hopeful. God Almighty. Aron's hands were sweating. He remembered the golden thread she had given him once. Maybe now she'll give me the real present, he thought. Grandma Lilly wagged her head, shaking off forgetfulness, fatigue. Her face turned sallow with effort and frustration. Aron sank back in his chair.

That day Papa didn't go to work at Edna Bloom's. Maybe Mama's accusation worked and now he was frightened of himself. After they

THE BOOK OF

put Grandma to bed in her alcove, Papa tiptoed around the house, and Aron tried to stay out of his way. With Papa in the house, even the door frames and the furniture, everything looked tiny around him, and Aron reckoned the days that had passed and knew only a miracle would save them now; something had to happen, one way or another, it had to, he was about to explode: the food he swallowed in tiny bitefuls clogged up his stomach, and how long would his heart be able to pump with all that mush inside him, it did seem to be beating more sluggishly of late, he had actually noticed that, maybe food particles were filtering into his bloodstream, congesting the chambers, the auricles and the ventricles; Aron could picture it clearly: the atrium, a muscular pouch, filling up with liquid food, and his heart struggling to pump it, barely able to contract, it was so glutted with goop; and all night long he tosses and turns, burping those little burps that burn and smell like rotten eggs, and next his throat will fill up and push out his Adam's apple, and then the stuff will ooze into his face, and his cheeks will balloon, he'll look like a freak, and from there it will pass into his brain, and then he'll blow up, then they'll really have a mess on their hands.

In the evening when Mama went out to the Romanian pharmacy to buy Grandma her medicines, Aron sneaked down to the furnace room and got the fancy dress and the high-heeled shoes and the bathing suit and the thick braid and all the other stuff. Cautiously he walked up to Grandma, who was sitting rigidly on her bed. He smiled at her and displayed his heavily laden arms. There were no sparks of recognition. He kneeled with effort and put the shoes on her twisted feet, and the hairbands on her head, like seven rainbows shining after a storm. She didn't budge. She let him do what he wanted. Then he stood her up, and with great difficulty pulled the dress on over her robe. Why, he didn't know, he only knew it had to be done and that Yochi would be proud of him. And then he went back to his room and lay down on his bed. At ten past seven Mama returned from the pharmacy and walked into Grandma's alcove. Aron heard Mama give a frightened yelp, and after that she locked herself in her room, switched the light off, and didn't come out till morning.

That evening there was no supper.

For three days more, three hours a day, Mama sat in the torn and dusty armchair at Edna Bloom's. Still, she wouldn't speak an unnecessary word to Papa, but at least she behaved respectfully toward him and also a little fearfully, as though watching the slow, awesome fall of a giant tree. Wearily he raised the little tile hammer, and there were long spells when he sat motionless on the broken floor, trying to remember why he had come here in the first place. And then Mama would look up from her knitting and stare at him in silence, not even daring to rouse him with a snort. At night, as he lay sleeping on the Gandhi mattress in the salon, he would groan so deeply he made the milk curdle, and Mama had to let his clothes out day after day to accommodate his expanding musculature; she slit his sleeves and sewed large strips of cloth into his trousers, but to no avail.

And then one day there were no more piñones in the rice, and Mama slackened her knitting. Edna served the dinner tray and stood abjectly by. And the following afternoon there was a chicken wing on the plate instead of butter-soft tongue of veal. Papa finished eating and picked his teeth as usual, only this time he neglected to cover his mouth and a feeble belch escaped it, tarnishing Edna's face an ashen gray. Maybe that was the moment a voice whispered to her that she'd been fooled. That in some mysterious way, by some twisted conjugal logic, husband and wife had both been using her to reinforce their bonds. That all unconsciously, perhaps, they had sacrificed her to their union. Edna gave a short, fainthearted laugh. Mama and Papa examined her together.

The day after, it was a Thursday, Papa looked up from a meager drumstick and gazed reflectively into Mama's eyes. Mama returned the gaze, reading what she read therein. When Edna left to get the dessert—for two days now this had consisted of watery peaches from a can—Mama said to Papa, "I'll go home now, Moshe, for the thorough cleaning." Just like that; and she walked away.

Papa waited for Edna Bloom. He stood up and wandered around the ruins till she returned, absently kicking the broken bricks, stamping lightly on the dust heaps. The first green leaves were budding on the plane tree in the yard. The warm sun tickled the most intimate corners of the afternoon. Aron stood on the sidewalk, looking thin and bowed from the back, his feet spread ridiculously wide as he gazed out at the valley. A sudden pain shot through Papa's heart. Like a splinter from a nightmare piercing his memory in the middle of the day: he remembered his movements as he demolished the first wall. The unearthly winter he had drifted through alone for so long. He tried to recall what it was he had been looking for, and shrugged his shoulders in disillusionment, in helpless grief; what else could he do.

Edna returned from the kitchen and her eyes sought Mama. Her face lit up for an instant, till she realized it was a sign of her final defeat. Papa took the plate from her hand and their fingers touched. Nothing happened. Except that Edna turned to stone. She felt it in her feet first, then her knees, and her thighs, and then the slow petrifaction of her sapless pubic mound. She had just enough time to imagine Mr. Kleinfeld digging her out of the marble that formed over her childless breasts, but by then there was so much stone in her heart and on her lips, and in her brain, that she didn't hear him explaining, calmly and rationally, This has been dragging on too long, Miss Bloom, it's too complicated, I never expected this, and I won't take money for the floor in the hallway, it was a great honor to make your acquaintance, but now I have to go.

25

The bathroom door flew open, and everyone listened. A moment's silence, and then the hoarse and languorous voice said, "Achh, a mechayeh, that was good."

Ruddy and shining and fragrant with soap, Papa shuffled into the salon and lay facedown on the Bordeaux, bare-chested, with a towel around his waist. Mama waited in the bedroom, clasping her hands in front of the mirror. She took a deep breath to brace herself and muttered good riddance. Then she sent Yochi to bring Mamchu in to help, and went to get the massage lotion in the bathroom.

Aron finds it difficult to concentrate on peeling the potatoes. One by one he picks them up and weighs them in his hand. They all have different faces, weird human-looking faces, but distorted and miserable, and sometimes when the knife cuts into them, he can actually feel them wince. Slowly he starts Aroning. But Papa's groans from the salon penetrate even there. And it isn't easy to practice these days. Oh please, let him never lose the gift. The trouble is, there's no room left inside him. He's utterly stuffed. His eyes are bulging, his lungs are drowning in mush. His breath stinks of it. His thoughts are smeared with it. It's heavy as lead, it burns, it's nauseating. And him in there with his moaning and groaning, achhhh, achhhh. It's been a long time since we heard the like of those. Aron tries with all his might to seal himself off from the noise. Seated in the kitchen he can see Papa's hand dangling from the sofa, with the thick, hairy fingers, *tsss tsss tsss* goes the chirring

218

in his head, addressing him in the pinchy voice, through the mouthpiece of the gland: Watch it, your fingers are limp, soon they'll spread and you'll drop the knife. Aron pouts with concentration and quickly cuts. The little red peeler, runt of her kitchen knives, comes menacingly close to his fingers now, and he loses half the potato for a change. They're all turning out like pygmies today. *Tsss tsss tsss*, why must you be so stubborn. Why are you fighting me. You don't stand a chance. Because everything in the world is me. There's nothing in the world that isn't me. I'm the things of the world and the people who use them. I'm steel and rubber and wood and flesh. I'm cranks and valves and gears and pistons. I'm the blade that cuts. I'm the screws you have to remember which way to screw in on the first try. I'm the knots in your shoelaces and the cord for the blinds. Yes, I'm everything, a coded message, a secret experiment. Aron veers angrily away from the little red knife, which has suddenly started bobbing around with a life of its own. He focuses his gaze far away from here, on the fingers in the salon, for instance, and it's a good thing Papa's nostrils are big enough. Mama opens her mouth to alert Yochi and Grandma about a big one hiding slyly in a tangle of hair on Papa's shoulder. And I am the scourge of the broken plate and the light bulb exploding in your hand and the glass that shatters when you clink l'chaim. And the sweater you put on inside out. And the buttons you button wrong. And the door you slam on your finger. This runt keeps trying to cut him, without even bothering to hide it. He pauses a minute and looks down at his hands, the pink little hands that always reminded him somehow of an inner organ exposed to view. He used to play the guitar once. But it broke, oh sure, uh-huh, and Yochi bought him a new one, but he can't bring himself to take it out of the case. Just give it a try, why don't you, see what's left in your hands and your feelings. Once they promised him that when he was older he could take guitar lessons with a real teacher. Then they said he didn't have talent. A Mozart you're not, said Mama, and she smiled for some reason. So what was he? What was he? The wunderkind has lost his wunder. Because he used to have such a knack for things. Once he even fixed the toaster Mama wanted to throw out. And Papa used to let him pour the kiddush wine on Friday nights, but now his hand trembles and everything spills. He reflects about this with an eighth of a thought, as though skating on very thin ice. He knows his mind plays tricks on him and uses him against himself. It locks him in. Lock by lock. If only he could remember how he used to do things, without even thinking.

In the salon the women are going over Papa. They have matching skin, he thinks, as though they were cut from the same cloth. Even Grandma resembles them now. Not in looks so much as the expression on her face while she works on Papa: at least she won't be singing those songs to his back anymore; Papa's face turned purple that time when they had the fight and Mama screamed at him, You promised, you promised, and his Adam's apple bounced up all red, and a long, frightening moment later it began to slide back, and Aron stared, mesmerized, at the way it pushed down on his Polish, his language with Grandma Lilly; even when Mama wasn't home they didn't dare speak it anymore, they would sit in silence. Why did you let Mama have her way? Aron is seething. Why did you give in?

He goes to the sink and washes the cut on his finger. The faucet doesn't shut all the way. There's a leak. He sucks the blood from the cut. It'll heal in time for your wedding. Heal, nothing. Wedding, nothing. Why did he have to inspect each stupid word, measuring it against his problem. But he'd barely thought about himself in the past few weeks. Where have you been and what have you been doing? Nothing. Just disappeared, that's all. Went into hibernation. He saw a whole show in his dreams at night, for adults only. But how come they let him see it, why did they allow him. Hard and fast he peels the potato. What if, could it be, they wanted him to see. Go on. It's the truth. They did it in front of him. They concealed nothing. Right from the first, after Papa's return. Quartered potatoes squirt out from under his knife. A vertical furrow of outrage cuts the space between his eyebrows. They wanted him to see. They forced him to watch. Like the wrestling matches on Lebanon TV, the titans tangling and grappling together. Watch them and learn how to fight. He stares at his hand, which is empty. Pieces of potato lie scattered at his feet. Nonsense. All they did was tear down some walls, the rest is only in your mind. But what will happen to Edna now? Maybe he ought to inform someone. Like her parents. But I don't know Hungarian. And a wave of indignity surged through him, as if they'd left him stranded among the islands of debris, and he nearly ran out to the salon, gasping with distress, needing to be hugged. But he did not run out. He did not move. He merely shuddered at the thought that he wasn't running out to them. That there was no longer a boy

THE BOOK OF

who went running out to the salon whenever something troubled him, that he might never insinuate himself into their hearts again, how could he bear to touch their flesh, and now the chirring returns: I am one, it says to him, I am one and everything is one, and there is no law except for mine: there are no two ways of connecting electric wires. For every button there is but one hole. There is but one direction to turn the faucet. That is how it is and that is how it will always be. Nevermore will you fall into error and confusion. I've had my eye on you for quite a while.

Mama takes the cap off the lotion and begins the massage. Papa's back is so enormous there are places left for Grandma and Yochi. Grandma lays her hands on him, and Mama watches tremulously. It's a miracle. A miracle. And Aron has to make. Now of all times he feels it coming. He checks, astonished, vaguely hopeful, he's had false alarms before. In his sleep a couple of times, but as soon as he noticed, it went away. His mind must have forced it back. So maybe this too is a false alarm. He sits up. Listening inward. Yes: a fluttering. A stirring, deep and winding, with a sticky blob of goo at the end, and a drop of moisture condenses there; oh help, Aron is aghast, why now, when he's trapped in the kitchen, it's getting stronger and stronger in there, whirling around, overpowering him, then receding, like an oval whisper, but it's there all the same, strange, it came on just after the pounding stopped. Why didn't you plan ahead, idiot, why now, when it's a thousand times harder to run out of the house squeezing your legs together, and it's scary in the valley and in the hiding place at the Wizo Nursery School, and where will you find an alternative to Edna's?

Papa is groaning hoarsely. You can hear his body relaxing, flowing, and Aron winces and fidgets on the edge of the tabouret, and the pain draws in like a wave, you can feel it starting, here it comes, bend over, crouch, oowwwww, his back and shoulders are so tense they hurt, okay, we made it through that wave, but he feels another one already, far away, maybe he should try making at home this time. Well now, that helped, thinking that, but just stop thinking about it, plan ahead! He looks up, pale-faced, with tiny beads of sweat on his forehead. Cautiously he peeks: Mama's smearing a ton of lotion on Papa's back. The cap on the bottle twists open in the same direction as the faucet. And if you twirl a spoon of honey around very fast it'll stop dripping. Would you believe that inanimate objects are capable of laughing? Well, would you? It's a whistle-like laugh, like Michael Carny giggling with Rina Fichman, *tsssssss*, what a clown. And you turn the key in the lock to the right, not the left. The way you twist the cap on the toothpaste. *Tsssssss*. Or the cap of the massage lotion. Just as spring follows winter, just as a donkey can only give birth to a baby donkey. They look so busy out there, poking and squeezing and sighing. Their faces are inscrutable. Not that they really resemble each other; well, they do, actually but they're different too; not in what's in them: in what isn't in them. Each has her own particular area to rub and knead which singles her out from the other two. Almost cruelly they press down on him. And they know it hurts, though he doesn't complain. Look: they twiddle his flesh between their fingers like dough, tearing him to pieces. Melting him down. And the only thing he dares to do is groan. In submission. In repentance. Just don't let their fingers become tangled in the forest of hair on his back or they'll pull it out, skin and all. And suddenly Aron feels a whirlpool of pain sucking him irresistibly down. It takes every last bit of strength to escape it, and he sits leaning hard against the wall, perspiring, his eyes opened wide. What's happening to him? Having to crap at a time like this. How long will he be able to hold it in? He jumps to his feet and turns off the leaky faucet. But there's another drop swelling there, he stares at it with horror. Don't look. Sit down. Bend over. No! Just the opposite! Get up. Stand straight. Hands in the air. Breathe deep. Press your cheek against the refrigerator. Hush now. Calm down. What were we thinking about? When? Never mind when, what were we thinking about, oh yes, about that kid in *Ripley's Believe It or Not*: 300 incredible cases, who also suffered from a terrible stomachache, almost died of it, and when the doctors operated they found the undeveloped fetus of his twin inside. What inventiveness. And he makes a mental note that Hanan Schweiky has a visible mustache already. Today we had our third proof, in broad daylight, and what did we find on Gil Kaplan, pimples on his forehead and his chin; wait, no, that was Asa Kolodny, you're getting confused, where's your head, you used to have a good head; well, at least Gideon is still pure. Okay, he has an Adam's apple and his voice is pretty much a lost cause, but we've managed to stop the rest of it for the time being. Aron sneaks back and sits down on the tabouret, holding the knife, *tsssssss*. Like babies start walking when they're one, lose their milk teeth when they're five. Like children always grow taller than their parents. Everyone progresses point by point. Stage by stage. So this victory with Gideon is worthless anyway, maybe he still has some purity left, but the way he acts, he's so competitive, and he gets embarrassed whenever Aron opens his mouth in front of other kids. You talk like a professor, he says, you talk the way they talk on the radio, he says, and this coming from Gideon, whose whole life—only when they're alone together is he nice to Aron, like a mensch, and the minute other kids join in, he starts lecturing them, and Aron has never, but never, criticized him for it, so what's left of that friendship, Aron muses sadly, it's like all I ever worry about is his body, the rest I've lost. And we're very fast at catching spies, says the pinchy chirring voice, we test them: can they slide a straw in the bottle on the first try, for instance. *Tsssssss.* Soon, the week after Passover, Gideon would go for tests at the clinic, they wanted to find out why he's always so tired. A couple of times he almost fell asleep in class. All Aron needed now was for them to find something in his blood, traces or residues of something. Suddenly he's up, choking, wanting out. Where to? You're under house arrest. The foursome in the salon notice his impulsive movement and look up, taking him in at a single glance, and he slinks back to the kitchen. Sit down, you have more than half the potatoes left to peel. He used to be such a pro at this, yeah, yeah, who cares; what did he want from Gideon anyway, to keep him safe a little while longer, safe in a bubble of the present continuous, and once more he rises and nearly runs out. Here it comes again, what made it start, I ought to be grateful, and he sits back down, intent and molten, what's going on, it feels like a little earthquake inside, shaking him up from head to toe, everything is erupting, everything is changing shape, a great sharp pyramid is slowly revolving in his guts, and say he was willing to compromise about one of his problems. Not that he would give in so easily, but let's just say he—limped a little, okay? Limping is simple. Plenty of people limp. They have an accident, or maybe they were even born like that, with one leg shorter. And they limp. They can move the foot a little, like a broken screw. But limping is pretty clear-cut. It's like an appliance breaking. It isn't a curse. It's not as if everything died inside. Come to think of it, Binyumin the gimp has pimples on his face. And he tries to imagine himself limping, and instantly it's as if someone handed him a long list, and he can see himself tripping on the stairway or on the soccer field, or roller skating, or riding his bike, or folk dancing, right, we get the picture, or having to decide which foot to set forward as you step off the bus first so no one will notice, or going to the water fountain when they start playing chicken, and dropping out of the honor guard when they stand at attention beside the memorial plaque for fallen alumni on Independence Day. Enough already, he submits, angrily, wearily shaking his head. Or what if you were blind or deaf, or fat, or you stuttered or had a birthmark on your face, oh please, but what's going on in his stomach, what were we thinking about, nothing, oh yes, how once, on the school trip to the Sea of Galilee, the best school trip they ever had, they visited a studio in an old Arab house and watched a potter at work throwing slabs of clay into slender urns or pudgy crocks. The clay decides, said the potter, and he let them feel it with their fingers, and the clay decided: a clumsy blob turned into a smooth and graceful pitcher with parted lips, don't peek!

Papa groans with pleasure and asks them to scratch a little higher, nu, by the whatzit. The spine, the spine, Aron corrects him in a whisper. You'd think he'd know a simple word like that. Mama and Yochi start from opposite sides and work toward the middle, till he's positively bursting with bliss. Imagine Papa trying to pronounce something long and complicated, like hippopotamus, or that word in the health book —hypothalamus, or even an easy word, like firefly: could a big fat tongue like his pronounce it without flubbing, and wouldn't it be awful if it tied itself in a knot forever trying to say flierflifflfflff! Aron wants to jump out the kitchen window right now, run to the Wizo Nursery School, and squat in the dark, but the windowsill is full of jars, jars of pickled cucumbers and pickled peppers and sauerkraut and pimientos and olives and pearl onions, even carrots; there's nothing she doesn't pickle, no vegetable is safe with Mama around.

Nimbly snipping, he tries to be careful. Only his fingertips move. And the women are busy massaging Papa from top to bottom. You could melt just thinking about it. They've never given him such a long one before. It's impossible to see the whole of him from here; maybe they dismantled him and later they'll put him back together again, only this time they'll decide how. And if you throw back your head a little you see a section of shoulder and Mama's fingers lingering on the muscles, examining something, scratching with her fingernail, trying to find out if it's real, and then she gives another little scratch. Hey, what kind of massage is this. And her fingers start tickling, coochie-coochie-coo! And

THE BOOK OF

Papa squirms and squeals with laughter, and she tickles him all the way up his arm, accidentally shoving Yochi and Grandma out of the way, allowing herself the liberty of a little smile, she hasn't smiled like that in weeks, and Papa's mouth is squashed against the Bordeaux sofa in a saggy grin, you could easily mistake it for a frown, and the question is whether that mouth could manage a word like "thread," and Aron pictures a golden thread shining in the sunlight, dripping honey, like a guitar string still aquiver with the melody a moment after it was strummed. Threa-d, murmurs Aron with fine-drawn lips, with deep devotion, threa-d, like a string plucked out of his depths, lyrical and sweet, but airy too, and hazy like the halos around those people in his negatives, and he can easily slip through any crack, through a needle's eye. He tilts his head, eyes shut, lips parted like the mouth of an urn, uttering "Threa-d," like the whistle of the wind, gentle but cutting, and he smiles to himself: Papa can't get in, like a thread with a knot at the end. Ha ha: Aron the passing thread, thready-Aron passes, while Papa, the knot-man, with his face and his body and his blackheads—wham! Aron is all the way in now, alone inside where everything is soft, translucent, simple as a diagram, pure and simple, all aglow with a firefly light; there is a little light in everything, even the steel wool for scrubbing panels has a mysterious spark, even dark purple grapes have a dusky gleam, or a thick drop of blood on the tip of your finger, that too, if you say it right with deep devotion, "a drop of blood," you see a beacon flashing forth as from a distant lighthouse, and certain words, if you know how to pronounce them in a special way, not from the outside but as though you were calling their names, right away they turn to you, they show you their pink penetralia, they purr to you and they're yours, they'll do anything you want; take "bell," for instance, he rolls it over his tongue as though tasting it for the first time ever, "bellll," or "honeysuckle," or "lion" or "legend" or "coal" or "melody" or "gleam" or "velvet," melting on his tongue, sloughing off their earthly guises, till suddenly there is red heat, a cinder of memory spreading its glow as it slowly disappears into his mouth, for *Lo, this hath touched thy lips, and thine iniquity is taken away, and thy sin is expiated.*

He pushes himself on the tabouret which Mama likened to King Farouk wearing a fez, and leans forward to watch, carefully so as not to let anything leak out. He observes the salon: the three women working on Papa's back like cranes on a water buffalo. Grandma seems to be getting tired. Even now that she's had an operation, the power controlling her mind is pretty weak. Mama settles her on the Franzousky, so she'll rest. She sniffs her from behind in case she made. Grandma's eyes are covered with a membrane. Just don't let her die in the house. And Mama mutters under her breath, How long can we go on keeping her at home like this? And if Grandma makes in the middle of the salon, he thinks, they'll kill her for certain. And after the "thorough" yet, when everything's shiny and clean. And on such a special day, the day Papa came home. Mama will murder her on the spot. He cringes and freezes all over. Only his lips are still Aron, and he slowly puckers them till they let out a whistle, the secret ultrasonic whistle only females can hear, and then they follow you blindly and do whatever you want. But he didn't believe Giora, not even at the time. He puckers his lips. Concentrates. Forgets the rest. Forgets what's building up inside him, dense and ugly. His lips weave a web.

The three women sat up with a start, as though someone had tickled them inside. As though someone had whispered their names. Even Grandma quivered. Only Papa lay inert and didn't notice anything. Deaf and heavy, he sprawled on the sofa. Aron stopped in alarm, and the women went back to their task. Again Aron set his lips, forming his snare of a whistle, and with faithful precision wove his mighty web. Again the women turned around as in a trance, moonily picking up their colorful dusters, and while Papa rose on his elbows with a "Huh?" and a "Whuh?," they surrounded Aron with mincing softness, fluttering by him like feather clouds, titillating the creatures of his writhing back, rippling with the pleasures of the intimate tickle, with helpless, jellylike giggles of laughter, and Aron whispers "lion," "honeysuckle," "melody," "legend," and one by one the words present their sleek underbellies, giving out a reddish glow, revealing a tiny vibrant tongue inside that tintinnabulates with longing for his own supple tongue, his tongue unbound, his lump of flesh, and Aron grew sublimely giddy with self-transcendence, and one twilit moment later, swathed in darkening shame and the stench of primal disgrace, he slid off the tabouret onto the floor, where, strangely cool, he passed the runty knife over the cut on his middle finger again, watching the timorous spurt, and in his bowels, an amazing void, an emptiness like nothing he can remember, the emptiness of somebody else. And oh, the unbearable sting of bliss at that moment, long as eternity, when he flowed and flowed; giving

THE BOOK OF

birth to himself, a small, beloved, stinking self; rid at last of the horrible anguish, the harsh dark secret, not his own, he had been forced to keep inside. Circumspectly he lay down with his cheek to the floor. The stench filled the kitchen. A fire in his pants. The blood trickled out near his open eye and he observed it. Like somebody else's blood dripping into the cracks. In fact, everything was somebody else's. He felt so light. Light enough to float. With naught to encumber his immortal soul. Aury. Aery. Ari. There was no doubt: from now on everything would change. To tell the truth, the ordeal has weakened him. Not just the events of the last few weeks. Forget that. But everything he's been through in these three years of waste. His brains have weakened too. He forgets things. He's not on the ball anymore the way he used to be. He finds it hard to concentrate. He scribbles nonsense on exam papers. It's as if the whatzit in there were bloating up and crowding out everything else, pressing down and squashing it flat. He used to be known as a comedian. He could really make them laugh. Do impersonations of just about anyone. Now even the laughter center had pooped out on him, and he was gray and boring. Other kids were growing up while he—yeah right, he made lists of Adam's apples and hairy legs and armpits and pimples and body odor. But Mama's noticed something. She sits up suddenly. Her forehead wrinkles. And he will be redeemed. Oh yes, no two ways about it. He will remember all he has lost. And she blurts out a question to Yochi in Yiddish: Do you smell anything, Yochileh, and Yochi sniffs and says no. Because so help me, if she just made on the Franzousky, I'm taking her to Emergency first thing in the morning and leaving her there, a thousand doctors won't persuade me to take her back, and Aron doesn't even have to reach into his pocket and touch the onion strip to hear her thinking: No more happy times with Mamchu here. But Aron will be a good boy. He'll change. He'll learn how to play the guitar again, he'll play his new guitar for them, he will play a golden flute and lead the other children in a song, he will be crowned a prince, tell stories, interpret dreams, fend off famines, trap the lustrous auras of this world in glassy marbles. Mama rushes over to Grandma and forces her to her feet, sniffs her from behind, and stays fixed for a moment. And to each and every aura Aron will give a name, a secret name, and he will string the names together on a fine golden thread, he himself will be that thread, and he will draw forth the soul of things and hide it between his lips . . . Again Mama sits up.

Disconcertedly she pushes Grandma down on the Franzousky, and her nostrils quiver, scanning, tuning in, homing in on the kitchen, bouncing back to Grandma, then stubbornly returning to the kitchen, advancing, shrinking, and flaring slowly in double perplexity, in disbelief, in re- vulsion, until a lightning bolt of pagan horror flashes on her face.

THE BOOK OF

26

Nevertheless, that spring Aron fell in love. One evening, on his way across the yard of the Wizo Nursery School, he caught a glimpse of Zacky Smitanka making out with Dorit Alush on the bench. Aron ducked off the path before they noticed him, slinked along the hedges till he found the hole in the fence, and slipped through. He hurried home and sat around in the gloom of his bedroom, silent, empty. Reluctantly he dragged his feet in to supper. Mama came over to him right away and pressed her lips to his forehead, and for a minute he thought she was going to kiss him because she knew what he was feeling, a mother's heart, so he closed his eyes helplessly, nearly bursting with the softness of her lips on his forehead, where they lingered, hovered a moment, pressed down again; she hadn't kissed him in ages and he never dreamed he wanted her to so badly, but no, he didn't have a fever, she reported dryly, sitting down again. So why do you look like that? growled Papa, suppressing his annoyance. Like what? asked Aron weakly. Squashed like a pacha, said Mama. Like someone sat on your face. He sighed and shrugged his shoulders, imagining Dorit Alush's long brown leg jerking up and down with pain or pleasure, who knew how many more smutty surprises were lurking out there. Papa was silent. Mama was silent too. Aron left the table and said he didn't feel so good, and he put on his pajamas and got into bed, and tried with all his might to fall asleep, to sink deeper and deeper, deeper than his mind and memory, and he must have succeeded, because through the alchemy of despair, the only philosophy he really knew, Aron's first love blossomed overnight.

Aliza Lieber, Miri Tamari, Rina Fichman; dizzily he circled among them on a mystic quest, a seeker of love. Ariella Biltzky, Osnat Berlin, Tammy Lerner; everyday girls lit up from within, shyly inclining their sunflower faces; Ruthy Zuckerman, Hanni Altschuller, Hanni Hirsch, Orna Agami; he loved them all despite their flaws, and presently, because of them, those minor imperfections that seemed like secret clues intended for him alone; Ruchama Taub, Gila Shalgi, even chubby Naomi Feingold for ten days (till he found out her brother had six toes on his left foot); he loved them whole and he loved them piecemeal; sometimes he lost his heart to a cheek, the grace of a hand, the lilt of a giggle, and ignored their cruder appendages; he became infatuated with Varda Koppler for a week of illusion and dark jealousy over her soldier pen pal, when he noticed her lisp. And then he discovered a dimple on Malka Shlein and the crater of a vaccination on the adorable arm of Adina Ringle, and it filled him with wonder that in every girl he studied closely there was something worthy of his eternal love, and he circulated like a courier bursting with the secret knowledge he carried, speaking out to them in his quiet way; Esty Parsitz, Aviva Castlenuovo, Nira Vered . . . the glass slipper worked overtime.

Yaeli Kedmi was a year younger, in seventh grade, and for the past few years she'd been walking home from school with him and the other neighborhood kids. She was small and demure, but her cheeks were full, and better than he knew her face or voice he knew the shiny black mantle of her wavy hair. Since the age of nine she had trailed along, and they were used to her silence, her modesty. Rarely did anyone address her, nor were they particularly careful with secrets in her presence: she was What's-her-name Yaeli whom they were supposed to keep an eye on at the Bet Hakerem intersection till she drifted away without a word at the corner of Bialik Street.

But one afternoon Aron accompanied Yochi to her ballet class in the Valley of the Cross near the new wing they were building at the Israel Museum. What interested him there were the blasts of dynamite every day around five and the shock waves that filled the air, and when Yochi went to change into her costume, Aron watched the younger girls just finishing their lesson, among whom he suddenly spotted Yaeli. She wore a tight black leotard, and her arms and legs didn't look skinny anymore,

THE BOOK OF

they looked gracefully slender as she danced, like the swiggles of a sharpened pencil, and the billowing hair which had always seemed heavy and overlavish on such a tiny frame, flowed around her now as she pirouetted, glorious, sublime.

Aron stepped back in confusion and stood by the entrance door, staring at Yaeli. Rina Nikova, the aging ballet mistress, clapped her hands and gave him a start—he thought she was going to point at him. He tried to assume an air of indifference, but it melted in the heat leaking out of him. Madame Nikova explained something to the girls in her thick Russian accent. Yaeli did not look his way. Again the music played, and they practiced the arabesque as Aron devoured Yaeli's face, so lovely and delicately drawn with a sharp quick line; and her gaze of concentration when she practiced the "cat step"; and her milky skin; the note of defiance in her nose; her slanty almond eyes, which seemed unable to decide whether to be brown like his or hazel; and the smile that hovered over her full red mouth, the netherlip swollen. Aron could feel his heart pound, it was happening, a burst of light; Yaeli danced before him so airy and free—free as a bird, the words beat through him like wings in flight—and then he knew, he knew with certainty that she was a vegetarian as he had been, and he also knew that this time, for her sake, he would assert his vegetarianism, and then, most miraculously, with a single look and a single heartbeat, Yaeli was redeemed.

Yochi came back wearing her leotard, moving leadenly. By now it was impossible not to notice she was fat, and the only reason Madame Nikova didn't kick her out was that soon she would be going into the army. Her legs were flabby, and her buttocks fairly burst out of the leotard. Approximately two years before, though she had perfectly smooth legs inherited from Grandma Lilly, Yochi started waxing off the hair so it would grow back thicker and she could remove it like all the other girls. Now, as she slowly twirled before his eyes, he could see the black dots on her calves and for a moment he was angry with her, hostile even, but it wasn't her fault, poor thing, what with Papa's appetite and Mama's constipation, and still he felt angry when she was pushed back into the third row with the beginners, a dove among the sparrows.

Madame Nikova clapped three times. Lesson over, she declared, and a stream of girls burbled out to the dressing room. Aron backed off and leaned against the wall, blushing with shyness and excitement, dizzy with the mingled scents of orange blossom, perspiration, kittens. A pair of legs paused in front of him as he stared fixedly at the floor, two legs he had once thought scrawny, bony, which were now most definitely slender and shapely, and for a split second he glanced up at her with a trembling heart and wobbling knees, and the expression she wore was gentle, but also defiant and playful and self-assured: I saw you looking, said her eyes, I was dancing for you, can you believe it's me?

The next day, on their way home from school, Aron didn't dare exchange glances with her. Zacky and Gideon walked in the lead as usual, arguing boisterously, with Aron at their side lagging slightly behind, listening to them through Yaeli's ears. How well she must know them all, he realized, she had absorbed so much over the years, and he wondered what she thought about him, and about his problem. Zacky told a joke he'd read in the book about Prime Minister Levi Eshkol, and Gideon grumbled that jokes like that ought to be banned because they're bad for national morale, and Hanan Schweiky hollered, Stop lecturing, Strashnov, and let Zacky give us another one. Aron was disgusted at their coarseness and vulgarity, how would he be able to protect Yaeli's innocence, and when Zacky started making fun of Morduch, the blind beggar, and tossed him a nail instead of a coin, Aron drew away from them in protest. Yaeli trailed behind the group as usual, weighed down by her school bag, drooping under the crowning glory of her heavy hair; he glanced at her furtively. She dances even when she's standing still, he thought, not just at Madame Nikova's, and who had been idiot enough to suppose she was tagging along; his eyes lingered on her sprightly feet, she had a little red scar by the buckle of her sandal and it made him burst with love. When the rest of them went into the supermarket, he almost dared to lag behind and go through the automatic door all by himself, he could do it, because with every breath he felt a new fullness inside him, and still he hesitated, maybe he wasn't quite ready yet, and he sneaked in with a young woman pushing a stroller and caught up with the other kids. He waited his chance to say something to Yaeli, to make contact with her somehow. As they were crossing Bet Hakerem Street he hung back, and when she barged ahead he blurted, almost gruffly, "Look out, car coming," and saw her neck turn rosy.

Love made him gentle and happy. He suddenly remembered how

happy he could be. In the morning, before dressing, he would lie in bed with his hand under his head and stare up at the bright blue sky, feeling as though about to return from a long, long journey. And then he would jump out of bed to greet the new day. One evening, when he got a splinter in his finger and Mama was sterilizing a needle over the burner to take it out for him, he almost started crying, his throat felt choked, and Mama thought he was scared or something and started teasing him, though he was really moved to tears that she cared about him and loved him so. From one day to the next he dropped his secret experiments, forgot about them, blotted them out. Once when he found a couple of cigarette butts in his school-bag pocket, he blithely tossed them away. As though they happened to get there by chance. He dismissed the things of the past. Even that strange last summer and his winter hibernation. A new leaf. A new leaf. When they sent him out to buy something at the corner grocery, he volunteered to go all the way to the shopping center just to be able to pass her house and smell the flowering honeysuckle in the yard. There was a place in his stomach, under his heart, that would glow with pain whenever he longed for Yaeli, and at recess one time he agreed to join the kids for soccer, and showed them how a real champion plays, and reveled in the game, running and kicking, and even scored a goal, and everyone sighed: what a waste that someone like Arik Kleinfeld should hang up his shoes, maybe there's some way we can convince him to start practicing with the team again for the eighth-grade cup at the end of the year. He left the field flushed and exhilarated, and ran to the water fountain, where out of the corner of his eye he saw she had broken away from a cluster of girls and was coming over to drink. His courage failed. He leaned over nervously and took a sip, and saw her wavy black mane so near he closed his eyes, and drank up vigorously, till he remembered the falling water level in the Sea of Galilee.

They peeked at each other, and Aron blushed as he blurted out, "I saw you at Madame Nikova's." Her lip swelled, and her teeth sparkled like pearls for him. How could she be so calm. Calmer than he was. Quietly she said, "I want to be a dancer when I grow up." "I used to play the guitar," said Aron, all aflutter. "But you quit." She didn't ask. She knew. Maybe she was even chiding him for it. She knew everything about him. It was no use trying to improve his image in her eyes. I stand before you. Help me. You must have noticed what I'm going through. It's a good thing I don't have to say it in words. But I am getting better now, it's still a secret, Yaeli, but I feel I really am. Everything is opening up inside me. Thanks to you-know-who. "I'm going to take it up again," Aron mustered the strength to answer. "I got a new guitar for my bar mitzvah and I'm going to start playing it soon." Yaeli smiled at him. She believed him. The magic would work. Their hands lingering on the water fountain were twins, and Aron, who knew exactly what his hands looked like, didn't pull them back, with all his strength he didn't pull them back, so she would know everything about him, from her he would keep no secrets, so that a standard of absolute truth and sincerity would prevail from the start, even if it hurt. "My name is Aron," he foolishly blurted, but it wasn't foolish at all: he was offering his name to her, his name with everything in it. She smiled. Again her netherlip protruded, curiously, affectionately. The janitor rang the school bell.

It was the same the day after. And the day after that. A fine, transparent web. The kids walked home amid the usual clamor, laughing, shouting, fooling around, with every word a silent clue, the cooing of a carrier pigeon: Did you hear what he said? Remind you of anything? What do they understand, these dimwits, these outsiders.

And meanwhile, unconsciously, unintentionally, Gideon slows his pace from time to time, hanging back till Aron catches up with him, and then, what do you know, he wants to talk, it's been months since he and Aron talked so familiarly, in front of everyone yet, and Zacky Smitanka stares at them dumbfounded, shrinking and lowering as if the spark of life has gone out of him, his little black eyes drying up in the desert of his face, and then he punches gangly Michael Carny on the back of the neck. What's happening, Giraffe, how's the weather up there? And a minor skirmish follows which Gideon doesn't even notice; he's talking to Aron, peering into his face, inspecting it so closely Aron has to practice some complicated maneuvers to win a glance from her eyes, but subterfuge is also a spice, she's ready, at last, and Aron feels rewarded for having kept himself pure throughout the difficult times; he never once sullied himself, in word or deed, was never so much as tempted to rub down there; he knew how he would feel if he did it without a real urge, and even in the days of the maddening fear, his heart had told him how much he would hate himself if he ever gave in like certain others who sell themselves with lust and shame and receive

THE BOOK OF

their sticky voucher in return; but not him; he never succumbed. Never cheapened himself. And now therefore his joy is resurrected, the dead letter of his childhood lost so long in the mazes of bureaucracy had at last been delivered. Careful now! A chill was sneaking up; a beady eye, a cruel Cyclopean eye slowly opened inside his head, searching for him: What's all this happiness? Who's that there being so happy? And right away—like a spy destroying his documents before the authorities catch him—he banishes Yaeli from his thoughts. And walks ahead with a swagger. And then it flickers tentatively deep in his stomach, exactly where it burned when he used to think about his problem; yes, that's where his joy is coming from. Hush, that's classified, he must never let anything imperil his love; he will fight this time. Indeed he will.

"Hey, what if"—he says at the top of his voice to Gideon, who is trying to catch up with him. (What if what? He only said that to distract them)—"what if there were these people, see, people you could rent your pimples to if you wanted?" Gideon laughs. "You and your ideas," and turns to Michael Carny, who has approached for protection against Zacky's punches, saying, "Kleinfeld and his zany ideas!" The first kind word in a long long time. "No, seriously, Gideon, what if there were these people who could take over your pimples and pains, say, even for a week. So if you had a school trip to go on and you broke an arm, all you'd have to do is deposit it with this person for a week . . ." Gideon laughs again and pats Aron on the shoulder. Aron, deeply thrilled, peeks over and knows she's heard, and, best of all, that she's witnessed Gideon's hand touching his shoulder, the electric circuit closing between their bodies, without a hiss; it was like, say, in physics, with object A and object B, any two objects, only one of them was Aron's body, and it was so bright, so accessible and unreserved, that another boy, a certain object A, could simply reach out and touch him, pat him on the shoulder. And overwhelmed with joy, he leaps up waving his hands in the air, doing his impersonation of Rodensky, the comedian, and Gideon, who has been watching attentively, responds with his own rather lame imitation.

And now that astute and sober-minded Gideon had given the go-ahead, they started romping, flying like a storm through the paths of Memorial Park, frightening a group of kindergarten children, shaking down the fruit from a carob tree, and Hanan Schweiky and Meirky Blutreich flanked the war monument with an empty bottle in one hand

and a rolled-up sweater for a soccer ball, and everyone guessed what they were spoofing and shouted the movie advertisement in unison, "We call it near-beer!" And Yaeli watched this hullabaloo with a placid expression, a smile tapering at the corners of her mouth, as though she guessed whose anonymous presence had launched this merry ship. But don't think about it, not in your head, under the gaze of the evil eye. Still the firecracker whistled, flashed red in his belly, scorched beneath his heart, where it might yet spontaneously, effortlessly, burst into being amid many little pinpricks of pleasure, exactly where it burns when he eats an omelette fried in oil; forget the details, look over there, see Hanan Schweiky jumping up on the bench to do that routine from *Comedy Night*, puffing his cheeks and sticking out his stomach, and Aron and the others join in, oh, please let his voice crack now, please, God, it's coming, it's coming—and Gideon casts an anxious glance at him, flowing back to his friend over bubbly streams, detecting the gleam of a tiny vein in the heart of a derelict gold mine.

27

Gideon and Aron are friends again. He repeats this in various ways to himself: Hey! They're friends again! Or (coolly offhanded): You know those two guys, What's-his-name and What's-his-name, who used to hang around together and then sort of didn't, well, now they do again. He laughs happily to himself. Open-armed they ran toward each other like actors in a movie, like children in a drawing with O-shaped mouths, as if they hadn't seen each other every day for the past two years, as if there hadn't been an understanding between them throughout the separation that once or twice a week Aron would hand Gideon a yellow pill which he swallowed without water, oh, if only he hadn't, but now they met like travelers returning from afar, unpacking their suitcases together: naturally Gideon did most of the talking, because Aron didn't have much to say. But Gideon didn't mind that: he told Aron about being a leader in the youth movement, and about his brother Manny's maneuvers in the Fouga Magister squadron, and about Manny's new girlfriend and about the Lambretta Zacky put together out of junk; Aron merely nodded his head and listened intently, and again Gideon told about Manny's girlfriend, who was from Kibbutz Bet Zera and who slept overnight in his and Manny's room, and he told him about the air force youth battalion, and that after Independence Day they were going to learn how to shoot a Czech rifle, and about how Manny kicked him out of the room when his girlfriend slept over, and Aron listened and kept silent. Together they rambled through the streets of the workers' neighborhood, and Gideon told him casually that a boy and girl in his youth group had started going together, and he intended to have a serious talk with the kids about the social implications of pairing up at their age. Aron let nothing show on his face. Then Gideon launched the subject of Anat Fish, who did in the end go with her boyfriend Mickey Zik to the beach in Eilat, and shared a sleeping bag with him; this wasn't Gideon's usual way of speaking, he seemed to be winding himself around Aron and pleading for help, but Aron couldn't figure out why. He said nothing. Gideon too fell silent and yawned widely. For a moment their new thread of intimacy seemed to slacken, everything turned gray and saggy, but it was enough for Aron to think Yaeli, to pull in his stomach so that it tickled in that new place under the heart, hush, mum's the word; but now Gideon was warming up to him again, displaying exuberant signs of closeness, gabbing about some girl from another class who dropped out of the youth movement and joined the social set, and Aron thought, After all this time, Gideon doesn't shave yet either, still has last year's peach fuzz over his lip, though his eyebrows are thicker now, soon they'll grow together over the bridge of his nose and then Gideon will look more serious than ever, but there's plenty of time till then, okay, his voice has changed, but that's not new, we're used to that, when Aron would phone him —in the days of their estrangement—and hang up right away, he wasn't always sure who'd answered, Gideon or his father, Gideon had taught himself to speak in an indifferent, expressionless voice without a smile or question mark at the end of a question, and then there was the matter of height; he was almost a whole head taller than Aron by now, though maybe he would stay there for a while, and if you looked at it objectively, he really wasn't that far ahead of him, he just had a little more confidence, that's all, a few more bones in his face, and he walked like a cowboy, spread-legged, and if God forbid the pills worked, but they wouldn't, would they, his heart contracted, they were way past the prescription date, so they couldn't affect him one way or another, and there was another explanation, just a hunch really, which Aron whispered to himself in a language he didn't know: maybe, deep down inside, Gideon was waiting for him to catch up. And with a wild burst of enthusiasm Aron suggested that they go to Mandelbaum Gate tomorrow and watch the police convoy come down from the Israeli enclave on Mt. Scopus after a two-week shift; he always liked to read the newspaper

THE BOOK OF

description of the tension in the air as they crossed through Jordanian territory, peering through the holes in their armored vehicles till they were safely over the border, but Gideon didn't seem to be listening and started in again about Zacky Smitanka, who made himself, yeah, we know, a Lambretta, how could Aron forget, they were out there every Friday, Zacky and his new buddies, hoody types like him with Lambrettas and motorbikes and leather jackets, driving the neighbors crazy with the noise, and Papa comes down in his undershirt and says, Hey, gang, what'you doing, busting our heads with all that noise, but they know him and they're not afraid, they crowd around him like puppy dogs, ask him for advice, and he teaches one guy how to tune the carburetor and change the plugs, and eventually he hops on for a trial spin, and the biker rides behind him, hugging his waist, and Papa tears down the street like a hooligan, roaring with laughter, and don't forget that Zacky let Papa take the first run on his illegitimate Lambretta; Aron was peeking from behind the curtain just then and saw the look on Zacky's face, the way Papa smiled at him and the way Zacky smiled at Papa, like a real moron who finally manages to bring home a good report card; and Gideon said that, by the way, he heard it from reliable sources, Zacky himself, what Zacky did with What's-her-name, that cow, Dorit Alush, something called "between the legs." He blurted the news out quickly, looking away, desperate for Aron to say something quickly and dispel the foul sound of those words, the kind of words that had never passed between them, and Aron didn't respond; so that's what Gideon was getting at, that's why he was beating around the bush, he had broken their tacit agreement again, he was a traitor, always stretching the delicate membranes of their friendship to the limit, he was getting to be so darn tough, growing from the inside and breaking out, and Gideon sensed that Aron was withdrawing from him and tried to repair the damage by saying that in his opinion kids their age weren't mature enough for real love, and that he'd vowed not to fall in love until after flight school, and then he would marry his first girlfriend, not someone easy like Manny's girlfriend, uh-uh; Gideon turned to Aron, his face aglow with inner conviction, his sincere and honest face again, and he swore to him that he would never debase the most sacred thing of all; friendship with a girl—sure, definitely, but nothing dirty or nasty, and Aron nodded with all his might, to signal Gideon that he was on the right track, and Gideon kept watching Aron's expressions, which guided him, and then said slowly, as though deciphering a secret bulletin from deep inside Aron, that he wished he could persuade the kids in the movement to obey the tenth commandment of socialist youth, sexual purity, and Aron almost shouted, Me too, I swear it, and his eyes were moist and shiny as Gideon looked into them and remarked much to his own surprise, You notice that kid, What's-her-name, Yaeli, she's really starting to grow up, isn't she?

Aron turned aside and looked into the distance, feeling a little like someone trying to keep the pupil in the next seat from copying, but since this was Gideon, his good friend Gideon, he forced himself to turn back and asked weakly if Gideon really thought so, and Gideon said, Absolutely, haven't you noticed, there's something about her, she keeps to herself a lot but she has this quiet smile, too bad she's a bourgeois Scout instead of a socialist. Well anyway, she's still young enough to win over to the movement. Aron could no longer contain his myriad emotions and fervently confessed his love for her to Gideon, telling him about their secret glances and the conversation full of hidden meanings by the drinking fountain. He described the nights he lay awake and saw her dance before his eyes. He told him about the scraps of paper with her name written on them that he stuck in his sandwich at school and swallowed, sitting right next to her during recess, and how he went to the nurse's room with some excuse and stole Yaeli's dental records, and then hid them, and look, these are flowers from the honeysuckle bushes in front of her house, I keep them in my handkerchief.

Gideon slapped his knee with a loud laugh, and Aron too began to laugh uproariously, listening to himself in pure amazement, and they ran together, breathless, on fire, all the way to their rock in the valley, where they sat down with tears of laughter in their eyes; what a laugh that was, not the kind he could squeeze from the glands in his armpits and squirt out through his mouth in a dirty artificial spray, and Gideon was all eyes, his pupils darting around in search of the fine gold vein. Go on, tell, describe some more, and Aron, drunk and princely, prodigal as the forces of nature, told everything: about her face when she danced for him, the way she suddenly appeared in her leotard, extending her slender leg in the air, noble and free, the way, the way, the way; as he spoke he felt the agreeable prickling sensation in the new place, her place, somewhere to the south, as they say in the army, the root of the

THE BOOK OF

secret shining over the point he had established there, beware! The cruel eye is watching, the wind of ruin blows hither, freezing everything, and down below, a round new world is floating inside him, an adorable bubble, with a tiny dancer tapping her toes inside it; wait, she isn't really in there yet, she keeps disappearing every minute, maybe he'd been too explicit in his thoughts, maybe the suspicious eye had stirred beneath its marbly lid, tracing every spark of light, tracking radarlike after the waves of heat and joy; this is nonsense, gobbledygook, so he told Gideon only what he was allowed to tell him, and used his mouth to etch the lips pouting over her chin, to whittle the arching muscle of her calf, the sweet little space between her big toe and the others . . . Gideon's eyes grew round as he watched Aron's lips dripping the first words of love he had ever spoken aloud, words imbued with what they described, and Gideon too could taste her skin, her rounded cheeks, the sweetness of her childish lips, the lower one swollen and smiling. Sometimes Gideon seemed to be trying to control himself, to protect himself, to draw comparisons, whether out of pettiness or concern, between Aron's description and the girl he knew, but gradually the pendulum stopped swinging, he forgot the little girl and her slender legs, absented himself completely from the green eyes in which only Aron was reflected now, a tiny figure paddling relentlessly, and Aron too could not help marveling how the words coming out of him not only showed Yaeli as she was but beautified and refined her, transforming her into a vision of who she would shortly become, eliminating a flaw or two, the proud smile as a possible foreshadowing of conceit, a certain note of resolve and worrisome striving in her nose, and even her wonderful lower lip, which at times, from a certain angle, appeared too full, too earthy for a girl like her; these he mercifully concealed from Gideon, erased them with a wag of his magic tongue, and now he was worthy to love her unto death in the rosy future to which they would jointly aspire.

Finally he stopped talking, dry-mouthed and breathless, surprised to see evening had already fallen. Gideon's eyes remained fixed on him, with a thread of spit between his parted lips, and Aron vaguely recalled a different mouth, gaping at him thus, with the same thread of spit, and he felt a tickle of pride inside that he, Aron, was being looked at like this, he and his words had accomplished this, and the thread of spit was not disgusting, not in the least, for Aron and his words had created it, and Gideon's face resumed the cast of the child he was, shucking off its bony hardness.

"Listen." Gideon spoke at last in a voice so quiet it sounded like his old melodious voice. "If you're so crazy about her, why don't we walk her home sometime?"

"You mean both of us? Together?" Aron's eyes lit up. "You want to?"

But the next day, in the first few minutes after they joined her on their way home, a stupid argument flared up between her and Gideon, so that instead of talking as Aron had imagined countless times, about her and her parents and her girl friends and her ballet class and her ambition to be a dancer and his to play the guitar, Gideon started lecturing them, as usual, preaching to the world, and never once looked at Yaeli. She walked with them in silence, as usual, and if it thrilled her that two boys had dropped out of the group to follow her home, she didn't let it show. A blush spread over her throat, not the shade Aron treasured in his memory, but a louder pink, with an unbecoming red at its center.

"The whole class will break up!" Gideon summarized his argument and sniffed with fury.

"Aren't you exaggerating slightly?" said Yaeli with a self-assurance that took Aron's breath away. "Look, if you have enough backbone as a class, what's the harm in letting kids try out different things."

Aron exulted inwardly: Good for you!

"Different things!" Gideon practically shuddered at the words, raising his arms and still not looking at Yaeli. "What do you mean! All they want to do is sit on the railings on Saturday night and whistle at girls!"

"That's their privilege. There's no law that says you have to spend Saturday night at a youth group or Scout meeting arguing about politics." Aron gloated with an inward chuckle. Wow, she's really letting him have it.

"Great! Terrific!" cried Gideon, and his voice cracked twice. "Next you'll tell me you're planning to drop out of Scouts so you can be completely free!"

"Not me." Yaeli answered him with a powerful stare. "But I would certainly understand someone else wanting to try something different."

"Phew! Great! Copying America! That's what results from a lack of

THE BOOK OF

idealism among today's youth!" shouted Gideon, his collar fluttering. Aron waited tensely for Yaeli's answer. Her wavy black hair was full of electricity, he could almost hear it breathing over the clamor. But instead of answering she broke into a silent smile which Aron found himself mimicking unconsciously.

"Go on, laugh." Gideon turned to him with stifled anger, in his seemingly indifferent voice. "What are you laughing at, huh? Why don't you let us in on it instead of laughing under your mustache."

He meant no harm by it. That's how all the kids talked. But Aron's heart sank.

"I . . . don't . . . I haven't thought about it much."

Idiot. Jerk. Why didn't he make something up? Now she'd think he had no opinions. That he was shallow. Actually he wasn't sure what he thought about the matter, and at first, when everyone was joining a youth movement, he tried going to a couple of meetings, but then he quit. He couldn't stand those assemblies and standing in rows, and the ceremonies and the anthems, and doing everything together like a bunch of robots, so he kept making wisecracks and joking around till finally they kicked him out. And now it was too late to join again. They were all filled up, and anyway, by now everyone knew he was—was what? What was happening to him? He ought to be getting ready for his great awakening, approaching it with giant steps, how come he couldn't answer such a silly question? And why were they arguing about it? He had planned this very differently. And now look at him, so listless, almost paralyzed. But even after the scolding he couldn't open his mouth, not just because he was excited that they were walking her home, but because of something else, something inexplicable that was going on here, the way Yaeli was talking, for instance, and the way Gideon was answering her, only, how would Aron be able to guide his love when Yaeli was so far ahead of him, she must have been honing her opinions for quite a while, and she certainly did look feisty with her lip sticking out like that. Hey, they're arguing like grownups, he thought unhappily, they were getting all that practice in their youth movements while he spent his time daydreaming or playing with Pelé and Gummy, or hunting spies.

Aron wilted. They spoke so confidently, with the verve of the wise and experienced. So why was it so hard for him to utter words like values and ideals, responsibilities, institutions . . . "I personally believe," said Gideon, flaunting his seniority, "that you fail to grasp what happens to a society made up of isolated individualists without a frame of reference or a guiding principle."

"Do you know how to dance, Gideon?"

Her tone of voice as she spoke his name. The fact that she spoke it. He had to get hold of himself and work his way into this phony conversation.

"You don't have to know how to dance to know what goes on."

"Maybe you should try dancing sometime, then you'll see it isn't so terrible."

A tiny figure danced in the center of his little world and retreated on the tips of her toes. Malice flickered in the sleepy Cyclopean eye. Everything was sinking, sinking.

"I appreciate that it's fun to dance," he said, more cautious in his strategy.

"I personally like ballet, but I can still go crazy over the Beatles."

Uh-oh, thought Aron, now Gideon's going to start up again.

"All I can say is, thank God the Ministry of Education wouldn't allow them in the country!"

"I was sorry about that, actually."

"Oh right! I can see you now, screaming and fainting with the rest of those birdbrains!"

"Uh-huh, and scratching my face! And then I'd come home and laugh at myself, and be happy I'd been there, because when will we get another chance to kick up our heels? When we're forty?"

"Oh right, and you don't give a darn what impression we'd make on the youth of other countries, going haywire over four lousy beatniks!"

She smiled dismissively. Will you listen to the two of them arguing, mused Aron with a trace of satisfaction. He had to stop clamming up like this. He had to get his feet wet. Five steps more and he'd take the plunge. At the next cypress tree. Around the corner. Again and again he swallowed and opened his mouth, but nothing came out. What should he say? Where should he start? In his loneliness of late, words had come to be utterly inward, whispering a grammar so intimate and tortuous they could never break forth into the light. He cleared his throat, mumbled something in preparation, something about rock 'n' roll, Beatles, youth today, but it only wearied him, so he stopped before

THE BOOK OF

the words could reach their ears. What now? He walked beside them with downcast head, angrily tonguing his stubborn milk tooth. He neither spoke nor listened to them, heeding only the girl on her toes, the dancer in the leotard who was everlastingly redeemed because he had chosen her, again and again; but what about the outward Yaeli, and the outward Gideon too, for that matter, and who was Aron anyway, this outward Aron walking beside them, moving his arms and legs; how could they fail to see into him, to see what was going on? Seething with rage he lagged behind them; he would win the lottery and enroll himself at the music academy, and then someday he would play for Yaeli and she would dance to the music of his guitar; his fingers strummed the air, and Gideon would be there too, of course, little Gideon, his green eyes flashing, his eager high-pitched voice, and his warm smile the time they made the covenant in the cave. Aron mumbled to remind his inward Gideon, but the question remained, what price would he pay for being with them now, here, on the outside, in the phony world? What was the penalty for this betrayal? His lips moved, his face knitted belligerently, and over him closed the frozen steppes; how would he get out of here, what if he never could, who would be left inside, abandoned forever? He would, he would be the one who was abandoned, and again like a parrot he mimicked Gideon, the transistor generation, the "go-go" kids, what did any of it have to do with what was going on within, and who knows, maybe by now he had ceased to exist on the outside. Hey, wait up, he shouted, why're you stepping on the gas, you two? Even these simple words rang in his ears like a bad translation, an unfaithful rendering of himself. He pursed his lips and hurried to catch up.

"What's wrong with that," Yaeli answered Gideon imperturbably; how patient she was with him, why didn't she just tell him to shut up already and say what she should in that soft voice of hers: *I want to be a dancer. I used to play the guitar. And you stopped. Yes, but I'll soon start playing again. I know, I believe in you. It's kind of hard to explain it. Never mind, Aron, I understand you without words*; that's how she'd spoken to him the other times. That's what she beamed at him from the place under his heart—maybe he ought to give it a code name to confuse the enemy—the place that hurts when you eat a fried omelette or after a long run. "I don't see any reason why young people with ideals, as you call them, should have to wear blue shirts and khaki trousers. What do you think, Kleinfeld?" What did he think? Caught in a dream again. He'd barely been listening to them. Why were they getting so worked up? What was that she called him?

"Kleinfeld gets bored whenever anyone starts talking about ideals," muttered Gideon.

"That doesn't mean he's morally inferior to you," retorted Yaeli, flashing her eyes at Aron and setting his heart aglow.

"Well, I personally think it's pretty egotistical not to care about values," said Gideon in the same biting tone, and Aron regarded him with a crooked, tentative smile to show he bore no grudges. He had a fleeting vision of himself, dimly depicted as a weak old man, near death perhaps, with a flustered young couple at his bedside asking for his blessings and forgiveness. "I personally would be interested to hear what His Majesty has to say about this!" fumed Gideon, his face looking strangely red all of a sudden, and Aron braced himself and quietly, truthfully, expressed his opinion: "Kids our age don't understand what values are, all we do is imitate the high-sounding language we hear from grownups." He said it simply and sincerely, really and truly he didn't know what these values were that everyone kept talking about, at his house nobody ever discussed them and that didn't make his parents any less decent; they never stole from anybody, for fear of being caught, and the only time they ever cheated was on their income tax, which was a mitzvah, but then there was that stuff about if you find something in the street, you keep your mouth shut and put it in your pocket, and Papa's special telephone token with the string tied to it, which had already saved him a heap of money, or their sending Aron to the door when Peretz Atias and his wife came over, to lie and say his parents weren't home; outside of that they were honest, though, never harmed anyone, all they wanted was to be left in peace. So what are values, Aron wondered, and how exactly do you raise children to have these values; for instance, was Mama's warning not to tell strangers what goes on in the house, considered a value, and maybe their not telling a doctor about his problem was a kind of value too, but what if Gideon was already more adept at values than he was? "I think," he added faintly, "that until we grow up—when we're, like, mature—we won't be able to understand for ourselves what values are."

"I totally agree," Yaeli thrust at Gideon, and with that the argument died down. Aron throughout had teetertottered on the changing expressions of her face: when she addressed herself to him she was soft and fluid, but while letting fly at Gideon, there were flames of war in her almond eyes, and when Gideon caught fire, a smile flickered brightly in the corners of her mouth and the glow of a blush spread over her throat.

They walked her home and dawdled in the yard, the two of them talking, arguing really, bickering endlessly, needling each other and making up again, and Aron engraved her gestures in his heart, the way she spoke, the way she smiled, nurturing his own Yaeli and filling her with more and more life, till eventually her mother stepped out and with a smile just like Yaeli's asked if they were planning to come in or to stand there waiting for the Messiah, and only then did they say goodbye.

They walked on in silence, Gideon pensive, Aron ecstatic: all his doubts had been dispelled by the smile she beamed at him before turning into the house. Their glances had generated an electrical storm in front of the honeysuckle bush, and Aron had won, he had won the final glimpse from her almond eyes. She was his. She was his. Inside and out Yaeli was his. And Gideon, really, he would have to be taught how to behave around a girl. Aron picked a honeysuckle blossom and sniffed its fragrance. You have to know how to love, he mused, you have to love to know what life is. Love conquers death. Orblike words revolved inside him, and he decided to note these emotions in a secret diary so he would remember them forever and ever: and you have to be open to love and the pain of love, he thought. But then of course Mama would peek in his diary and find out. You have to be willing to pay the most terrible price of all: your own life in martyrdom for the sanctity of love. Maybe he would write it in code and conceal it from her that way. He stole a glance at Gideon, who was engrossed in himself, blushing slightly as his lips moved in private speech. Aron smiled: Good old Gideon, even to himself he has to lecture.

"Why did you have to argue with her like that," said Aron loftily. "What do you care if she thinks differently?"

"Me argue with her?" Gideon was startled. "What, you mean it looked like I was arguing with her?"

Aron laughed. He punched Gideon in the shoulder. Gideon blushed harder, and smiled at his friend with shining eyes. "Hey, what do you say, let's ask her to the movies."

"You mean Yaeli?"

"Sure, why not? We'll go together, the three of us. It'll be fun."

"Okay, but which movie?" asked Aron. "Some of them are restricted, you know."

"Your choice."

There, Gideon understood.

"*Uncle Tom's Cabin* is playing at the Smadar."

"Whatever you say. Even that."

"And we'll go half and half on her ticket?"

"Half and half."

"She probably won't let us pay for her."

"Yeah, probably not," said Gideon, smiling. "She's a girl of principle."

"So how will we tell her? Do you have the nerve to ask her?"

Gideon halted a moment and kicked the asphalt with his shoe. Then he shrugged his shoulders.

"You ask her," he said. "You'll know better how to persuade her to go."

"Who me? What do I know? You."

"No, you."

"No, you."

They stood there shoving each other, jabbing each other lightly on the arm, and Aron even landed a weak punch on Gideon's elbow the way he saw them do in Tel Aviv, and Gideon retaliated gingerly and giggled; it was Gideon's embarrassment, in fact, and his fairly weak fists that cheered Aron, he wasn't at all the tough guy yet that he fancied himself to be, and their school bags rested between them on the pavement, nestling together like puppies who had cleverly brought their masters together.

"What do you think?" asked Gideon with a grin. "Does she wear a 'thingy' yet?"

"Don't know." Aron instantly cooled off, crushed and offended by the crudeness of the question. He picked up his school bag, followed by Gideon, who didn't notice his glowering face. No, he wouldn't, he had already betrayed their understanding with its threadlike nuances, and you have to pay for being on the outside, you have to sacrifice something to be able to ask a question like that, in a voice like that, about Yaeli. " 'Cause I've never noticed a stripe across her back, have you?"

28

How long were they together? Five weeks, maybe six, depending on whether you counted work camp or not, time enough for Gideon and Aron to lavish the treasures of their childhood on Yaeli, the profusion of their stories and secrets and plans, and sometimes Aron worried they were sharing things before they were ready to, but he tried to persuade himself that here he could count on Gideon, on his confidence and instincts and brains, because Gideon probably knew better what was okay to tell her and what wasn't and where to draw the limits, and Gideon told her quite a lot, almost everything, in fact. And the way he talked, you'd think it was all a big joke, that nothing was serious to him, and he kind of bragged too, at Aron's expense sometimes; he even lied, though Aron never said a word, because he didn't want to embarrass him.

On Thursdays they walked Yaeli to her ballet class in the Valley of the Cross and waited outside for her like bodyguards. One time Madame Nikova passed by them, diminutive and wrinkled, and stopped and turned. "Always the two of you are with her, no?" she asked in her thick Russian accent. They nodded. Madame Nikova glanced astutely from the boys to Yaeli. There was a flicker of amused approval in her eyes. Her crimson mouth assumed a smile, and Yaeli bowed her head as though feigning modesty. The old ballet mistress seemed about to say more, perhaps she was reminded of her past, but she seemed to think better of it and turned away again, and Aron had a sneaky suspicion that such things were not unknown, that theirs was not a unique and unprecedented relationship; that the outcome was inevitable.

Later, when they walked her home, Yaeli's mother invited them in. Yaeli had three big sisters who looked so much like her that through his half-closed lids, Aron could enjoy a vision of the mother and her daughters, Yaeli times five, like milestones over the years to come.

Yaeli's mother was pretty. She was petite like Yaeli, smily and direct, maybe too direct at times. She walked right into Yaeli's room and sat down cross-legged on the rug with them. And although she was a Bible teacher she talked like a young person, not like his parents. It was even a little jarring sometimes, once he heard her say "Son-of-a-bitch!" and didn't know where to bury himself. She let Yaeli call her by her name, Atara, and they shared each other's clothes and hugged and cuddled in front of everyone, and her cheeks turned pink, he was pleased to discover, whenever she talked about her boyfriends in the Haganah, or when she made them listen to all six sides of *The Magic Flute*, and hummed along with Papageno and Papagena. And her eyes glistened with a joy and a longing she didn't even try to disguise, so Aron, who was amazed that she and his parents were the same age, wanted to ask his mother and father what they did in the days before the War of Independence, when Yaeli's mother was out on night raids and fighting Arabs face-to-face. Gideon told Atara he really envied her and her generation for living in that glorious time, and she ruffled his hair and said, Don't talk nonsense, she hoped to God his generation would never know anything like that glory. Aron knew Atara's choice would strongly influence Yaeli's, and he tried his best to show her he was worthy of her daughter, that he was reliable and neat and clean and came from a good family, but he couldn't help feeling she didn't like him. She seemed much fonder of Gideon, even though he put his feet up on the table and imitated different accents, things he'd never done before; he even let Atara teach him to dance the debka properly, and she pranced around the salon with him, barefoot and jubilant and young, and Aron looked down at his hands. She's so light on her feet, he thought to himself, nothing weighs her down, and he peeked out shyly through his lashes at the dancing presence and the flashing mysteries, and his spirits flagged as he suddenly imagined Yaeli and Gideon having happy memories like this someday, because of their childhood and youth camp and school trips and dances and even their stupid arguments, while he—what was he but a shirker like his parents. Always Aroning.

Once a week he and Gideon took Yaeli to the movies. They went halfsies on her ticket and she sat between them. After the movies they would treat her to a falafel or a shewarma, which she quickly devoured, and then they'd buy her pumpkin seeds in Bahari's Lane, furtively peeping at the prostitutes but never saying anything. Then they'd go to Café Allenby for a frozen custard, a Creambo, and chocolate twisters; she had an alarming sweet tooth, and Aron worried about those pretty white teeth. On the bus home they always stood up so neither of them would miss the chance to sit with Yaeli. They tried their best to be fair to each other: when Gideon was sick, Aron skipped walking Yaeli home in order to keep to their three-way agreement; on Saturday nights, when the kids from Gideon's youth group passed Yaeli's Scout troop in the street, the two of them ignored each other, out of loyalty. Aron, who was probably in bed pretending to read just then, tortured himself with the thought that although he could trust them both wholeheartedly, Gideon and Yaeli existed together, even apart, in a world from which he was excluded. He and Gideon, when she wasn't there, could speak of nothing but Yaeli. She filled their lives, and they carried her between them in gentle wonder. Every day she seemed to grow wiser. Wiser than either of them. They would go over and over her seemingly innocent remarks, looking for hidden meanings, discussing her taste in movie stars and pop singers; they went out and bought her a book of poems by Esther Kal, and read it aloud together before presenting it to Yaeli, and then they had a long conversation about it and felt how mature they were becoming. Every Thursday they would check her horoscope in *Woman's* magazine, and peek at each other's birth signs to find out what their love life held in store, and then they would listen to the Hit Parade on the radio and send in a postcard with Yaeli's name on it for the big drawing, and because Yaeli had a subscription to *Maariv Magazine for Youth* they would read it cover to cover so they'd have something to talk about, and spend more time together, more and more and more.

But there was one thing marring Aron's happiness: the bickering and arguing between Gideon and Yaeli. They drove each other crazy, those two, and God only knows what might have happened if Aron hadn't been around to smooth things over with his silences and serious demeanor. Anything Yaeli said about public issues would set Gideon off, and his promises to Aron were promptly forgotten when she answered his orations with some smiling, skeptical remark. Even on Gideon's birthday, when they went to Café Nava, they got into an argument. It started—who cares how it started, there was always some reason—Gideon said something about musicals, that they were stupid and superficial, and it was disgraceful the way they were starting to catch on in Israel, and Yaeli said she thought they were fantastic, that she'd give anything to dance in a musical someday with costumes and scenery and a huge cast, and when they'd finished exasperating each other, they fumed in silence, looking off in opposite directions, and then flared up again so suddenly Aron hardly noticed, till he heard Gideon say that school uniforms give youth a healthy sense of group identity and Yaeli stuck her tongue out: *pffff!* she made an offensive noise, that goody-goody outfit made her feel like a prisoner, and Aron stopped listening, bored with them, and looked up at the gray-blue sky, the evening sky of Jerusalem, as he waited patiently for the quarrel to subside, and tried to think of a special way to celebrate Yaeli's birthday two weeks from now, she and Gideon were the same sun sign, and next winter all three of them would celebrate his birthday, and he stirred the tall glass before him, annoyed with Gideon for ordering filter coffee; Gideon didn't like coffee, how could anyone like coffee or beer or cigarettes, no one in the world could stand the taste, it was all an act, he would never pretend for them, not even when he was eighty, so why did Yaeli have to order grain coffee, and he woke up to the sound of tempers flaring. "I personally wouldn't use makeup," Yaeli chafed. "But if an unattractive girl wants to help nature out and make herself look good, I say why not." "By painting her face?!" Gideon exclaimed, turning white and sitting forward, his eyes glaring green and his voice aquiver. "Nobody will be able to scrape it off and get to the real girl underneath!" "I take it you speak from personal experience, Gideon?" Silence. Aron guessed he'd better say something quick to clear the air and pry Gideon's face away from Yaeli's, but something was wrong, there were muddy-green whirlpools in her eyes, and Gideon's eyes were so deep inside them, so fixed and smoldering, the waves of fury receded and the strange muddy green gave way to an eerie catlike gleam; Aron was bewildered, he didn't know how to conciliate them, for though it seemed to him that

THE BOOK OF

he had listened to their every word, as usual he was left out or, rather, he had sunk into a cherished memory, a familiar memory, yes, about how he felt when Yaeli emerged like a butterfly at ballet class, because by falling in love with someone you save them from death in a way, not to mention yourself. "So what do you say, Kleinfeld, can we hear your opinion on the subject?" asked Yaeli, tearing her face from Gideon's with cool impatience in her voice. "Would you like to share your thoughts with us now, or go on stirring your milk shake like a loon?"

He stopped abruptly and stared at his still fluttering fingers. Then he glanced at Yaeli with a helpless grin. Her face before him, her beautiful angry face; the defiant cast of her nose making her look almost predatory. And her eyes had never shone so fiercely green before, where did she get that green, and Aron gazed into them, trying to understand, to correct an error, diving and vanishing into himself and reemerging with unexpected vigor, with a life-or-death intensity, in a torrent of words and declarations. "I want to decide at what age I'll die! I want to die when I reach thirty! On my thirtieth birthday! While I'm still young and strong, before old age sets in!" Shut up, will you shut up already, you're making a big mistake, look at the expressions on their faces. "I want to commit suicide! When I hit my peak! I mean it, that way you can be happy, because you always know the end is coming, so you live your life to the fullest, you're never bored, you never waste time . . ." His voice was fading. He mumbled, turning pale. Why didn't I shut up. A hollow silence followed, people at nearby tables stared, all around his error loomed, his social gaffe, his breach of the rules of conversation, of the boundaries separating him from others. Shame and humiliation filled his heart, for his self-betrayal, for having divulged something unacceptable. "Kleinfeld the philosopher," said Gideon, with a quick glance at the surrounding tables, and the three of them laughed a little too much, and Aron thought all was lost, all was illusion, he was not redeemed, not yet redeemed. Unconsciously he wound his fingers tightly around his wrist and began to squeeze, counting in silence, but he shook himself out of it. Enough of that! No more! Yet something had shifted in the distant darkness, stirred as if under the sea.

As Yaeli's thirteenth birthday approached, Aron came up with a brilliant idea—they would bake a huge sweet challah in her likeness. Gideon was ecstatic and called it the most dynamite Ari plan ever. Aron treasured these words in the round little place that was like a miniature planet earth inside him, where he could be really happy sometimes at night watching a misty apparition with peach-colored cheeks and almond eyes take on life and substance, but mum's the word.

They went to Aron's father and asked him to help them bake the challah, telling him only that it was for a girl in their class. They didn't mention her name. Papa chuckled and gave Aron an affectionate slap on the shoulder, you could see he was pleased, and he said, "Never fear, Moshe's here," and that they did right to come to him, with his experience, twelve years at Angel's bakery; he hadn't always been a pencil pusher at union headquarters, no sirree; up until the accident, he had an honest job, breaking his back under the flour sacks and sweating like a demon on the night shift.

And so, for two feverish, flour-dappled hours, they commandeered the kitchen and went to work. Papa whistled while he stirred in the flour, eggs, margarine, and water, and then he showed them how to knead and roll the dough till it rose. As usual, he overdid the quantities, and squishy balls of cloven dough lay scattered around the kitchen table. Then he greased the baking pan with margarine, reveling in the movement of his hands, while the two boys shaped Yaeli's face, her healthy cheeks, the defiant nose, and the smile of amusement on her lips, the lower one pouting slightly—oh, that willful mouth—and then they stuck in two almonds for her eyes, and Aron studied them, shook his head, slanted them a little more, and smiled: there she was, Yaeli, looking up at them, a veritable replica of herself.

Then they shaped her slender neck. Aron felt sweet all over as he rolled it between his palms, so fragile, too fragile to bear such happiness. At times like this, when he could feel his soul grow deep and wide, he was sure that soon, very soon, the depth and width of it would be all-pervading. His love empowered him, even when it hurt; and his gift for loving was equal to anyone's: no one could hide this sky from him. Papa chuckled and said maybe it was time to steer the tanks around and head south to the interesting places, and Aron, who never lacked for inspired ideas but was often weak on execution, began having second thoughts.

Papa ignored his hesitation. He asked if the little lady had titties yet, and were they shaped like this or like this? Or maybe like this? He squeezed the puffy balls of dough: Like this? Like pears? Like grapefruits? Huh? Whuh? Spreading his fingers he dug into the dough, his

THE BOOK OF

face glistening with perspiration. Aron buried his eyes in the table, and Papa said playfully, "Don't tell me you fellas are blushing, huh? You know, if you wanna make a statue you gotta do it right. *A la naturel!*" Gideon blurted out that she didn't, well not yet anyway, and Papa shrugged and said, "Flatfooted, huh?" And smacked the balls of dough with his open palm. "Never mind," he said consolingly, pinching out a pair of sweet childish nipples. "They'll grow. Even Sophia Loren was flat as a board once." They continued in silence. Aron made one arm and Gideon the other. Aron formed the tender wrist and was almost tempted to lick it into shape. Now and then his eyes darted to the two flat patties of dough on the table. Papa took the arms from him and Gideon, and joined them precisely to the body. He used a knife to smooth the shoulders and examined his handiwork with satisfaction, and Aron remembered the old days, before Mama turned Papa into a clerk with tenure and a pension plan, when he used to get up at 2 a.m. to go to work. Aron, aged four or five, would slip into Papa's place in the double bed beside Mama; Yochi, her eyes still closed, would curl up in Aron's bed, with its thicker, softer mattress; Grandma would stumble out of her alcove, looking small and bewildered, and sleepwalk over to Yochi's warm, empty bed, where she would nestle, sucking her thumb till she fell asleep again. Papa would stand in the doorway in his overalls, watching the rustling traffic of quilts and nightgowns, holding the cold door handle, refusing to be torn away. Will you go already, thought Aron before the door closed behind Papa, pressing himself into the hollow he'd left in the bed, cuddling up to his softly moaning mother, who drowsily offered her warm behind while he—a fervent Jacob— stole Esau's blessing from his blind father, Isaac, with a twinge in his heart, snuggling closer as the hushed "Gooodbye" sounded forlornly from the hall—let him please just leave—and an icy draft made them shiver in their beds.

The kitchen, with the door shut to keep out his indignant mama, was filling up with steam. Aron modeled Yaeli's leg in dough, compassionately forming the still-childish knee, then sliding down to work on the ankle till it was trim and shapely. When he caught a glimpse of Gideon scrutinizing him, he quickly changed expression. Papa took Yaeli's legs from them and laughed: the contrast was so striking! "You like 'em zaftig, huh"—he elbowed Gideon—"with lots of meat on 'em, huh? Wuh? Something to grab!" But Aron wasn't listening. He noticed that

Gideon had forgotten the space between her toes. Gideon didn't love her like he did, he reflected, he wasn't committed to her all the way.

"We finish her tuchis and we're through," said Papa, turning to the oven.

Aron peered at Gideon and both of them blushed. Then, in unison, so neither would be first, they picked up the remaining balls of dough and started shaping them. Aron could almost feel it arching under his fingers. Gideon worked intently, his eyes a little blurred. Aron molded an apple-shaped buttock and placed it on the table. Gideon set his creation down beside it and Papa laughed again. "You wanna tell me these are from the same girl?"

Then he said, "Now, close your eyes. From here on in, it's adults only." He laid the buttocks in the well-greased pan, joining them at the hips. Then, leaning forward over the froglike limbs, he gravely cut a slit between them with the horny curve of his yellow fingernail.

"Schoin, gemacht! Now we cover her up good so nothing shows!" And he sprinkled sesame and raisins all over like a farmer sowing seed.

Then, with a he-man swagger, Papa shoved the sweet challah into the oven, and before long, the fresh, intoxicating fragrance of baking challah filled the air.

29

"So what say, Aronchik, do we start sewing a wedding suit?"

At supper they teased him. Papa joked about seeing him down by the rock with Yaeli and Gideon, and Mama said someone reported spotting the three of them at the movies. They were positively glowing: the dreary gray curse of recent events seemed to have suddenly lifted. Papa poked his face into Aron's and inquired, amid howls of laughter, what the lady's father did for a living, and Mama reflected that Yaeli's family name—Kedmi—sounded, eppes, like it might have been changed to cover up what it was before. She interrogated him closely about their house: when did they last redecorate, how big was their refrigerator, and was Yaeli's mother the same Kedmi who bought an expensive wig from America, because, you know, she hastened to explain, her eyes shining, sometimes a woman wants a wig to make the neighbors jealous, but sometimes it's to hide her baldness, which may run in the family; she pursed her lips self-righteously. "Nu, enough already, Mamaleh," chided Papa. "It's a little early to talk about hair and balding, I think, but how's about inviting your girlie home to meet us, Aronchik, so we can take a good long look at her."

Mama broke out in a smile that Aron detested, her fawning female smile, and Papa asked again what the little lovely's name was, and Aron turned bright red and hid his head between his shoulders, terrified they would repeat her name with their mouths full. "Go on, eat, ess!" urged Mama, heaping the mashed potatoes on his plate. "Your time has come!

You have to start gorging yourself!" And Papa carved a thick hunk of rye bread with his deadly knife and stuffed it into his hand. "My own Aronchik," he cheered, "you'll never know how glad I am!" They were truly exultant. Suddenly they looked carefree, radiant with youth, as Papa raised his plate and scraped some beans out on Aron's plate. "There, have a little fasoulia! Gonna meet your girlie tonight, huh?" And Mama and Papa burst out laughing and shared a look he'd never seen before, and when Mama served the meat her hand rested on Papa's arm. "Have another thigh!" she insisted, passing Aron the chicken from her own plate. "You've got to make up for lost time now! Eat! Don't store it in your mouth! I said eat!" They buzzed around him, filling his plate with the choicest morsels, their hands hurrying back and forth, canceling the features of Yochi's face as she chewed her food in silence; and Aron too averted his eyes, letting her down when this new pride trickled through to him, as though all by himself, with a snap of his fingers, he had opened the window they had their noses pressed to and let in a stream of wonderful fresh air. For a moment he yielded to a sense of elation, but catching sight of Yochi's downcast head and the face of his mother greedily drinking in the breeze, he suddenly remembered the shoes he wore for his bar mitzvah, those elevator shoes. His shoulders drooped. His eyes sought Yochi's, and his tongue cleared a path through the warehouse in his mouth, to touch his milk tooth. Mama and Papa went on chewing and talking, but he didn't hear them anymore. Mama forgot to feed Grandma with a spoon, and Grandma sat before her plate of mashed chicken, a thread of saliva dripping down to her bib. Aron stuffed his mouth but couldn't swallow. He shunted the warehouse from cheek to cheek, dug into his piece of bread, nervously picked out the caraway seeds one by one, and set them out in an arrowhead formation, like a flock of storks; from now on he'd better eat halvah and mashed potatoes every day to fortify himself so he'd be able to hold on to that place inside with the dancer, and at least seven squares of chocolate besides, not so good for the teeth but it would strengthen his internal Gideon, the Gideon who used to be, and he gravely checked the list again; the sugars of friendship and the starches of perseverance and the carbohydrates of loyalty, his own personal nutriments, and he smiled to himself; two weeks ago there had been nothing there, it was just another unfamiliar place inside his body, and now he could feel it alive and throbbing; and he woke up to Yochi

THE BOOK OF

pushing her dessert plate away and going over to spit in the sink: Yuck, what did you put in that? Mama glared at her and tasted from the tip of her spoon. Her face turned yellow. So nu, she said, I must have switched the plates; if you helped me serve instead of sitting around like a princess with her feet in the air, a thing like that would never happen, she muttered, flushing red as she passed the dessert with the crushed medication to Grandma. Now sit down and eat your compote, nothing happened, why did you blow up like that; and Aron looked around bewilderedly, he'd been dreaming again, maybe they'd asked him a question or ordered him to do something that had to do with the future, his future; he nodded in anguish, what did they want from him; he stared down at the table, discovered the arrowhead of caraway seeds, flicked them away, and shook off the seeds that stuck to his fingers, all he needed now was for Papa to see what he'd done to a good piece of bread.

But neither Papa nor Mama noticed, they were so full of their happiness, they took long, loud slurps of compote, how he loved to watch Yaeli sipping from a glass, because then he could see her pretty mouth double, but now their lips curled in convulsive laughter and they looked like prisoners jeering at a newcomer to the cell who is trying to pretend he doesn't belong there. The words they used rotted in their mouths: wonderful words like "pleasure" and "love"; he would have to abstain from those words for a full day now. No: for a full seven days. Till they were clean again. "There's one thing I still don't get," said Papa, unbuckling his belt and spilling out into the room. "You walk her home from school with Gideon. You play in the valley with her and Gideon. You go to the movies—with Gideon again! He'll probably tag along on your honeymoon and hold the candle for you too."

Papa heaved with loud, heavy laughter, but in Mama's eyes there was a strange metallic glint. "If you wait too long, he'll snatch her away," she said in a humorless voice. "Remember, Aron, when it comes to things like this, no friends and no favors! It's first come, first served! Nice guys finish last!" She threw a sharp glance at Papa and there was sudden silence as an onerous memory filled the room, almost as if it had burst in through the walls and the floor.

"Take it from me, Aron"—Mama repeated the warning, whetting her voice to rip the silence to shreds—"when it comes to things like this, if you wait like a lamb you'll end up bleating like a lamb! *Beeeeh!*"

Her mouth formed a fleshy crescent. "You understand what I'm saying?" And all the while she was feeding Grandma, her hand rising and falling from the compote dish, catching a drop every three trips under Grandma's mouth. Yochi couldn't stand it anymore.

"I won't have you sticking your nose up, young lady!" Mama fumed at her. "You're a real authority, you are! So where are the beaux in your life? In their envelopes? Under the stamps? Let's see them!" "Sha, enough, Mamaleh. Leave the girl alone!" With Yochi's matriculation exams coming up, Papa protected her with deep solicitude. He would get up in the middle of the night sometimes and tiptoe to the kitchen, caress her head as she dozed over the notebooks, and make her coffee and a nice, thick sandwich, and then tiptoe out again so as not to distract her. "I will not put up with this from her," grumbled Mama. "When she gets a husband let her do what she likes, not here."

Aron buried his face in his plate and chewed the mush in his mouth. The potatoes will go in and some of them will come out in my shit and the rest will stay inside and become a part of me. So, in fact, I am eating a part of myself, before it has actually become me; it's strange to think that any old potato, or even a cucumber or an egg, might someday become a part of me, Aron Kleinfeld, or a part of someone else, for that matter, but I still can't tell what's mine and only mine and not from someone else and not available to anyone else even if I wanted to give it to them, because it can't exist in anyone but me, and when I find out what it is I will cling to it with all my might, because the rest will be taken from me, I know that already, or else I'll give it away, and maybe it wasn't really mine in the first place, but that which is mine and mine only I will cling to until my dying breath; he didn't want to listen to Mama's insinuations, or the urgency in her voice, as if his entire fate depended on winning Yaeli, on conquering Yaeli, but how can you conquer someone you want to love, how can you conquer someone you love precisely for being free and independent. He stuffed more and more food into his mouth just to avoid looking at Mama's bouncing chin, and he vowed never to be jealous of Gideon on Yaeli's account, because that was the beauty of their three-way friendship: without a word they had made an equitable division, they each got all of Yaeli, and at the same time, the Yaeli of each of them was a different Yaeli, because Gideon knew the Yaeli everyone else knew, the more public Yaeli, whereas Aron was in love with a different Yaeli, the Yaeli

THE BOOK OF

she would have wanted to be, and no one knew her the way he did, deep inside.

No, he wasn't jealous of Gideon, if only because he didn't really know which of them gave him more happiness—Gideon, who made it possible to get close to Yaeli, or Yaeli, who made Gideon open up to him again. Or maybe his great happiness came from the two of them combined? He stole a glance at Yochi, all hunched up; she'd probably hate him now because of Yaeli, but Yochi glanced back encouragingly, and his heart went out to her. Don't give in to them, li'l brother, said her eyes. Neither of them has ever experienced the twin joys you feel in your heart. They know nothing. They know less than a fourth of what you know. Maybe that's why they're abusing you now. But Mama spurred him on with her prickly tongue, and listening to the way she sounded, seeing the fierceness in her eyes, you might have thought she was the one competing with Gideon around here. "Take some money, go on!" She stuffed it into his hand as he was about to leave for the movies. "And if he buys her a falafel, you buy her a shewarma! Don't skimp! Everything's on me!" And later, when he returned from his evening out, she would be waiting for him in her bathrobe, looking ruffled as a bird of prey, interrogating him down to the smallest details: what did she say, and what did he say, did it seem to be coming to a head yet, were there any hints of a decision? She wrung her hands, muttering the monosyllabic answers along with him. Sometimes when she dunked him in her bitterness, and painted a lurid picture of the trouble there would be if he wasn't careful, if he let Gideon snatch her from right under his nose, he had a strange suspicion that she derived a twisted pleasure from infecting him, from lashing his ear and forcing him down to earth, her earth. "And next time you see your doll," she warned him, sparks flying out of her eyes, "don't show her you're interested! Not on your life! She'll only want to humiliate you if you do!" She squinted at him narrowly and her voice was solemn, resonating with age-old innuendos. "And don't act like a pipsqueak around her, the way you usually do! Don't let her see what you're thinking. Don't sell yourself cheap, don't give yourself away. Play with her a little. Why not. Women like that. I'm telling you!" Aron thought of his innocent Yaeli and the rosy blush that spread over her throat, and he almost burst out laughing.

"Don't laugh like that, nebbich," she raged. "Your little doll isn't the innocent lamb you think, not if she knows how to twist the two of you around her finger like that; you listen to me, Aron, she knows very well where legs sprout from."

She shook her head self-righteously, and again he saw the bewildering contrast between the pious expression she wore and her actual face, which was handsome and animated, almost provocative. For a moment he felt trapped in a maze of illusion. Then he shrugged his shoulders and tried to wriggle out.

"And just where do you think you're going, stand up straight." She lowered her voice. "Over to her house?"

"Leave me alone. I was about to go to Grandma's room. To read the newspaper to her."

"What, are you nuts? Going to read to Grandma? A fourteen-and-a-half-year-old shmo spending time with his grandma? You think she understands anything you read to her? Why don't you go out with your doll instead?"

" 'Cause . . . 'cause Gideon isn't home now."

She hooted at him: "You poor little sap! And what if he's there, by some strange chance? What if he's with her in her house, in her room now, sitting on her bed with her and laughing at the fool?"

"He isn't."

"Oh no? And you think he'd come running back to tell you if he was? Go on, fly off to her, grab her and run! You have money?"

"What about Grandma—"

"Forget Grandma! Why bother with Grandma? Grandma's finished, believe me, she wouldn't bother with you for half a minute!" And she pressed a pound note into his reluctant hand. "Go, go, suck up all the life you can out there, because if you don't, somebody else will."

His nostrils constricted like a camel's in a sandstorm. And still she tried to push him out, then finally gave up. He could do whatever he wanted. She, thank God, was no longer responsible for him. She could get along just fine, thank you. Her fingers squeezed the dishtowel. She walked out and left him alone. He wouldn't go. He wouldn't go. He walked out to the balcony and looked around. There were no kids outside. Yesterday's newspaper was lying on the floor. Aron leafed through it to the obituaries. Abraham Kadishman R.I.P. was his choice for the day. He played around with the letters awhile, dish, ram, main, radish; then he proceeded to Pessia Sternberg, but soon got bored, he'd finish later in the evening. He went back to his room and sat on the windowsill, one foot propped on the kerosene heater. He opened his box of negatives and looked through them. It had been months since he added anything to his collection. He searched the film for the hazy aura. Some primitive people won't let themselves be photographed because they're afraid of losing their souls. Maybe he would ask Uncle Shimmik for a negative of himself. That would be interesting to see. He already knew what his aura looked like. Round with a soft orange glow. What nonsense Mama talked. Gideon and Yaeli, really now. For the past few days they'd been arguing a lot less, thank God. You could actually walk between them without going deaf. And if Aron hadn't opened his mouth, they might never have talked at all. What did Mama know, anyway. He jumped up, grabbed his soccer ball, and ran downstairs.

The street out front was deserted. He played here, played there. By the fig tree stump he noticed something and stopped. He hugged the ball to his chest and drew closer: a leaf. A small green leaf was sprouting out of the stump. His eyes darted up to the blinds on the fourth-floor window. Where was she now? He walked around the stump. Leaned over and gently touched it. What a winter. Someone, possibly even Mama, had telephoned Edna's parents and told them to pick her up. The whole building peeked out and watched her walk rigidly away between her two small parents. Edna disappeared into a waiting taxi. He half expected her father to turn around and shake a fist at the neighbors' blinds, hurling curses that would all come true, but he didn't turn around or curse; the three of them quietly drove away forever, they probably took her home, or found a more suitable environment for her. Another person I've betrayed, he thought, and then jumped back and charged up the street as the crowd roared, but all of sudden he stopped in his tracks. Enough, he didn't need that make-believe stuff anymore. Thanks to Yaeli he was in real life now. Again he glanced up cautiously at the fourth-floor window. And thanks to Yaeli he no longer felt the emptiness of Edna Bloom's, or the fluttering thing that was trapped inside it forever, beating its wings against the walls. He tore his eyes away and fled, hopping on one foot, mildly bitter, and thanks to Yaeli he had been spared a whole variety of future ills. But where were all the children? How strange. Softly he called Gideon's name. Silence. Maybe he would stroll to the shopping center. Maybe Mama needed something. A bottle of oil maybe. She was surprised to find the bottle almost empty yesterday. He was eating everything fried lately. Suddenly he was running up the stairway of Entrance C. He tiptoed past Zacky's. Went up to the third floor. Pressed his ear to Gideon's door. Silently called his name. From inside came angry sounds of shouting and Aron drew back. Mira, Gideon's mother, yelled: "What are you doing to us? You're really enjoying this, aren't you?" And Gideon's father answered her in his viciously noble tone: "It's your happiness I'm thinking of, my dear. What could be more important to me than that?" There was a moment's silence and then Gideon's mother sobbed: "Don't go, I beg you. Don't leave me here alone with him. You're pushing me into it. Why? Why?" And Gideon's father answered with cold amusement: "A new love will do wonders for your complexion, darling." Aron fled, devastated, disgusted. Everything they touched, these grownups, became contaminated. He sat down on the steps behind the building and hid his head between his knees. He would never be like them. Never. His love would be pure eternally. Thus he loved Yaeli now, and thus he would love her till his dying day. He only hoped he would die before she did, so he would not have to live a single day of his life without her. He tried to visualize a world she did not inspirit. The fingers of his left hand tightened around his right wrist, but he noticed what he was doing in time and scolded himself. We don't do that anymore. That, thank heavens, is behind us. Now we have Yaeli. Because life means nothing without Yaeli. Yes, it was dangerous to be dependent but maybe that's how he'd learned to love the way he did. An all-or-nothing love. But his fingers kept sliding up to choke his wrist. What was Mama doing to him? Why was she like that? What did she know about him or Gideon or friendship? How could you explain to her, for instance, that Aron had written a poem to Yaeli, the most beautiful and love-filled poem ever written, a poem written with his heart's blood, which he would never under any circumstances give to Yaeli or even allude to, because Gideon doesn't know how to write poems. But what if she's right. Maybe he really is naïve. Maybe in momentous biological matters like this there is a powerful instinct at work which he hasn't developed yet, which is why he remained virtuous. Or naïve. Deeply disgusted, he found the pound note she'd given him in his pocket. He ordered himself to bury it in the yard. Her voice inside him tried to bargain, sawing and hissing in his brain. Aron tightened

THE BOOK OF

his stomach muscles against her. Yaeli, he thought, Yaeli, and he dug into the earth with rigid fingers and buried the money there. Good. It was like a sacrifice, only he didn't feel purified. On the contrary. How come she always made him feel so disgusted with himself. Where could Gideon be? A cobweb glistened on the rosemary bush. How many dead insects were hiding there? He tossed a twig at the cobweb. At the invisible spider. Maybe there was no spider. He couldn't go to her alone. He'd rather die. He loved his Yaeli and he trusted her. There was something else too, something important: thanks to his love for her he knew he liked girls. Females, that is. Because sometimes the terrible thought occurred to him that perhaps, among other ideas and inventions of the disaster in his body, he would start liking boys. Males, that is. Such things were known to happen. A kid reached this age and suddenly there was a kind of order from his glands, so what could he do, argue, plead? Because what's inside is also outside, like potatoes strewn over a distant field, cucumbers and lettuce and onions, a stranger who didn't belong. What time was it, where did everyone go? Gideon, Gideon.

A pale butterfly, a brownish-gray moth really, came to rest on a nearby leaf. Aron reached out and caught it and, without pausing to think, stuck it on the web. Its wings fluttered. A barely perceptible stirring. In an instant the spider was there. Huge, with long legs. Aron gasped. But surely it won't crawl out on the dry leaves! he screamed in his heart. What fault of mine is it that the moving moth attracted it? Before his eyes the spider besieged the moth. Swiftly, methodically, it spun a web around the frail, stunned body and Aron didn't lift a twig to stop it. He didn't want to disturb the spider. He sat and stared at this little murder, guilty and agitated. Why aren't you stopping it? But if the moth hadn't done that the spider wouldn't have noticed it. Done what? Showed it was alive. You're crazy, you're cruel, you're not yourself anymore; now hit the spider with a twig so it will run away and leave the moth alone. The spider isn't even touching it, just spinning a web around it from afar. What have you done? Don't you see, you're enjoying this. Enjoying what? Helping, cooperating with death.

It was over in a flash. The moth drained out of itself. It twitched its antennae one last time, like a last request or warning to Aron, and then expired. The spider stood over it, somber and still. Only the web breathed. Aron trembled. He hugged himself and tried to calm down. How did it happen? Yes, but what if they were cheating on him in there. What if they were laughing at the fool. Sudden footsteps approached. A hand touched his shoulder. Gideon stood over him, looking stern, drawn, hopeless.

"What's up, Kleinfeld?"

"Nothing. Just sitting here."

"I went out looking for you. Come on, let's go to her house."

Aron stood up. Stood up in front of Gideon. Stood up to him. "Listen, listen . . ."

"What's wrong, Aron, tell me."

"Come here . . . first let's do something." He didn't know what he was talking about.

"What, what do you want to do?"

"I need your help with something." Oh please, let him say it right. "See, I've got this tooth—"

"What tooth?"

He giggled apologetically. "I have a milk tooth left."

"No kidding. You mean it's still in there?" Gideon was so amazed he let a question mark into his voice.

"Yes. Just one. I want to pull it out. Now. My father told me how."

"Why now?"

"Well, because. Because it's really wiggling." Because you waited for me. Because you and I know how to be friends. Because we'll never be like our parents. "You take a string and tie it to the tooth, and then you tie the other end of the string to a door and you slam it shut."

"That's what your father told you?"

"Yes, that's what they used to do when he was a little boy in Poland. You have the nerve to do it?"

"I . . . Well, yes. But what if . . . it might hurt."

"It's about to fall out anyway."

They ran together, side by side, silent, serious, all the way to the shopping center, to Zadok's hardware store, where they bought three meters of nylon string.

"We can't do it at my house," said Gideon hastily.

"Or at my house either. How about the shelter?"

"What if somebody walks in?"

Help. Don't let it stop. Where were his ideas when he needed them. Oh, come, oh, come, ideas. "Y'alla." "Where are you off to?" "Let's go."

They arrived panting at the junkyard in the valley. Aron had been pressing his tongue against the tooth all the way there. To loosen it. To pry out at least a millimeter of the root. But small and white, it was fixed immutably. The surrounding teeth were big, healthy meat teeth, only it was a runt. Gideon wouldn't look at him. He was restless. Three times already he'd asked if Aron was sure it wasn't dangerous. Aron tingled with excitement. Please don't let him chicken out now. I'll make him such a covenant, oh God, oh God. But when he tied the string to the handle of the Tupolino, it crumbled into a rusty powder in his hand. So did the other handle. Gideon was peering anxiously in the direction of the building. He'd already blurted out that Yaeli was probably waiting for them. Aron looked around in desperation. Wait a minute. What a couple of jerks we are. If you want my advice, said Gideon hesitantly, just leave it alone. But Aron forced the door of the old refrigerator open, and recoiled at the stench that came out of it. The stench of death. For years it must have been closed like that. He peeked inside: it was a little thing, a puppy of a refrigerator. You don't see dinky ones like that around anymore. He tied the end of the string to the heavy steel handle. Just imagine, he giggled to Gideon, doing the Houdini in an old refrigerator like this. Don't you dare, said Gideon, eyeing him strangely. Just kidding, said Aron. He finished tying the string and backed off a few steps. He felt too shy to ask Gideon to tie his tooth. He tied it himself. He pulled it tighter at the base and already tasted a drop of blood. This would really hurt. In one split second it would pull out the tooth. Everything inside him would be shaken up. But this was the perfect time. And the perfect friend. Cautiously he backed off a few more steps. The string was taut against his lower lip. Now quickly, slam the door, he cried through stretched lips. Are you sure it's okay? Yes, yes, go on, let's get it over with. Are you positive it's loose enough? Yes, positive, don't chicken out now. Gideon ran a careful finger over the string. He studied the knot around the handle. Suddenly he turned serious, protective, but not like a friend: more like a grownup watching over a child. Who cares. Don't let in a single negative thought. You have to want this with all your heart. You have to believe, you have to surrender. There will be one instant of terrible pain, the way there is when they brand a new calf joining the herd. "Get ready," said Gideon, extending his arm in front of the open refrigerator door. "On your mark, set—" Gideon closed his eyes. So did Aron, chin out. Gideon's chin was pressed to his chest. There was a loud bang. A white blade slit Aron's lip. His jaw cracked. Blood ran. Maybe that was good. He foundered, stunned, crouching over till he was lying prone, numb, but soon there would be pain, where was it, where did it come from, oh, let it come already; and for one endless moment Aron hovered, slowly igniting, spreading, vanishing, hanging by a thread, draining inward, backward, soon to be no more, without any strength left to save himself, to fight it, giving in to it with a flutter of wonder; it came on slowly, like a dream, and he divined it there, a kind of tangled web, a fine, strong mesh at the base of him, revealing and concealing itself under the turbid waves, something made out of *her*; in fact, out of Mama, that never showed in her face or voice but was her nonetheless, and when he fell he was swathed in it, enveloped in a swoon, a magic cloak that melted into his skin, merged into an already familiar and not displeasing whisper: *Death is right*, and all the rest is error; never revel in what you find, it isn't yours, just put it in your pocket and keep your mouth shut. And when the pain throbbed suddenly he was almost relieved. He was still alive.

Gideon ran around him in a panic, shouting his name, scampering off, returning, approaching cautiously, sobbing: "You tricked me! You tricked me! It wasn't loose!" And Aron, with a mouthful of blood, with a broken heart, his faculties waning, shook his head. It didn't hurt at all, and it was loose too. He was suddenly alarmed to be lying flat on the ground like this with Gideon standing over him. Exhaustedly he pulled himself together and sat up. His jaw felt heavy and huge, and something was stubbornly piercing his temple and his ear. Gideon kneeled beside him, remorseful, angry, saying over and over that he was sorry. Aron wiped his mouth with his hand. There was blood everywhere. He touched his wound with the tip of his tongue. But no new tooth was growing in its place. Empty. An empty space. And there before him, hanging from the string tied to the refrigerator door, was his tiny milk tooth. Nothing earthshaking. Just a tooth. For fourteen and a half years it had been inside his mouth, and now it was hanging from a string.

30

"You be the man. You lead!"

So his mother commanded him, taking his reluctant hands and putting them firmly around her middle. "Go on, lead!" She smiled at him. He could feel her breath on his face and his body stiffened. "Try to relax! Loosen up!" She panted, maneuvering them both around the floor to the record of *Swan Lake*, which Yochi had once used for her ballet exercises. "You're not leading! One two three! You're letting me lead!" Yochi was sitting on the Bordeaux sofa with her arms crossed. She watched them blankly and made Aron feel uneasy, as though she could see the present in the past and could therefore be detached, turn renegade. "Nu, try again," sighed Mama, wiping her brow. "You have to show her, two three, that you know how to behave, two three, with girls, two three, otherwise that friend of yours is going to snatch her from under your nose, two three, you mark my words!"

He tightened his arm muscles and tried not to notice the beads of perspiration glistening wantonly over her lip. Once, he loved the smell of her breath, like a whiff of a secret, subliminal self. "And quit jerking your head around like a water sprinkler." From deep inside her it came out, how dare she blow air at him from in there. "I'll bet he knows how to dance, doesn't he?" "He" being what she called Gideon now that she knew he and Aron were sharing Yaeli. Aron said Gideon didn't know how to dance yet either. Not social dancing anyway. "We're not quite up to social dancing." Mama laughed over his shoulder to Yochi.

"This is just a waltz. We'll get to social dancing soon enough!" Yochi crossed her legs and scrutinized them with that neutral expression she'd adopted lately; there were only a few months left before she went into the army, and she could hardly wait; this she told Aron in deepest secrecy; oh, to be surrounded by strangers, people who wouldn't know how to interpret her every fart and sigh and silence and use them against her in devious ways. "But what do you mean, the army," Aron gasped, "you asked for a deferral, didn't you?" "I don't want a deferral, she can shove it, she can forget about me going to the university." "But you asked for a deferral, you asked for it!" Aron hopped up and down, confused about why he was so offended. "I did, but a little birdie told me I didn't do so well on the essay part of the matriculation exam," she informed him dispassionately. "What? You failed the essay question?" "Hmm, I guess I must have had an off day in essay writing." She smiled at him coolly, and he envisioned her staring dully at the face of the examination monitor. "Come on, don't fret about it, li'l brother." She tapped him between his disconcerted eyes. "I can easily fix it after the army, but not a word, you hear?"

Whenever she spoke that way he was alarmed at the amount of hatred in her, and now, seeing the look on his face, she added, as if to hurt him even more, that her only worry was losing control and exploding at Mama before her call-up date. And then all the filth would burst out of her and smear all over the floor and the walls and the furniture. "I'm holding it in with all my might," she said. "That's my biggest test now, not to give her the satisfaction of a knock-down fight, oh no no no . . ." She stretched her short neck out in a crude gesture of contempt. "That she will never get from me." She squeezed out a laugh, surprising him with the bright blue flame in her eyes. "I . . . don't . . ." he stammered, "I don't think you have a right to be so angry with her." She sneered in reply, and for a moment he saw her double chin swelling out like a bladder of resentment. "You defend her, you Goody Two-shoes, after all she's done to you, you still defend her?" "She hasn't done anything to me," he mumbled. "She only wants what's best, and every family has its problems." "Listen to me, li'l brother," she said, coming closer. "Hear the word of the prophetess Yocheved: A day will come when you will hate your mother, you will hate her with an intense black hatred and do anything you can to get out of her clutches; to the ends of the earth you will flee, you will live in the Sahara Desert just

THE BOOK OF

to get away from her." She paused a moment, her face in a weft of wonder, of prayer, looking through him as though she saw him from afar, and then she giggled. "And the worst part is, in the end I'll be all she has left." "No!" exclaimed Aron in a strained, stubborn voice. "I won't hate Mama. She's my mother. No matter what she does, I'll never hate her." "Watch out," said Yochi, her voice cool and calm. "Beware the day when it's a matter of honor not to hate her."

Mama pulled away from Aron's arms. "You're letting me lead again! Stop dreaming! How do you expect to be a man?" Again they tried. He laid a tentative sweaty hand on her shoulder, and she grasped it, pressing it masterfully around her fleshy waist. "This is how you lead! With your hand! This is how you let your girlfriend know a man is holding her! Otherwise, *psssss*, she'll run away from you!" And she hiccupped a little giggle, a slimy giggle out of her depths, and her breath blew in his face from that place inside her, as Aron turned away, tightened his grip, and led her three steps left, two steps right. "Not like a golem, one two three." She heaved. "Put some feeling into it, some style, move me around like butter. Turn it up a little, Yochi, will you?"

Oh no, just what we need, thought Yochi, leaning over the record player and watching out of the corner of her eye as Grandma Lilly hobbled into the salon, groping half-blindly for the source of the music that woke her up. In deep amazement Grandma surveyed the scene, then turned around, trailing the hem of her oversize bathrobe across the floor. Yochi hurried to her and grasped her arm. She seemed about to take her to her alcove, but on second thought drew her gently, indifferently over to the Pouritz, where she sat her down, smoothed her bathrobe and her wispy gray hair, which was starting to grow out now; it was a long time since Yochi let Mama cut Grandma's hair, maybe she would even grow a braid. Do sit down, Grannykins, she whispered in her heart to muffle the Mama inside her. Come watch with me.

Mama caught on right away. "Hold me tighter!" she blared at Aron, who was inattentive for a moment. "Not like a nebbich!"

Her shouting startled him out of a dream. Obediently he led her around the room, trying his best to please her, but something inside would not be appeased, it protested. Stop thinking, he told himself, forget everything, surrender, be reckless, and his limbs relaxed, his shoulders and arms and the painful, petrified muscles of his legs. You see you can do it; if you want to, you can do it. And he let his eyelids droop, loosened the grip of his fingers, now it's final; a timorous leap went through him from head to toe, something melted and began to flow. I'm really dancing, and with a quiver of amazement and delight he felt his mother washed out of his arms and carried by the dance like a fish by water, and she fluttered her eyelashes and threw her head back as though a masterful fist had grabbed her by the hair, and then her hands groped their way up his arms till they were firmly gripping his shoulders, and she gave a little laugh as if in her sleep and lifted his hand and twirled around under it, her dress belling out, showing her thighs and the hem of her slip, and her armpits unlocked and blinked their curly lashes at him, and he gazed at her in helpless revulsion, at her lips splitting further and further apart, and he grabbed her hand, pulled it too hard, lost the beat, stumbled into her . . . Slowly, sadly, she regained her senses, and the old expression reappeared in her eyes. Wearily she shook her head at him. "You simply won't let yourself go," she whispered, prolonging their ungainly dance, and he couldn't understand why she was whispering. "That's the problem with you, you cramp yourself, you freeze up, no girl's going to look at you twice if you stay the way you are." Versed as he was in her intricate patterns of voice and expression, he looked over his shoulder, and when he saw Grandma Lilly there, watching them, he tripped over Mama's feet and disgraced himself. Grandma sat up in the *fauteuil* and followed their progress as though straining to hear them better. It's lucky for Mama, thought Yochi, that Grandma can't open her mouth. "Dance! Move your feet! Klutz!" rasped Mama, holding on tightly and dragging him around, and he suddenly remembered the spit on the lips of that man in the picture watching Lilly dance, and again he lost the beat and was no longer dancing: he was capering in jerky confusion, and Mama twirled him around and around to keep out of Grandma's sight, but though she tried to maneuver away from them, her eyes kept encountering Grandma's and Yochi's, like swords clashing in midair, and sparks flew out of Grandma's seeing eye, the sparks of double derision: at Aron for being such a clumsy oaf and at Hinda for wasting her future on such a son. "Now listen to me, Aron," Mama blared again, he always cringed when she started off like that. "A wallflower at fifteen stays a wallflower for life. Oh yes!" Yochi bit her cheeks: Mama grabbed his hand and held it out in front of her face, which suddenly tightened: she was unbearably herself again, emanating a shrewdness of appraisal which made whatever her gaze happened to rest on seem cheap, shoddy. "Because at your age, Aron, parties are IT!" she said, puffing at him in her dickering way till he felt as though he were standing naked on an auction block. "When you dance and neck and lollygag! You'll see!" Oh, if only she could help him cross this river with her wisdom and experience, if only she could help him to be himself for the duration of these "critical" years. "And believe me, when it comes to that, you're either in or you're out! And when I say out, I mean out!"

What did she want from him. How far would she hound him. He traipsed home with Gideon and Yaeli. Today it was Gideon's turn to carry Yaeli's school bag. Lucky thing too, because she had a geography lesson and the atlas weighed a ton. They walked in silence at his side, and Aron told them that he'd decided to learn Esperanto when he grew up and help spread it all over the world, so that everyone would speak one language and understand each other and there would be no more secrets in society. They listened and nodded, and Aron grew elated and told them his other plan, to write a letter to the Secretary-General of the United Nations, requesting that Esperanto be written in Braille instead of regular letters so that people everywhere would read it exactly the same, and there would be no discrimination against those who couldn't read regular writing. Yaeli said it sounded like a good idea. A dynamite idea, really. Gideon said yes, Ari comes up with some brilliant ideas. Aron blushed as he walked between them, inflated with pride, lapping up their praises. Walking with them now he knew how absurd what Mama said about Yaeli was. She and Gideon didn't argue anymore. They seemed calmer now. Maybe even a little more open to Aron, overflowing with goodwill, smiling at him, putting him in the center. Pensively they strolled beside him, looking off in opposite directions, stroking the bark on the trees. And if they continued, thought Aron, very soon he would be able to unravel the knot inside him, to pull out one end of the string and tell them everything, so they'd understand the hell he'd been living through. Till recently. It was scary to think how recently, how short a time separated him from those terrible days. Soon. At the next cypress tree. At the car after that. Later.

They stopped outside Yaeli's and crumbled honeysuckle leaves. She and Gideon were silent. Gideon looked down at the tips of his shoes. Aron said that if capital punishment were allowed, Menashe Anwar would hang for ruining three families, can you imagine, waking up one day and murdering three innocent people, but still Yaeli and Gideon said nothing, they had no opinion on the matter, and Aron too was silent now; the poor victims, living peacefully, never suspecting that somewhere a man like Menashe Anwar existed, while they were growing up and going to school, and that everything was leading up to their deaths, maybe he'd even passed them on the street once, but they were totally unaware of their doom. But Aron didn't want to sink into such dark ruminations, so he told about a special key ring the Delek gas company was handing out in honor of Independence Day, a key ring in the shape of a Mirage jet, his father had a whole collection of key rings from various stores and companies, and lately, since Edna Bloom, he had been devoting himself seriously to this wonderful hobby, he even put red plastic hooks on the salon wall to hang them up in a little exhibition, Mama was all for it. Better this than his other mishegoss, she said with a smile, and she even let him mar the newly painted walls with his collection, which kept him busy every day after work, trading with Peretz Atias and Felix Botenero, but Gideon and Yaeli still said nothing; why were they so quiet, why did they look so sad? He decided that if that's how they were going to be, then he would be quiet too; sure, he was terrific at being quiet. Quiet was his middle name. Ha ha. But suddenly he couldn't stand it anymore, this wasn't normal quiet, this was a deep silence. Better they should argue, because what did he have to talk about, what would he say to them now; that he wanted to know exactly when he was going to die, he'd already told them that and it made them uncomfortable and they started teasing him about it, but he didn't care, let them laugh, as long as they broke the silence and returned. "When I die," he began in a quiet voice, and they looked up uncomprehending, "I want my death to be long and drawn-out." They stared at him in dismay. "No really, I'm serious, don't laugh!" But they didn't even smile. "I've given it a lot of thought: I really want to get to know my death. To die very slowly. I mean, that's the important thing in life, isn't it? I mean, isn't it? No, seriously." Again they looked away. Shut up now. Watch out. There's something going on here. "I mean, usually when your time comes, you're either too old or too sick to understand, and it's all wasted, no, really, because at the most important times of life you're too busy worrying about trivial things to notice what's happening and understand the important things." He began talking fast, frantically piling on the words: "I mean, that's how it is when you're born, you're too young to understand the importance of being born and living life, and at our age too, we still don't really understand what's going on, so obviously it's like that when you get old and mixed up, which is why I want to die at my peak, so I'll know death as an experience, no really, I'm serious: it's the deepest experience you can have!" Enough. There were no words left to fill the silence, and his tongue dipped into the crater left by his milk tooth. Traitor, selling himself like that, always willing to pay more for less, and he hung his head and waited. Then suddenly Gideon blurted, "Listen, Kleinfeld, you know that youth movement camp we were supposed to go to in the Carmel mountains before Independence Day . . ." Aron listened.

"Well, in the end, because of the recession and the kibbutz situation, they've changed it around, see. All the groups are going together. The decision came from the central council. It wasn't our decision. You see?"

He didn't see. He asked Gideon to explain it to him.

"That's how it worked out, we're all going to the Jezreel Valley, and there they'll spread us around on different kibbutzim. To help in the fields." Gideon looked up a moment and then quickly looked down again. "It's because of the recession, see. It's only because of that. We're going there to work, not to have fun."

Aron turned to Yaeli, but Yaeli studied the honeysuckle blossom in her hand, then sucked it intently. Don't worry, he told himself in a mature and reasonable voice, you'll understand eventually. But inside there was panic: excuses, explanations: how could he get them to call off the camp; how could he persuade them not to go away; how could he make it all a dream. Slowly he descended into his secret place; if he really concentrated he'd be able to shield himself, though maybe first he ought to put up some more defenses, because the hour of the test was drawing near. A little dancer wearing a leotard was in there, and when Aron sat down beside her, tired and gloomy, she looked at him and smiled. Peaches, he reflected, at least two peaches a day for her cheeks. And choconut ice cream, brown and green, for her almond eyes. This time he would put up a fight, though. For her he would give it everything he had. He'd fight to the death. Not even the outward Gideon would ever be able to take her away. The girl inside danced the cat step for him. He smiled as she did. He couldn't speak of her yet. For that he would need words of greater purity. With his eyes he asked her for something: she turned around and, concentrating sweetly, raised a rosy blush over her throat.

"What Gideon means is that all of us in the various youth movements are going away for a week. Sort of. That's all. We just wanted you to hear it from us."

We wanted. His gaze lingered on her, weakening steadily. She shook herself from his eyes with a twinge of annoyance. "I told Gideon we ought to talk to you and get it over with."

"Oh?" He still hadn't fully understood. "When?"

Yaeli looked at him. "When what?"

"When did you tell Gideon?"

"That's beside the point." She waved her hand impatiently. "The point is, you'll be staying here, and we don't want you getting any silly ideas."

"I'll be staying here? And you . . . Where?"

"Weren't you listening? What's the matter with you? The Scouts and the youth movements are going together."

He turned his leaden head from Gideon to Yaeli and back again. Something inside him creaked and groaned. Slowly, like a clumsy submarine, his disaster surfaced from the darkest depths.

"We just wanted you to know that nothing's changed as far as we're concerned," said Yaeli, sounding relieved, and she added with a little giggle, "Would you believe we've been debating how to tell you for a week already?"

Aron stumbled backward till his foot hit a low stone wall, which he found himself sitting on. What an idiot he'd been to feel happy. Would he never learn.

"The first night we're sleeping at the Kadouri Agricultural High School near Mt. Tabor, and from there they'll send us to different kibbutzim." Yaeli chattered and her eyes shone. "Listen, Arik," Gideon interrupted anxiously, more familiar than she with Aron's silences. "The three of us have to trust each other, that's what counts, we can't let anything spoil that for us, that's more important to me than anything, Ari."

Ah, he's bribing me with "Ari." What his mother said had come to pass. Something inside him, like a dim ray of light, sank down down down, to the bottomless depths of eternity. They've shot a bird, he thought. It's over, he thought, as the cold, shadowy grid of his mother's prophecies hovered over him and clanked down upon his dream. Yes, she was right. She won. And what was worse, he wasn't the only one she had vanquished.

"Listen, Ari." The tips of her little shoes were facing his. She had never called him Ari before. "If it means that much to you, I'll stay behind. We've already discussed it. Gideon has to go because he's a youth group leader, but I could stay if you insist."

He shook his head, listening to the intimation of closeness in these plans they had made without him. "No no," he said, mustering his strength. "You go, both of you." He really was that old man on his deathbed, giving his blessings to a guilty young couple.

"But you have to promise us not to torment yourself, okay? We do know how you get."

He smiled crookedly. Now he could stretch his neck over the lump that was choking him. "Go, go. Why are you making such a fuss about it? How long is it for, anyway?"

"No time at all," said Gideon hastily. "About eight days. Maybe a bit more. From just before Independence Day till a few days after." "But what about school?" he asked in despair. "Aa-bullshit, they're letting us off because it's work. Hey, don't get the wrong impression, we're really going to hustle there."

A minute ago she said one week, thought Aron, and they'll be staying at the Kadouri School, a place Yaeli's mother told them about, having parties and campfires and stealing chickens and showering together in the middle of the night.

"Go, go."

"What did I tell you!" cried Yaeli, clapping Gideon on the shoulder, her underlip swollen, inflamed. "I told you we were making a mountain out of a molehill!"

His fingers groped between the stones of the wall. Come on, snake, bite me. Eight days. If Gideon betrays me, he thought in silence, and gulped, "No sweat." His tongue went back to the empty hole where the tooth had been. His heart sank. At school they read a story once about a woman who slaved her youth away to pay for a string of pearls she'd lost, and in the end she found out the pearls were fake. Suddenly he felt her hand fluttering in his. Gideon turned away. Aron squeezed it, imploring. But she freed herself from his grip.

She's playing with the two of you, she can twist you around her little finger, thought Aron, and loved her more than ever.

"Why are we so glum all of a sudden?" wheedled Yaeli. "Look at you, your faces are as flat as a pita! And we still have a few days left before the trip."

"The work camp," Gideon and Aron corrected her in a whisper, each one to himself.

They said goodbye to Yaeli and turned the corner together. Silence surrounded them, and neither spoke. Gideon ran back for a sprig of honeysuckle; he practically tore off half the bush, crushed it and spread it over his face, and suddenly started talking, lecturing non-stop in a forced-sounding voice as he fanned himself with the leafy branch. And then he stopped, let the fan drop, and in a different voice, a friendly voice, said he hoped Aron would let him have a couple of pills for his eyes, to take with him to work camp, and Aron thought, What's the point? For some time he had suspected that Gideon threw the pills away, that he only pretended to swallow them, probably a good thing, too, but he knew he'd let him have some anyway, did he have a choice? Then Gideon started again, saying that in his opinion a work camp joining Scouts and youth movements was the perfect implementation of the Zionist ideal. Aron chewed the sticky words over in his mind but still couldn't figure out what they meant. He was trying to convince himself that he could trust Gideon. That Gideon was perfectly trustworthy. That his mother would turn out to be wrong. That the world would turn out to be wrong. And that thanks to this switch in the way of things, an evil spell would be lifted from the world and Aron too would be redeemed. You idiot, you jerk, he jeered at himself; they were laughing at the fool, yet in the very same breath he was angry with himself because even if he were to lose everything else, he would still have something no one could take away from him, the love he'd known over the past few weeks, a love which they could never corrupt. Oh? Couldn't they just? You child. You child. He strode ahead on iron legs, barely noticing that Gideon had left him, slowing down steadily as he approached the entrance. Surely she was home, he thought dejectedly, waiting with his lunch. And she would take one look at him and know. He quietly walked out to the asphalt strip behind the building and sat down on the crooked stairs, covered with dry leaves. He slapped his knee and watched it kick. His lips moved quickly as he talked to himself, made plans: too much time wasted lately. Now he had to start everything all over again. More daring would be required. More ruthlessness toward himself. Where are your ideas; but how would he make it from one minute to the next in the weeks to come? They laughed at you. Enough. Stop feeling sorry for yourself. He pursed his lips and made a mental note to look for cigarette butts. He wiped the sweat from his brow with the back of his hand. That gesture was from Papa. At least something was. Again he slapped his knee. It jerked. It's an involuntary movement, it's a reflex. It isn't the brain that wants it but Aron who makes it happen with his hand, like switching on a machine. And he went on rhythmically slapping his kneecap. It jerked. And jerked again. No doubt his brain was ready to pop because it couldn't stop it from jerking. And he slapped again. Jeering aloud. With all the contempt in him. So it would hear and know Aron was mocking it. A weak man's weapon, but at least it was something. A little revenge for the suffering it had caused. A few more slaps. Precise and baneful. And now he felt the bubble filling with life down there, and the warm blood circulating through the membrane that covered it; and a rustling inside, his secret headquarters preparing for battle. Mutiny, mutiny, groaned Aron, slapping his knee and forcing himself to watch with open eyes: there was nothing even faintly humorous anymore about the knee jerking up and down. Again he slapped it, and a faint, far-off nausea threatened, but nausea was his inner weapon, which he used to scare it away, to keep it from sticking its nose in where it didn't belong or from accidentally divulging secrets, and now he slapped some more, moving his hand up and down like a conductor, like a general, like a little tin soldier in the service of love. Over and over the knee jerked in his trouser leg, bouncing, twisting, he never knew it could bounce like that, bouncy bouncy, bouncing backward, in time, in space, into the mist, with a slap, his kneecap jerking, unrelenting, because when it bounced like a toy, with that soldierly woodenness, it began to spill the secret, to admit what it was in reality, and he slapped it again and again and again; oh, please don't let the nausea break him down now, because it's sickening to watch it jerk, and his hand moved up and down and jerked his knee while the aborted fetuses of misbegotten notions ran through his mind, as though his leg were madly spinning a reel of film, and through the blue of daylight he envisioned hazy shadows you could guess about like clouds; maybe in the shadows there were chained black men stumbling over each other while a villain whipped them like in *Uncle Tom's Cabin*; and then he saw a man in rags lying prostrate in the street of a distant land, and the indifferent parade marches past and then halts, exclaiming in unison, saluting in unison, and marching on, and when they have passed he suddenly spies a distant field where overgrown men and women, giants maybe, or maybe they were just healthy peasants, were celebrating something, having a wonderful time; again he slapped and then again, maybe they were torturing someone, but who?—a tiny unknown animal, without a skin, and their mouths brim with brutal laughter, and their ears grow longer and longer with the pleasure that could find nowhere else to lodge, and he sobbed in silence: Stop, stop, stop it right now, but he didn't stop, no, he wanted more, more, but his hand hurt, and his knee was turning red, and he slapped it again, alert with fear: Stop it, stop it, but all the while, all through the disaster there had been a comforting aura about him, a corridor of hope, the secret wish of a tunnel from which he would emerge a new and different being, and maybe somewhere, amid the darkness and confusion, a miracle would occur, an invisible hand would reach out and switch the suitcase, and wave a wand and change the secret orders, so that when Aron reached the light he would meet the new him out there; yes yes, Aron slapped his knee as hard as he could. Maybe it's all a dream, maybe he was only in prison for one night, for one tunnel length, and then maybe he would be like a blind man when the great surgeon takes off the bandages and hands him a mirror and says, Look, here is your face, a human face like everyone else's; that's how he always wished it would happen, that's what kept him sane; and now he whacked and thwacked, and lucidly, with helpless grief, began to realize that this was just the prelude, that night for him was day, and that there would be no vindication for his abhorrent body, it would emerge from the tunnel with Aron, as himself, not the exuberant, solid piece of life he used to be, and inwardly he still hoped to fuse again, to unite unto death, in a oneness of flesh; and still he continued smacking his knee, thirty times, forty times, till it was raw, a slab of meat and bone, fifty, seventy; and every time it jerked, involuntarily, with no relation to him, it was coming to seem more and more like an artificial limb, all of his body was artificial; the real Aron would force it to confess, he would put his soul into the mutiny from now on, with new ideas and inventions, with a life-or-death cruelty and contempt! The inward Aron cried and cried, and through his sweat-blinded eyes and twitching face he imagined a gloomy little cloud there, a puff of loss and loneliness, and he smacked it harder, ruthlessly, with a groan from the heart, torturing the hostage of the hated enemy, the faithless lover who gradually stopped pretending, and confessed a horrible thing—that she had never ever been his; whose then? He bashed her, feeling nothing in either hand or knee, dry leaves and gray dust swirled beneath her; whose then? Somebody else's? Up and down she went, loath to answer, forced to answer in the end, Another being's? Tell me, tell me! Yes yes, another being's. Whose, whose? I don't remember. And before that? What were you before? Before, before, what was she before, oh yes, perhaps, quite, yes, before that she was probably the death of the other being. He groaned. And before that? What were you before that? Before that and that. And that. Out of the void she spoke, jerking out the monotonous answers: more, more, more, his death, his death. He stopped. All at once. With a long groan. His body collapsing. What was happening? Someone might see him like this. Like what? Like this, acting crazy. Cautiously he glanced at his leg, sticking out from the curb. He got up, putting his weight on the other. He didn't want to stay here alone. Alone with her. Again he laughed with astonishment. He wished someone would call him: "Come to me," or punish him for being a naughty, stupid child, even if it wasn't fair, a punishment that would make him cry bitterly and stagger away sobbing into the thick of sleep, till at last he reached oblivion, nestling in the sweetness of consolation, sucking his thumb, hugging a cuddly puppy, protected by the talismans of childhood . . . Wearily he climbed the steps, trying to iron his face out with his hands. Mama would know right away that they went to camp together, that was the kind of thing she would feel in her bones. He stopped at the door and coughed his cough, preparing himself to hide from her eyes, from the look that would see and understand, immediately, without mercy.

31

As a matter of fact it took her a week to find out what happened. She ignored him and started preparing for the Independence Day party. Almost a year had passed since she and Papa stopped playing rummy on Friday nights, but it was their turn to give the party this time and she didn't want their friends to think they'd quit just to get out of it. Aron was furious at her for being so calculating. You call that friendship, he cried when she said she would throw such a grandiose party their eyes would pop. What kind of friendship is that, you hide things from them and want them to be jealous and never talk about anything important. He screamed and stamped his foot, startling Mama, who said with a sideways glance, Oh sure, at your age it's easy to have friends and be palsy-walsy, but wait till you get to be our age, let's see what you're willing or not willing to tell each other then. She didn't stay around long enough to scoff though, she was too busy cooking and baking for the party and making lists, and it wasn't till later, a few days before they left for work camp, that something inside her clicked, and even then she only suspected. She asked him indirectly, Where is he, why aren't you with *him*? I just don't feel like it today, I'm a little tired, we ran the thousand in gym class, and she transfixed him with a penetrating stare, not saying anything as yet, but next day she barged into his room while he was sitting on the windowsill, looking out and concentrating with all his might on the sumo trick, you can stop tears that way too, and she yelled at him, What are you doing staring out

THE BOOK OF

like a stone, why aren't you with *him*, you used to be thick, the two of you, a knife wouldn't cut between you, and Aron blurted some lie or other, though he knew her brain was already at work, and the following evening, when Gideon and Yaeli had left, cleared out, skedaddled, she suddenly understood; Aron was lying on his bed just then, staring at the ceiling, and she walked into the room and started pacing around him without a word, you could hear it fizzling inside her, and he waited patiently on his bed. Would you mind telling me where he is, that friend of yours? she finally asked through zippered lips, so it wouldn't burst out of her all at once. The two of you used to be tight as a tuchis, what's going on, I'd like to know, and Aron took a deep breath and told her quietly, casually, as though he hadn't just boiled half a cup of stinking oil and drunk it down to feel the Yaeli place in his stomach again. So how long have they gone for? she whispered, her lips turning white and her face sinking under the ash of defeat, Oh, five or six days, he answered voicelessly, and saw how like an avalanche the zap in her heart began. From love and concern, he thought, raising his hand to cover his face, though she wasn't going to hit him, she merely stumbled backward, her eyes gaping at something in him she'd refused to acknowledge up to now, and then she shut herself in her room, and when Papa came home she called him in and they stayed in for a whole hour, and when they emerged at last they wouldn't look at him, and for the last two days she'd been running around like crazy, hardly troubling with the party at all; twice now when Aron came home and coughed at the door he found her with Papa in the corner of the kitchen, and right away he sensed there was something going on, this was new, the way they stood there, hugging and kissing with all their might, glued together from top to bottom, so he thought it best to stay out of their sight.

At five in the afternoon Aron was playing Pelé on the narrow asphalt behind the building, with the legendary Gordon Banks as goalkeeper for the rest of the world, the only obstacle between Aron and the shining trophy on the desk of the head of the Olympic committee. Pelé was having a fairly weak day: the playing field was too narrow for him to use his powers to the fullest, especially his swift charge up the pitch, as if Aron was used to the green lawns of Wembley and Rio. Yet all the same, when they invited him to play the match of the century on this seemingly modest field, in Jerusalem, as it happens, a benefit game for Elanshil, the polio foundation, he didn't hesitate for a moment, to hell with them. He sat down on the stairs and sulked, and when that didn't work he groaned and hugged the ball, sinking into himself. He stayed like this for a couple of minutes until the wave subsided. A standard soccer ball. Made of leather, with the faded autographs of the Jerusalem Hapoel team all over it. Papa knew the players personally because of his job at the workers' council. Every Saturday there were two tickets waiting for them at the box office. Zacky used to come along and stay outside till halftime, when he could get in free and join them in the bleachers. And how the fans roared whenever Ben Rimozh scored. How they swore at the referee's mother, and the vapors of their sweat condensed in the air, and from under the stands came the reek of urine, and the men rose up and sat down in a body screaming, "The ref is a son-of-a-bitch, the ref is a son-of-a-bitch," and Aron went up and down with them, chanting inwardly, "The chef is a son-of-a-bee," because what did the referee's mother have to do with anything, and Papa sat beside him, sunburned and sweaty, with a big bag of sunflower seeds between his knees, spitting out shells, roaring with the crowd, and quickly winking at Aron and Zacky: Don't worry, fellas, it's all in fun, huh? Whuh? And now a hush fell, as though there were no one in the building. As though the city'd been evacuated. The children were gone. Someone came and led them away, playing a pipe only children that age can hear. Again without noticing it he began to slap his kneecap nervously. It would be interesting to know what Papa did with the other ticket since Aron stopped going to the games with him. Nobody talked about that either. Only silence. Again he slapped his kneecap and suddenly lurched out and charged, dribbling the ball from left field, with the entire defense of the rest of the world after him, and the ball practically glued to his foot, in a continuum of motion; never looking back, because they were running behind him, trying to catch up, surrounded by frightened, angry faces; everyone was avoiding him, even Yochi disappeared all day and came home only late at night, when everyone was in bed. Where did she wander, he knew she didn't have a boyfriend or girl friend to be with so long, she was probably walking around, counting the minutes to her army call-up, half a year from now, and what would he do on the eve of Independence Day, where would he be, where would he go; in the old days he used to go to town with Gideon and their classmates, but then he couldn't stand the crowds and the noise and the crudeness in the street anymore, he would stay home with Yochi and play Scrabble, going nuts, and this year the three of them had planned to go together, he, Gideon, and Yaeli, to the show downtown and the folk dancing, and now, because of his parents' party, he couldn't stay at home either, so he had to make plans, to think of a hideout; if only he could do something with Yochi, but where was Yochi, where was he, everything was falling apart, and last night he had that dream again, better not think—suddenly he veered around, only a fool lets himself be lulled to sleep by such sad concerns, and skipping lightly over their outstretched legs, he twirled like a dancer, and the crowd went wild. Lithely juggling just for the fun of it, to break the monotony, to thumb his nose at the human race, and he ran around the mound of bricks and plaster and broken tiles left there two months ago, exchanged a pass with Atias's gas canister, lost the ball, caught it, tussled with the forwards on the rival team, their furious jaws snapping behind him as he streaked across the lawn and positioned himself in place to kick a goal with a spin to the left, but alas, too hard, too high, maybe he was wearing his jinxed shoes, excuses, excuses, and meanwhile, as the coach, Sir Alf Ramsey, calls the players in for a briefing, Aron dribbles with his famous left, concentrating on the automatic hophop, dribble-dribble; "dribble" is a wonderful word; and there's something else he doesn't understand, but who can he ask, it's about anger, their anger at him; he dribbles precisely, he's good at that, once he held the school record for dribbling, thirty-seven times with heading and shouldering, now it's working because of the word, dribble, dribble, hopping inside him like a tiny frog, *ribble, ribble*, their anger at him, why, their contempt, even; to some extent, their hatred; he needs his ball now, he hugs it to his stomach with all his might, he'll never surrender, never, and break down here in front of a million spectators, but why their anger, that's the interesting question. So who do you want us to be angry at, smarty, who do you want us to blame? Oh right, I forgot: it's everyone for himself, like rats on an interminably sinking ship, but you do love me, don't you, we're such a loving family, not like the Sephardim or the goyim or the Arabers, who don't care if their children play in the middle of the traffic; no, you always look after me, you're always there to tell me, Dress warmly, button your top button, eat, eat, look both ways before crossing, and don't talk to strangers, so why are you acting like that. Like what? Giving up on me so easily. Without a struggle. And then he stormed ahead, in fear, because the words came out so clearly, and he feinted forward and kicked the ball through the opponents' goal posts, and gave an overly jubilant cheer, even went down on his knees and crossed himself secretly like the goyishe players do, what did he care, we aren't any better than the goyim, but then he realized that he'd missed the goal, and noted inwardly that he was having a weak day, an off day; Pelé, the black diamond.

And very slowly—he was familiar with this process, the heart contracts before the mind catches on—the answer came to him that maybe there's something in the brain like, say, a soccer center, which was closing up on him for some reason, and he checked himself again, with tremulous composure, noting that there did seem to be some deterioration in the brain center for triangle kicks, and he conducted several more experiments, double-passing with the Atiases' and Kaminers' gas canisters, only to discover that he was off in his estimate of the bounce, and he was astonished that in the midst of a war his brain should find time to harass him with something so trivial, and he headed for the stairs, concealing his temporary weakness from the fans.

He sat down, calmed himself. Pounded his kneecap nervously. A lubberly piece of flesh. Come on, get up, play another game, a corrective one, but he didn't have the strength for it. I'm on the bench, second string. It's five-thirty already. Where are they—by now they've finished working in the fields and croplands, or in the barns and silos, with the plowing and the gathering, the mowing and the grape picking. He never could remember which came when. And they'd all go in to shower together, Aron among them; he would approach the leader and gravely show him the sore on his foot which prevented him from getting his body wet for the duration of work camp, either in the public shower or the swimming pool or water tower. But there were other ways; for instance, he could say he was allergic to the chlorine, it made him break out in ghastly hives, or he could fracture his arm again, like he did last summer in defiance of the trip to Tel Aviv, yes, there goes Aron, strolling through the kibbutz, his arm in a sling, a mere broken arm couldn't keep him from going out with the rest of the class, colorful doodles and scribbles cover the plaster, just like last time he broke his arm, a chart for crossing out the days till the cast comes off, words of encouragement and the barely legible autographs of friends on the curve,

THE BOOK OF

it isn't easy to write left-handed on your right arm; and after the shower we go in to eat, you should see how they feed us here, not like at home, here nobody coddles you, unpeeled cucumbers with all the vitamins and the natural taste of earth left in, and at midnight we steal chickens out of the coop, or catch a fat pigeon and wring its neck, ping its peck, ding its deck, with a single twist they wring it, they're capable of that, you know, already they're capable of it, they aren't tortured as he is by dreams of a moth implanted in a sticky web, its antennae twitching accusingly; he slapped his knee, hop to, poor flesh—like if you shine a light in your eye, the pupil contracts in seconds, that's a reflex too, that too is something Aron can perpetrate against his body; "pupil," now there's a word for you, Gideon's father has a flashlight he uses for his coin collection; he groped in his back pocket, the coin was still there, he'd had it for almost two years now, couldn't get rid of it, and his knee jerked up and down, what will happen when they come back from work camp and notice his latest chendelach, making his knee jerk over and over. And now they're probably in the dining hall, it's self-service, there's a basin on the table for leftovers, and a groundskeeper and a dairyman, and boots and mustaches, and the children's home, and they smoke in the shadows so the leader won't see, and at night they have fun painting each other, but only after the campfire, or after skinny-dipping in the pool, don't skip that in your thoughts.

He ran. Ran across the Wizo Nursery School, up Halutz Street and Bialik Street, all the way to the tree-lined house where she lived, and into the yard where the laundry hung, cool sheets that draped around his face, caressing his cheeks as he slashed his way by them, and they let him pass, led him gently from one to the next, as though helping him out of there. It's no use, child, go home now, there isn't anyone here for you. Breathless and exhausted he swept through, emerging at last with a frightened backward glance at the armada of sheets billowing in the wind. He pressed his burning face against Yaeli's window, peeked through the blinds at her little room. It was dark. No Yaeli in there. But even with his eyes closed he knew this room. There was the bed and there was the bureau and there was the closet and there was her desk. And there was the shelf with her doll collection from when she was a little girl. He smiled. And up there, the cardboard box where she kept her collection of fluffy bits of yarn; Aron himself had supplied her with threads from every sweater he had, the orange one with the stars, the brown checkered one, the abadayat sweater from his bar mitzvah; Mama noticed, when she changed the mothballs, that the sweaters were a fraction of a centimeter out of place, and she waylaid him and caught him in the act, she would skin him alive if she ever found him pulling threads out again, she used the same wool over, year after year, was she a Rothschild, no, she was a balebusteh who could knit the old into new, but he risked his life to pull out more threads for Yaeli, even from the green one, his newest, with the big white triangles; he plucked it out and gave it to Yaeli, to hide in her treasury of fluff, like a woolly nest with carousel colors; and in his mind's eye he saw her messy desk, with the ink spot the shape of an apple, and the clipping from *Maariv Magazine for Youth* which she'd tacked up over it: *Love is calling. The flame of love is calling to you. You must love the trembling lips that say it: Love. You must notice little things, a smile that plays upon tender lips. A dreamy gaze. A teardrop hiding a mute and bitter pain.* He read through the slats in the blinds, with mouth a-tremble: *You must desire to tread this earth in search of its profoundest secrets, the riddles of the night. You must gaze into a young girl's eyes, ready to feel the warmth of love, though it burns you till you cry out in pain. True love is single-hearted, a great, strong surging of the blood. Tears wrung out of sacred sentiments* . . . He was worried about this last bit of youthful eloquence by our correspondent in Ashkelon, Ziona Kapach, hanging there before his innocent Yaeli's eyes; what if she wasn't ready for such a burning love yet, and was tempted by the pretty words into trying something cheap and phony, love isn't a game, you know, it's a matter of life and death, you can save a life with love, and maybe Yaeli's feelings were lighter than his, a little shallower, maybe she wasn't committed the way he was; oh, if only he could learn from her the wisdom of that lightness of feeling. As he backed away from the window, something touched his head and frightened him: the laundry again. Sleeves and hems hung limply now. The sheets were like empty sails. He walked through with his eyes closed, lost among them, how did Ziona Kapach from Ashkelon learn to speak so true. He wound a shirtsleeve around his hand, a towel, a pillowslip, meandering through this grove of ghosts, drawing profound secrets and tears and sacred sentiments after him, words to be purified inside before he said them aloud, lightheartedly; and he tasted the name of the stranger from Ashkelon, Ziona Kapach. Who was she? Not one of ours, judging by her surname, and he secretly fleshed her out in a shack full of barefoot children wading in the mud and a drunken father, and in the corner of the shack, by the light of a kerosene lamp, sits a slender girl with a serious, delicate face and glasses, writing the profoundest secrets of her heart, and suddenly her father comes up and starts beating her and yelling, Get out of here and earn some money, and her mother laments that Ziona doesn't know how to cook and sew, she has two left hands, who would ever marry her, a blot on the family, and Ziona looks up, entreating, despairing: from whence will her help come, is there anyone in the whole world who can understand her in her loneliness? If only he had the nerve to send her a letter. She would understand him. He could tell her everything, simply, without digressions. And she would read his letter by the light of the kerosene lamp, transported to him out of her life. She would have stayed. Yes. She would never have left him like that. He was frightened. Because of the betrayal. Again he whispered, Yaeli, till he felt the ember spreading circles of warmth inside him. He reached out. He ran his hand over the clothesline with his eyes shut. He grabbed something. He stuck it in his pocket. Ran away. Ran for his life. At the corner of the boulevard he stopped. He ducked into the bushes, took it out of his pocket: her sock. The green-and-red stocking. He sniffed it: the good smell of laundry soap. He inhaled deeply. Good. Good. Everything was good. Then he wrapped the sock around his fist and was amazed: was her heart so small, then? How could such a heart contain the heart of one who tried to win it? Run, get help, go to Mt. Tabor and rescue Yaeli in a daring night raid. But already he knew that he was too weak, he wasn't what he used to be, so what was he, so who was he, who was the real twin and who was the one who had slyly taken over, because sometimes while he was pissing he would cover his face with a towel and listen to it streaming out with a different sound, a deeper sound, as though it were someone else's; what did it mean, who was pissing out of him? He stuck the sock in his pocket and began running helter-skelter, awash with sweat, seeking refuge in the crowded shopping center, pretending to be calm, like a normal boy. But they noticed him right away. He was the only child there. He and the barber's son Binyumin, who leaned against the door of the barbershop and watched him with interest. And Aron hurried by. As if he had somewhere to go. Straighten up so they won't think you're a hunchback too on top of everything. Surely Binyumin would hit him now. Now that he was a head taller than Aron he would get revenge for the beating he'd taken from him way back when. But Binyumin wasn't thinking about hitting him. He merely watched him and hinted with his eyes: Over there, over there. Where? There. But there's nothing there. Except Morduch, the blind man. Sitting, moving around. And Aron turned away with his head held high. Mosco the iceman's cart horse swerved around and looked into his eyes. Aron tried to fight it, to control himself, but his fingers dug deeper and deeper into his pocket, touching the rotten onion strips: on Moshav Aderet a two-headed calf was born, read the horse through the onion strips, and bared its teeth in wild laughter. Aron recoiled and walked blindly by. Someone turned on the loudspeaker in the square, whistles and squeaks filled the air. A song started and suddenly stopped. Remember our names forever. Preparations for Memorial Day. And there was Morduch again. In the exact same place. Muttering over his rusty tin can. The can of Richard Levy corned beef they always took on the yearly school trip. But why was he here looking at Morduch again, wasn't he going in a different direction? And he quickly strode ahead wearing a troubled expression, following two big guys who were juniors in high school, and one of them who looked like Mickey Zik, Anat Fish's boyfriend, said in a loud voice: "So anyway, when the other animals saw it was no go they decided to send the rabbit in to show the lion how you do it." And Aron froze. It was crowded. He took a few more steps.

He dallied in front of the new supermarket. No one happened to be going in. The automatic door stood there innocently, pretending it was only glass. Daring him to enter. Come on, prove you're a man, it said in Glass-dooric. He looked around. Not a soul was heading that way. To save him from the door. All right, he had no choice. He stepped up slowly, sure that all eyes were upon him. Now he'd have to stall for time: he bent down to tie his shoe. An old woman was approaching. Thank God. He waited for her, crouching, watching her out of the corner of his eye, and, at the right moment, stood up and joined her on the rubber mat. The door slid open, for both of them together, and Aron distinctly heard it hissing, *ssssee* . . . he hurried by the crowded shelves. In a blur he saw the fruit and vegetable counters, so much color and abundance, but he still had to get out of here. To exit through that door. And nobody else seemed ready to leave yet. He lingered by the newspapers, casually sneaking up on it. Menashe Anwar's attorney argues that his client was temporarily insane at the time of the murders. What kind of country is this anyway: a person can murder, rob, be a spy, and if they say they were crazy all is forgiven. Come on, pay attention, run! He made for the door just as a young man with an armload of shopping bags was about to go out. Aron shuffled over, hands in his pockets. Just an ordinary boy, on his way out of the supermarket. But the young man stopped. Uh-oh! He stopped! The cashier called him back to the checkout line, waving a slip of paper, and the man turned around, leaving Aron stranded at the door, the automatic glass door that senses people, senses their bodies. It can't be fooled. It's as cruel and uncompromising as an infirmary scale, emitting invisible rays through the skin to see whether your body is real or not. He cringed. Again he leaned down and tied his shoe. The whole shopping center was probably licking its lips by now. Oh God, please let someone come in. Even a dog. But no one did. Aron stood up. He set his foot on the rubber mat. He felt as if he was floating. As if he couldn't quite land with his full weight. He hunched his shoulders, walked through.

Sure it opened, dum-dum. Did you really think it wouldn't. What's wrong with you, huh, tell me, what is wrong with you. Wearily, unresistingly, he looked up and met the gaze of Binyumin. Binyumin, who said nothing but ordered Aron over there. What does he want from me? Over there, and Aron complied obediently, reaching into his pocket: what could he throw the beggar that would sound like metal; he kept one of Papa's old razor blades under the sole of his shoe, and the piece of saw he swiped from shop class hidden in his cuff; Mama kneeled with pins in her mouth, taking his trousers up, cheating for him, so no one would notice, and the small nails and the long black lead nail he carried around, the equipment he always had on him, in case there was an opportunity to do a Houdini act, which there hadn't been for over a year, but where are we? What are we doing here? And Binyumin, yes, yes, we saw, he stuck his leg out indicating: There, over there, and Morduch the beggar shut his mouth, raised his bony head with the twisted veins, looking for something in the air, groping around, his mouth open wide to reveal his rotten teeth; of course! Finally Aron understood! What a dimwit he'd been not to catch on sooner, and he reached into his back pocket and pulled out the coin he'd won in the water, which had preserved its chill over such a long time, and with heavy resignation he dropped it into the rusty can in Morduch's hand.

For a moment everyone in the square seemed to freeze. His heart pounded once, like an enormous gong announcing the entrance of a mysterious guest, faceless and nameless, whom everyone knew. Aron closed his eyes, reeling as he stood over him. When he opened his eyes again he saw that everything was back to normal. No one, apparently, had noticed anything. Anxiously he glanced around: people walking by with bags and briefcases. Shopping for the holiday, hurrying home. Cars drove past, honking for no reason. See, it's all in your mind. You're the one who's abusing you. Put that pumpkin head to work and plan what you're going to do tomorrow evening: where will you hide, how will you pass the time. See, everything's normal. Except that Morduch the beggar was staring at Aron with his empty eyes, nodding his veiny skull, his hands fluttering this way and that, and Binyumin too was shifting his weight in the doorway of the barbershop, as though in prayer, as though they were tying an invisible knot together from opposite sides of the square. Aron fled. He ran for his life, past the drooping trees along the boulevard, home, home; he barely made it up the stairs, paused at the door, and gave his little cough, but when it opened they were in there glued together with all their might again, only this time he knew it was different, there was not the slightest trace of a nasty smile on their faces, and a fragment from a recent dream floated up, pieces that didn't quite fit, two animals chasing each other gently in circles, creating a kind of moving wholeness, a full revolving circle, though luckily for him he was sound asleep at the time, peeking out of his dream at Yochi's back; she was pretending to be sleeping, and she was frightened too, things like that had never happened around here before; luckily he wasn't a light sleeper, he could curl up in his sleep with an imperceptible contraction, you can practice even in your sleep, you can stop the flow of fear through your body, you count their breaths and gather scientific data, all arranged and classified; one person chases the other around and around in a circle and suddenly they crash; no, at the last minute they don't crash, a hand reaches out and catches them; at last they noticed him, standing in the kitchen, and slowly they separated, glaring at him, but why this anger, it choked him inside, and they blamed him yet, as if it were his fault, as if it were anybody's fault, and she said he'd wasted his growing years, bullshit, baloney, and yet —who knows, she can dish out the sarcasm, oh yes, she's a pro, but if only she'd tell him what to do about it. They were even ashamed to admit to the doctor that something like this had happened in their family. And they blamed Aron for it, as if he had betrayed them or brought some plague into the house that isn't mentioned in the Bible, and ruined everything, the quiet life they led, even Yochi was distant these days. He could feel it, she and he were not as they used to be. He was becoming extremely sensitive to people who acted distant. People whose expressions changed. He knew of course what she was thinking inside: that if she ever did find a husband, they'd have to hide Aron so he wouldn't think it was hereditary. There was no doubt that's what she was thinking. Even if she still loved him a little and was ashamed of thinking that, that's what she was thinking. Because that's how they'd brought her up to think. But how could he fight his damn biology single-handed; he pleaded with the thing inside his brain, the particular gland responsible for growing: Okay, you've had your fun, you've had your laughs, three years you've been fooling around with me, we get the point, now do something, give me something, stop being so mean, just one little drop, from here to there, one teeny-weeny drop flowing no more than half a millimeter, and then everything will change, the world will change; for the past year and a half he had been praying to the gland, he had nothing to hide anymore and no strength to hide it, yes, for a year and a half now he had been secretly putting on tefillin under the covers, chanting from his bar mitzvah portion: *Lo, this hath touched thy lips, and thine iniquity is taken away, and thy sin is expiated.* Because maybe he had sinned, maybe he needed to atone. But what could he have done. He was pure, the purest member of the family. He couldn't even shit in the toilet at home, for fear of pulling the chain too hard and causing a flood. And he never rubbed himself; who needed that when he could barely drag himself around. Still, maybe he was guilty of something. Like the time he gave Binyumin a beating and held him down and walked over him saying, "May you never grow." Or maybe he had sinned in his imagination. At times he liked to imagine that he wasn't really their son but the son of, say, a nobleman or a king. People from England or maybe Sweden, tall and slender, gracefully attired, speaking English quietly, wearing gold-rimmed glasses as they play the piano, because sometimes he suspected this would not have happened to him in a different family, as though it were something here, in their house, that cramped his soul, but no matter how he prayed, how he pleaded with the gland, it wouldn't answer him; no matter how he banged his head against the floor trying to jolt it— No answer, no answer, mumbled Aron, trudging through the busy streets as noisy shouts and patriotic songs blared over the loudspeakers, and the smell of burning in the air after the fireworks, how the night sky suddenly burst into color, with a pang of longing he thought of Yaeli, and people kept bumping into him, saying, Hey, kid, watch where you're going; he was out of step, out of sync, he always ruined everything, someone hit a sour note on the accordion: "Sing, oh water / Flow to the Negev." "Flow," that's nice, and there are public showers there, but what about the flow of blood, and carefully he extricated the word "flow" from the general clamor, stripping it gently and whispering it backward thrice with great intensity; "Wolf wolf wolf," his mouth clamped shut so none of the outer pollution would infiltrate, the tumult and the smoke and the crowds, till the dusty, sweaty sheath of "flow" dropped away like a cast-off skin, with its shrill notes and dissonances and random undertones; he hid it inside him, in the intimate new center, quickly checking over the other words he had smuggled in over the past few days: "supple," "lonely," "gazelle," "profoundest secrets," "sacrifice," "tears," words that welled out of an endless stream, and now "flow"; for seven days he would refrain from saying it aloud, till it was purified, till it was his, his alone. He struggled through the crowd, what a mob. Look at him, see the way he walks, he's talking to himself. What's the matter, kid, have you been drinking cognac? "Wolf wolf wolf," it was hard to concentrate, hard to hear it over the noise. If only they'd shut up a minute, he would be able to organize his thoughts and wander through the streets again, free from worry, enjoying the music, having fun, if only he could get rid of that monotonous buzzing, that neverending lament in his head, no answer, no answer, the gland was indifferent to him, it wouldn't answer, and it was so hard to keep the rhythm as he walked through the crowd; maybe there's a course in public walking like they have in public speaking, obviously you've never taken it, you stop, they move, they stop, you bump into them, and for almost an hour now they're the ones who've been deciding where you go, they push and crush you like food passing through the alimentary canal, and now he found himself in front of a high platform, with a loud, incessant roaring in his ears as the crowd hemmed him in on every side. He turned and tried to flee, but the crowd was like a solid wall of fortified flesh

294   THE BOOK OF

around him. No chinks anywhere. Folk dancers in colorful costumes were doing the hora on the platform, while below the platform teenage kids were unabashedly doing the twist to the rhythm of the hora; "the social set," he raised his weary head, having fun, living it up. Great bunch, he muttered aloud, to fool whomever it was necessary to fool, and meanwhile, with an expert eye he squinted at them tracking down the stowaway, the enemy he instantly identified as he went on counting Adam's apples and sideburns and mustaches and breasts; it wasn't easy either, they kept moving all the time, they really were enjoying themselves, playing with their new toys, idiots, they don't belong to you! You've been had! But wait, maybe he was the one who didn't understand, he, Aron, who wouldn't allow himself a single moment of illusion or self-forgetting; maybe they go together, those things and the pleasure they bring. If only he could win the struggle with himself, get around himself, forget himself for five minutes, maybe that's all he needed, five little minutes when his brain wasn't watching, five free minutes. Okay, we heard you the first time, and you know what would happen then? You'd be just like they are. Huh? Whuh?

He stood there mumbling and shuffling his feet, pushed by the bodies that crowded around, puffing their breath at him, and he stared entranced at the shoes of the dancing boys, his right hand tightening around his left wrist, as he counted at a precise and moderate tempo. They looked so big. Tremendous. Shoes betokening massive bones, like the jaws of a prehistoric animal, and a word floated past in the rushing stream, "youth"; he felt it instantly, a lovely word, dive in, why don't you, and fish it out. I'm too tired. Dive in and get it, now, he ordered, and dully obeyed, his head hanging down to his chest. Now fish it out, "youth," all bubbly, happy, swingy, springy, free, htuoy, htuoy, he mumbled, and something inside him groaned, but he had taken a physician's oath: yet he couldn't do it all by himself; too bad, he had responsibilities; so many words pounding at the doors of the secret hospital he had established in the bush. Htuoy. Words streaming by, from people from the radio from newspapers from billboards from popular songs from the onion strip. Htuoy. It sounds Japanese. In urgent need of treatment, Aron operates, counting twenty-five seconds; when he gets to thirty usually the pins and needles start in his wrist and fingertips. Again he tried to break through the stifling ring of flesh, floundering but unable to budge, not even Houdini could help him here;

he turned his head with difficulty and for an instant saw his face reflected in a store window, a small white face like a spot of brightness in the crowd, like an absence: Yaeli, where are you, what are you doing now? Thirty-one, thirty-two, he could feel the blood throbbing frantically against the barricade of fingers around his wrist, his poor muddled blood, he'd been driving it nuts in the last few days, thirty-seven already, thirty-eight, thirty-nine, and the worst of it, as usual, was the nausea: in every experiment the body's ultimate weapon against him. But here too, Aron was training himself, sticking his finger down his throat for one second, then almost two, ho hum, this finger isn't him, neither are the nausea and the gagging and the vomiting, he was himself in spite of these, forty-three now, don't give up; for once he had to get through the nausea, because if there's something beyond it, the body has its reasons; now the nausea is coming in waves, but maybe beyond it, or beneath it, at the bottom of the swamp there was someone imprisoned in a bubble, banging his head against it, begging him to go all the way as a matador and a partisan, but any minute he would vomit or faint, it was coming, fifty-one, don't give in, this is the body against the soul, so don't give in, but he does give in. As usual. His hand lets go of his wrist. Another minute and he would have vomited all over everyone, too bad, too bad. Pins and needles in his hand. Too bad.

He drooped among the sturdy bodies supporting him, covered with sweat he collapsed and slowly recovered: still, he did manage to hurt it a little, he did get revenge. But then his vision cleared, and what was this, what was going on, only now did he spot the familiar faces, how come he hadn't noticed before, how was it possible; he'd been standing here all this time while they were dancing, and now he recognized them, before he didn't. As though someone had played a trick on him: he'd been here for the past quarter of an hour, how did that beautiful girl suddenly turn into Anat Fish? He shrugged his shoulders, past hope of understanding: here she was, the beautiful Anat Fish, dancing barefoot in the street. He stared at her, trying not to look at the others, Anat Fish, in the black stretch pants the boys call fuck-me pants, and if you look carefully you see she really has lost something; she's faded, who knows why, maybe because of what they said about her and that guy, the one she went to Eilat with, yes, yes, we know all about it, and maybe she's lost some of her charm because David Lipschitz isn't around anymore to adore her, and there's Adina Ringle and Aliza Lieber, the

THE BOOK OF

kids in the social set who didn't go to work camp, and look, wow, Michael Carny, what's he doing here, he's not a "socie," not in any youth movement, either, pareveh, but he's dancing too, look, he's danc- ing with chutzpah right in front of the unperturbable Anat Fish, stealing a dance like a hungry beggar; but at least he dared, watch and learn, his gland has secreted that special substance that enables you to forget yourself and deceive yourself for a minute, look. Aron forced himself to look directly at Michael Carny undulating camel-like. Watch what happens; he watched, withering inside as Michael Carny revealed his body, rocking around with a startled joy, with a curious violence, to and fro he danced, watch and learn how— Wait a minute! Because in the middle of his ungainly dance Michael turned to Aliza Lieber, the redhead, and asked her to dance, and she refused, naturally she refused, look at her and look at him, but he doesn't despair, how well Aron knows the importance of not despairing now; he can't stop dancing even for a moment, and carefully, as though guiding a sleepwalker across a roof, Michael offers himself to Rina Fichman, who is standing there with Miri Tamari and Esty Parsitz and Osnat Berlin and Varda Koppler; what's this, half the class is here, and Rina's dressed in a miniskirt like a real doll, he's never seen her like that; if he saw her in the street and didn't know her, he'd think, There goes a real doll; if Mama saw her, she'd smile that smile and elbow Papa in the ribs and say, "Husti gezein? Did you see that?" And Rina and Michael have been sitting next to each other in class for years, always passing notes, like two gigglepusses . . . Aron muttered as though telling himself an old old story . . . htuoy, htuoy, and Michael drew nearer, hopping and dancing over to adorable Rina Fichman, lightly, as though carrying a trembling candle in the storm, and timidly touched her hand and said something to her Aron couldn't hear, with all the shouting and singing, the crowd was all, and out of the crowd Rina Fichman raised her startled eyes to Michael Carny, and smiled at him and began to sway her supple body; "supple" was also in isolation, being purified inside him now, tomorrow its turn would come, for seven days he had been careful not to utter it aloud and tomorrow he would put it back into its natural surroundings, he would be permitted to use it in his silent communion with Yaeli and Gideon, and the weary doctor paused, removed his pith helmet, wiped the sweat from his brow, and carried on with his dedicated work, never taking his eyes off Michael Carny's glowing face, words like "dance," "jubilant," "bliss," "darling," and he forced himself to gaze at this mystery, this ineffable moment of emergence, the butterfly moment when a shiny thread went out between Michael and Rina; but how did half the class get here, when did they plan it, was there a notice up on the bulletin board that he hadn't read, and all the while he kept worrying he would bump into Yochi, he sensed her presence nearby, knew that she too was wandering through the streets, avoiding their parents' party. He stared at the dancing shoes in the street again, potent-looking boys' shoes. They're gaining this thing called mass, he explained to himself, yes, their bones have a higher density now, they're full of marrow, it must be that, and through their shoes he sensed the soles of their feet soaking in the iron dust of the fecund earth, but did that mean they also *existed* more than he did, who could say, who could measure, but yes, he guessed dispassionately, they probably did exist more, though what exactly did that mean, did they feel something he didn't? What was it like for them? Is it like muscles of steel in the pit of their stomach? And does the blood fizz through their veins and practically gush out of them like soda from a bottle when you shake it up? Yes, could be, he consoled himself with a scientific hum, but the thing is, what did they have to give up in return? Huh? Whuh? Good question. The sixty-four-dollar question! Ask again! Did they give up something in return? Yes! Yes! He almost howls it, clinging to the vaguely comforting hope that by accepting the awe-inspiring code of mass, the canon of the flesh, they had chosen the path of enslavement and drudgery, directly and without digression, step by step to the bitter end. Death. And then he sneered at himself and stifled the filthy laughter in his armpits. Har-de-har-har-har, who do you think you are, oh, high-and-mighty one, do you think you're safe because you're different? Even now you're sinking, sinking, you're worse than they are. Look at you. Like the living dead. Everybody's watching you. He hunched his shoulders even more, muttering wolf, htuoy, ssilb, a Dr. Schweitzer of the jungle, a Dr. Dolittle of language. Get out of here, quick, breathe.

He broke away, slogging through the crowds, ducking down a half-deserted alley where three little children accosted him and bopped him with their plastic squeak hammers, calling after him, "Pumpkinhead! Pumpkinhead!" But he just kept walking to avoid a fracas, smiling inwardly at their mistake, they thought he was their age. Then two skinny hoods grabbed his arm and dragged him over to a deck of playing cards spread out on the sidewalk: Bet one pound, take home ten, everyone's a winner here. He wriggled free, nauseated by the wine on their breath, and darted off again, sealing out the music that blared at him from the tall buildings and puffing out the smoke he had inhaled from the air so it wouldn't pollute him inside; what's the time, they were probably having a campfire about now, charred potatoes on a wire, blackened fingers smudging an autograph on somebody's cheek, the smell of smoke in her hair, her quiet laughter. Take the hair out of my mouth, would you please, Gideon, my hands are covered with soot. A gangly old man without a face emerged from the shadows and walked up to Aron, holding out his hand. I thought you weren't coming, he simpered. Didn't Simo tell you to be here at eight? Aron stared at him uncomprehendingly, shivering down his spine, the voice sounded familiar, and suddenly he felt a skinny hand on the back of his neck with squidlike fingers, and heard him snicker in his ear, Shall we go for a little walk, Simo tells me you're new around here. Aron veered around and sank his teeth into the slippery hand; he snapped at the fingers hard as he could till he felt the flesh break, and didn't stop there, flesh and blood, he bit down murderously, to kill, to annihilate once and for all, but when he tasted the blood he spat it out and fled for his life, shuddering and shaking, while the faceless man collapsed in the alley, howling with pain and bewilderment, and Aron kept running, spitting out every drop of saliva in his mouth, maybe the man had a contagious disease, what was that all about, maybe he wanted to force him into joining a gang of robbers; Aron didn't know where he was anymore, the din from the loudspeakers pursued him through the alleyways. The streets had no names, the houses no numbers; he trembled so, his hands started fluttering at his sides; if only a miracle would happen and Yochi would appear now, calling to him with open arms: Come here, li'l brother.

At last he found himself in the crowded street again and heaved a sigh of relief. The faces of the people streaming in on every side shone red and yellow under the colored lights. Aron stopped to glance at his watch. It would be six or seven hours before he could go home. He sank exhaustedly on the curb. People bumped into him, stepped over him, cursed him angrily. He cradled his head in his hands. Through the legs of the revelers he saw another group of children. He studied them carefully: this time they were strangers, but so what. They all looked the same when they were dancing. Cavorting. With wild exuberance. He searched for the most attractive couple. Two by two he examined them. Swallowed them longingly with his eyes. He caught his breath, stretched out on the sidewalk. All tired out, but no malingering, he had to check them over by the book. No exceptions. He cleared his throat. Sat up a little. He chose a few more couples out of the crowd. He swore to be honest with himself. To admit the truth, even if it hurt. But no matter how he tried, he couldn't find any real happiness in them. He felt the urgency in their steamy shouts of jubilation, to be as alike as they possibly could, to know that which Aron—like a deaf man watching faces in the audience—could only surmise by their quivering movements, that they wanted to surrender to it, crying out in airy rapture, in sheer oblivion, before the alarm buttons went off in their horrified hearts.

So he stared at their dancing feet, his face bare and his secrets scrawled rudely upon it. A group of children noticed him sitting there, moving his lips, and pointed at him conspicuously. Someone spilled the dregs of a juice bottle over his head, drip, drip, it leaked into his collar. He ignored it. Easily. What did he care if he was wet. There, they quit and walked away. Relieved, as if a vicious hand had suddenly let go of him, he stretched his legs out and leaned back. Relieved of the pain, of the unbearable heaviness in his heart. Just like that, for no particular reason, a brief respite. Who knew what he would have to pay for it.

And in the midst of this, in the split-second interval between the blow and the pain, with the instinct of an elderly fourteen-and-a-half-year-old, he knew that the dancers were just as miserable as he was. That having a body is itself a defect. That even this gaiety they yielded to, this frenzied urge, was inwardly childish and playful, not deep, not really theirs, he sensed without words for it, in the darkened cell of his nascent mind: and all they have is a consolation prize, wonderful but strange and callow, the kind you use up quickly, in the shadows, with humiliating greed, with dark forebodings; this, like a letter, they would pass on to others . . .

Sometime later, around midnight, he headed home from the center of town. Slowly plodding through the streets, he continued his little experiment, forced to add the new blister on his foot to the repertory, to time the yelps of pain; how long did it take them to reach his brain, did they mingle there like echoes, and sometimes he would count how

THE BOOK OF

many times he could hop on one foot before his thigh muscle started shaking, or he would stare directly into the blinding streetlamps, observing the influence of light on his pupils; what does that have to do with anything, though maybe it did have something to do with it, maybe he would draw sudden insight from it, a flash of brilliance from the pupil of his eye. He repeated the facts again, he would have to juggle them in order to solve the riddle, to break them down and build something new, healthy, lively; it would be interesting to know what was going on there now, maybe at midnight everybody kissed, maybe they've gone even further, maybe they kiss with their tongues by this time. He tore a hair out of his cowlick. Three seconds of pain. That's interesting: this morning it was five.

When he finally approached the house, he heard raucous voices and music inside. There were Menachem and Aliza Bergman on the balcony with Yosaleh and Hanna Stock, snorting with laughter at something or maybe someone, not him, of course, though he did hear them say "rarin'" to go, which sounded for a minute like "Aron"; but their voices had that tone he knew, and he retreated deftly into the shadows, where he saw them suddenly switch to the code; Yosaleh Stock lit a cigarette and there was suddenly red lipstick on Aliza Bergman's lips. Maybe they did notice something after all. How long was the party going to last? He wandered around the neighborhood. What if he went upstairs and rang the bell and said hello to everyone and walked through the hall to his bedroom: We all went home so we'll be able to wake up fresh at 4 a.m. to watch the sunrise, and he turned away in shame. Maybe he'd wander around for a while. Maybe he'd go do a mitzvah at the hospital where Grandma used to be. The night shift was on now. He could volunteer to change sheets, for instance. This party might last till morning, and when he said goodbye nobody even asked where he was going. What an idiot he was not to take his passkey. Then he could have taken a little nap in the shelter. Or sneaked into Edna Bloom's, he thought with surprise, shivering as he fled from the empty space of her apartment, with a backward glance at the imaginary thing that might jump out and grab him and lock him up inside, and so he ran to the end of the street, and only then slowed down, out of breath, with a stitch in his side, and shambled aimlessly, hugging himself with cold, and again and again he thought about Yaeli, but he was so tired, so tired, his jealousy and pain were muffled. Maybe this was the moment to start the separation. Be realistic, she's not for you. He even evoked an unpretty picture of her as she emerged from the oven, bloated and puffy, and for a moment he could imagine how she would look one day. She's not for you. You need someone different. Someone more . . . More what? More sad, he thought. Tentatively he spoke her name: Yaeli, Yaeli. Nothing. Only a dull and distant pain passing through him, and so he continued, careful to stay half-asleep throughout the operation, and he tried to decide rationally who his next love would be; he felt so logical, he began by crossing off all the ineligible women of the world, like Mama, for instance, and Yochi and Grandma Lilly and Gucha and Rivche and Itka, and women who were out because they were too old, like Golda Meir and Bebe Idelson and Henrietta Szold, yes, go on, and how about the ones in hospitals and mental institutions, like Rivche's Lealeh; there, you see, so many women who can never be yours, one Yaeli more or less won't make any difference, and how about the millions of women in China and Japan whom he would never even set eyes on, or the Arab women he had to disqualify because they were enemies and stank, and he came to the conclusion that his love would have to be Jewish and live in Israel, because how else could they meet, and as he sleepwalked through the darkness under the bowing cypress trees, he eliminated all Jewish women of Moroccan, Kurdish, and Turkish descent, he knew Mama would never let him bring one home and he didn't have the strength to fight her now, and after brief consideration he eliminated Bulgarians too, and hesitated over Romanians, she always warned him that Romanians are almost one of ours but not quite, that they try to marry up, she had this complicated hierarchy of Ashkenazim and Franks, and finally he went through the list of suitable girls he knew, checking them off one by one, like Rina Fichman, she could definitely be right but it seemed she was taken already; Naomi Feingold might be the best one in fact, except what about that brother of hers; and then, as he traipsed back along the narrow road that led to the building project, surely they were gone by now, he realized after all that the only girl who was eligible to be the love of his life was Yaeli, and the thought of it woke him up with the pain of an open wound when the bandage is torn off, and he heard the chirring in his ears again: No answer, no answer, no answer, and now he stood in front of the building where the noisy party was still in full swing. Now where? Down to the valley, maybe, dare he go there in the dark, to hide in the cave till the party was over. He shuffled along, turning down the side street that led to the valley, skulking near fences every time the headlights of a passing car rushed by, but at the end of the street, on the edge of the valley, the utter darkness filled him with terror and he couldn't go through with it. He sat on a rock, laid his head on his arms, and dozed off, awaking in a panic every minute, where am I, cruelly banging his kneecap, tearing out hairs, muttering, This is war, this is life or death, and dozed off again, tired out, and life, if he ever lived it, if his disaster didn't portend an untimely death, would in all likelihood force him to be constantly alert, constantly juggling, without pride, without distinction, what would such a life be worth. But what choice is there? He heaved a bitter sigh: Calm down, you're becoming hysterical, you're exaggerating, there are plenty of kids your age who haven't started growing yet, you might start growing any minute. Right away, in fact. But what about his measurements, he argued with himself; every morning he measured himself, in the morning the cartilage between the vertebrae is still unabraded, which makes a difference of about three millimeters in his favor, and thanks to the marks Papa drew for him once on the door, Aron knew for a fact, every time he left or entered his bedroom, that he was no taller now than he had been at ten and a half, he was exactly the same height and weight; so what, stupid, he didn't need measurements, he knew from the pangs in his heart and the coded communications, the idiom of his most intimate grammar, that this was no temporary delay, it was becoming, God forbid, the thing itself, and just as he had felt *chosen* somehow before his problem started, now he felt chosen, too, same difference, which gave his disaster a certain dark and twisted logic: it was *his* disaster, out of which he had been fashioned.

A car slowed to a halt very near him, with its lights dimmed, and the couple in it started writhing and moaning, but Aron didn't wake up, he slept like a stone, counting their breaths; by ninety-one it's usually over, sometimes ninety-five at most; he knows these things, it's always the same, with minimal variations. A long bare foot jutted out through the open window, and in important matters they have no choice; when it comes it comes, it grabs them by the claws and won't let go, and it's seventy-five already, and the clumsy back goes up and down, why do they always groan like that, and maybe it has to go in and out a few times before it connects, and soon we'll hear the krechtzes; ninety-one, ninety-two, what's this, a hitch, some technical difficulty, ninety-nine wow, a hundred already, and he continued to count in sheer amazement, awakened by the sight of the bare brown foot with the painted toenails which began to squirm, one hundred and thirty-seven already, here come the krechtzes, thank God, maybe he miscounted, maybe he was so tired that he counted faster than he usually did at home, one two three and four groans jumbled up; now she'll whisper to him, Pull out, and five and six; what's the matter with her, she's supposed to scream, Pull out, arois, it's been like that for nights already, and then he'll cling to her with all his might, he won't want to pull out, and she'll push him and scream in a whisper the whole house can hear, Arois arois, be careful, pull out, arois charois marois parois, but the lady in the car doesn't push him away, she doesn't scream, Pull out, they just keep panting and groaning, going up and down like a giant piston, with the bare foot wriggling and squirming out the window, and the long toes stretching out farther and farther, soon they'll stretch all the way to Aron, maybe she can't hear him, but the whole world can hear him now. Aron counts the groans in astonishment, seven, eight, nine, maybe he'll find a use for these details someday, maybe someday the question that has been plaguing him for so long—ever since he saw that curious amber glob in the handkerchief—would be answered once and for all: when exactly do they decide to piss the sperm, and he sat up, suddenly excited, that is, if they do decide! As if it were something they could decide! You stupid idiot! And he started banging his kneecap with one hand, sticking the other between his teeth and biting it hard, to keep from sobbing, and the darkness whirled before his eyes as the animals ran around and around and grabbed each other's tails in their mouths, chasing faster and faster; what timing and precision were needed here, to prevent them from crashing, because just as they're about to, a long hand, a reliable hand, will reach out and grab them in midair, but what if it misses them, what if someday they explode into a thousand pieces, or maybe it happened already.

He jumped up, forgetting they might see him, and ran with a pounding heart all the way to Memorial Park, but here too there were groans and whispers and sucking sounds; where could he run now, where could he rest awhile and understand his mounting fear, how long would they go on dancing up there; again he stumbled back toward the building project, beating his temples with his fists to silence them, it's nothing, it couldn't be, it's all in your mind; he could hear the music from afar, Mama was dancing too. Who with? Whose arm was holding her, whose masterful hand was guiding her to the beat like a fish through water. Hello, hello, he whispered from his hiding place, what are you doing, what have you done, you already have a girl and boy, right? But there's no answer, no answer, muttered Aron to himself, retreating half asleep, hungrily drifting through the drowsy streets; no matter how he tried, there was still no answer; why this anger, why this hatred, hadn't he been trying his level best for the past three years, sitting for hours in front of a faucet that dripped once every second, he thought that would have an effect, collecting cigarette butts in the street and smoking them secretly in the bomb shelter, breathing in and out through his nose so the smoke would get in and make him sneeze so hard it would jolt it; and he would go to building sites and open his mouth and inner self when they dynamited the rocks, and once he swiped a huge magnet from the science lab at school and slept with it under his pillow all night, though he knew it could cause terrible damage, what if the good came out with the bad in one big hodgepodge, did he have a choice, and nothing happened; it was enough to drive you crazy, so near and yet so far, a fat little mound with a drooping eye in the middle and pouting lips, and little warts all over, the memory center and the laughter center and the speech center and the sports center, and maybe there's a love center and a happiness center too, glued to it, dependent on it alone; now we will hurt this mound, we will injure this gland, this Hitler, we will stick pins in the veins of our hands and feet, ice on the jugular, you won't get any blood or any air, a total blockade; he put his hands around his neck and choked himself for thirty seconds, forty seconds, forty-five seconds, black circles whirled around in his head, dark birds, wake up, bitch, wandering around the house with an up-turned lid; granules penetrate it. Infection. Pus. He smeared a drop of nail-polish remover inside his nose and screamed when the burning started. But he didn't give up, how could he, this was life or death.

A week has gone by since Independence Day and they're still not home from camp, where are they; he poked little things into his wounded nose: a tiny piece of dough with a Trojan horse of yeast inside it and a note with the ineffable Name, like the Golem of Prague, and nothing. Please, wake up, give a sign of life, say that someday everything will work out. Even if it's ten years from now, I don't care, just let it work out okay in the end. He wrote with his finger in the sand, in the air, he didn't care that people were staring, he wrote begging letters, appealing to its common sense, and what did it answer, nothing, it ignored him. So he had no choice, he sat down and wrote out a vicious threat, cutting out the black letters from the obituary notices, *It shall be neither mine nor thine*. His hand trembled as he folded the paper into a tiny ball and pushed it up his nostril with a matchstick, ten times at least the gland tossed it back to him with a sneeze, till he managed to push it in beyond the sneeze line, and for three days now the letter had been carried upward by a courier or the shadow of a courier, or a child, white and pure and tiny, running with the letter in his hand, winding in and out of the nasal cavities, onward, onward. Aron to Aron, where are you now, over; Aron to Aron, still far away, over; and so day in day out, whether he was walking in the street or sleeping or eating supper or Aroning, inside him burned an ember with a little dancer and a green-eyed boy whose ears were pointed with seriousness and responsibility, and Aron was with them too, three friends, three in one, quietly planning how to salvage the one, and meanwhile, the misty courier crosses the white plain, the ossified reticulation in the forehead, and works his way upward, over a scaffolding of bones and pipes and cords, and suddenly stops in fear: before him, all alone in a red-black sea of cool clotting blood, floated a large marble egg, or was it a pale-yellow coral, forsaken, full of fissures, covered in a frosty film. Aron to Aron, how will I cross the sea, over; Aron to Aron, an anonymous paper boat is waiting at the dock to take you, over. A misty boy floats in a paper boat, rows quietly across, careful not to wake the Cyclopean eye in the middle of the fatty mound on top of the coral, and the sea is thick, its tides slow and lazy, and before the boat lies the sleeping coral, and coming closer he can see it was swollen, yellow, you could scarcely feel it breathing, and the three-in-one awaited the news, silently cheered him on with the loveliest, purest words in the world, putting their heads together, fusing into each other, never to part; they have a single language, rings of warmth spread out from them to his stomach, to his legs, and in birds' nests lined with colorful fluff lie the invalids, squeaking through their gaping mouths at Aron the savior; today's arrivals are "longing" and "wandering" and "heron" and "diamond" and "autumn" and "lonely" and "a purple scarf" and "beauty unadorned" and "Jerusalem of gold," all culled from the Hit Parade on the radio, an excellent source of words; in the middle there was news, Nasser Kasser Basser Yasser, and later that afternoon he would be releasing "lamb" and "twilight" and "train" and "midnight" and "kiss me by the sea" from that pretty new song, so he must send them off with supplies for the journey, three squares of friendship sugar and a spoonful of royal jelly, and he opens the jar of sour cream and licks off the buttery coating; Mama was standing behind him but she didn't say a word, she saw he opened her refrigerator without permission, but she watched in silence, she wouldn't dare say anything now. He crosses to the sink. Turns the tap. Turns it some more. Her eyes bore into the back of his neck. He doesn't turn it off. Stomps away; the water gushes, splashing him as far as the pantry. There's a tap in the bathroom too. And a flushing toilet. The water comes from far away, from deep wells and vast cisterns, and electricity reaches us from distant cataracts, and whirlpools and rushing rivers, and gas to cook the chicken soup with noodles gushes out of the earth, in the beginning there was tohubohu, he runs his finger over the gas switch, he can feel a giant rig boring into the sea, into the ground, he hears a high-pitched whistle, and sniffs a pungent smell, and the spirit of God hovered over the face of the waters; slowly he walked out of the kitchen, directly in front of her staring eyes, and a mighty stream of water flows, and the courier in the paper boat has secretly reached the shores of the coral island, tied his boat to a blighted bush. Aron to Aron, have reached shore, am on my way, over; Aron to Aron, what do you see there, over; silence. The only sound coming through is the sound of his astonished breathing. Aron to Aron, I repeat, what do you see, what is it like, tell me, tell me, over; silence; and the tender boy, misty and white, fades out as he slithers over the chilly ash-or-frost-dabbled earth, creeping cautiously over the crimpled terrain and the pearly-gray craters. Aron to Aron, you wouldn't believe how horrible it is here, over; Aron to Aron, I hear you, over. And a little boy crawls through crevices and crannies with a black letter in his hand, and withered bushes scratch his face and crumble at his touch; once everything was full of life here, the bushes flowered and thrived, there were four flowing rivers, blue and clear, he had original ideas, innovations, children enjoyed them. Where am I today and where are they, thinks Aron, lying on his bed, staring at the ceiling, there are no children here, they all stayed to fill in the dwindling ranks for the harvesting or reaping or gathering or gleaning or whatever, and at night they sit around the campfire, singing to the strains of the accordion, and there was only one important question left, namely, was Gideon still loyal, was he still waiting for Aron, and the courier presses on in silence, his eyes open wide, and he ran his grief-stunned hand over memories and sights and reflections and laughter now gray and musty as withered fruit, the Aron it had cursed and turned to stone by growing over his life and stifling it; and suddenly the ember in his stomach glowed with a soft red light that spread through his limbs, warming him inside, trickling down to his feet. An idea, an idea, he had an idea, eureka, we're saved, ideas were coming out of his new place now. Aron to Aron, an urgent message: pick up everything you can, do you read me, over? Aron to Aron, message unclear, repeat, over; Aron to Aron, collect whatever you can and smuggle it back here on the double, everything must go, remove it and evacuate, over and out; and Aron jumped from his bed, bewildered, why hadn't he thought of it sooner; and now we have to help him, muster our forces, call up the reserves, the volunteers and the civil guard, and declare emergency measures; the windows were crisscrossed with black masking tape already, Mama and Papa did that yesterday while he lay abed watching them divide the sky into squares; that's how life prisoners see the world, but he would escape, he would slip out of his cell and break through the siege, through the naval blockade, the fire brigade, the bire frigade, he ran back to the kitchen, the taps were closed and Mama was staring into the open refrigerator, holding two bottles of milk, weighing them in her hands, and suddenly she sensed him there, she veered around and let out a scream, an unidentified expression appearing on her face; Aron stares at her, perceives a primitive stratum, and freezes, shocked; who is she, who is she, reaches into his pocket, and Mama recoils as if he were about to pull out a knife; he gropes in his pocket and doesn't find it, though he understands well enough without the onion, it's flickering at him, out of the depths of her Cain-like guilt, a needle of rage and retribution. It's all your fault, said the onion, you brought it on us, you have only yourself to blame for what happened between me and Papa, and he drew back from the animal look in her eyes, farther and farther back, his hands flying out behind him to keep from bumping into anything, he could knock something over, now let's see how fast you catch. He bumped into the wall and stopped. Get out, he shouted, moving toward her, get out of here right now, and she retreated, not looking at him, yes, suddenly he saw: she couldn't look at him. Or maybe she could, and now she did, so what did it mean, groping her way backward. Aron, Aron, come back and be yourself again, she murmured; her voice, she was afraid of him now, let her say more: Aron, I'm asking you, I'm afraid but I'm also worried, what's become of you lately; if only she would go on looking at him, but she looked away, she did, what could he do to make her look at him again, how would he make her give him that long, deep gaze she used for calming him and winning his forgiveness, now he would really shock her; *Eef you vant to be a bradher*, he nearly screamed at her, though he didn't dare, how could she help but guess what was frightening him, when once, before the problems started and her heart was open and quivering to him, he had a horrible dream about her and the whole next morning he could barely look at her, he was so frightened and remorseful, and she guessed, naturally, and sat him down on the edge of the bathtub and said, You dreamed something, didn't you, and he nodded. Something bad? Yes. And she tilted his chin back and peered into him, through his eyes, and rolled herself inside like a little ball, and washed through him like a storm, through the caves and crevices in him, and came out again and sat facing him like before, only now she was panting; You dreamed I was dead, tfu tfu tfu, and now everything is all right again and I forgive you, and he snuggled up and cried and cried till all the knots came out of him; she knew how to save him, it was easy for her; but don't you see, she's trying now too, her eyes transfixed him, her lips suddenly trembled, searching for the words in her mouth to save him. They'll put you in the crazy house if you don't start being yourself again, Aron, she implored in a whisper, and in her throat, or was it his, he felt the stab, the spears of all the tears she had swallowed. Ice baths they'll give you there; he knew: it was her love talking; he listened for the tumult in her voice riding the crest of a tidal wave of tears. Electric shocks they'll give you there, Aron, and only he and she understand this language, and if not for the pillar of tears Aron and she would be drowning all the time, in a never-ending, a primal scream. And I suggest you get hold of yourself while it's still possible; but why doesn't she look at him, who is she protecting, it can drive you crazy, but she has been looking into him, clasping the two milk bottles. Maybe I've made some mistakes too, she whispered, we're all a little tense these days, with Yochi going into the army and the military situation, and you're not so easy to get along with either, you know, maybe you are a special child like everyone says, with your brains and your talent, kineahora, and maybe we're not smart or educated enough to understand what's happening to you, Aron, and we haven't read books or studied in the university, but what, you think I don't worry about it all the time, and even though your papa never had a father himself and doesn't know how to be a father and makes mistakes sometimes, and I grew up without parents for most of my life too, we try; so why wasn't she looking at him again, she remembered suddenly and looked away. And you know we're only thinking of your good, don't you, even when we get angry at you, what do we have in this world but you and Yochi. Oh please, let her say it again, let her swear it on the Bible, and now both eyes are definitely on him, big and open wide, swallowing him in; so what's real, what's true, let her say it already, let her say definitively, is she or isn't she, and everything will stop and he'll relax, and she continued looking at him, taking him in, her arms going out to him, and he too went toward her, everything collapsed inside, but at the last second before he fell into the whirlpool his hands fluttered at his sides and flew out at her and struck the bottles hard; he knew she'd catch them, though, he simply had to do it before the reconciliation, her eyes already promised she would catch them easily, so what did he need this for, and he continued to bellow and lash out at her, blind with rage and humiliation, at her, at himself, and the milk flowed out, all over her body, milk and broken glass, and he pushed her and pushed her: Get out, get out of here, whore, spitting and screaming, and he returned to the refrigerator and stuffed his mouth full of sour cream, and halvah by the handful, to fortify his new place, to defend it and expand it, there was a lot of work to do. Aron to Aron, what have you found, over.

THE BOOK OF

32

The evil Cyclopean eye. Fixed half-open on the pale child, the silent child burrowing frantically in the lifeless earth. He digs with his fingers, throwing anxious glances over his shoulder at the immovable eye. Is it watching him? Far in the distance the wind is wailing, ululating, and the child, white as a leper, cracks his nails on the stony clods. He is a misty child, the child in the formaldehyde, who for three or four years has been banging his head against the glass, blinking at his fellow in the neighboring jar, or is it his own reflection, nebulous, like absence, like a cloudy human fetus slowly disintegrating; but not Aron, oh no, Aron will fight, he will find new life, a land of the living, he will flee the solitary and deserted land inside his brain; but the eyes of his fellow fetus start to flutter, the filmy lids on his polliwog eyes conceal a wan, ironic smile. Aron to Aron, hurry, hurry, over; and in the room next door Mama is blowing her nose with all her might, fearful of him, afraid to come out. Even now you don't hear crying out of her. And he remembers, he's been neglecting his tear experiments, the effects of a single grain of salt in the corner of his eye, precisely at what distance from the olive tree in the valley does it start to tear. Aron to Aron, I've found something, over; because the coral island puckers around his broken nails: leave it! The bubble ember inside him burns. Jars of formaldehyde float in space with a somber reddish glow. Stillborn fetuses heave a deathly sigh. Faded umbilical cords swing limply, searching for something to fasten on, to suck. Aron to Aron, what did you find, report at once, over; the leprous child runs through the cracks of the canals, the sorely puckered mounds, pursued by electrical chirring, and in his hands, the slowly flashing beacon light of a diamond, a waking memory, how he used to get lost when he was little, never missed a chance to, at the market, at the seashore, even in the street sometimes he would let go of her warm hand for a moment to look at something, and suddenly he could no longer see her through the curtain of strangers that intervened, she was carried away from him, but then he would hear her, desperately calling his name, and he would stand there listening to the motherliness that issued forth as if through a secret conch inside her. Never had his name sounded so clear as then, and he wasn't frightened, wasn't alarmed, even that time in Tel Aviv when she actually did disappear and someone led him to a policeman, who ruffled his hair and bought him a bottle of orange soda and took him down to the station, where everyone fussed and joked with him, and at just the right moment Mama and Papa walked in together and ran toward him, calling his name in a very special voice, with an animal whimper, and they hugged him with all their might, and he laughed and cried with them, and in his heart he knew he would get lost again at the earliest opportunity, but after that they watched him like a hawk and neither lost nor found him, and today if he went missing the radio announcer would probably say, "And here is his description." And then he'd know what he looked like to them, because "And here is his description" is uncompromisingly scientific, it tells about you like an automatic glass door. Aron to Aron, load the boat and return to search again, over; Aron to Aron, must I take everything with me? the bad with the good, over; he reflects a moment. Hesitates. I don't need it all, why should I spoil the new place too? It's bad enough as it is. But Aron to Aron, you have to take it all. Leave nothing behind. A wholesale exodus. Over and out.

He hurries to the back yard. It'll be dark soon, getting chilly. Did she pack a sweater for camp, I wonder. What if she says, Gideon, I'm cold. He lurks in the shadows so no one will notice him. Avigdor Kaminer is going to empty the garbage with a little transistor radio pressed to his ear, can't miss a minute of his program, even for the garbage. Hi, Aron, says Avigdor, so what do you say about the latest developments? Which latest developments? asks Aron reticently, he doesn't feel like getting into a conversation now. You know, all the brouhaha in the news, with the Straits of Tiran-Shmiran. Aron cocks

THE BOOK OF

an eye and smiles at him cautiously. Hey, maybe Kaminer knows something, thanks to his dead wife. Slowly he answers him, in code, like a spy talking to an allied agent in enemy territory: Tiran-Shmiran Firan-Liran? But Kaminer didn't hear him, he walked away, wagging his head in consternation. You have to be very careful now. That was a grave mistake. They could find you out. He skulks along the fence, half whispering, "Gideon, Gideon." But why aren't they back yet? Lucky for them they aren't missing any classes, most of the classes have been canceled, the men teachers are away in the army. The seventh-graders volunteered to deliver mail. The sixth-graders are helping fill sandbags. Everyone is occupied. Everyone looks busy and worried. His own class has scattered and disappeared. Sometimes he opens the classroom door in the morning and sees the chairs overturned on the tables and the remnants of a grammar exercise on the blackboard, a lesson on exceptions to the rule. He tries out various seats. To see how other children view the classroom. Tries this seat and that. Experimenting: Gideon's naturally, but also Michael Carny's, Zacky Smitanka's, and Eli Ben-Zikri's. Even David Lipschitz's. A creased map of the Middle East hangs on the wall, and you can barely find Israel on it, it's so small. Maybe it's shrunk even more, because of the recession, or because Egypt and Syria and Jordan and Lebanon are swelling up around it. Just looking at that map was enough to suffocate you. He ran a reluctant hand over it, fingering the cracks and wrinkles: like skin. Then he hurried out so no one would catch him there and ask questions. On the school bulletin board was a notice from last week. Grade 8-C, his class, would meet in front of the supermarket tomorrow, and be sent to dig trenches. Dig trenches? he was aghast: trenches for what?

He heard a scream and ran to the front of the building, his entrance, where a group of neighbors had gathered by the open shelter. Papa stood among them, shouting at the top of his lungs: he had gone down to check the shelter and make sure it was ready, and what did he find? Everything had been stolen! See for yourselves! Half our belongings were down there! Chairs and mattresses and the old buffet! And the neighbors crowded around and gaped in dismay, they too had been using the shelter for storage all these years. Malka Smitanka began to cry, she kept a folding cot in there. Peretz Atias discovered that his son's bike was gone, and Mrs. Pinkus, the divorcée, screamed, Where's the box with my feather quilt, it was an heirloom from my mother.

Papa turned red and said it had to be someone from the building project, someone who had a key, and he started looking at everyone's face. If I ever catch the traitor, I'll chop his arms and legs off. Sha, sha, said Mama when she came down to see what all the commotion was about, she'd changed out of the dress with the spilled milk, and Aron saw that her eyes had sunk in their sockets and her face was ashen white. Silently he hid behind Felix Botenero. Botenero was standing there with a transistor at his ear; what could they be saying on the radio now? It's no use screaming and getting all worked up, she said in a numb and weary voice. The dirty thief, said Papa, he's left us bald as a baby's tuchis. Mama noticed Aron and pretended not to. Mira Strashnov, Gideon's mother, rushed over to find out what the shouting was about with Eddy, the lodger, watching her like a puppy. Where's Gideon, why doesn't he come back? Maybe she received a letter from him, everything would be different if Gideon were here. Mira looked around at the frenzied neighbors, but she was obviously preoccupied, and a moment later she walked away with Eddy at her heels. Mama and Zlateh Botenero exchanged looks. Malka Smitanka called after her softly: Mira! and hurried to catch up.

None of the men noticed. Only Aron saw it, as though watching from the wings. The women. The men. Papa cooled off and started a conversation with Atias. You'll see, just wait, we're going to clobber them till they learn how fishes piss. Maybe so, answered Atias, I sure wish I could believe you. What do you mean, you don't believe me? Papa steamed up again. You listen to Moshe Kleinfeld, Atias, you listen good, I hope that midget of a King Hussein joins in the war so we can let him have it, and show him who's a man. Sure, right, mumbled Atias under his mustache, which suddenly looked shriveled and gray. But you know, Mr. Moshe, once these things get started, you never know where they'll end. And now they've closed the straits, said Botenero quietly, and Atias and Mrs. Pinkus nodded in silence, and Aron could see how scared they were, and felt a catch in his throat as though someone were trying to choke him; only Sophie Atias, her little one in her arms, seemed full of fighting spirit, and the whole time Papa spoke she kept nodding and looking at him with shiny eyes. Don't worry—Papa patted Atias on his shoulder—this is why we have an army and Moshe Dayan, you'll see, we'll clobber them like in that song they play on the radio. "Aiaiai, aiaiai, Nasser's waiting for a war," Papa sang hoarsely. "Rabin's going to beat him sore," Atias chimed in with drooping lips, and Aron saw that Atias junior, who had been crying over his stolen bike, and his feet didn't even reach the pedals yet, was mouthing the words along with them; how does everyone know this song, Nasser's waiting for the war, Rabin's going to deat him gore, meat him bore. He went back home and lay down on his bed, troubled, clearing his throat in anguish, it's hard to breathe in this country, looking at Yochi's empty bed, she's been away for five days already. Aron to Aron, what do you see, over; Aron to Aron, I've picked up the first days with Yaeli, but maybe you aren't up to it now, over; Aron to Aron, let me have it. Let me have everything. The bad with the good. Her eyes and her lips, and her smile, and the way she danced for me that first ballet class and the way she smelled when we were running through the valley and she waved her arms, and the space between her toes, and the way when the weather turned summery she wore a miniskirt, I thought it was too short, you could see everything, but it was nice that she was dressing in the latest style like the other girls, her time has come, and Aron doubles over, practicing sumo, to stop the pain washing through his body like a river. Retrieve everything, smuggle it out of there, the bad with the good, like a breath of fresh air, anything you can save, we'll establish a new place, you'll see, fresh and pure and natural and friendly, where we'll know what has to be done and how to do it, there, it's over, the wave.

He lay in bed till nightfall. He didn't even go in for supper. He had what he needed hidden in his room. A small jar of royal jelly, a bar of chocolate, chunks of Sabbath challah, a bottle of kiddush wine, a perfect, unblemished peach. Tomorrow he would steal a couple of potatoes from the pantry and make starch. He relaxed. He could hear Mama putting Grandma to bed in the alcove, covering her up with the Scottish plaid. Then there was silence. Where was Yochi now? Go know. The evening before she left she kissed him goodbye and whispered in his ear that his hair was almost brown now. What do you mean, brown, I'm blond, aren't I? he asked weakly, and she brought the mirror over so he could see. He didn't know whether to be happy or sad about it: brown. Maybe that was a good sign, though. Maybe he would stop being so special. Cigarette smoke drifted in from the balcony. Papa's smoking like a chimney again. Mama screams at him not to stink up the house. She can't stand him smoking around her these days. She's being careful suddenly. What's there to be careful about? It's all in your mind. Control yourself. And after the cigarette he'll take a shower and then she'll tell him what happened in the kitchen today with the milk. No, she won't. She'll be afraid to say those things out loud. He lies down and chokes his wrists and ankles one after the other, counting inwardly, reciting the results. Then he puts the pillow on his face and tries to choke the jugular vein with his hands. At the last minute he's saved. He takes a gulp of air. Checks the clock. Here too the results are in accord with what he already knows. So constant and predictable. You'd think by now he'd be able to control the thing from outside. The whole idiotic machine. But in the end it's still baffling. The fact is, he never succeeds. And what if the answer isn't in the body. What if it's in something else. Like, well, the soul. But what is the soul? Maybe it's what the Torah says: God blew the breath of life into the dust He fashioned; all right, but what if God ran out of air at a certain moment? Aron lets out a real laugh: oh, he can think of several people who must have been created just then. Again he laughs. A bad laugh. He orders his fingers to squeeze the laugh glands under his armpit. Laugh, you rats. Yes, but suppose God had accidents of the opposite type as well, maybe sometimes He blew too hard and the flesh and bones and everything flew up in the air and could never be glued back together again, except for some of it, leaving a big naked soul to flutter around in desperation like a pink turtle without its shell. Then he remembers the big picture on the wall in Edna's bedroom: all the broken, misshapen bodies, and out of them, a big mysterious soul bursting forth. Aron rolls over and sighs. But the soul is him. It is him. It's that place inside him, it's his essence. Now he can feel it distinctly: through the pangs inside you feel a small flame burning, spreading light and warmth, and his stomach and feet fill with heat and life, and there, down deep, is his Yaeli, and his little Gideon, and Aron, yes, his soul is what he used to be, in his childhood, and in the early dawn when he woke up frozen and torn with everything leaking out of him, he would simply take out a couple of friendship-sugar cubes and courage proteins from the hiding place under his mattress, and at the last minute he would be saved. But does anyone really understand this body-and-soul thing? he asks himself in anguish, rhythmically pricking his naked tummy with a pin, watching the little red dots spreading over his skin till they slowly tear open and begin to bleed; but it isn't fair, the sides are unevenly matched, in his case the soul is thoroughly subservient to the body, it has to throw itself

THE BOOK OF

at it all the time and beg for attention, and the body just ignores it. But maybe the body is right. Maybe there is no soul, thinks Aron, and something inside him suddenly dims: what if he's been wrong all along? Has anyone ever actually seen a soul? Maybe people like Winston Churchill and Albert Schweitzer and Ben-Gurion have souls. Okay, they're spiritual giants, but what about the others? Does Papa have one? Does Mama? And what about Grandma, who's more dead than alive? If they opened up their bodies and searched through their hearts and brains and everywhere, what would they find? Anything? Maybe nothing? Not even a few desperate scratches on the inside? But it must exist. There's got to be a soul. Oh yeah? Says who? Says no one, I just hope so, I have to. Then please explain, great genius of our century, how the soul is connected to the body. How is it separated from it when you die? And how does it enter life eternal, and how is it redeemed from human suffering? Huh? Whuh? Y'alla, Kleinfeld, you and your philosophy, go to sleep now, go to sleep.

Grownups' mouths are ugly, thinks Aron, stealthily approaching to watch: they're asleep. A warty, humpbacked sleep, a grumpy grownup sleep, a sleep as rough as labor. They lie far apart, and Mama's swollen foot is tangled in the blanket. Her lips move sometimes as though she's talking to someone. Arguing. What is she dreaming about? Maybe she has different children in her dreams. Maybe she has someone else in there already. There's quite a space between her and Papa. Aron draws closer, stands directly before her face. With all his might and fear he plants himself in front of her. So she'll see him in her sleep. So he'll infiltrate her dreams. Her blood. Like a curse.

But suddenly she sighs and he scurries away. He stands in the hall for a minute. Peeps in again. The orange boiler light throws eerie shadows. Papa's mouth droops open. Snoring like a saw. The driveling red mouth, how it twists when there's shaving cream around it, like a little animal bleeding in the snow, bait in the trap for other animals. Look at his fillings. Aron doesn't have a single filling. Aron is pure. He draws nearer. A vague terror of death seizes him as he watches their sleeping bodies. Maybe he'd better scream. To wake them up. But Papa would break his bones for that. Look at his mouth. It never stops moving. Curiously supple. Squirming as though he were talking to Aron. Come here, son, come to Papa, get in quick and let's be done with it, it'll only hurt for a minute and then . . . Aron shudders: if not for the smell in there he really might have let himself be swallowed up. He steps back. From the foot of the bed their faces are even stranger-looking. Their wrinkles, the mole under Mama's chin, Papa's cheek squashed flat on the pillow, his cheekbones standing out from the flesh. Aron leans cautiously over him and sniffs: after his bath Papa's feet always have that special smell. That sweet, clean smell. Aron to Aron: Now! Hurry! Over. He brings his nose closer and inhales. A good warm smell. Exactly what he was looking for without knowing it! This must be why he woke up and came in here. And now Papa is shifting his position just for him. He lies on his back with his feet spread apart, and they're long and rounded at the toes like loaves of bread. Aron smells them timidly. Breathes in. The toes are fresh like little rolls. He remembers this smell from when he was little. That is—young. But the Cyclopean eye is slumbering. He sniffs them hungrily. Falls to his knees at the foot of their bed. And a cold wind, black and cutting, blows over the forsaken steppes. And a spent, despondent child creeps over the steppes, and the evil eye, the spiteful eye, rolls slowly under its fatty lid, beware! Papa groans in his sleep. The blanket drops away. The scar is revealed, like a pale hiatus, a silky gap in Papa's brawn, but maybe at night it opens up, unravels: Come here, child, and a tiny child kneels fearfully, delving into the dust to pull out the bloodlike threads of embroidery, the tatters of slumbering flesh, and he runs along the cracks of the canals, over the palpitating mounds. And a diamond light beacons slowly in his hands, and the Cyclopean eye stirs. An extinguished volcano cracks open. A sardonic smile perhaps. And the child jumps into the anonymous paper boat, quickly, through the veins and the arteries, Aron to Aron, causing the heart to beat faster for you, over; and the heart pounds and the boat with the child inside it and the memories, like the smell of Papa's feet, sails from room to room, and the heart is pumping, and beating and throbbing, he could have a heart attack like this, and his quick, soft breathing caresses Papa's feet; now his feet smell a little sharper, a little clearer. A childhood smell. And maybe the true invisible Papa begins at the legs and grows downward from there. Maybe the person growing upward is a different man who is only a friend sometimes, but most of the time an enemy; a man who never looks at Aron anymore. Who has given up on him. Breathlessly he reaches the secret place, the new brain he has endowed himself with below, and he falls over its threshold, stretches out his hand, and delivers this smell. Now

THE BOOK OF

go back up and bring the rest. Hurry. Time is running out, the straits are closing, they're strangling us; run, run, bring more and more in and let us breathe, it's life or death in here. Wait. Have to rest.

And with all his might Aron clings to the smell. If only he could re-create everything out of this good-old-smell. Papa sighs and rolls over voluptuously, like a giant cat, and Aron sniffs and sniffs the naked feet, and in the middle of the blanket a strange little mound begins to grow, and Aron draws into himself and savors the smell of Papa, the smell of Papa's roots. But suddenly it's over, run for your life. Like a raging red moon, Papa's head rose over his feet.

33

And at the end of the month, after nearly two weeks away at work camp, Gideon returned; Aron knew he was coming home; the night before as he was getting ready for bed, he had this feeling, this hunch, and he took a long bath and washed his hair and tried to comb his eyebrows so they'd connect over the bridge of his nose, and he looked into his eyes in the mirror and silently asked himself the one important question: was Gideon still loyal to him, because the outer Yaeli was fading fast, and Aron acknowledged without too much pain that he no longer cared whether she was loyal or not, it was Gideon who counted; if Gideon had waited for him, that was all that mattered.

He slept deeply and peacefully for the first time in weeks, and when he woke up the next morning he put on clean clothes and left for school, but he took the back path, and between the buildings he caught sight of Gideon, looking very tan, his walk more vigorous, more arrogant than ever, but what did that mean; in itself, nothing.

At Memorial Park Gideon was joined by Meirky Blutreich and Hanan Schweiky and Avi Sasson, who marched alongside him, listening intently as he talked and waved his hands around, and Aron scratched his forehead on a branch; even from this distance he could see Gideon was lecturing about the war, that's all anyone cares about these days, why doesn't it just start already so they can get it over with, and it wasn't hard to guess what he was saying, that we have to smear those Arabs once and for all, he knew Gideon, he knew he would go out and

THE BOOK OF

volunteer today to join the Red Magen David Society, or to fill sandbags, but more important, Gideon hadn't actually changed that much in all the time he was away, except for the shadow of a mustache over his lip which did appear a little darker and thicker from here, and his eyebrows had just about connected, though not completely yet; maybe he was still taking the pills every day. Aron winced with guilt.

He followed him up to the school gate, unsure whether to go over and show his face and talk to him as if nothing had happened, so what had, and if God forbid it had, Aron wasn't the one who ought to feel guilty, and there would be one definite answer to a million questions, and there would no longer be any need to ask or to hope, but he didn't go over to him or show his face, he slinked behind from tree to tree, from post to post, discerning a change in Gideon, after all; he did look sturdier or something, more sure of himself, conceited even, it was hard to say what. At the school gate Gideon turned around, and for a moment there was a troubled look in his eyes, as though he was searching for something, yes, as though he was missing someone, and Aron gasped as a quivering heartstring snapped with pain, he nearly burst out of his hiding place to show Gideon that if he did wait for him, Aron would be there, only at the very last second a viperlike message hissed through his mind, maybe it wasn't Aron he was waiting for, and he froze and waited for Gideon to disappear into the school, and then, shrinking off, he grabbed a handful of friendship-sugar cubes from his back pocket, popping one after another into his mouth, to hell with his teeth. On his way home he stopped to pick the three leaves on the right from the bottom of the big ficus tree by the path to Gideon's entrance; I'm sorry I'm sorry I'm sorry, poor things, here they thought it was an ordinary day, they were happy and green in the sunshine, and without any explanation someone came and plucked them. Why? Because, that's why. And then he went home, to bed, and worked on his laugh glands for a while, just for the record, so they would say he always tried to be cheerful, and then he put a little nylon bag over each of his middle fingers to compare the sweat, for no particular reason, what was the point, he was only running around in circles, breaking himself down, because he needed something new, fresh fuel to burn inside, but he didn't have strength anymore, he couldn't go on, and he wondered if Gideon had come home yet and seen it. And at four in the afternoon, not one second earlier, he went down to their rock in the valley and walked around and around it until seven o'clock, but Gideon never showed up, maybe he took the back way home and didn't see the leaves missing on the ficus tree; well, that was the first try.

And the morning after Aron used two stones to twist open the tap on the little pipe behind the building, and made it drip with the hollow whistling sound you could hear from far away, and at four o'clock he went down to the rock again, and again he traipsed around, all the way to the junkyard this time, but no one came, maybe a neighbor had heard the dripping and closed the tap before Gideon came home from school; second try.

And on the third day Aron took sand from the Wizo Nursery School and blocked up the holes in all three sewer covers behind the building and poured in water to make it goopy and wiped his hands and was satisfied. But he kept smelling something, he checked his shoes, no, he hadn't stepped in anything, and still he smelled it, maybe it was coming from the sewer. He stepped on the round cement cover and laughed for real; oh, the hours they had spent here playing aju, the thousands of apricot pits they had traded, he and Gideon and Zacky; I wonder if Gideon noticed this time, maybe I should have thought of bigger, more obvious signs back then; when you're a kid you notice these things right away, and when you grow up you have other things on your mind and you don't walk around with your head down, searching; so in fact, if Gideon hadn't noticed the signs, that in itself was the answer, there was nothing more to say. And at four sharp Aron went down to the valley and dozed on the rock shelf, as the warm sunshine quickened the Yaeli and Gideon inside him, faceless but both there, setting off a kind of vibration like two strings which he tried to play on so they would blend inside him, and he felt the strings twang so that when he opened his mouth he made their sound. By the time he woke up it was five-thirty, he'd certainly developed a flair for naps, at least that, and he walked down to the junkyard and checked around and did his calculations, and opened and closed the door at least ten times, and decided the problem was that the tongue of the lock stuck too far into the socket, which made it pretty hard to pull the pin away from the inside, not to mention the problem of lighting, because what if he dropped a nail or hinge with his perspiring fingers, how would he find them on the floor in the dark, he wouldn't even be able to light a match in there because there wouldn't be enough oxygen, maybe he could tape a little flashlight

322 THE BOOK OF

under the freezer compartment, and by now it was seven o'clock, so Aron went home; he wasn't totally discouraged yet, not at all, though there was a kind of sadness gnawing at him, the sadness of parting, but what if Gideon never went out behind the building and didn't notice the wet sand in the holes.

The next morning he picked up a piece of chalk and followed the arrows on the sidewalk, at first he thought he would have to draw the arrows himself, he'd forgotten that every generation draws arrows and all he had to do was add two slanty lines to each of the existing arrows; he was enjoying this as though he were part of the game, and for a moment he even thought of following the arrows past the building project, but he ran out of curiosity, what did he care where their treasure was. In the afternoon he went down to the junkyard and climbed inside the little refrigerator, and discovered that the freezer compartment forced him to work with his chin on his chest, this was an unexpected problem. He crawled out and closed the door, and tried to stick his hand in through the rubber insulation strips, but they didn't stretch enough and snapped behind his fingers with a moist, wormy swish, and Aron thought maybe he'd have to grease it with something, but suddenly he had a better idea, he would bring a big can opener from home, the kind with ball bearings, and he'd wind it up the rubber insulation strips of the refrigerator, the way you open a can, only from the inside out. And he patted himself on the shoulder and said, Dynamite idea, Kleinfeld, but there remained the problem of the tongue in the socket: he tried to poke in the skinny little Yemenite, the runt of Papa's screwdrivers, but couldn't even fit that in. What to do? He sat and thought a minute, his feet dangling out, not touching the ground; on the bus he liked to practice finding the seats over the wheels at a single glance, they were higher, and suddenly a loud siren pierced the air, maybe the war had started already, and it stopped right away, they must be testing them, but the shrill wailing sound had annoyed him, he jumped out and slammed the door; the squatty refrigerator wobbled as though absorbing the shock.

At supper that evening everyone ate in silence, concentrating on their plates. Papa's army knapsack was packed and ready by the door, and Aron wondered what would become of him if Papa left too and he stayed home alone with Mama. Grandma coughed and spat a little mashed chicken on the table, and Mama slapped her shoulder, hard, too hard. For a moment they all stopped chewing, Grandma gasped, and Aron thought it was all over. But she recovered. It wasn't her time yet. Who wants some more mashed potatoes? asked Mama wearily. Papa did; she got up to serve him and Aron saw she was walking peculiarly, sort of dragging herself a little bowleggedly. Oh please, give me a break, she's walking the way she always does, and Aron quickly asked for seconds too: More mashed potatoes, thanks, lots of mashed potatoes, he said too loudly. She made a face, who cares, and she wouldn't look at him directly; that is, she looked at him, but from the side. He devoured the starch of perseverance and asked for thirds. Yochi's chair stood empty, and everyone kept glancing at it, even Grandma. A couple of days ago, at such a time as this, right in the middle of supper, Yochi opened her mouth and announced that her continued efforts over the past few months had finally paid off, the town major had agreed to give her an early call-up date, and with a smile of triumph, of sweet revenge, she described how she had sat outside his office every day, morning till night, for three solid weeks, till he finally gave in and signed her up six months ahead of schedule, and Aron, the food in his mouth a tasteless mush, retorted inwardly what Mama said aloud: What, you're so miserable here you have to run away to the army, and Yochi said nothing in reply, she was silent, and everyone kept silent with her, they ate their soup and swallowed, ate and swallowed, and Mama sighed, she was on the verge of tears sitting next to Yochi, but she controlled herself, maybe she regretted the deferral she'd wanted so badly for her, and he peeked up and saw Yochi surveying the scene, as though pressing down on a seal to engrave it in her memory: the little kitchen with the narrow Formica table and the tiles with the flower decals where Mama stuck the wax paper and the nylon bags to dry, and Mama herself, and Papa and Grandma and him; everything was converted to the past tense by the sheer force of her gaze, and the next few days were so insufferably oppressive Aron couldn't wait for Yochi to leave, and on the morning of the third day Papa took her down to the recruiting center and she disappeared as if she'd cut herself out of the house with a knife, and then late last night she finally called; they woke him up and sent him running to the phone in his pajamas to talk to her, he was sleepy, he heard the exultant voice on the other end of the line and didn't know who it was. She said that due to the situation she'd been transferred to a field unit. She spoke

THE BOOK OF

fast, didn't call him by name, didn't say li'l brother, and when she asked how he was, it sounded as though she didn't want to know.

Now he lay in bed planning tomorrow, trying to guess what Gideon was thinking; suppose he hadn't seen the signs, could be, maybe he was busy concentrating on the preparations, but why hadn't he come over to see Aron after camp, what was he afraid of, what did he have to hide, all he had to do for God's sake was to say one word; was he loyal, yes or no, and it wasn't as if Aron would do anything to him, all he needed was his answer, and after that, Gideon would be free of him forever, because if the answer was yes, if Gideon had remained loyal and waited, then Aron would be instantly redeemed. He was absolutely sure of it. Like Sleeping Beauty waiting for a kiss; like the Independence Day parade that doesn't begin until the Prime Minister gives the signal. Aron was ready. One word and everything would zoom ahead.

The smell of Papa's cigarette drifted in from the balcony. He was bursting with impatience. At least ten times a day he called his unit, the military police, and they kept saying they didn't need him yet. From the salon came the sound of mumbling: Mama. There was something in her tone of voice, a wrinkle of secrecy and subterfuge. Aron jumped up, always prepared, and tiptoed to the hall for a peek. But he was wrong this time: there was nothing out of the ordinary going on. Mama had sat Grandma on the Pouritz with her right hand on the armrest. She rotated it to the desired angle and then placed Grandma's paralyzed left hand on the support she'd made with two volumes of Winston Churchill. Aron watched, trying to remember what had excited his attention. On the balcony he saw the broad shadow of Papa's back with a slender column of smoke rising above it. Mama wound the yarn on Grandma Lilly's outstretched hands. Now try to remember, Mamchu, she whispered so low he could scarcely hear, Leibaleh's brother, What's-his-name, the one you told us about who was killed by the Germans, remember? Nod yes or no, the one you said there was something wrong with, do you remember what it was? What? Show me by nodding. Was he, eppes, deaf? Was he epileptic? If yes, nod; was he crippled from polio? Was he a midget? And she began to wind the yarn from the double pack on Grandma's hands into a ball, sputtering questions Aron strained to hear: Was he missing any fingers or toes, Was he an albino? Was he feeble-minded? Aron stared at the growing ball of yarn, and Mama's nimble fingers, and her lips moving in the monotonous interrogation, till at last she fell strangely silent, though she seemed still to question Grandma wordlessly as her hands flitted right and left, stretching and winding, her little face receding to the monotonous winding rhythm, and Aron watched the green wool stretch and wind, stretch and wind; he knew that color, it was his sweater! The green sweater with the triangles she knitted him last winter, that still fit, what was she doing, her eyes were turning glassy, shining coldly. Aron took one step forward, even if he went in and stood in front of her now she wouldn't notice, she was completely out of herself, her hands worked on mechanically. Now, now, go in and scream at her: Why, how dare you, it was a perfectly good sweater, but he said nothing and only stared at her glassy eyes over the green ball of yarn, her tongue sticking out between her teeth, small, pointy, very pink; she took short whistling breaths, her hands never stopping, like a human spinning wheel. Unless someone stopped her, she could go on like this forever. Grandma stared blindly ahead, maybe she would stay in her condition for years, maybe death had forgotten her, maybe she was already dead, maybe this was death, and when the yarn was all gone, then Grandma herself would start to unravel, and then the Pouritz, and then the Vichtig carpet and the Methuselah *fauteuil* and the Bordeaux and the buffet and the wallpaper and the walls, everything would start to unravel, it wouldn't die, it would unravel into one long thread, and just then the tail end of the green yarn passed through Mama's fingers and she twiddled the empty air. Her shoulders dropped. Her face fell. She sighed.

The next day Aron went off with his school bag and a sandwich and an apple, but he hid at the Wizo Nursery School till he saw Mama leave to do the shopping, and then he hurried home. First he made sure Grandma was still breathing under the tightly tucked Scottish plaid, then he went to piss and smelled vomit in the toilet; somebody barfed in there, well, they probably had an upset stomach, that's all, maybe the herring yesterday was spoiled, why twist everything around, they're old, at their age it's impossible, yes, but what about that woman in Egypt, the one Yochi mentioned. Quickly he climbed up on a chair and started rummaging through the top shelves in his closet. But he forgot, why had he climbed up here and what was he looking for, and then he started groping around, unfolding his old clothes, all the shorts and long trousers, the checkered flannel shirts and the pullovers and pajamas, from last year and ten years ago, even his baby clothes; we never throw anything out around here. With this pair of pants he won the fifth-grade jumping championship, on these pants there was a permanent bloodstain, he had worn them the time he tried to find out how a blind person feels riding a bicycle, and here was the Trumpeldor shirt with the cut-off sleeve for the plaster cast, and here were the pajamas he wore as a five-year-old when he slept over at Gideon's for the first time, and here it was, this was what he had been looking for, the red T-shirt from day camp, the time he and Gideon had their big feud, when Aron was the captain of the volley ball team and had to choose his players and he picked Gideon last, not because Gideon wasn't a good player, he just wanted the suspense to build up before he rescued Gideon in the end, like when he pretended the Arabs conquered Jerusalem and the Egyptian Colonel Shams, out of esteem for Aron, let him save his five best friends from the firing squad, and Aron went down the lines of beseeching faces; he only did it to increase the excitement and Gideon's relief and happiness, like Joseph confessing to Benjamin and his brothers at the last minute, but that started their big feud, for a whole month, the worst month of their lives, which was when Aron devised the secret sign system, to guarantee that no future fight of theirs would endure for more than a week, and now he tried to fold the clothes and straighten up the mess he'd made. Hmm, how long would it take her to notice, he wondered, and then he washed the red shirt with water and ran downstairs to hang it as conspicuously as possible on the line behind the building, only a blind man would miss it there, and then he went back home.

He sat down at his desk and started writing to Yochi: he hoped she was well, taking good care of herself, things here were fine, nothing new at home, her bed was waiting for her; and he started wondering about her pen pals, they must all have been called up by now, and blithely, as though someone else were doing it, he opened her drawer and weighed her padlocked letter box in his hand, she'd taken the key with her to the army, and as he was closing the drawer he found a page sticking halfway out of the box, and he couldn't resist, he pulled it gently and read the strange list of names there, the names of all her pen pals, with unintelligible directions next to each in a tiny scrawl: lover killed in action, poet, daddy longlegs, dreamer, athlete, adopted, twenty-five years old, attempted suicide, romantic invalid; and beside the name of the cripple from Australia, printed clearly: the truth. Aron read up and down the page, but it made no sense to him and he didn't have the energy to fathom it. Quickly he scribbled out a few more lines to Yochi: Keep up your morale, the nation is behind you.

He arrived at the rock at four o'clock and sat there waiting patiently, but no one came down the path to the valley; maybe Gideon was at home getting ready, getting ready for what, all he had to do was say whether he was or wasn't, even if he didn't say the words out loud, if he just nodded, it would be understood. And Aron reviewed the signs he'd left so far, maybe he'd skipped one and Gideon was confused, but no, he'd left them in the proper order. From the bottom leaves of the ficus tree to the red camp T-shirt. Hmm, interesting, even then he'd had the brains to think of all those signs, and at a time when there was nothing to worry about yet; on the contrary.

He stood up and stretched as though from boredom, and started pacing this way and that, wondering about that list of Yochi's. Someday when it was all over, he would have the time to think about things, like Yochi, and historical things like the Phoenicians, or science and flights to outer space, and discoveries and inventions and animals, and the lives of Thomas Alva Edison and Abraham Lincoln, which had interested him for years only he didn't have the time, or about Louis Pasteur and about explorers, and about the voyage of the *Kon Tiki*, and about the Gypsies and the Aztecs, and about dirigibles and zeppelins, the world is full of knowledge, and once again he found himself in front of the little refrigerator and he climbed in and noticed that, once inside it, he was less aware of the stink coming out of him, the stink of his breath, and he decided to go through a trial run, without actually closing the door, and then he looked around and found a cardboard box to put his rescue tools in, and set it down on one of the shelves, and, using the little Yemenite, unscrew to the left, lifted out the two small side shelves where you put the eggs and margarine and jars of sour cream and the horseradish and mayonnaise, so they wouldn't get in the way of his elbows, in any case he could move only his left hand in there and with that he had to untie his right shoelace and remove Mama's nail file from under the insole, since it was probably the only tool that could fit between the tongue and the metal pin. He let it drop deliberately from pretend-sweaty fingers and groped around the floor with his eyes shut; it took him at least ten seconds too long

THE BOOK OF

to find it again, he would have less than sixty seconds to act in a clearheaded way. Again and again he practiced dropping it, training himself to think coolly so he would know by the sound where to find it immediately. Then he went back to the rock and waited till exactly seven o'clock. Tomorrow, he thought, it would be three weeks since Independence Day, since he said goodbye to Gideon, the waiting, the baiting, the grating, the skating; maybe Gideon had forgotten him, he had other things to think about now, at a time like this it was easy to forget some kid you knew, nobody at school seemed particularly upset that Aron hadn't turned up in a couple of weeks; they hadn't noticed at home, for that matter. And suddenly evening fell and it turned cold and he rushed home and burst through the door in the middle of supper; they hadn't waited for him, they had started without him. He sat down at his place and ate without appetite, and Papa said he called his unit again and they told him to wait patiently, first they take the younger men. As if I'm old, he fumed, I could show those guys where their legs sprout from, and he swallowed an enormous hunk of bread. "Get this, Hindaleh, at work today we were listening to the Voice of Thunder on Cairo radio, and the meathead who reads the propaganda in Hebrew said Nasser's going to make us 'lick the bust,' you hear? He said 'lick the bust,' " and he split his sides laughing, spraying spit and bread around the table as Mama watched impassively. "Ah, you're all alike," she said. "Arabs, Jews, you're all alike."

She stood up with a sigh and dragged Grandma off to bed. A few minutes later she returned, with a hasty glimpse at Aron still sitting at the table all by himself; he didn't even bother to hide the blue-and-purple stains on his knuckles from her. Mama cleared the table. She set about baking a cake to send Yochi. She worked in silence beside him. More wearily than usual. When the silence grew unbearable she turned on the transistor. The management of the Sport Toto wishes to announce that due to the recruitment of many players to military service, all upcoming lotteries and National League games are hereby postponed. Tickets will be refunded at their place of purchase— She switched it off angrily. Aron was shocked. What did they mean, postponing the games. He shook his head in anger: It's not fair. They're not fair.

Mama groaned as she cracked the first egg, and her face turned very pale. Aron watched her, not daring to move. She pressed a frightened hand to her belly. Slowly she took off her kangaroo apron and hung it on the hook. Aron didn't get up, and didn't ask what happened. He saw her totter to her bedroom. He was left alone in the kitchen. He cupped his hand around his nose and mouth and smelled the stink, and he knew it came from inside him, from his putrefying brain; soon all the thoughts and words that went through it would come out sick, covered with white patches, stubbed like a cigarette butt. Nervously he switched on the transistor, heard that the Helena Rubinstein Corporation wishes to inform the women of Israel that we are doing everything possible to continue production in this emergency state, to help you look your loveliest for that special man in the army. Kibbutz Or Haner announces that the wedding scheduled for next Tuesday has been postponed until— He switched it off. Soon he would go to sleep. To muster strength for tomorrow. He looked for a clean glass to drink water from but didn't find one. Drank from a dirty glass instead. In the sink was the egg with the big bloody spot. He felt exhausted again and sat down. He thought he could see Papa on his knees at Mama's bedside, hugging her, his head buried in her body. Over and over he grumbled to himself, What do they mean, postponing the National League, what harm would there be in letting the players out of the army for a day, for a measly few hours, instead of shutting them in there with those stupid Helena Rubinstein people. Furiously he smacked his fist.

And what's that stink coming out of you? said Mama in a new voice, loud and impervious, when she came to wake him the following morning, and rudely, gruffly, raised the blinds before turning back to him for a better look. You've had it for a couple of days already. Notice that she's looking straight at you, she isn't afraid of you anymore. And he curled up and hid his face in the pillow; what's changed her, why is she acting strange? She leaned over him and began to sniff suspiciously, from his feet up to his head, the way she used to sniff Grandma from behind, and suddenly she squinted. Aron to Aron, run for your life, danger, danger, over; he'd seen that look in her eyes before, the flash of horror that time in the kitchen after the thorough cleaning when the shit came out. Roughly she turned him over on his back, pushed away the hands he held up to guard his face, sniffed hard, then zeroed in on his nose. You're insane, what have you done to your nose, meshuggeneh; it was bad enough without adding this chendelach to your list; in case the blind can't see what you are, at least they'll be able to

THE BOOK OF

smell you? And the doctor at the first-aid station said there was no need to worry, that's the smell you give off when something gets caught in your nasal cavities. Did he by any chance remember accidentally sticking something small up there? Aron only shook his head. Aron to Aron, get out, get out, run for your life, over. All around the station there was tumult. They were getting the stretchers ready, packing bandages, taking an inventory of medicines. From the corner of his eye Aron saw two seventh-graders he knew strutting around in white coats. Everyone looked busy, as though they were hurrying to an important meeting, even the children wore that expression on their faces. It's a matter of a day or two before the thing starts, breathed the doctor, sticking a fine pair of tweezers into Aron's nose and poking around. Aha, got it, ho there, that's in pretty deep, here it comes, we'll force it out of you, don't move, it might hurt for just a second, and slowly and carefully he removed the vile-smelling glob and waved it in the air, but his smile of triumph quickly vanished as he peered more closely at the glob, smudged with letters. A boy your age, putting something up your nose, shame on you. The doctor was aghast, tilting his head at Aron, *tsss tsss tsss*, that's something you'd expect from a three-year-old, not a grown-up ten-year-old. Silence. Mama froze. Now let her tell him, let her tell the doctor everything and the doctor will tell us what has to be done. This was the last chance. And maybe there was a perfectly simple solution. An electric shock or something. A moment of pain and it'll be over. Now, please, before the war starts, because afterward who'll care? He's twelve, mumbled Mama, shamefaced. Aron stared at her. She didn't set him straight. And before his eyes, caught in the tweezers, waved the letter that would never arrive at its destination. Aron to Aron, what now, over. He winced at himself. He had no right to complain about her. Wasn't he too standing here not daring to open his mouth, any more than he had when she bought him elevator shoes for his bar mitzvah. He had said nothing to her then, and hated himself for it, for having betrayed himself. Twelve and a half, she mumbled lamely, tucking her head between her shoulders, dark with disgrace.

And the next day was the last day. At four o'clock Aron went down to the valley wearing a clean pair of pants and a crisply ironed shirt, his hair slicked down with water. He left the house without a goodbye, for fear that the sight of them would hold him back or set something off inside. He had all his equipment with him. He even remembered the big can opener, which he hid in his pants. He arrived at the rock and climbed up it, and at the highest point, with the help of his little red mirror, he flashed the reflected sun at Gideon's open window; three short flashes, then three long ones, and three short ones again. Three times over he did it, his hands trembling slightly but scrupulous with the rhythm, and then he sat down on the rock again, feeling weak, curling up on Gideon's part of the rock shelf, trying to stop what he was feeling, the draining out, and he must have fallen asleep then, wishing someone would touch him on the shoulder and say, You rang? But at exactly five o'clock he awoke all alone, and stood up languidly and flashed the mirror again three times, aiming at the ceiling in Gideon's room, because maybe the first time Gideon was sleeping and didn't see, and right away his knees buckled and he slipped off the rock and lay beside it; he'd had this stunned and hollow feeling, right here, the time he broke his arm; he had been crazy with despair then, much more than now, now was nothing in comparison, now was almost over. Back then he had jumped up and down for over half an hour. Maybe an hour. Waiting for just the right moment when his ofzeluchi brain would stray. When it would neglect to order his arm to bend in time. Back then he'd gone over all his troubles: Giora trying to drown him to save himself, Giora's hand-me-downs, the looks people gave him everywhere he went, the insults, sly or obvious; and nothing helped, until he imagined round little Uncle Loniu standing before him at the bar mitzvah, repeating "Body-building, body-building," and suddenly it happened, he heard a crack, and felt the pain, the worst he'd ever experienced, shooting through him as he realized he'd done it, he'd actually done a thing like that, and now they would never send him to Tel Aviv, and that's when he started to get scared.

Again he looked at his watch and saw that almost an hour had gone by. Strange how fast time was flying, and now to signal for the third time. With what remained of his strength he climbed to the top of the rock and tried to stand up straight—his legs were trembling—to flash a final SOS; maybe last time Gideon was lying on his stomach and didn't see the moving light-script overhead, because surely if he had seen it he would be here by now, it was an unignorable call for help, even if it came in the middle of a feud. Even when they were both grown up, living apart in foreign lands, lying in bed in their new homes, or palaces even, if they suddenly saw a light flash on the ceiling, three

THE BOOK OF

dots, three dashes, three dots, they would leap up and pack their bags and, without so much as a goodbye to anyone, hop on the first plane and get there just in time to rescue each other. They had sworn it.

He leaned against the rock, trying to steady himself, to put on a happy face. Why appear weak and repulsive? Trying to fill up with life from the rays of the setting sun. Let's say he was in Komi, up to his knees in the ice, longing for this moment by the rock, but he didn't have the strength to imagine Komi, Komi and the taiga were fading, shrinking. Aron to Aron, I've found something else, over; Aron to Aron, I almost forgot you were there, over; I hardly am anymore, I'm hardly there, it's the end of the road, isn't it, over; Aron to Aron, what did you find, over; I found, I found, deep down, under the dust, under the ground, another thing maybe you'd like to take with you, a gift, maybe it will help you, maybe it will last like the oil that burned for eight days; she used to buy a carp for the Sabbath, but it was a special carp. You're the one who made it special, before you came along it was an ordinary carp swimming around in the bathtub, opening and closing its mouth, all fat and shiny, and you sat on the edge of the bathtub and watched it; it looked kind of silly, with its tough little body, opening and closing its mouth like a toy, swimming laps up and down the tub, and suddenly you stood up, yes, now I remember, you ran to her closet, climbed on a chair, and opened her jewelry box with the necklaces and bracelets and rings and pins, till you found what you were looking for, the shiny red bead that had dropped off, a shiny red bead, you were sure it was a ruby, and you ran to the bathtub with it, carrying it high in the air like a torch, your shiny red ruby, and then you caught the carp; it tried to wiggle out of your hands but you held it as tight as you could, though it floundered and flapped its tail and fought you, and you pushed the ruby into its mouth and down its throat with your finger, and it looked at you in furious amazement, but the ruby was in its stomach by then, and all day long you strutted around feeling proud of your secret: I have a fish with a ruby inside, and you waited for Mama to cut the carp open on Friday and find it there and make a wish, and whatever she asked would be granted instantly, so okay, it didn't turn out the way you planned, things never do, especially not when you're a child; it's better not to believe in magic, so you don't get disappointed, but now, nevertheless, on the path to the valley from the building project, here comes Gideon, just in time, at the very last

minute, walking his walk, his bowlegged walk, maybe I'm dreaming.
Aron to Aron, maybe I'm dreaming, yes, maybe I am.

Hi, Kleinfeld, what's up?

Hello, Gideon.

What are you doing here, all hunched over?

What, you saw my sign?

No. Move over. Let me sit on my side.

THE BOOK OF

34

... And it will be a story about an ordinary boy, like us, a boy our age, see, I've been planning it for a long time, I jot my ideas down in a special notebook I bought, uh-huh, seventy pages, I'm always writing, it's full of ideas, anyway, there's a good chance it'll be made into a movie, no really, about a kid like us, approximately our age; I can't tell you everything yet, it's still secret, but I will tell you one thing, there'll definitely be spy stuff in it, and maybe something about a circus or Houdini, for entertainment; it isn't finished yet, it takes a while to plan, but the truth is—the lies burst out on his tongue like flaming pimples—the boy's name happens to be Gideon, and the plot involves airplanes, he's really keen on airplanes, this Gideon kid, maybe he wants to be a fighter pilot; I haven't written all of this down yet, or figured out how a kid can be a pilot, because, I mean, what if they do make it into a movie, don't laugh, the kid will have to fly a real plane. No way, forget it, I'm not using doubles in my movie; this isn't one of your James Bond deals; in my movie, everything is real and authentic from beginning to end, when the plane crashes and the kid is wounded in the leg, the leg, the leg. Aron licked his lips and peeked again at Gideon's bare leg bouncing on the rock, he'd run out of words. He gasped for breath, how did he get himself mixed up in such a lie when all he wanted was to ask Gideon a simple question, the question, without mentioning any names, because it wasn't her so much as whether Gideon was still loyal, only that would save him, but now he'd botched it, though later when Gideon offered a loyal helpful hand up, Aron thought, Yes, I'm sure he waited for me, and almost melted with joy and relief when he clapped him on the shoulder warmly, and Aron asked with a choked voice, So what's new, how's it going? remembering too late to pull his puny shoulders back, and Gideon said, Hey, it could start any minute now, today or tomorrow, and Aron asked, What could? and Gideon ignored the question and solemnly whispered that his brother Manny had told him in strictest confidence what the secret call-up code for our defense force would be, and he glanced around to make sure no one was eavesdropping. If you swear you'll keep as silent as a grave, I'll tell you too. Aron groaned inwardly, the basalt stone, there was a time when Gideon wouldn't have had to ask him to swear it, and why was he going on about the secret code, what did that have to do with anything now, why was he offering trivial bribes, why didn't he just say it: Was he or wasn't he? and Gideon looked serious and said, Red sheet. Red sheet what? asked Aron faintly, sinking, lost. So the answer was no. He wasn't, red sheet, that was no. And Gideon laughed. The secret code, dum-dum, what'd you think I meant, and if you ask me, it's dynamite, red sheet, like waving a red sheet in front of a bull, get it, those Arabs are going to end up like a lot of dead bulls. Aron shook his head no, he didn't understand, what was Gideon talking about? What did all his words amount to: are you or aren't you? And Gideon said, What are we standing here for? and raised himself up on the rock, trying vainly to cross his long legs in the niche, till he finally gave up, dangled them over the ledge, and lay on his back, and Aron heaved a sigh of relief, Gideon was talking of nothing but the war. But just when Aron thought he still had a chance, he noticed a dark shadow, new and kinky, where Gideon's thigh met his groin. There, see, over the leg. Why are you so jumpy, I just wanted to show you where the wound is. Who's touching you. I mean, see, it's a serious wound, shrapnel from antiaircraft, and for half the movie his leg will be bandaged, maybe even in a cast, though come to think of it, where would he get a cast in the desert? God, I'm dumb, see, I'll change it immediately, and he took a pen out of his shirt pocket, tremblingly, with an earnest expression, and scribbled something on the palm of his hand. Gideon watched him blankly. You couldn't tell what he was thinking. Maybe he remembered that once, long ago, Aron used to have these crazy dreams that all came true. But you had to believe in them. No: not in them, in

336   THE BOOK OF

Aron. In his enthusiasm. But Gideon said nothing, revealed nothing. He had truly matured in that respect, and Aron didn't know how to read his expressions anymore; there was only one hope, it didn't even have to be an answer in words, it would be enough if Gideon would let him see clearly and definitively yes or no, that's all he wanted: for Gideon to be a real friend, a friend through and through. And you know, just now as we were sitting here I had this dynamite idea, maybe you'll be the star of the movie, yes you, why not, sure, a real movie, but for that we'll have to put a bandage on your leg or a plaster cast all the way up to there. Hey, where are you going, stay, wait a minute, man. "Man"—I'm talking like them now, talking like them and lying like them. Give me a second to explain, where were we? Oh yes, it's like this, the kid flies south on a rescue mission and suddenly the Egyptians fire their antiaircraft guns at him, or better yet— Listen to this, his closest friend, no, his brother, he's a pilot too, see, and when his brother is shot down over Egypt, the younger brother, this Gideon, decides to rescue him, because no other pilot is willing to risk his life. So what do you think?

Breathlessly he studied Gideon's inscrutable face, alarmed that Gideon had allowed him to become so completely embroiled in his own lies, but he went on delving for new words to offer him, not that words were so important; only Gideon was sitting there, pursing his lips and waiting to see what would happen next. Why wasn't he talking or lecturing anymore? Why this utter silence? Okay then, he would be silent too, silent like a man. And then, see, this Gideon kid, he's a born flier, always building model planes, a member of the air force youth battalion, so when the squad commander asks for a volunteer to fly behind enemy lines and rescue the pilot who was shot down—and at this point Gideon might have hinted, indicated by a mere gesture that he was fed up with this pathetic, transparent lie, and Aron would have quit then and there, he would have laughed loudly and told him he was only joshing, goofing around to relieve the tension of the military alert; he had kept the option open the whole time, over the years he had learned pretty well how to maintain his dignity, how to hide the erosion inside, but Gideon didn't speak, didn't try to make it any easier for him, he forced him to take it further and further, to the point where it would be almost impossible to retreat with a laugh and a joke, so he sat there with his legs pressed together, watching him with cold, scientific eyes. And then there's this scene in the movie when Gideon finds his brother in an oasis, and they both swim naked, sure, naked, how else are they supposed to swim? With their clothes on? God, you're a baby. But you only see them from the back. Right. So what are you saying, the cameraman should close his eyes? Are you embarrassed to take your pants down for half a minute? The kids in our class? What about them? Look out, he thought, Gideon's bluffing, pretending to be interested, but he isn't. He's a stranger already. He's one of them. And Aron tried to appear calm and innocent, and not to twitch, though he knew he was falling deeper and deeper into Gideon's trap, but what choice did he have, it was life or death like never before, and just in case, in case there was a minute particle of the real Gideon somewhere, willing to share this moment with him, he said, Who cares about the kids in our class, imagine how jealous of you they'll be for starring in a movie. Gideon pretended to listen. You could see he was planning to tell everyone that Aron had lost his mind, as if a thing like that could happen in our family. All right, if you insist, we'll restrict the movie to sixteen and over, but for your information, they won't let us see the movie then either, or maybe they will, if we promise to close our eyes when that scene comes on, at the grand premiere with the Prime Minister and the President and the air force commander. What are you laughing at, why are you laughing like that? Of course they'll be there. Now Gideon was laughing to tears. Wiping his eyes, groaning, slapping his thigh. Here was his chance to retreat. To say he was only goofing around. Putting him on. What a gas. But he didn't have the strength to talk that way. He didn't have the strength to retreat. He had to see it one more time, in broad daylight with his own eyes. To see what had happened to this body he knew almost as well as his own. And how could he have been fool enough to think Gideon was waiting for him all these years, that he was a friend through and through. What remained of Gideon in the boy here who moved and walked and talked as if he wasn't afraid of anything; if they dropped him down in the middle of China he would know instinctively how to behave; he bowed his head: it was true. What was left of his Gideon? Even the loyal old Gideon inside him was almost gone by now. A whole bar of chocolate he had to devour, twenty-four squares of friendship-sugar a day to preserve the memory. And from close up it was obvious that Gideon had stopped taking the pills: you could see he had made incredible progress: those muscles in his arms, the big strong veins sticking out on his hands, and his voice, it was so deep, and his Adam's apple bulged, as though the five milligrams of Valium twice a week really had been holding him back all this time. And here you are, making such a big fuss about showing your tuchis on the screen when I'm talking about a grand premiere and Academy Awards and your picture all over the papers; you make me laugh, Gideon, you actually believe I'd pick an actor without making sure he's right for the part? Suddenly Gideon's ears pricked up. Not a good sign. Gideon's sincere, responsible family ears. Sure I've seen you, why are you laughing, but that was ages ago, go on, laugh! What are you laughing at? I'm not speaking as a friend now. Forget we're friends: I'm speaking as a professional. You know what? Don't show me, okay? Don't do me any favors. Skip it. Let's go home. Actually, you go on by yourself. I want to stay here awhile longer. To plan the filming. Who cares about your tuchis.

But Gideon didn't budge. He sat on the rock watching Aron with heightened curiosity, like someone waiting for the next performance to begin, though he looked a little surprised, a little cruel too. Aron was appalled to recognize the malice of Gideon's father's face in his expression: Gideon was using everything he had. He was unbelievably cool. He was mature. Aron gave up in silence. From the street above they heard a raucous horn. The Lambretta was coming. Zacky Smitanka, thought Aron resentfully, Zacky Smitanka. Once we were friends. Whole chunks of my life have turned white with mildew. So what were you saying? Didn't you just say something? So will you or won't you? So are you or aren't you? Yes or no? Just let me have a quick look, to see if you're right for the part. Sure I'm serious. Do I look like I'm joking, or what?

And just then Gideon came round. Or pretended to. Who could tell. Nobody thought, nobody planned it that way. It just sort of happened. Thank God, said Aron, it's about time. Get behind the rock and strip, and I'll only peek for a second. As if anyone ever walks down this way. It's almost dark. For pity's sake, Gideon, you're such a baby.

Slowly Gideon slid off the rock and stood beside him with a sidelong glance. He considered for a minute, straightened up, turned away un- hurriedly, and went behind the rock. Please, please, begged Aron inwardly. Never mind the shame and humiliation. The important thing is to see whether it's yes or no . . . After that they can all drop dead as far as I'm concerned, they can all drop dead.

Gideon emerged from behind the rock. He looked at Aron with an unfamiliar expression: goading, disdainful. Then, quite simply, he turned to leave. He was dressed. He hadn't taken his pants off. He'd been mocking him all along. Aron froze, then flew at him. Gideon started running, running lightly, effortlessly. The distance between them remained the same, no matter how hard Aron ran.

He pursued him through the valley, amazed to see Gideon so far in the lead, seeming to enjoy the chase, to be merely trying to wear him out and show him how quickly his little legs would tire. They ran in silence for a moment or two, the distance between them never diminishing, around the soccer field, and past the cave, and across the junkyard, circling widely back to the rock, where suddenly Gideon stopped running and veered around, and Aron too came to a standstill, panting and red and goggle-eyed. Gideon's face wore a puzzling expression: neither masculine nor quite feminine either. As though taking his time about deciding, savoring his right to choose, leisurely and calm even as it crystallized. Then, with a strange lingering movement, he began to pull his pants down, offering Aron a glimpse of that heartrending weft of gloom. Twice, in broad daylight, thought Aron. Gideon's eyes glinted with the vicious relief of the survivor, it was almost as if he had been eagerly anticipating this performance all along, that he had an impure urge to mingle with the secretion of Aron's brain. Again he turned to leave, only this time he didn't bother running, and Aron pounced on him with a bitter scream.

They grappled on the ground, panting and snorting and groaning, unable to stop. Gideon was tougher than he was, but Aron's screaming and spitting like a cat were enough to render him powerless. He barely recognized the little animal with the teeth and nails and foaming mouth, tearing into him and puffing his corpse-like breath in his face, as though trying to break his skin so he could merge with what was inside it. Gideon held on to his pants for dear life as Aron struggled to grab them. His strength was giving out, and a sense of resignation, stuporlike, slowly pervaded him. Helplessly Gideon watched as the rabid creature dug his claws into him, pawed his face, mauled his body, and seemed to be fighting for his life, till suddenly he let out a squeal of fear, appealing to him with a forgotten nickname, not Kleinfeld, not Ari, but as their kindergarten teacher used to call him, Neshumeh, little soul; only Aron didn't answer, maybe he couldn't hear anymore; he stripped the pants off the sobbing youth, pulled them down to his knees. Looked, examined. Then nodded as his eyes began to dim. Gideon sprawled on the ground, wounded and violated under his gaze. Aron got up and turned away with downcast eyes as Gideon dressed himself, bawling and shrieking, glancing fearfully in Aron's direction. Then he took a few steps forward, broke into a run, and fled toward the building project.

Aron stood cringing a moment or so longer. Then, with cautious tread, he set off through the darkened valley, fixing his gaze on a patch of white, a leprous glow in the shadows of dusk. Farther and farther he wandered, away from the building project, from the street noise, the clanking of pots, the crying of children, till at last he arrived and collapsed on the ground, leaning against the refrigerator door. Slowly, as though trying to remember something, he ran a finger up his body, from his feet to his neck and shoulders. Detached from all emotion, he investigated his flesh, tracing the geography of the unfamiliar zone of hell. Then he stood up, pulled the cold door handle, opened the refrigerator, and breathed in the stench. He folded himself into the lower shelf with his legs dangling out and looked up at the spangled sky. Perfect stillness all around, silence as far as the building project. There in the darkness, beyond the ring of light, he felt the whole nation waiting for the first shot, the great jump-off. Who would win and who would lose? How many would die? Which of those he knew would be wounded? Like Papa, for instance, and Yochi, who was stationed someplace, and he ran through the list of relations, near and far, and acquaintances and teachers and neighbors, and older brothers of his friends, and the soccer players who had been mobilized. He was worried about Manny, the pilot, sorry the scheme for fossilizing faces in the rock had fallen through. Because if anything happened to one of them, God forbid, at least that way there would be something to remember them by. Slowly he began to drain the morass that filled his soul. His clarity of mind returned like blood to a tingling limb.

Then he set his cardboard toolbox down beside him: through the crack in the sole of his shoe he pulled out the nail file and the rusty razor blade, from under his belt he fished the nail. Then he found the piece of saw in his trouser cuff, and the matchbook Uncle Shimmik got on the airplane, but decided to throw it out. To leave a trail for them. He felt along the curve of his spine, tore off the fake plaster, and caught the shiny lead nail between his fingers. Then he closed his eyes and gently ran his hand over his things so he'd know where they were in the dark. And all the while a child's voice inside him asked, Is this it, is this it? He didn't believe he would do it.

When he was ready he raised his legs, and slowly, like a pro, he crossed them carefully under him, first the left, then the right, with his right hand on his thigh. It occurred to him that if he did succeed, and of course he would, this would be his greatest Houdini performance, now of all times without an audience, but he didn't need an audience: he was performing for himself alone. And if he did succeed, and of course he would, if he did get out of here, and of course he would, no one would know. Not even Yochi. Maybe in twenty years it would be all right to tell. But not for twenty years. Even those nearest and dearest to him wouldn't know: not for twenty years.

And when these words ran through his mind—not for twenty years—he felt a shock of pain, as though the electricity had gone haywire in his head, and he pressed down on his eyes till the pain faded, till sparks flew out of them, growing into a blaze of light, and his head was filled with a dazzling dawn, and he hunched down in wonder, pressing harder with his knuckles, till he saw the sparks he knew, and then the little angels of light, and then he went even further, was even crueler to himself, because soon, he understood, he would arrive, and his eyes really did fill with something from inside him, a great shining essence, glowing brighter and brighter, like a distant explosion, but gentle, beaming, bursting like the sunrise, and under his clenched fist curled a smile of amazement, a movie show in his eyes in spite of the pain, in spite of the tears that dimmed his vision and trickled down his arms, but he didn't stop; he wondered why in all his past experimenting he had never tried to reach such a moment, a moment like this, a gift from his body.

And then, when he couldn't stand it anymore, he stopped pressing and quietly endured the pain of opening his eyes, of wiping away his tears, watching the slow return of the familiar world. And someone called his name. Mama was out on the balcony, calling him. Papa came out and called him too. Why were they both calling him? Maybe they

THE BOOK OF

had noticed something after all. Maybe Gideon had run home to warn them. His somber name hovering over the valley seemed barely able to reach him here. He could sense its presence like a heavy cloud floating slowly toward him, beating the air with the vowels of his unbeloved name.

Haggard with grief they called to him, his mama and papa. Caught in the soft mists, their voices sprinkled over him. A wail of pure anguish. A lamentation. He arranged his feet on the shelf. Bowed his head on his chest under the freezer compartment. Placed the fingers of his left hand firmly on the Houdini tools.

Translated by Betsy Rosenberg